Advance Praise

"*Houses of Detention* explores with uncanny wisdom, humor and compassion the travails of one large Jewish immigrant family's attempts at finding its place in American society. The shadow of the Old World and War hang over the characters psyches, whether they were born in the United States or in their small, segregated village in "bloodlands" between Russia and Germany. Jean Ende gives us a compelling inside view into this chaotic and loving family, the elders wanting nothing more than to leave a legacy of stability and success for their children. A fabulous read that illuminates the issues all immigrants from disparate countries and backgrounds face."

> — Kaylie Jones, author of *A Soldier's Daughter Never Cries and Lies My Mother Never Told Me*

"To read Jean Ende's remarkable debut novel is to pull up a seat to a dining room table in the Bronx of the mid-20th century, a table packed with colorful characters and their plentiful gossip. Beneath all that kibitzing, however, is the real story: the essential and often heartrending tale of one family of Jewish immigrants searching for a new American life in the shadow of genocide and exodus."

> — Stefan Merrill Block, author of *The Story of Forgetting and Oliver Loving*

"Jean Ende's *Houses of Detention* takes us deep into a historical American Jewish experience and a family working through the generational trauma of the Holocaust. Maybe they could be called typical, but every family's tsuris is complicated. Ende has portrayed the lives of this family in a raw and unvarnished way, bringing a rare truth to this engrossing novel."

— Judy L. Mandel, *New York Times* bestselling author of *Replacement Child – a memoir*, and her most recent book, *White Flag*

"Jean Ende weaves love and bitterness and confusion and compassion into a saga with characters so rich you'll wake up thinking about them."

— Julie Maloney, author of *Matter of Chance* and director of Women Reading Aloud

Houses of
DETENTION

Houses of

DETENTION

a novel

Jean Ende

Apprentice
House Press
Loyola University Maryland

Chapter 3 of *Houses of Detention*, "Hocus Pocus" originally appeared in Stories Through The Ages, Baby Boomers Plus, 2018, published by Living Springs Publishers.

First Edition

Casebound ISBN: 978-1-62720-557-3
Paperback ISBN: 978-1-62720-558-0
Ebook ISBN: 978-1-62720-559-7

Library of Congress Control Number: 2025932638

Design by Apprentice House Press
Editorial Development by Sophia Strocko
Promotion Development by Rylee Miller

Published by Apprentice House Press

Apprentice
House Press
Loyola University Maryland

Loyola University Maryland
4501 N. Charles Street, Baltimore, MD 21210
410.617.5265
www.ApprenticeHouse.com
info@ApprenticeHouse.com

To My Son,
JOSHUA ENDE KEATING

CONTENTS

1.

GIRLS HOUSE OF JUVENILE DETENTION (1958)

The Girls House of Juvenile Detention in the Bronx was where underage girls were kept until authorities decided what should be done with them. The building looked as if it had never been new. The cinder block walls had always been coated with grime, the steel mesh covering the dirty windows, always rusty.

A few girls were smoking in the corner of the fenced-in, asphalt courtyard. In a small playground area a broken swing hung from the crossbar, a deflated ball rested against a rusted pole with a hoop but no net and the see-saw seat was splintered.

Saul had driven his wife, Helen, and their daughter, Sarah, from their home in the leafy north Bronx to this place in the slums of the south Bronx. "You're sure Harvey shouldn't come?" he had said to Helen before they pulled away from their house. "He is her father."

"You think we didn't discuss it? Everyone agreed this is best," Helen replied.

Saul glanced into the rear-view mirror. His daughter was

staring out the window, trying to look as if she wasn't listening to her parents' conversation. "And Sarah?" he said. "She's not too young for this?"

"They're friends. I don't want Rebecca to think she's not still part of the family. Go already."

They quietly drove through unfamiliar neighborhoods. "Well, here we are," Saul said after an hour. "Right on time."

They stared at the garbage-strewn sidewalk and watched a shabby man stumble towards them. "Everyone lock your doors," said Saul. But before the man reached their car, he stopped walking, leaned against a building, slowly slid down the wall, and stretched out on the street.

Saul glanced at the dashboard. "I need gas," he said. "How long do you think this will take?"

"Longer than it takes to get gas," Helen said. "Go fill up the car, come back and stay right here. Right here. Sarah and I can't be alone in this neighborhood."

"Give Rebecca my best," said Saul and drove off.

Sarah was 13 years old, too old to hold her mother's hand, but she didn't pull away when Helen reached for her. They walked together across the yard towards the building's entrance. They were wearing their good coats, Helen's had a silver fox collar, bright against the black wool, Sarah's was pale blue with black piping that curled around the shoulders and down the front.

It seemed to take a long time to reach the detention center's entrance. They opened the scarred, grey, metal door and Helen approached the large man in a guard's uniform sitting behind a dirty Plexiglas window.

"I'm Helen Rosen. I'm here to see my niece, Rebecca," she said. "This is my daughter. We have an appointment." Helen pulled a paper out of her purse and slid it through the narrow slot at the bottom of the window.

The guard glanced at Helen and took the paper. He opened a large book on his desk and ran his finger down the page, then turned to the next page. Helen watched him carefully. Sarah looked into the booth, trying to see if he had a gun.

The guard finally found the listing he needed, picked up the phone, mumbled something, nodded, and hung up. "Go to the end of the hall, last room on the left," he said and pressed a button on his desk. A buzzer rasped loudly. Helen pulled on the door leading to the hallway. It was heavier than she had expected.

Inside, the walls were painted seasick green, the floors had speckled grey tiles, and there were large corkboards on the walls covered with yellowing notices. Everything was clean, ammonia scented.

Helen and Sarah walked slowly down the hall until they reached the room that the guard had indicated. It was empty. "I'm sure they'll bring Rebecca soon," Helen said as she entered. "We'll just wait."

The room had five rows of chairs facing the blackboard, the type of chairs with an arm that curved around and served as a desk. Sarah wondered if her stout mother would fit into it. But Helen just walked to the front row, pulled out a chair and slid in. She stared ahead as if there was something to read on the chalky blackboard.

Sarah was too nervous to sit still. She walked across the room and looked at the texts stacked on a bookcase. She thought about a movie she'd seen with her friends, *Rebel Without a Cause*.

Natalie Wood played a teenage girl who got picked up by the police. Just like Rebecca. But, at the end of the movie, Natalie

Wood went home to her family and kept James Dean as her boyfriend. She wasn't sent to a house of detention.

2.

BRONX CHEER

So what was a nice Jewish girl doing in a place like that?

The Girls House of Juvenile Detention was not where you'd expect to find a girl like Rebecca, a smart girl, part of the Rosen family, a good family by all neighborhood standards. They generated their share of gossip, but nothing special, not until Rebecca pushed the boundaries so far that the police became part of the family's story.

The Rosens lived in *a shtetl*. Not an area of poverty-stricken Jews crammed into dilapidated wooden buildings like a community in 19th century Eastern Europe. This *shtetl* was pretty high class, well, at least upper middle class. There were several Italian families in the neighborhood, but it was primarily populated by Jews like the Rosens: parents, aunts, uncles, cousins, grandparents and miscellaneous other relatives, all living within a few blocks of each other.

Some of the oldest members of the Rosen family had fled Europe in the 1930s, before the worst of the Holocaust. Others endured war times, torturous times, and came later. By the 1950s what was left of the entire clan had settled in sturdy, two-family, brick houses in the Pelham Parkway section of the Bronx. There were back yards for kids to play in, a mink stole in every hall closet, a car not more than three years old in every driveway.

Saul and Morris Rosen, brothers, were partners in a business where there was always a job available for a cousin or a *landsman*. When they'd arrived from Poland they had been hired by someone from their village who'd come over a few years earlier and started a small factory that sold equipment to neighborhood stores. The brothers had been merchants in Europe and they quickly learned this business. Soon they opened their own factory and started selling their own line of merchandise.

Most of their business was done in poor neighborhoods and involved other refugees, sometimes other Jews, much of the time with Hispanics, Blacks who'd recently arrived from the south or the Caribbean, or with Asians, Greeks and others. The refugee mentality created a common vocabulary.

Both brothers had stubble covered cheeks by the end of each day although they shaved every morning. They were totally grey by their forties, but their hair remained thick and they felt superior to contemporaries who had little or no hair. Saul was the older, shorter, heavier one; Morris was taller, slimmer, better looking. Despite these differences, people got them confused because they were always together. The brothers sat in adjoining seats in the synagogue and drove the identical model car. They saw each other every day at the shop and preferred to sit together at social events so they could continue discussing business.

When someone encountered either Saul or Morris by himself and asked which of the Rosen men he was, the brother would say, "First you have to tell me why you're asking. If you're here to pay, I'm the man you want. If you're trying to collect, you want my brother and I don't know where he is."

The Rosen women were homemakers, the ultimate occupation as far as they were concerned. Technically they were sisters-in-law, emotionally they were sisters. Helen, the only member of the immediate family born in the U.S., was married to Saul, Rachel was married to Morris and Elaine, nee Rosen, was Saul and Morris' younger sister. Her husband, Harvey, had joined the Rosen's business when they married.

All three were compact women who generally wore polyester pant sets in pastel colors. Every Saturday they met at the neighborhood beauty parlor located under the El where they had their hair teased and shellacked into neat, helmet-shaped domes.

Helen was the shortest, but her strongly voiced opinions made up for her lack of stature; no one ever overlooked Helen. She had thick, very dark, almost black hair that didn't grey until she was very old. At the beauty parlor, she carried a paperback novel in her purse and would read while she waited for the others to be finished. Helen had bad vision and always wore thick glasses with plastic cats-eye frames.

Elaine had a few highlights put into her light brown hair, trying to brighten up her pale complexion. She spoke in a softer voice than the other two, was thinner and often unnoticed. But when she had something important to say she always managed to get others to consider her point of view.

Rachel, the tallest, was the glamour girl of the group. She never went out in public without a full face of make-up and a coordinated outfit. She had come to the US as a teenager and told people she'd been a model in a hat store before she married. Occasionally, someone who had known her during those years said they thought she'd been a salesperson in the store, not a model, but Rachel ignored such people. No one remembered her natural color; Rachel's hair morphed from red to brown to blonde as her mood, the seasons and her beautician's advice changed.

The Rosen offspring were close in age and went to the same schools. They grew up knowing that, in their *shtetl*, there was always an aunt or uncle or grandparent watching them, an adult who would report any wrongdoing and be available to help if anything went wrong.

These children were Jewish-Americans, the hyphen an essential part of their identity. They were part of a generation imprinted by what had happened in a country they'd never seen. They were replacement children, expected to replace a generation that was sent into gas chambers.

Don't waste your life, they were told. Compensate for those who didn't have a chance. It was a worthy goal. Impossible to accomplish.

Children of Jewish refugees don't need to be told about the boogey man. They'd heard about the Nazis. Most children who look under their beds to see if monsters are lurking below eventually feel foolish.

But of course, some monsters are real.

3.

HOCUS POCUS

When Elaine got sick there was no question about who would take care of her and her children or supervise her household until she was better. That's what family was for, especially a family like the Rosens.

Helen and Rachel explained to their husbands that their brother-in-law, Harvey, would need increased take-home pay for a while so he could afford the full-time housekeeper they'd hired to cook and clean for Elaine's family. It never occurred to Morris or Saul to object.

During the day, Rachel kept an eye on seven-year-old Marvin, and Helen watched 12 year old Rebecca.

"Marvin's no trouble at all. Such a good boy I hardly know he's there," Rachel said to Harvey when she brought Marvin home. "Not like my wild savages." Rachel had three sons. She knew what little boys were like.

Rachel and Saul lived only two houses away from Elaine and Harvey. The family matriarch, *Bubbe* Golda Rosen, lived in between. This was a great arrangement as far as Marvin was concerned. His aunt's house was crammed with toys outgrown by her boys and at least one of his older cousins was usually willing to play with him.

Bubbe Golda, could usually be counted on to take the side of any grandchild who had an argument with their parent while dispensing the rock candy she made herself because, "you need some sweetness in your life.

"Be careful not to swallow the string," *Bubbe* would warn her grandchildren when she cut off a piece of the smoky crystals she carried in her pocket along with tiny nail scissors. "You don't want it to get tangled in your insides."

At Marvin's house his sister Rebecca bossed him around and some adult was always shushing him. His mama was very sick they reminded him; she needed her rest. At Aunt Rachel's house, they were all used to noise.

Everyone agreed Helen had the more difficult job. Elaine's oldest, Rebecca, was a handful. She was always on the move, taking off for someplace she wasn't supposed to go, showing up late and inconveniencing the adults, failing to clean her room or help with household chores. But Helen didn't mind taking care of her niece. Rebecca and her aunt had been close, even before Elaine got sick.

Helen's daughter, Sarah, wondered why no one asked what she thought of the arrangement, if she minded having her mom always dashing out in response to an emergency at her older cousin's house.

One day Rebecca fell off her bike, started screaming and said she couldn't get up. Helen was so frightened she ran to the corner and pulled the handle on the red fire alarm box attached to the telephone wire pole.

Rebecca didn't stop crying until she heard sirens but as soon as she did, she sat up and smiled. The men in the ambulance said it was just a badly scraped knee and elbow and quieted Rebecca with a lollipop and two big bandages with stars on them. They let her look around the ambulance and turn the siren on and off. When

Helen told the story, she said she thought she was going to have a heart attack from all of the commotion, but she always hugged Rebecca at the end of the telling.

Not long after this incident, Sarah fell off her bike. She'd been going twice as fast as Rebecca who had hit a crack in the sidewalk. Sarah hit a lamppost. Sarah's leg was throbbing when she slowly limped into her house. She got yelled at for tearing her pants.

When he wasn't at his Aunt Rachel's house, Marvin liked to spend time in his mother's room. He climbed into Elaine's big bed and she read stories to him or they sang songs together. Sometimes she talked about Poland, where she and his papa had lived when they were young.

"My family was poor but we lived in a big house," Elaine told Marvin. "The girls slept in one room, the boys slept in another, and spare rooms were rented to travelers who sometimes told us stories about what was going on in the rest of the world.

"And this wasn't the only business we had. My father and brothers were always involved in some clever scheme," Elaine said with a smile. "Sometimes they got in trouble and the family was short on money, sometimes they came out ahead and we'd celebrate with special treats.

"Your papa's family was different, much more pious, much more learned. Your papa spent his time studying at the *shul*, so did his father. Everyone respected them."

While his mama slept, Marvin sat quietly in the corner with a pad of white paper and a large box of crayons and drew pictures about the stories he'd heard. As soon as she woke up, his mama looked at the pictures and praised him. She showed Marvin where to hang the new pictures on her bedroom wall and which of the older pictures he should take down and put away. She told Marvin,

"I want these to be the first thing I see when I wake up and the last thing I see when I fall asleep."

Sometimes grown-ups forgot he was there. They would say things like "bad prognosis" or "palliative care," words he didn't understand. But he understood his mama was very sick and getting worse and no one knew what to do about it.

One day, Aunt Rachel took Marvin and her boys shopping and he stopped in front of a toy store.

"Whatcha lookin' at?" asked his cousin Kenny. "Those baseball gloves are pretty nice, huh? Think you're ready for a big kid's glove?"

Marvin pointed to a large, brightly colored box. "I need that," he said. "*Bubbe* Golda gave me *gelt* for Chanukah. I have to go home, get my money, come back and buy it. Right now."

Kenny looked where Marvin indicated. There were magical symbols on the box, a rabbit coming out of a hat, a bouquet of flowers emerging from a boy's sleeve and a wand with stars shooting from the end. He looked at the label on the box. "It's 14.95," he said. "*Bubbe* only gives $2 for Chanukah. You need another $12.95."

Marvin ran over to Aunt Rachel. "Please give me $12.95," he said.

It had been a long day. Rachel was tired. It was time to go home and start dinner. "I don't have $12.95 to spend on more toys for you boys," she said. "No more shopping today. Ask your parents. Maybe for your birthday."

Marvin didn't argue with her. But as soon as his papa got home from work Marvin asked to talk to him.

"I've had a hard day, Marvin," Harvey said. "Let me wash up and say hello to your mama. We'll talk later."

"I need to talk now."

Harvey smiled at his little boy. Marvin didn't smile back.

"I guess this is an important matter," Harvey said. "Okay. Let's go into the study and talk. Man to man."

Harvey sat in the big armchair and Marvin sat on the couch, his feet not quite reaching the floor. There was a big desk in front of papa's chair and behind Harvey were bookshelves up to the ceiling. Many of the books had Hebrew words on their spines, gold or silver characters pressed into the leather binding. They looked old, well worn.

"I saw something in the toy store I need to buy," said Marvin. "It costs $14.95 and all I have is the $2 *Bubbe* Golda gave me for Chanukah. My birthday is a long time away. Can you give me $12.95? Now? Please."

"Well, you're a very direct young man," said Harvey. "You know, money doesn't come easy. I work very hard to earn money for our family's food and clothing, for all of the toys you already have."

Marvin had heard this before.

Harvey thought for a minute, then his face lit up. "You could earn money for your new toy," said Harvey.

"But I don't have a job. I'm too young to get one."

"I was about your age when I started studying with my father," Harvey said. "I wanted to be a scholar like him. I was honored that he would help me. But for you it's different, I know. To live in America, you need money. But maybe you could study with me and make money at the same time. Would you like that?"

Marvin looked skeptical.

"I could teach you the Hebrew alphabet. There are 22 letters and every time you learn to write and pronounce a letter properly I'll pay you 10¢. Then we can put the letters together and make words. Each time you learn a word you'll earn a quarter. Pretty soon we'll put the words together and make sentences, you can recite prayers." Harvey was grinning enthusiastically. "You can learn the blessings said at mealtimes and then other blessings. For every blessing you learn by heart you get 50¢.

"Lately I've stopped saying these prayers when we eat, I've been busy with other things. That's my mistake. I apologize. Once you know the blessings we'll say them together at each meal. Soon you'll learn other prayers. You can come to the *shul*. We can *daven* together. Everyone will envy me for having such a learned son."

Marvin didn't change his serious expression. "How long will it take to earn $12.95?"

"Ah, your mother's blood is speaking," said Harvey. "Focusing on the money, not the knowledge. The men in your mother's family were always in business, always hustling. But in Europe I was too busy studying the holy works to worry about such things. In those days a man could spend his days on what was important to his soul, not worry about his wallet."

Marvin had heard this before. "How long will it take for me to get $12.95?"

"The answer depends on you. If you work hard you'll make money quickly. If you don't concentrate it'll take a long time."

"Couldn't you just give me the money?"

"That wouldn't be fair to your sister."

Marvin looked down at his shoes. He scratched his head. He shrugged. "Okay, I'll do it."

"Maybe you should have just gotten him the toy," Elaine said when Harvey told her about the arrangement. "He asks for so little. Rebecca is always carrying on and winds up getting more than her share. What does he want so badly?"

"What does it matter?" said Harvey. "Some silly toy for a child to play with for a while and then forget. In this country too much fuss is made over children having fun, not enough attention to their learning. No, this is the best way. I'll study with my son, just like my father studied with me. He'll realize how rewarding it is. Once he has the baseball glove, or whatever it is he thinks is so important, I'm sure he'll want to continue studying." Harvey laughed. "An American *tsaddik*. Our son can be knowledgeable about baseball and about holiness."

Marvin and Harvey worked together every evening after dinner. Harvey printed each Hebrew letter on a large index card. He had Marvin copy the letter a few times in his notebook. Then Harvey would make the sound of the letter and Marvin imitated him.

"Now Marvin, let's see you print a lamed," said Harvey

Marvin drew a wiggly line.

"That's close," said Harvey. "But it has a straight portion in the middle. Here, watch me make it." Harvey drew the letter, then took the paper. "Now you do it."

Marvin scrunched his eyebrows together just as Harvey did when he was annoyed.

"Almost," said Harvey with a sigh. "Let's try something easier. Yesterday I showed you the samekh and the kaf. Do you remember? Write them for me."

Marvin scratched behind his ear with the pencil and drew two boxes. He erased one side on one of the figures.

"Which is which?"

"Uh, the samekh is the full box and the kaf is missing the side," Marvin said hesitantly.

"Well, that's right," said Harvey. "But the kaf is missing the left side. You erased the right side." Harvey shook his head. "Here's the chart with all of the letters. Copy them again, pronouncing them as you write."

Marvin did as he was told.

Harvey was disappointed that Marvin didn't catch on faster, but he was impressed by his son's determination. He tried to be patient, convinced Marvin would soon learn to love this work. Harvey had been recognized as a Torah prodigy when he was not much older than Marvin. Surely his son also had this ability.

"I haven't seen Harvey so happy since I got sick," Elaine told Rachel soon after the study sessions started. "I just hope he's not working Marvin too hard."

"Marvin's determined to learn, and he's convinced his cousins to help him," said Rachel. "It's a regular yeshiva in my house these days. Whatever Harvey is paying Marvin, I should pay him double for getting them all to keep quiet and stop tearing up the place."

Soon the whole Rosen family was talking about Marvin's Hebrew lessons. No one forgot about Elaine's gloomy prognosis, especially Harvey, but now when people asked him how things were at home, instead of mumbling about Elaine going downhill, Harvey would talk about his son's progress. He didn't stop asking the doctor if anything else could be done, if there was another specialist they could see. He still stayed awake at night, praying and triple checking that Elaine had taken her medicine, that she was as comfortable as possible. But now his day had a high point—the time he spent studying with Marvin.

He began humming long-forgotten Hebrew melodies to himself as he drove home from work. He smiled more often. He allowed himself to imagine that all the doctors were wrong.

"When Elaine hears her son praying her whole face lights up," said Harvey to anyone who inquired about her health. "This is the best medicine possible."

Harvey sometimes thought how people would admire the beautiful picture Elaine and Marvin would make at Marvin's Bar Mitzvah. Of course they'd invite the doctor and be gracious when he apologized for his mistakes.

Harvey paid his son promptly. Each time Marvin learned something new, more money went into the cigar box he'd gotten from the candy store. Every night, before he went to sleep, Marvin carefully counted his cash. Then he went into his mother's room to say goodnight, and, if she was awake, talk to her for a little while. Each night his mother looked a little paler and Marvin left her room determined to study harder and make her happy.

It took Marvin two months to earn the money he needed.

"Will you take me to the store tomorrow, Papa?" Marvin asked as soon as he deposited the final coins in his box. "It stays open late on Thursday. We can go when you come home from work."

"Okay, I'll try to come home early."

"And don't tell Mama I've got all the money," said Marvin. "I want it to be a surprise."

"I know she's proud you're earning your own money for your toy and she'll be impressed by how much Hebrew you've learned," said Harvey. "You know there's lots more to learn. Do you want to continue our lessons?"

"I have enough money," Marvin said. "I don't need any more lessons."

"You're sure?" asked Harvey. "The more you know the more interesting it is to study."

"No more," said Marvin, shaking his head.

"Okay," said Harvey. "I'm sure you'll change your mind when

you're a little older."

When they got to the toy store Harvey was surprised to see Marvin run past the baseball equipment to the boxed games. "That's it," said Marvin. "That's what I want. It's still here. I was afraid someone else would buy it."

He was pointing to a large red and gold box. On the cover, in big silver letters, were the words, *I CAN DO MAGIC.* The boy on the box was wearing a black cape and tall black silk hat and holding a black wand.

"A magic set?" said Harvey. "That's what you want? Isn't that a little too old for you?"

"I need it right away. I can't reach it. Get it for me. Please Papa, reach it for me."

Harvey handed the box to Marvin. "You're going to put on a magic show?" he said. "That's what all of the fuss is about? Your mama likes magicians? I never knew. Well, I'm sure she'll enjoy your show."

Marvin ran to the cashier and carefully counted out his money. "Now, let's go home," he said to Harvey.

At the house, Marvin tore off the cellophane wrapping, opened the box and stared at the contents, confused. Under the hat and cape and instruction sheet were a bunch of cellophane bags, bags with rings, paper flowers, small scarves and other items that made no sense to Marvin.

"Let me help you," said Harvey. "This is really a toy for an older child, I'll show you how it works."

Harvey read the instructions to himself while Marvin squirmed. "See," Harvey said. "These rings have very thin cracks, you can barely see them. Just tell people they're solid, wave your wand, and say hocus pocus. Then you bang them together and they join. You can make a chain. And this wire lets you hide the colored scarves in your sleeve, so you can pull them out and surprise people. The main thing is to keep talking and move quickly, wave the wand around and get people to look the other way so they don't notice what you're doing."

Marvin looked at his Papa. He looked at the contents of the box. He looked at the illustrations on the direction sheet. "That's not magic! It's just tricking people," Marvin yelled. "I wanted magic! Real magic!"

Harvey had never heard Marvin yell so loudly. "Calm down," he said. "What's the problem? Of course it's tricks. What did you think it was? If you practice and do the tricks well, you'll look like a real magician."

Marvin picked up the box, held it as high as he could and threw it to the ground. "I don't need tricks. I need magic!" he screamed. Marvin jumped on the box again and again. "I need magic to make mama not sick anymore."

He kicked the box so hard it flew across the floor and crashed into the wall. Rings and scarfs and flowers and glitter scattered all over. Marvin ran over to the box, kicked it again and the box crashed into the opposite wall.

Marvin was crying. His nose was running. "Mama has been sick too much. I wanted to make her better."

"Oh Marvin, my poor little boy." Harvey got on his knees and put his arms around Marvin until the boy stopped sobbing. He went into the bathroom and got a glass of water and a tissue. "I know it's hard to have mama be so sick. But there's no magic cure. The doctor is doing all he can to help mama feel better."

"The doctor can't do anything more," said Marvin. "I heard him say so."

"You hear so much, don't you?" said Harvey. "You sit there quietly, looking so busy while the grown-ups talk. I'm sorry we don't notice you. There are things you shouldn't hear, things you can't understand."

Harvey got up and went to the bookshelf. He pulled out one of his books, a black leather book with Hebrew words printed in gold on the cover. "The doctor is still working hard to cure mama and meanwhile we can do our part and pray for her. The Lord is more powerful than any doctor, than any medicine, than any magic trick."

Harvey opened the book to a page in the middle. "Look here," he said. "This is a prayer to ask for help for a sick person, to ask that their pain is eased, that they don't suffer, that they regain their health. You already know many of these words, I'll help you with the others. Should we say it together right now?"

Marvin blew his nose. He glared at Harvey. "You pray all the time. It doesn't do any good."

Marvin grabbed the book out of his papa's hand and threw it down. Then Marvin kicked it so hard the book flew across the floor just like the magic kit. He jumped on the book and broke its spine.

Harvey ran across the room, his face red, his eyes bulging. He was screaming Hebrew and Yiddish words Marvin had never heard. He grabbed Marvin's arm and jerked him off the floor. Harvey was a big man. Marvin was a small boy. Harvey held Marvin high above the floor. He shook Marvin hard. Once, and then again.

"No papa, no," Marvin yelled.

Harvey looked into Marvin's eyes and carefully put him on the floor.

"I'm sorry," said Harvey. "Are you okay? I didn't mean to hurt you."

He picked up the Hebrew book, examined the broken spine, kissed the book quickly, wiped it on his shirt and put it back on the shelf.

Marvin was sitting on the floor where Harvey had left him. He was quiet, trembling slightly, his nose running again.

"You know it's a sin to mistreat a holy book. It's called a desecration, it's a terrible sin. Many bad people have destroyed Jewish books. Just like they tried to destroy the Jewish people. That's why I got so upset. But you're a child, you didn't know what you were doing. I'm sorry I forgot, sorry I scared you, sorry I hurt you."

"I'm okay, papa. I'm sorry I hurt your book."

Rebecca and her mom were upstairs in their bedrooms and they heard the yelling coming from Harvey's study. Rebecca was simultaneously talking on the phone and watching TV and easily ignored the disturbance, but when Elaine called out, she rushed into her mother's room.

"Help me get downstairs," Elaine demanded.

"I'll go find out what's going on," Rebecca said. "You stay here."

"No, I want to see for myself," said Elaine. "I just need a little help."

Elaine made her way slowly down the stairs, leaning on Rebecca. When they arrived in the study Marvin was still on the floor, Harvey standing over him. Pieces of the magic kit were scattered all over the room. Glittering strings that had been attached to the wand had broken off and there were sparkles on the bottom of Harvey's pants. Marvin was absently wiping his nose with a piece of a multi-colored scarf.

"What did you do to him?" Rebecca yelled at Harvey. She ran to her brother.

"What's going on here?" said Elaine softly. "Are either of you hurt?"

It took a few minutes for Harvey and Marvin to explain what

had happened.

"You goofball," Rebecca said to her brother. She sat on the floor and put her arm around Marvin's bruised shoulder. "You really thought you were going to yell 'hocus pocus' and mom would instantly be okay? You're really a jerk. You know that?"

Marvin smiled at her and nodded.

"I didn't mean to hurt him. I would never intentionally cause harm to my child," Harvey said. He glanced at the bookshelves. "But that was a holy book. A book that contained the name of the Lord. There are commandments about how such objects should be handled."

"Come here, all of you," said Elaine. Harvey sat down on one side of her, Marvin on the other. Rebecca sat next to Marvin. "You both were trying to do a good thing, but it didn't work the way you wanted it to. It's no one's fault. I love all of you. I know you're all doing your very best to help me get well and I thank you all."

Elaine hugged her husband and then her children.

Rebecca and Marvin went upstairs, and Rebecca let him win three games of checkers. She noticed Marvin rubbing his shoulders and saw his bruises.

"Did Papa do that?" she asked Marvin.

"It's okay, he was mad," said Marvin.

"He should pick on someone his own size," said Rebecca.

"It doesn't really hurt," said Marvin. "Don't say anything to him."

The next day, worried about her sisters-in-laws' reaction should they notice Marvin's bruises, Elaine told Helen and Rachel what had happened.

"Before you start, I'm telling you, don't say a bad word about Harvey," she said. "He's Marvin's father, and he loves him. He prays for guidance to do the right thing."

"Well, I'm not going to listen again to the story of Harvey's superior knowledge, how well he did in his studies in Europe, what a great sacrifice it is for him to live like a normal person in America," said Rachel. "He thinks just because he memorized the Torah, God smiles at him and he can do no wrong. I've known plenty of religious people, in Europe and here. Most of them are good people, good to their families. They say prayers, they don't beat children."

"You don't know what it was like for him in Poland. It was worse than what you went through," Elaine said to Rachel, who had left Europe five years before Harvey. "He watched the Nazis burn his synagogue, watched when his father tried to save the Torah and the Nazis pulled off his *payes* with their hands and laughed as they threw that pious man, and the Torah, into the fire.

"It was far worse than you heard about in America," she said to Helen.

Helen and Rachel sat silently, one on each side of Elaine's bed.

"He's a good man. He wants to be a good father, he just doesn't know how," said Elaine. "He'll need your help when I'm gone."

"Stop talking like that."

"You're getting stronger all the time."

Elaine held up her hands. "Medicine is not going to cure me. Prayers are not going to cure me. Now I know even a magic wand cannot cure me. I'm ready. But for me to go in peace you have to promise you'll both watch over Harvey and my children."

Helen and Rachel nodded.

The three women joined hands, tears in their eyes.

4.

MAY HER MEMORY BE A BLESSING

A few months later, at almost 3 a.m. on a cool October night, a nurse's aide was sitting in Elaine's bedroom reading a Spanish language fashion magazine by the dim light of the medical devices. The equipment made a soft humming sound, a light blinked on and off.

Elaine took quiet, shallow breaths.

And then she stopped.

A shrill beep startled the aide. She jumped up and went to Elaine, took her pulse, checked all the equipment. She called the doctor.

Then she went downstairs and knocked on Harvey's door. He'd started sleeping in his study when his bedroom filled with machines and medicines and caretakers.

There was no answer, so the nurse called his name and entered the room. She touched Harvey's shoulder, shook him softly. When Harvey was awake, she told him his wife was dead. She suggested he tell the children so they could say their goodbyes while they waited for the doctor. And for the undertaker.

Harvey pushed the young woman away, ran upstairs and grabbed Elaine's limp body. "How could this happen? How could you leave me?" he cried. "My darling, my sweet wife, come back to me."

Harvey turned to the young woman who had followed him into the room. "Why didn't you call me before she was gone? I wanted to say goodbye," he yelled. "Were you too busy with your silly magazines to keep an eye on the machines? Did you forget her medicine? Or were you sound asleep the whole night, neglecting your duties?"

The nurse had seen distraught families before. She quietly left the room.

Harvey started yelling at God, looking at the ceiling and waving his hands. "Didn't I pray hard enough?" he demanded. "Didn't I suffer enough in Europe? Haven't you seen how everyone in this country laughed at me for keeping my faith while they broke your commandments? Why did you do this to me?" Then he apologized to God for doubting His wisdom, hung his head, and started reciting prayers.

The commotion woke Marvin and Rebecca. They'd been told that their mother didn't have much time left, but they weren't prepared for the noises they heard coming from her room.

Marvin ran into Rebecca's room. "What's going on? Is Mama dead?" he asked.

"I think so," Rebecca said, hugging him. "That's why Papa is yelling. Remember, we knew this was coming. She's not in pain anymore. We've still got the rest of the family with us. We're okay."

"What is Papa doing?" Marvin asked.

"I guess he's praying."

"What should we do?"

"Do you want to say goodbye to Mama? We'll go together."

Marvin nodded and he and his big sister held hands as they

walked down the hall to their parents' bedroom. The nurse was still standing outside the door.

"Call my aunts," Rebecca said. "They'll know what to do."

The children walked into the room and found their father standing by their mother's bed, swaying back and forth, loudly praying while tears rolled down his cheeks. They looked from their father to their mother. Harvey walked over and put one arm around each of them. "Your dear mother has left us. It was God's will," he said. "Kiss her goodbye and come say a prayer with me. We'll mourn together."

Neither Rebecca nor Marvin had ever seen a dead person before. They slowly walked over to the body lying on the bed. Their mama's body. Lying perfectly still. Rebecca had the strong desire to poke her mother, to see if she was really dead, to see what a dead person felt like. Rebecca clasped her hands behind her back to make herself stay still.

"Maybe she's just sleeping," Marvin said. He turned away from the body and looked up at his sister. "Maybe Papa was yelling to try to wake Mama up."

"I wish that was true," said Harvey. "I also wish for a miracle. But I checked, there is no life in her. The nurse checked the monitors. The doctor is on his way to certify her death. All we can do now is pray. Say goodbye to your beloved mother and come join me."

Marvin didn't move.

"Don't be frightened," said Rebecca. "It's just mama."

She took one of Marvin's hands. He squeezed her fingers tightly as he leaned over Elaine's body. "Good-bye," he whispered through tears. "I love you."

Rebecca took a deep breath. She wanted to bang something and yell as loud as she could, but she knew her mother would want her to be strong and help Marvin. I can scream later when I'm alone, she told herself. It was important to keep it together now. Rebecca smoothed her mother's hair, whispered goodbye and kissed her cheek. She took a tissue from the box next to Elaine's bed, wiped Marvin's tear-stained cheeks and put her arm around him. The children went over to their father. He nodded, briefly hugged them and started saying a prayer very slowly. Rebecca and Marvin haltingly repeated the Hebrew words.

Helen and Rachel arrived quickly, coats thrown over their nightgowns. They ran upstairs and each grabbed one of Elaine's hands and started to cry. They hugged Harvey and the children. "Elaine's at peace now, no more suffering," said Helen.

"Let's go downstairs," said Rachel. "Marvin, you'll stay at my house tonight."

"Maybe," he said. Marvin looked up at Rebecca, still holding her hand.

"I'm staying with him," Rebecca said. "We should be together."

"Of course," said Rachel. "You'll both sleep at my house. And you, Harvey? You're welcome too."

"I'm staying here," said Harvey. "The Lord will be my companion."

"Whatever you want," said Helen. "I'll be downstairs making calls while Rachel gets the children settled. Let me know if I can do anything for you."

Harvey turned away, picked up the prayer book he'd put down when his sisters-in-law rushed in and interrupted him. He started to recite prayers loudly, swaying back and forth, pounding his chest. There was no way to give Harvey another hug. Touching him would be intrusive. They left him alone.

Rebecca and Marvin were already in their pajamas, so Rachel

told them to get their toothbrushes and some clothes to wear tomorrow.

At the front door Helen took Rachel's arm. "Should I call the old lady now or wait until morning?" she asked softly. All the Rosen children knew that 'the old lady' was what Helen and Rachel called their *Bubbe* Golda when she wasn't around.

"It'll frighten her to have the phone ring in the middle of the night. I'm worried how she'll deal with the shock," said Helen. "Maybe Saul and Morris should go to her first thing in the morning. They can stay with her."

"She'll want a chance to say goodbye before her daughter's body is taken away," Rachel said. "It won't be such a shock. She knew the end was near."

Rachel was right. Old people don't sleep very soundly, especially old people who know their child's life will soon be over. A few minutes after Rachel and her grandchildren passed her bedroom window, Golda was opening Elaine's front door. She hadn't waited for her phone to ring. She had seen the lights going on in Elaine's house and knew what that meant.

Golda didn't say anything to Helen, just went upstairs to Elaine's bedroom and told Harvey she needed time alone with her daughter. He left the room and stood in the hall with Helen. They heard Golda murmuring softly in Yiddish.

"That's not a prayer," Harvey said.

"It's a lullaby," said Helen.

After a few minutes, Golda came out and asked Helen to get a basin, soap and a clean washcloth. "Lukewarm water," Golda said. "Not too hot, not too cold. Be sure you check it."

"We've made arrangements for the cleansing, there'll be someone at the funeral parlor to watch over Elaine's body all night," Harvey said. "You don't have to do that."

Golda ignored him.

She took the basin Helen handed her, tested the water and nodded. "It's fine," she said, went back into the bedroom and closed the door behind her. Golda washed Elaine and combed her hair as she sang. It only took a few minutes. Soon she was outside and motioned to Harvey that he could go back into the bedroom.

"How are my grandchildren?" she asked Helen.

"They're spending the night with Rachel. They had a chance to say goodbye to their mother."

Golda nodded and kissed Helen on the cheek. "You and Rachel have been good sisters to my Elaine. I thank you. You know that this is the second daughter I've lost. My oldest died in the War. I didn't have a chance to say goodbye when she died."

Helen nodded, her eyes tearing up. She took off her glasses and wiped them on her blouse. She hugged Golda while the old lady stood stiffly, not responding. Then Golda walked down the stairs by herself.

The doctor came soon and, right after him, men from the funeral home took Elaine's body away. She was washed and dressed in a white shroud and professional mourners stayed with her throughout the night. Helen and Rachel called family and friends.

The services were held a day later. The sun was shining, the wind was blowing and Harvey was wailing. He'd been praying and crying since Elaine died and showed no sign of slowing down.

Golda sat silently at the funeral parlor. During the part of the prayers when people were expected to stand it took her a minute to get up, but she pushed away hands that tried to help her and stood straight. Relatives and friends gathered around Golda, offering condolences. She nodded, thanked them softly and turned away. Golda carried a freshly made bag of rock candy that she distributed to the youngsters. "On a day like today you need some sweetness," she murmured.

Almost everyone approached Rebecca and Marvin, told them how wonderful their mother had been, hugged and kissed the children. Marvin soon got tired of this and tried to squirm away. "I don't know a lot of these people," he said to his sister. "The women are getting lipstick all over me."

"Try to put up with it," Rebecca replied, handing him a tissue to wipe off the makeup. "Mama would want us to be polite."

She stood patiently beside Marvin, trying not to fidget in the drab, knee length grey dress her aunts had chosen for her. They'd shopped for the children's funeral clothes a few weeks before. Rebecca was and that the main thing her father had said to her that morning was a reprimand when he saw that she was wearing lipstick. Determined to set a good example for her brother, Rebecca smiled sadly while she tried to remember the name of the old lady with a thick white mustache who was smothering her.

From the funeral home, a long line of limousines made its way to the cemetery. Golda rode with Saul, Helen and Sarah in the second car, sucking on her candy. She didn't respond when they spoke to her.

In the back seat of the first car, Rebecca and Marvin spoke softly while Harvey stared out the tinted window. "Do you understand what's going to happen now?" Rebecca asked her brother. "We're going to bury Mama. Her body is in that box that was at the funeral home, they're going to dig a hole and put it in the ground."

"Why?" asked Marvin. "How will she breathe?"

"She's not breathing anymore. She died."

Rebecca put her arm around Marvin's shoulder. "But we're alive and we're going to keep her alive in our hearts by always remembering Mama."

Marvin looked younger than usual. Rebecca didn't know what she would do if he started to sob. She had a purse full of tissues, but she knew Marvin would be embarrassed. He always tried to be a big boy when he was with his older cousins.

"Will we go to school tomorrow?" Marvin asked. "I have a math test."

"Not tomorrow, in a few days," Rebecca said. "One of the aunts will let your teacher know about mama. There won't be any trouble. Anything else bothers you, you tell me. We still have each other and everyone else in the family. Remember that."

Harvey didn't say anything.

When traffic forced the procession to stop for a few minutes he stared out the window and quietly cursed the other cars.

Helen and Rachel had tried to prepare their own children for the funeral. "There's nothing to be frightened of," the mothers had said. "It's not like a *goische* funeral where you have to look at a dead body lying like a department store dummy on silk sheets in a fancy carved box. By us, everything is kept simple, natural. The casket is sealed, it's a plain pine box. Your aunt's body isn't stuffed with chemicals, her face isn't painted. At the funeral home people will talk about what a wonderful person your Aunt Elaine was and there'll be prayers, some in Hebrew, some in English. You just sit quietly, like in *shul*. When it's over we'll go to the cemetery."

No one thought to explain what a cemetery looked like and Helen's daughter, Sarah, was surprised when she stepped out of her parents' car and looked around. In the movies and on TV, cemeteries were always beautifully landscaped green fields with glistening white marble tombstones. But Jewish cemeteries aren't like that.

"What happened to this place?" she whispered to her mother.

"Why is everything so ugly?"

"Behave yourself," Helen whispered back. "Don't make me sorry I brought you. Go help *Bubbe* Golda out of the car."

Maybe Reform Jews have cemeteries that look like the ones in the movies, but in this cemetery there were no weeping willow trees, no stretches of verdant green lawn, no marble angels spreading grace from Heaven. No one brought flowers, no wreaths of white, waxy lilies, or deep red roses wrapped in ribbons and baby's breath. There was just earth and stones. The cemetery was crowded, one grave pushed in beside the next, laid out along a numbered grid, navigated with the maps provided by the office at the front gate.

When they reached the part of the ceremony during which the casket is buried, Golda got up, grabbed the heavy shovel, swung it around and sank it deep into the pile of loose dirt. But she couldn't get it out. "*Oy!*" she called loudly again and again, banging her fist on the handle of the shovel, which remained stuck in the dirt.

Rebecca immediately stood up and put her hands over her grandmother's gnarled fingers. Together they scooped up some dirt and dropped it into the waiting grave. Then Rebecca helped Golda back to her seat and kissed her.

When the service was over, Golda leaned heavily on Saul's arm, not looking where they were going, trusting her eldest son to guide her to the car. "Just take me home," she said. "I'll join the *shiva* tomorrow. My daughters are both at peace now."

Helen took Golda into her house and helped her change into a nightgown. She noticed the bottle of schnapps waiting on the kitchen table.

Harvey's house had been prepared for the week-long *shiva* period by funeral home employees while the family was at the cemetery. Mirrors were covered, vanity was forbidden; hard chairs were provided, no one would be comfortable. Neighbors brought food, took care of household chores and joined the family for prayers twice a day.

Rebecca and Marvin stayed at Rachel's house. Harvey didn't shave, didn't comb his hair, didn't wear shoes. When neighbors expressed sympathy, he just nodded his head, too involved with his own mourning to reply. Helen and Rachel kept track of gifts and charitable contributions, made sure thank-you cards were sent promptly.

When the *shiva* was over, funeral home employees came to the house and removed the mirror coverings, the hard chairs, the black drapes. The aura of death still hung over the house. Harvey barely noticed.

5.

A TIME TO GRIEVE, A TIME TO MOVE ON

Six months after Elaine's death Harvey was still grief-stricken. His sisters-in-law still took care of his children. His brothers-in-law grumbled that he still wasn't taking care of customers.

Helen decided to step in. The next time Harvey asked if Rebecca could spend yet another night at her house because he needed to be alone with his grief, she tilted up her head and looked him right in the eye.

"Harvey," Helen said, "enough is enough! You grieved, you sat *shiva*. You're the scholar, you know that at the end of the week you're supposed to resume your life. Soon you'll put up a gravestone for Elaine, you'll visit the cemetery, light a candle and say prayers. Of course you miss her, we all miss her, but you still have a life. And two living children."

Harvey tilted his head and looked down at Helen. He saw his reflection in her glasses. "You think I don't know this?" he said, sighing deeply. "But my heart has been torn from my chest. With such an ache how can I care for children? I have no choice but to ask for help."

Helen kept staring up at Harvey. "It's easy for me to take care of Rebecca. You know how much I love her. But it's not right. A child belongs with her parents. And in this country a father is also a parent."

Helen discussed the matter with Rachel. "We shouldn't automatically include Rebecca and Marvin every time either of us goes out. If Harvey insists on staying home, let him stay home with his children. He can talk to them, play with them, or not. But they'll be together. They're bright children, eventually they'll figure out something to do. A movie, the park, watch TV. They won't starve. Bad enough those children lost their mother, the way we're acting, they've also lost their father."

Rachel had doubts about this plan, but she didn't like arguing with Helen.

• • •

The front door banged shut behind Marvin as he charged into his Aunt Rachel's house, dropped his coat on the floor and ran up the stairs. "Sorry I'm late," he yelled to his cousins. "Had to take care of some stuff for my dad."

He stopped at the entrance to the room where his cousins were sprawled on the floor playing Monopoly. "What's going on? Why aren't you watching the game?"

"We can't," said Kenny. "We're being punished. These two jerks," he nodded at his younger brothers, "don't know how to behave. So, no TV for anyone. For a whole week."

"Like you were so innocent," said Bobby.

"I was trying to help," said Kenny. "You started it."

Kenny noticed a movement, glanced at his youngest brother who was slowly putting a green plastic house onto one of his own properties and, without a word, Kenny grabbed the piece and threw it at the younger boy who instinctively ducked. The hotel ricocheted off a lamp and fell onto the floor where Alan picked it up. Bobby twisted his brother's arm behind his back before he could throw it.

Marvin was looking for a way to join the melee when Rachel walked into the room. The boys froze. "What's going on? You can't stay quiet for two minutes? You want me to send you all to bed right now? Without supper?"

Rachel turned and noticed Marvin. "Oh, hello. I didn't know you were here. These three make so much noise I can't hear myself think. It's good to see you. You're staying for supper, right?"

"Sure. Sounds like I missed some excitement the other night. What happened?"

"I'll tell, I'll tell," said Alan.

"You're too young to get a story straight," said Kenny, turning to Marvin. "Last Sunday we went to the SeaHorse restaurant in City Island and while we were eating, this jerk," he nodded at Alan, "poured half a saltshaker into my dad's water glass."

"I thought it was Bobby's glass, he always does that to me," Alan said quietly. "I wanted to get him back."

"Dad took a huge swallow, got red in the face, started coughing and banging on the table. I ran over to save his life by pounding on his back. But while he was coughing dad had tipped over a saucer with melted butter.

"There was a small kid in a highchair at the next table. I slipped on the butter, fell down, knocked over the highchair and the baby fell on top of me. Good thing I was there, or that kid could have gotten really hurt."

"Yeah, you're a big hero," said Bobby. "Dad had almost stopped coughing when you reached him, but the kid and his mother started screaming at the top of their lungs soon as the highchair went over. I tried to give Dad my glass of clean water so he'd stop choking, but there was so much confusion I wound up spilling it on him. Mom tried to dry him off, dad's glasses slipped off his face and a passing waiter stepped on the glasses."

"Once things quieted down, Dad said he'd pay for whatever the parents of the kid who got knocked over wanted to eat. But he got mad when they ordered lobsters," said Alan. "And wine. They ordered a whole bottle, said they needed to calm their nerves. Dad glared, but the waiter had already heard that their meal should be on our check.

"My folks said that when you add the restaurant bill to the price of new glasses none of us will get an allowance for the rest of our lives."

Marvin was laughing so hard he couldn't stand up. "Gee, I'm sorry I missed that."

"Yeah, how come you weren't there?" asked Kenny. "You usually come to SeaHorse with us. We haven't seen you in a while."

"Well no one told me you were going," said Marvin.

The boys looked at Rachel. She turned away and started cleaning up the mess. "Marvin and Rebecca were having dinner with their father. They'll come with us another time." She looked at Marvin, "you're enjoying spending time with your father aren't you?"

"Sure, sure, lots of fun," said Marvin quietly.

The boys restarted the monopoly game and played until Rachel called them for dinner.

Soon as he got home, Marvin went to Rebecca's room. She was wearing a mini dress of Indian fabric embroidered with tiny mirrors, staring at herself in the full mirror on her closet door. "How do you think I'd look if I dyed my hair black?" she said to Marvin, not turning around. "I could paste a red crystal to my forehead, buy a sari, an Indian princess look, you know?"

"You'd look even weirder than you normally do."

Marvin pushed aside some of her clothes and sat on Rebecca's unmade bed. "Have you noticed we don't hang out with the rest of the family as much as we used to?" he said.

"You finally woke up, huh? It's Aunt Helen's newest bright idea. She's convinced we need to spend more time with our dear old dad. Thinks it's not healthy for him to grieve for Mama all alone, we should be consoling each other. Sarah told me."

"That's why we were eating that weird, curried beef casserole you made over the weekend instead of shrimp scampi at the SeaHorse?"

"Look, I followed the directions in the magazine. I don't know why it didn't come out better. I would have been happier at a restaurant. You think I jump for joy when Papa tells the housekeeper not to leave food for the weekend, that his wife was such a good cook he's sure his daughter will be able to make dinner too? Like you can inherit culinary ability. That it's in my DNA."

"I miss Mama's food."

"Yeah, I miss her too."

Rebecca went to her brother and hugged him. He held her for a minute before shrugging off her arm. "You think Aunt Helen's right? That we should be trying to make Papa feel better?"

"I think no one knows how to make things better for anyone. And it's not like we don't see the rest of the family at all. You've just come back from Aunt Rachel's house, right?"

"I guess."

"Don't worry. If this lasts too long, I'll tell *Bubbe* we miss our cousins. She'll get them to include us again. But getting back to domestic talents I lack, I walked past your room earlier and it was so immaculate it looked like no one lived there. What gives?"

"I've been trying to be extra obedient lately. Report cards are coming soon, and I don't think I'm going to do so well. Papa doesn't like messiness. I thought a clean room would encourage him to overlook my grades. He's been busy in the basement lately, says we need more bookshelves. I don't want him going at me because the only A I get is in gym."

Marvin looked at Rebecca's room where stuff was scattered everywhere. "You always get straight As."

Rebecca's eyebrows moved closer together. "Has he been hitting you?"

"No, no. Everything's fine. Forget I said anything."

"Let me see your back."

Rebecca tried to pull off Marvin's shirt, but he jerked away.

"Get your hands off me. Who do you think you are? I'm fine. I'm on the baseball team. Things happen. It's normal for a guy to have some bruises." His voice got louder. "And don't say anything. Not to Papa. Not to anyone. Not to our aunts or our uncles or our cousins or *Bubbe*. Understand? Everything's good."

Marvin started to leave. "I have to finish my homework." He glanced around. "Look, it wouldn't hurt you to straighten this place up. At least a little. The pile of spare material Papa has downstairs includes a couple of boards with nails in them."

Rebecca stood up. Not a good sign. She looked ready for action and that didn't mean hanging up her clothes.

"Hey, just kidding," he said. "Relax. I don't care how messy your room is. Okay? We good? You're going to stay here and make more of a mess. Right?" He walked out before she could say anything else.

Rebecca watched Marvin leave. Her mom would have expected her to take better care of Marvin. But how? Anyway, she had her own problems.

Rebecca was almost 14 years old and she felt ugly and abandoned. She hated her stringy, dirty blonde hair, her changing body. Maybe Aunt Rachel, with all her cosmetics and trips to the beauty parlor, could have helped her. But thanks to Helen's meddling, Aunt Rachel wasn't around much, and Rebecca was too embarrassed to ask for grooming tips.

When she tried to fix herself up, Harvey got angry. He called Rebecca a whore when she put on makeup or tried out a new hairstyle. Sometimes he slapped her. Rebecca just glared at him as she pulled out of his grasp, thinking, someday I'll get you back, I'll make you pay, just wait 'til I'm older.

Rebecca would run outside and walk around the neighborhood until their house was dark and she figured her father was asleep. He was always calm in the morning.

Everyone in the family thought Rebecca was doing so well because she got good grades. All of the Rosens had high hopes for Rebecca. She'd "made Science," been admitted to the academically prestigious Bronx High School of Science. All the girls at Science were smart and Rebecca was just as smart as any student in the school. But none of the girls at Science, and few at any other high school, looked like Rebecca. No one else had such big breasts.

There's one in every class. The first one to develop, the one who needs a bra while every other girl is still wearing an undershirt. The girl who slouches, wears oversized sweaters and carries her textbooks pressed up against her expanding chest while the boys make remarks and the other girls try exercises, creams and padding to remedy their flat chests.

To get to school, Rebecca took two buses and walked several blocks. The whole distance seemed populated by guys, teenagers and older men, none of whom had anything to do but stare at her and yell. And they didn't yell, 'Hey, look at that smart girl on her way to Bronx Science.' Sometimes they'd walk over and touch Rebecca, bump into her and make believe it was an accident. Sometimes they'd just grab and squeeze her breasts.

At first Rebecca was frightened, so ashamed she sometimes cried all the way to and from school. She thought about asking to transfer to a closer school, but her family would ask questions and make a fuss. That would be even more embarrassing than the things the guys were doing.

Rebecca decided her mom would have wanted her to protect herself, to get tough. She learned what to yell back so the men who had been making her miserable were the ones who were embarrassed, she figured out how to swing her book bag so they were the ones with bruises.

When she was no longer terrified to walk down the street, Rebecca realized that not all the guys who noticed her were creeps. Some were good looking, wanted to get to know her, to be nice to her.

She started sneaking out of the house at night, met a guy who took her to City Island, a short bus trip away where there were clubs that didn't bother carding her, where she could dance and laugh.

Rebecca learned what to wear to turn guys on, found shops that catered to young girls who wanted a social life. Of course, those sexy clothes weren't things her aunts would buy for her, and she didn't get much of an allowance from Harvey. She learned to shoplift.

Within a few months she was no longer the awkward, hunched-over teenager abused by men on the bus; she was the popular girl who could have a date anytime she wanted. She started having sex, assuring herself that it was okay because she only went with guys who were nice, who really liked her.

If things got out of hand, she just told the guys she was only 13 years old. She cried and said her father would call the police.

That stopped them. Usually. Almost always. They'd pull over and demand she get out of their car, turn their backs and yell at her to get lost. Rebecca would wind up walking alone in the middle of the night, and the cops started picking her up and driving her home.

Harvey told the police he would be stricter, that this would never happen again. He said his wife had recently died, that the family was in mourning. The police felt sorry for him. He was a respectable looking man who lived in a nice house in a good neighborhood. They let Rebecca go with a warning.

Harvey would wait until they got into the house before yelling at Rebecca, smacking her and saying her mother would be ashamed of her. The next morning he went to work as usual and she went to school.

No one said anything to the rest of the family.

6.

BY THE SEA, BY THE SEA

The summer after Elaine died, the Rosens rented a large house in Atlantic City. Aunts, uncles, grandmothers, siblings and cousins, all under one roof. The neighbors thought they were crazy. But Helen and Rachel had decided it would be easier to spend time at the beach together than for each of them to think of something to do with each of their children every day until school started again.

Harvey wasn't interested. He was too busy to visit on weekends, it was a waste of time to sit in traffic after a long day at work just to spend a few hours baking in the sun. He mentioned sending his children to sleep-away camp for the whole summer. Helen and Rachel didn't approve of strangers taking care of the children.

"Rebecca and Marvin should just come with us," Helen said. She had finally acknowledged that having Harvey spend more time with his children wasn't the way to resolve anyone's problem. "Marvin loves being with Rachel's boys and Rebecca can share a room with Sarah. Don't worry, I'll keep a special eye on your daughter. The sea breezes will be good for her."

When no one said anything about Harvey chipping in for the cost of the beach house he agreed to the plan.

Saul and Morris drove to the shore late every Friday night. The men recounted business problems, listened to family disputes, and ate extra-large meals cooked for them despite the heat. They took everyone on special outings that left children cranky and autos sandy. Early Sunday afternoon they distributed cash, advice, and hugs then drove off, claiming they were sorry to miss so much of the vacation, but wanted to avoid the traffic.

The Rosen family and all of their friends believed in the curative power of ocean waters. Grandmas waded into mid-thigh water and bounced up and down on arthritic knees while their black bathing suit skirts floated around them. Feuds were temporarily suspended, and they held hands as their toes sank into the sand, an attempt at balance which made their stances even more precarious.

Weekdays at the beach were calm, and Rebecca and Sarah grew close. Rebecca got Sarah to dive under the waves by threatening not to speak to her again if she didn't follow her cousin into the crashing walls of water. Rebecca wore tight, brightly flowered two-piece suits, and clutched her breasts and screeched in the water, saying she was afraid the waves would pull off the top. Sarah wore one-piece suits with ruffles on top to hide the fact that she didn't have a bust. The girls helped their younger cousins construct elaborate sandcastles.

Sarah was thrilled to have her cousin's attention. Back in the Bronx, she repeatedly heard the family talking about Rebecca, about the poor motherless girl. How often did she go out? Who were her friends? Where did they go? What did they do?

No one worried about Sarah. It was clear to her that Rebecca was smart and exciting and she was a loser. When she tried to ask for advice, Rebecca just said, "junior high kids are so immature" and turned away.

But at the beach Rebecca had no one else to hang out with

and decided her cousin wasn't so bad. Sarah was glad to hide the cigarettes Rebecca had started smoking since her mother's death. Adults never looked in Sarah's bureau. Rebecca showed her how to paint her nails and put on makeup. And when Rebecca caught Sarah trying on one of her bras, which hung limply from her shoulders, Rebecca laughed till she was out of breath and soon Sarah joined her.

At the end of their first week at the beach, Rebecca woke up in the middle of the night and thought she heard someone on the porch. She went downstairs and found Marvin having what looked like a very animated conversation with the sky.

She watched for a few minutes, wondering if he was walking and talking in his sleep, if she should wake him. Rebecca leaned against one of the porch rocking chairs and it creaked. Marvin jumped.

"Hey! Who's there?" Marvin said.

"Just me," said Rebecca softly. "Wondered who you were talking to."

"I'm not talking to anyone. There's no one here."

"Sure looked like you were talking to someone. Looked like you were enjoying the conversation. I'm glad you're having a good time."

"You won't tell?"

"Of course not."

"I'm talking to Mama. There are so many more stars here than there are in the Bronx I figured one of them was probably Mama and she was watching the house to make sure we were okay."

Conversing with their mother seemed to make Marvin feel good, so Rebecca didn't try to talk him out of it, even helped him sneak outside the next few nights. She sat quietly smoking a cigarette at one end of the porch while Marvin carried on his conversation at the other end. She never asked what he was saying to their mom, just let him stare at the sky, whispering softly until his eyes started to close, and then she helped him get back to bed.

About a week after he started having these midnight conversations, a shooting star streaked across the sky, and Marvin started to yell. Rebecca ran over.

"Why doesn't God catch her?" Marvin screamed. "She's going to get hurt. She's going to die again." Marvin looked at Rebecca, his eyes wide. "That falling star, that's the one I've been talking to. Mama slipped from her place in the sky. She's burning up."

"That's not our mom; you're looking at the wrong star. That's a clumsy person's star, someone who can't stand up straight." Rebecca held him tight. "Our mom is safe in heaven. She's still carefully watching us."

Marvin stopped yelling and looked up at Rebecca. "I guess you're right," he said softly and slowly nodded.

But he'd woken up the aunts and they rushed out. Rebecca said Marvin had been sleepwalking and had a bad dream. "He does that sometimes," she said. "Didn't my dad warn you? Not a big deal, just getting used to sleeping in a new place."

They gave Marvin warm milk, which he hated but drank without complaining, and went back to bed. The next morning, he was cheerful and assured everyone he was fine, and so the subject was dropped.

Later that afternoon, Marvin thanked Rebecca for covering for him. "I was a jerk," he said. "Of course I had the wrong star. Dumb mistake. Mom wasn't a *klutz*. She wouldn't fall. Anyway, God wouldn't let her die a second time."

Rebecca gave him a quick hug and he ran out to join the ball game in the yard. They didn't discuss it again. If he kept talking to the sky after that night, he did it alone.

Miscellaneous adult friends came to visit, spreading their blankets and beach chairs next to the Rosens. The boys pounded beach umbrella poles into the sand, but the umbrellas still fell over when the wind blew. The adults kept an eye on any child in the water. They yelled, "Don't go too far! Don't go too deep! Don't stay in too long!"

Sometimes the women pulled on colorful bathing caps adorned with rubber flower petals and ran into the ocean, laughing and shrieking that the water was too cold, the waves too rough.

Rebecca took Marvin aside. "Our mother wouldn't have made such a fuss," she said. "Our mother loved the water. She was a great swimmer."

Marvin nodded, although he didn't really remember going to the beach with his mother.

"Yeah," he said. "Nothing scared her. Our mom could do anything."

During the day everyone's skin glowed from repeated applications of tropical-scented suntan lotion. At night they smelled stronger, more medicinal, from thick globs of Noxzema on shoulders and noses that had turned red despite the lotion.

Helen and Sarah had dark skin that could soak up the sun without much damage, but Helen had pale circles around her eyes in the shape of the prescription sunglasses she never took off. Rebecca smelled like the lemons she squeezed onto her hair so it would turn blond. Sarah told her it looked lighter. Didn't say it looked like straw.

The beach was rarely crowded during the week, but one day the Rosens returned from lunch and found that another family had settled near their spot. There were a couple of teenage boys, a baby and a mother and father, all with blond hair and skin so pale it was clear they had just arrived at the shore. The Rosens studied them.

"What language are they speaking?" Sarah asked her mother. "It sounds kind of like Yiddish, but I don't understand it."

"That's not Yiddish," Helen said with a pained expression. "It's German."

Aunt Rachel noticed Rebecca eyeing the boys, who were playing paddleball near their parents. "Good looking boys," she said in a flat voice. "Very Aryan." Rebecca turned away.

Rachel turned to Helen. "You know, Beatrice Silverman mentioned she might meet us on the beach this afternoon. I think her father-in-law is visiting."

The whole family knew the Silvermans. In the Bronx, they lived around the corner from Helen and Saul in a two-family house. The grandfather lived in the downstairs apartment. He had a number on his arm.

No one said they were uneasy sitting next to a German family. For all they knew the people on the next blanket could have been German Jews. They all knew about "the righteous gentiles," non-Jews who worked bravely to save Jews during WWII, sometimes sacrificing themselves and their own families. But the Rosens were a family of Jewish refugees, and the adults scanned crowds to look for Jewish faces, didn't buy German cars and didn't appreciate German art and music.

Kenny listened to his mother's conversation. "How about moving our stuff closer to the water?" he asked. "Look, there's an empty spot not too far away."

"Good idea," said Helen gathering up the towels. "It'll be cooler over there."

Before dinner the whole family took long walks on the board-walk and waited for the evening breezes to cool the house.

They went to see "The Amazing Diving Horse" and were disappointed by the grey horse that jumped into a small pool, not a huge, winged, snow white horse ridden by a scantily clad woman as it soared through the clouds into a tiny bucket of water, which was how the act appeared on the billboard.

They had their pictures taken with Mr. Peanut, a ten-foot-tall peanut with a cane, monocle and top hat who tap danced in front of the Planters Peanut Store, scattering the pigeons who waited for people to throw them nuts.

Every possible sort of junk food was for sale. The family watched saltwater taffy being made on conveyor belts that wound through shiny steel machines behind the glass windows facing the boardwalk.

"Could we send some taffy to my dad?" Rebecca said, mesmerized by the multi-colored candies being wrapped and scooped into fancy packages. "I'll bet he's never had any."

"What a wonderful idea," Helen said in her *kvelling* voice. Everyone marched into the store and poured through bins of loose candy, looking for their favorites. The children were each allowed two pieces and didn't want to waste their choices on flavors they'd previously discovered were icky, like licorice or grapefruit. The grown-ups chose sugar-free candies.

Rebecca found an assortment of pastel-colored candies in a box ready for mailing. On the front was a picture of a smiling, bikini-clad woman holding a beach ball over her head and the words, Hello from Atlantic City, beside the space for the mailing address.

On the back of the package were a few lines where you could write a message.

I'm having a great time. Hope you're well. Enjoy this

49

candy. *Love, Rebecca*, she wrote.

The cashier figured out the postage, stamped the box and put it into a basket for mailing.

7.

ON THE BOARDWALK

Not long after they arrived, Rebecca became restless, wanted to go out at night. She snapped at the younger kids, kept changing the channel on the TV or listened to rock music on the radio at full volume.

"The other teenagers in this town are on the boardwalk at night," Rebecca complained to anyone who would listen. "I don't see why I should be treated like a child."

The adults didn't think it was a good idea to allow a young girl to wander alone after dark. "There are plenty of hoodlums out there," said Helen. "And just think what Harvey would say. He's so particular about everything.

"And a teenager with a figure like a grown woman, the boys notice her. That girl is more developed now than I was until I had my first child," Rachel whispered back.

Helen came up with the solution. She told Rebecca she could spend two hours on the boardwalk after dinner, as long as she stayed where it was well lit, and she took Sarah with her.

"You can't expect a teenager to sit around every night. This way, maybe she'll talk to a few other kids, but that's not the end of the world," Helen said. "Sarah idolizes Rebecca, so she'll stay close. How much trouble can a girl get into with a little kid stuck to her side?"

Sarah was thrilled by the arrangement. When she strolled along under the lights on the boardwalk with Rebecca, boys sometimes whistled, called out, "Hello beautiful, why don't you smile for me?"

She knew the boys were talking to Rebecca, who ignored them as they passed, and smiled broadly a few seconds later. But Sarah thought maybe a few of them believed she was pretty, too. It could happen. She was growing up. Rebecca was helping her become better looking.

At first Rebecca didn't care where they went. Sarah easily steered her to the huge arcade next to the amusement park with a large Ferris wheel where they'd gone during the day when it was full of families.

It was a different place at night.

Harsh fluorescent lights glared on the sunburnt skin, sprayed hair and lit cigarettes of teens determined to enjoy themselves. Shouting voices competed with pinball machines where clanging steel balls bounced off bumpers. Pow! Pow! Pow! Pow! Hunting rifles blasted tin duck targets, metal pucks struck miniature bowling pins and handfuls of coins dropped into machines that spat out tickets for winning scores

Along one wall a trinket-filled case displayed prizes a player could claim. For only five tickets you could get a keychain, a pen or a straw finger trap. For twenty-five tickets you could choose a pair of plastic sunglasses, a tiny puzzle with metal balls you rolled into holes, or a wallet with a mermaid painted on it. If you had over 100 tickets you got to shop on the higher shelves where there were large stuffed animals, straw baskets full of candy and jewelry in velvet cases.

Sarah desperately wanted the gold chain with a charm of Mr.

Peanut tipping his hat. It was on the very top shelf and cost 200 tickets.

Each night, Helen gave each girl one dollar. Rebecca saved her money to buy cigarettes and makeup. For Sarah, the money meant ten games and the possibility of accumulating enough tickets to get the necklace.

Her game was Skeeball. Sarah loved the sound of the balls rolling down the alley toward her when she inserted her coin and pulled the lever, and the way the bell rang when a ball landed in the target. But she wasn't very good. If she threw hard, she overshot the target and got zero. If she threw softly, the ball barely cleared the hump, and she got zero.

The second week, while Sarah was cursing the machine and Rebecca was trying to blow smoke rings, the girls met Sal.

"Looks like your little sister is having a problem," said a tall, dark haired teenage boy who was suddenly next to them. His hair was slicked back on the sides and his pompadour glistened in the light. His tight tee shirt clung to his muscles. He managed to talk without taking his cigarette out of his mouth. He was gorgeous.

"She's my cousin, and she's a *klutz*," said Rebecca, using the bored, sophisticated voice Sarah had heard her practice in front of a mirror.

They exchanged names. "Becky and Sarri, cute names for cute girls," Sal said. No one had ever called Sarah Sarri before. It sounded exotic.

Sal looked at Sarah, ignoring Rebecca. "Let me show you how, honey," he said, putting a dime in the Skeeball machine. He bent over to show her how he held the ball. Sal smelled like the aftershave she bought for her dad on his birthday because she liked the fancy bottle even though her father never used it.

Sarah and Rebecca watched Sal respectfully as he sent the first ball rolling down the alley. The ball went BAM! as it jumped over the hump and into the bullseye. BAM, bullseye! BAM, bullseye! BAM, bullseye! BAM, bullseye! All ten balls jumped into the small hole in the center of the target. The machine went Ding! Ding! Ding! and ejaculated a long stream of tickets.

Sarah reached for the tickets, but Sal grabbed her hand before she got to them. "Don't pull too quickly, the tug triggers the machine to stop giving tickets," he said. "If you pull slowly sometimes you can trick it into giving you a couple of extras."

She slowly pulled out the tickets, counted them and discovered he was right. Sarah had gotten an extra ticket. Sal put another dime into the machine. He picked up the first ball, put it into Sarah's hand and showed her how to hold it. She didn't hear a word he was saying. She was holding hands with a boy, a good-looking guy.

"Now you do just what I showed you while your cousin and I get acquainted," Sal said. Sarah watched as he walked around the arcade with Rebecca. He whispered in her ear and put his arm around her waist. She laughed and whispered back. A few minutes later they returned to the machine where Sarah was playing.

"It's too noisy to talk in here," said Rebecca. "We're going to get some air. We'll be right outside."

"You keep practicing," said Sal. He gave her a few extra dimes. "Just take it slow and soon you'll be able to pick the best prize in the place."

Sal and Rebecca strolled away. Sarah saw them settle onto the bench across the boardwalk from the arcade. In about half an hour she was out of dimes and had 10 tickets in her pocket. A lot more than she usually won. It was time to go home.

Sarah went outside and found Rebecca and Sal smoking cigarettes and laughing. Sal walked them as far as the ramp that led from the boardwalk to their street. He kissed Rebecca on the lips and kissed Sarah on the cheek.

As soon as they got off the boardwalk Rebecca threw away her cigarette and pulled out a peppermint life saver. "You don't have to tell your mother about everything that happened tonight, you know," she said slowly. "Your mom is a lot stricter than mine would have been. If my mother hadn't died, she would have let me go out with guys like Sal."

Sarah wasn't sure that was true. But there was no point arguing with her cousin, not when things were going so well.

"I'm not a baby. I know you're not supposed to smoke, but I don't care if you do. And if you want to have a boyfriend, Sal is okay with me."

From then on, Rebecca and Sarah went to that arcade whenever they could. Sal always seemed to be there, waiting for them. He smiled at Sarah, played a few games of Skeeball and handed her the tickets he won. Then he left her at the machine with some extra dimes while he and Rebecca went outside.

Some nights Sarah got tired of playing Skeeball, tried other games, or just walked around the arcade. She watched people go into the photo booth and thought about getting a picture with Sal so she could tell friends at home that he was her boyfriend, but she didn't have the nerve to ask him.

Sarah watched couples use the Test-Your-Love Machine. It had two metal handles on either side of a large wooden thermometer. Each person was supposed to grab a handle, think about the other person and squeeze the handle as hard as they could. A light moved up the thermometer measuring their relationship, from frigid to passionate. Someday I'll try this with my boyfriend, Sarah thought.

Before she left the arcade, Sarah went to the prize counter, made sure the Mr. Peanut necklace was still there and figured out how many more tickets she needed to win before she could claim it. Then she went outside.

Sometimes Sal and Rebecca were kissing. Sarah stood there watching them. Their lips moved as they pressed them together and she wondered how it felt.

When they became aware of her and stopped kissing the three of them would walk back together, enjoying the lights and the noise and the ocean breezes.

One day, her mom came into their room while Sarah was counting her prize tickets. She had 153 tickets; soon she'd have the necklace.

"How did you get so many tickets?" her mom asked, startling Sarah. Before she could think of an answer Helen said, "Oh, I guess Rebecca is giving you her winnings. Don't worry if she's better at the games. It's because she's older. You'll get there. Meanwhile, it's nice you two get along so well."

About a week after they sent the candy to Harvey, he called. Helen answered, greeted him warmly and assured him everything was fine before she loudly called upstairs, "Rebecca, pick up the phone, it's your father."

Instead of hanging up, Helen put her hand over the mouthpiece, listened to the call and frowned. She shook her head, and, about fifteen minutes later, softly hung up the receiver. Then Helen looked around, made sure no one was nearby and phoned her husband back in the Bronx. Without even asking what Saul had had for dinner, Helen told him about the call from Harvey.

"Who cares that there was a picture of a girl in a bathing suit on the candy box? Like I'd let Rebecca send him a Playboy Magazine. And who checks to see if candy is kosher? Candy is just candy.

"He kept asking Rebecca what she was eating. Maybe he thinks

I buy a freshly slaughtered pig every day so I can make bacon and eggs in the morning, and ham and cheeseburgers every night? And over and over he tells her to obey all the rules, like I'm running a jail here."

She paused for a moment but didn't give Saul a chance to speak. "Let me tell you, Rebecca is still missing her mother, and teenage years are hard for a girl, but she's a good girl. If he's having so much trouble with that child it's his own fault. She's been a big help here. She does the chores I ask her to do without any objection and she's been terrific with Sarah."

"Should I say something to Harvey at work?" Saul asked.

"No, no. Remember, I wasn't supposed to hear this call. So you don't know anything. You'll be here tomorrow. We'll talk then. Try to come a little early."

The next night, when the girls left for the boardwalk, Rebecca was wearing more makeup than usual, short shorts and a tight tube top. Everyone in the house was busy. No one noticed.

As soon as she saw Sal, Rebecca walked up to him and gave him a big, long kiss on the mouth. "It's always a treat to see my two favorite girls," he said.

Sarah smiled. Rebecca whispered in Sal's ear.

"Stay right here," he said.

Sal went to the change booth and was back in a few minutes carrying several rolls of dimes, which he unwrapped and deposited into the pockets of Sarah's shorts. The change was so heavy it pulled the elastic waistband down a bit. "This should give you enough games to win the whole place," he said.

Sal and Rebecca left the arcade and Sarah went to her favorite Skeeball machine.

Thanks to all the practice she'd had, thanks to Sal's generosity,

Sarah was now a skillful player. Every one of her balls reached the target, a few jumped into the bullseye.

They were leaving Atlantic City at the end of the next week and she was pretty sure she'd have enough tickets to get the Mr. Peanut necklace. If she was short, Sarah knew she could ask Sal to win some more tickets for her.

Suddenly she heard someone calling, "Sarah, Saraleh." It was her father. She was so surprised she dropped the ball in her hand, and it thudded onto the floor, sending Sarah scrambling among the other players' legs to retrieve it.

"Daddy," she said as she got up and hugged him. "Hi. You're early."

The fathers usually arrived around 11 pm, by which time Rebecca and Sarah were back at the house. "Does Mom know you're here?"

"Sure," he said. "I left the city early and there was almost no traffic. When I stopped at the house Mommy told me you and Rebecca were on the boardwalk. I decided to get some air and see if I could find my girls. Luckily this is the first place I looked. So, where is she? Let's get out of here and I'll buy you both some ice cream."

Saul looked around to see if Rebecca was standing nearby. He looked at the other machines. No Rebecca. Sarah just stood there.

"Maybe she went to the bathroom," Sarah said. "I'll go get her." She handed the ball to her father. "Here, you finish my turn while I look."

"Okay, I'll see if I can get you some tickets."

"That'd be great."

The bathroom was in the back of the arcade, but Sarah headed towards the front, certain Rebecca and Sal were in their usual place. But when she got to the door, she saw some other kids sitting on their bench. Sarah looked at the next bench, and the next. No Rebecca. No Sal. She didn't want to stay out too long; her father would have finished the game by now and would be waiting for her.

"She wasn't there," Sarah said when she got back. "Maybe she went for a walk."

"She leaves you alone?" her father asked. "Alone in this place?"

Sarah looked around and saw the friendly arcade now filled with people her parents called hoods and cheap girls.

"Maybe Rebecca wanted something to eat," she said. "They sell hot dogs, and pizza and all kinds of stuff around here. Maybe she's getting a soda and she'll be back soon. Do you want to try another game? I've got lots of money."

Sarah held out a handful of the dimes Sal had crammed into her pockets.

"Your mother gives you so much money?" said Saul. "Let's get out of here and look for Rebecca."

They turned left out of the arcade and walked in silence down the middle of the boardwalk. Saul looked at the benches on the water side; Sarah looked into the shops on the other side, wondering how they were going to explain Sal. A few times her dad went up to the railing and looked at the kids on the benches, at the kids on the sand, then came back.

"That wasn't her," he said.

After about 15 minutes they turned around and started back. This time, Saul carefully looked into all the shops and Sarah scanned the benches. When they reached the small amusement park he abruptly stopped.

There was nothing very special about the Ocean Avenue World O' Wonders Amusement Park. There were similar places every 10 or 15 blocks along the boardwalk, same rides, same smells of overpriced junk food, same sounds of roller-coaster-rider screams mixed with merry-go-round music and souvenir-hawker-spiels.

But this place had a large Ferris wheel, the Wonder Wheel, its name spelled out in red and silver tiles embedded in the wide steel beam that bisected the wheel. It wasn't very impressive during the day, but at night the tiles reflected the lights from the other rides and the whole structure twinkled. At each end of the beam was a large spotlight, green on one end, gold on the other, so, as the wheel slowly spun, the colored lights crept across the park.

The Wonder Wheel wasn't larger or gaudier than other Ferris wheels in other amusement parks. What made this park and this Ferris wheel so special that night was that the Ocean Avenue World O'Wonders was right next door to the arcade where Rebecca and Sarah had met Sal, and the moving spotlight on top of the Ocean Avenue Wonder Wheel traced a path from the roof of the arcade to its base, briefly illuminating the wall against which Sal and Rebecca had decided to take their romance to the next level.

When old Talmudic scholars debated the fine points of Jewish law they would sway back and forth and intone "and iiiiiiiiiiiiiiif that happened, then ....., and iiiiiiiiiiiiiiiif this happened then ...."

Today, some people still use this counterfactual style of argument. "And if bond prices go up, then stock prices go down. And if stocks go down, then real estate..."

Eventually someone gets annoyed and says, "enough with the if, if, if. If my grandmother had wheels, then she'd be a trolley." If they're really frustrated, they might say, "and if my grandmother had a penis, then she'd be my grandfather."

If Sarah and Saul had walked a little faster, or a little slower, then they wouldn't have reached the amusement park just as the Ferris wheel spotlight was pointing right at Rebecca and Sal. If the

Ferris wheel operator had not turned off the lights while he was taking a break a little while before Rebecca and Sal reached the wall, then they would have known the place they were leaning was right in the path of the beam and would have gone someplace else.

But Grandma Golda wasn't a trolley or a grandfather, and none of these things happened.

When Sarah and her father reached the amusement park the Wonder Wheel had just stopped to let people off. The bright yellow spotlight was shining, but not moving. It was pointing directly at the niche in the wall where Rebecca and Sal were standing, lighting up her long, straw-colored hair and his shiny black hair. Rebecca had her eyes closed, her head thrown back and her mouth open just like the actresses on the covers of the movie magazines she and Sarah secretly read in their bedroom. Maybe she was imagining she was a movie star and that's why she didn't mind the spotlight. Sal was kissing her neck.

Sarah's father didn't yell very often. But as soon as he realized what he was looking at, he started to shout. Loudly. "Rebecca! Rebecca! Rebecca!"

Standing next to her father, it seemed to Sarah he was screaming loud enough to shatter the glass windows of nearby stores, loud enough to get the crowds to stop moving and put their hands over their ears. But it was a Friday night in August on the noisy Atlantic City boardwalk next to an amusement park. Only a few people looked at him and then kept walking.

Saul grabbed Sarah's hand and they ran into the amusement park. They ran past the bumper cars, the Tilt-o-Whirl and the stand where a fat man was making bright pink cotton candy cones. They ran to the Ferris wheel whose lights were moving again to the place where Rebecca and Sal stood, now bathed in a slowly moving, green light.

Rebecca was still against the wall, Sal was still leaning against her. Saul grabbed the boy's arm with both of his and tugged with all his strength. When Sal stepped away, Sarah and her father saw that Rebecca's tube top was down around her waist and her large breasts were staring straight at them.

"Cover yourself!" Saul yelled at her.

"Hey, who do you think you are?" Sal said, easily shrugging out of Saul's grasp. Then he saw Sarah.

"Hey Sarri," he said. "What's going on?"

"This is my father, Sal," she said. "Rebecca's uncle."

"You know this boy?" Saul yelled. "You're not being attacked Rebecca? We trust you and this is what you do? And you're part of it, Sarah? You don't know any better?"

"Usually they stay on the bench," Sarah said.

"Not another word from either of you," said her father. "And you, young man," he said to Sal. "Zip your pants. Go home. And if I ever see you near anyone from my family again, you'll be sorry."

Sal started to say something. Rebecca shook her head and he stopped.

Saul glared at him.

"Don't get upset, old man," Sal said. "Nothing happened. I'm leaving." He strutted away, waving his hand over his shoulder, heading back to the boardwalk.

"So long, girls," he said. "Really nice meeting you both."

That was the last anyone saw of Sal.

Saul and the girls walked home in silence. When they reached the house, Saul asked Helen to come outside. Rebecca and Sarah followed. "I don't want the other children to hear," he said. Of course, by morning everyone knew everything anyway. It was that kind of family.

"There she was, no brassiere, nothing, just her boobies hanging there in the middle of the crowded park, where the whole world could see," Saul told Helen. He made large cups out of his fingers, stretched his arms in front of his chest and jiggled them up and down.

"And our Rebecca was making noises, not frightened noises, not angry noises, but noises only a married woman should make."

Helen looked at Rebecca and then at Sarah. Her eyes were glaring, her lips pressed together. She didn't say a word. Saul kept talking, his voice getting louder, more agitated.

"The boy's pants were open, but they were still on him. Was his *putz* out? I don't know, I didn't look. I just grabbed him off of her and threw him away like the garbage he is," Saul said. "I did notice Rebecca's shorts were on. Thank Heaven I got there before things went too far. Believe me, I gave that boy a piece of my mind. He knows he'll be sorry if he ever bothers us again."

"I wasn't going to let him go all the way," Rebecca said. "I know how to handle guys."

"No one told you to speak," Saul said.

"Wait, Saul," said Helen. "You forget we're dealing with a sophisticated, worldly woman here. This isn't an immature girl who doesn't realize how narrowly she avoided real trouble, maybe ruining her life."

Helen looked at Sarah. "And we're talking to a girl we thought had some common sense. A girl we thought knew when to let her mother know that something very wrong was going on."

She looked from Rebecca to Sarah, then back again. She shook her head and sighed.

"So, what do I do with you two? Do I punish you? Make you scrub the floors on your hands and knees? Yell at you? Hit you? For how long? How hard? What is the right action?"

Rebecca and Sarah didn't say a word.

"Maybe I shouldn't do anything. Maybe neither of you deserves the blame. Maybe the whole thing is my fault," Helen said. "What was I thinking? That the two of you were trustworthy? That you knew how to stay away from situations where you could be seriously hurt by dangerous men? Did I think that you came from a family where girls were taught to behave decently, not like tramps?

"How could I have trusted you both to go out by yourselves, night after night? How come I didn't spy on you? Why? Because I had confidence in you. That's why! How could I be so stupid?

"I should get down on my knees and ask the Lord for forgiveness for being such a terrible mother. I should ask for forgiveness from my dear Elaine in heaven whose child I promised I would take care of. How can poor Elaine rest in peace knowing she left her beloved Rebecca with such a terrible aunt?"

Rebecca and Sarah started to cry. Over and over they said how sorry they were. Helen reached out to the girls; Saul put his arm around his wife. Soon they were all hugging.

Saul kept repeating, "It could have been worse. Thank God I was there in time."

Rebecca assured her aunt and uncle she didn't know how to get in touch with Sal and wouldn't even think of trying to. She and Sarah promised that for the next week they'd do all the chores – wash and dry all the dishes, make the beds, clean the house and help care for the younger children. They promised to stay in every night and stay away from the arcade and the amusement park, where they never should have gone in the first place.

Everyone was exhausted when the girls finally kissed Helen and Saul and said goodnight. As they climbed the stairs to their room Rebecca suddenly turned around.

"Are you going to tell my father?"

Helen sighed and looked up at her. "I have to, sweetheart."

"Are you sure you have to tell him? Even if I do all the things I promised? Even if I do some extra things?"

"He's your father. It's not right to keep something like this from him. He trusted me to take care of you."

"What will you say?" asked Rebecca.

"I don't know," said Helen. "I really have no idea. I'll have to think about it. Think really hard. Now go get some rest."

Helen took a pitcher of iced tea out of the fridge, and she and Saul went back to the porch. They sat on the porch swing, not realizing it was located just below the open window in the room Rebecca and Sarah shared, where they crouched under the windowsill, listening.

"We could cut Rebecca's vacation short," said Saul. "I could take her back home with me on Sunday. Maybe it's not such a good idea for Sarah to spend so much time with her."

"And what would you say to Harvey?" asked Helen. "Tell him you caught his daughter running around naked like a wild woman with some strange man? No matter what you say you know he won't stay calm. I don't want him punishing her while no one from the family is around. Whatever happens, it'll be better if we're all there."

"It's not like we're not punishing her," said Saul. "We're taking care of the situation, doing what's proper. It's too bad we have to say anything to Harvey."

"I know, I know," said Helen. "It would be easier for everyone, maybe even better for everyone, if Harvey didn't know. But if Sarah did something wrong and Rachel knew about it, I'd be furious if she didn't tell me. Adults shouldn't keep secrets about children from their parents."

"You really believe that's true? In this case?" asked Saul.

"If Harvey were the type of parent Rebecca deserves it would definitely be true," said Helen. "We could tell Harvey what happened and remind him Rebecca is still mourning her mother. Another father might hear the story and say, 'So a grieving girl acted out, it's not the end of the world. I'll cut off her allowance, ground her for a while and try to be more attentive.'

"But that's not Harvey. You know it's not. So we'll tell him what happened so he'll know we respect him and his rights as a parent. But there's respect, and then there's respect. We can respect him without telling him everything."

"That's true," said Saul. "And I certainly don't want him to have a new reason to act superior. He spends too much time on his high horse as it is."

"I'll talk to Rachel," Helen said. "We'll figure something out. We have the whole week to work on a plan. But it won't be easy. We have to be careful. This isn't the kind of thing you can make go away by waving a magic wand."

Rebecca and Sara remembered Marvin's magic kit. They knew exactly what Helen meant when she talked about the impotence of a magic wand.

They shut the window and went to bed.

8.

WHAT TO TELL HARVEY

By lunchtime the next day everyone at the beach house knew that Sarah and Rebecca's nighttime excursions on the boardwalk hadn't been proper.

There was a lot of "tsk, tsking" and muttered Yiddish proverbs about the importance of a woman's virtue and the misfortunes suffered by a disobedient child. The younger children were delighted to learn that the girls had been bad and would be taking over their chores. Rebecca and Sarah did their jobs without complaint.

During that last week in Atlantic City everyone talked about how much they'd miss the beach, but they were ready to get home, sleep in their own beds, see their friends and prepare for the new school year.

Helen often looked distracted, mumbling to herself and having frequent conversations that started with, "So how do you think Harvey would react if I said..." If she noticed the girls nearby, she'd give them a look that meant they should move away.

Sarah didn't mind the extra work; it felt good to know she was making up for deceiving her mother. But she was very worried about one thing, a thing that confronted her every time she opened her bureau drawer where, carefully bundled and tied with rubber bands, were all the Skeeball tickets she'd won.

Sarah needed 18 more tickets to claim the necklace she longed for. She was now proficient in the game, sure she could win that many tickets quickly, in only a few games, it would only take a few minutes. Sarah had solemnly promised never to go into the arcade again. She didn't want to lie. She didn't want to risk getting in trouble again.

But then, one day her grandmother asked Sarah to go to the drugstore for her. Now that the weather was getting cooler, she needed the thick, flesh-colored elastic stockings she wore rolled up below her knees. The drugstore was just a block from the arcade, and it was usually busy in the early afternoon, when the arcade was almost empty. Sarah immediately realized she could run over to the arcade, quickly win the remaining tickets, claim her necklace and get her grandmother's stockings without anyone thinking she'd been gone too long.

That afternoon, Sarah was washing dishes while Rebecca made the beds. Helen walked into the kitchen. "So many dishes for such a young girl," she said. "Here, let me give my little girl a hand." She smiled and picked up a dish towel and started drying.

Sarah kept her head bent over the sink, pleased to see her mother smiling. Helen's anger had been giving her daughter stomach aches. Suddenly she thought of a plan that would allow her to do good and get the goods.

"I want you to know I've learned my lesson, and won't lie to you ever again," Sarah said while she put another dish into the soapy water. She described her plan to sneak into the arcade and get the Mr. Peanut charm and necklace while she was supposed to be getting her grandmother's stockings.

"But that's wrong and I don't want to be the type of person who does such things." Sarah looked directly into her mother's eyes so there'd be no doubt she was telling the truth. "Even if it were okay with you for me to make a quick stop in the arcade, and if I did get the prize I've been working so hard to earn, I still wouldn't wear it right away. I'd put it in my jewelry box and not touch it until you were 100% convinced I'm an honest person"

Sarah picked up an egg-stained frying pan and kept her head down while she scrubbed. It was important for her mom to know she was ashamed.

Helen stopped smiling. She carefully put the dish she was holding into the rack. "Tickets!" she yelled. "You think you win prizes for lying to me? Prizes for making me a liar to Uncle Harvey? For giving me a headache every night from trying to figure out what to do next? Sarah, go get me every single one of those tickets. Right now!"

How long does it take to tear 182 tickets in half? It couldn't have taken more than a few minutes. Helen worked quickly and tore several at a time, but it seemed to Sarah that she stood there for hours. She didn't say a word and neither did her mother. Sarah watched Helen tear up all her tickets and drop them into the garbage can on top of the eggshells, soggy tea bags, leftover cereal and coffee grounds.

"Now, finish the dishes and go get your grandmother her stockings," her mother said. "And if you make any stops along the way, or I ever hear one more word about that necklace, you'll be sorry."

The grown-ups worked out a plan. When it was time to return to the Bronx, Helen, Morris, Marvin and Sarah would be in the car that arrived first. Harvey could greet his son and hear a sanitized version of the story. Rachel and her children would arrive next, and she would reinforce the fact that the incident was "no big deal," if

Harvey asked for more details.

Saul, the two grandmothers and Rebecca would be in the last car. By then Rebecca's antics would be old news, lost in general conversation about the summer. Hopefully the presence of the old people would keep things respectful, at least while they were all on the street. What would happen after the luggage was sorted and everyone was back in their own homes? That was in the hands of the Lord.

"Drive slowly," Helen instructed Saul. "Make sure I arrive at least half an hour before you do. Hopefully that'll give Harvey enough time to calm down."

It wasn't a pleasant trip. *Bubbe* had insisted everyone eat a large breakfast to use up the leftover food; Marvin got carsick and threw up all over the back seat. They had to stop so he could change clothes and Morris could wipe down the car. Helen spent the rest of the trip urging him to drive faster, afraid Saul and Rebecca would arrive before they did.

She needn't have worried. There was no way a car carrying both grandmothers could move quickly. First one had to go to the bathroom, then the other needed something to eat. Then they both needed the bathroom again. In between, they told Saul he was driving too fast and repeatedly asked if he had enough gas, if he was sure of the directions.

Harvey ran out of his house as soon as he saw the first car pull up. As planned, Marvin darted out, ran to his father and hugged him. "Papa, I had a great time," said Marvin. "I can hold my breath and swim under water for a really long time and I can run faster than almost all the other boys." He was talking quickly, barely pausing for breath.

"That's wonderful," said Harvey. "You look like you've grown at least an inch. And so tan. And the sun bleached your hair until it's almost white. I hope you weren't any trouble. Now, go help with the luggage, thank everyone for taking care of you, and you can tell me all about your adventures as soon as we're in the house."

Harvey looked into the car. "And where's my pretty daughter who sends me such good candy?"

"She's in the other car," Helen said, stretching as she got out. "They should be here in a few minutes. Maybe they ran into traffic. Wait here with me."

Helen barely came up to Harvey's shoulder and she squinted into the sun as she lifted her head to look him in the eye. It was an uncomfortable position, but Helen didn't want to look like she was hiding anything as she recounted the vacation adventures. She told him about the waves, the boardwalk adventures made sure to add, "you look very good, Harvey, rested, relaxed, like you're the one who's been on vacation all month."

Wanting to be sure she didn't miss a word of what was going on, Sarah walked over to her mother and stood next to Harvey. "Did you have a good time, too?" he asked her.

Sarah didn't answer.

"That reminds me of one of the interesting stories I wanted you to hear," said Helen. "Seems our girls found themselves a boyfriend this summer."

Harvey looked at Sarah. "You had a boyfriend?" he said. "How old are you now?"

Sarah looked at her mother.

"No, they didn't each have a boyfriend," said Helen quickly. "Turns out they were sharing the same one between the two of them. Did you ever hear of such a thing? These kids, where do they get such ideas?"

"Who was this boy? Where was his family from?" asked

Harvey.

"Actually, I didn't meet the boy," said Helen. "The girls ran into him in one of those arcades. You know what I mean? Where they have all those machines. There's always such a racket in those places it's a wonder they can bear it. If it were me, I'd be deaf by now. I guess you have to have young ears to stand it."

"What are you talking about?" Harvey's voice got louder, his fingers clenched. "My daughter has been doing Lord knows what, with Lord knows who, and you want to talk about pinball machines?"

Harvey looked at Sarah again. "Tell me, did Rebecca go off with this boy? Alone?"

Sarah's eyes darted from Harvey to her mother.

"So maybe things got a little romantic once or twice. Come on, Harvey, take it easy. Don't you remember what it was like to be young?" said Helen. "I got the whole story, and it was just kid stuff."

Harvey turned away from Helen, took hold of Sarah's arm and stared at her. "Sarah," he said, not blinking. "What went on with this boy?" He was squeezing her arm. Hard. She winced but didn't say anything.

Helen lifted Harvey's hand off her daughter and pulled Sarah to her other side. "Turns out, the Lord was looking after our daughters," she said calmly. "The one time there was a possibility that things could have gotten a little out of hand was the night my Saul decided to take a walk. He ran into the girls, didn't like the looks of things and brought them right home."

Harvey's lips were pressed tightly together.

"Don't worry," Helen added. "I gave them both a piece of my mind. No more outings for those two. They didn't get off easy. They did enough work to make sure they'll be tired for the rest of the month."

Harvey took a deep breath.

"No," he said at last. "I don't know what it was like to be young like that. I spent most of my youth in the synagogue. I wanted nothing more than to surround myself with learned men who gave me the privilege of being taught by them. When I was young, I knew to behave like a decent, respectable person. I knew the importance of honesty, of keeping my promise. I don't know how a woman tells me she'll keep an eye on my daughter and then lets her run wild. But if that's the way your own daughter behaves maybe you really don't think it's wrong."

Harvey pulled his bushy eyebrows together until they almost formed one line.

"And this must have happened last weekend if Saul was there. How did Saul know something like this and not say a word to me all week? Could an honorable man work next to me and stay quiet about this?" said Harvey. "I thought I was a knowledgeable person, but it turns out it's easy to make me a fool."

Harvey turned his back to Helen and went over to Marvin. "I'm going to go into the house now," he said. "You wait here until Rebecca arrives. As soon as she gets here you bring her inside. Immediately." He started to walk and then turned back to his son. "Immediately, you understand?" Marvin nodded.

Harvey climbed the steps and closed his door.

Marvin stood still. His face had turned white underneath his tan. He was shaking. Helen put her arm around him, but he startled, and she took it away.

"Did you notice that your drawing pad and your crayons are on the shelf under the rear window?" she said gently to Marvin. "Why don't you sit in the car until everyone else gets here and draw a picture of things you saw on the way home?" Marvin didn't say anything, just walked back to the car.

Sarah looked at her mother and started to speak, but her mother held up her hand. "Don't say anything right now," Helen said. "I'm not ready to speak yet." She leaned against the car, took off her sandals and rubbed her calloused feet. Her hair was disheveled; she felt old.

Sarah and Helen stood quietly, listening to the passing cars. A large truck went by and for a few seconds all they heard was loud rumbling. A neighbor's dog started to bark and then abruptly stopped.

When the next car arrived, Helen hurried over and told Rachel what had happened. "I had to bite my tongue to keep from cursing him out," Helen said. "Imagine that man saying I don't know how to raise my own daughter. I only kept quiet because Elaine's children need me. Let him try to keep me away from them. Let him just try."

"Should I go speak to him?" asked Rachel.

"I'm not sure he'd open the door for you right now. Let's give him time. Maybe he'll cool down."

Saul's car arrived five minutes later. Marvin ran over, opened the passenger side door and tried to pull Rebecca out. "Papa said you have to come into the house immediately," he said. Rebecca ignored him.

Helen went over to the driver's door. The window was open, and Saul turned to her. "You talked to Harvey?" he asked.

"Sit inside the car with me, Saul," Helen said. "Rebecca, go over to the other cars and help sort the luggage. Don't go upstairs just yet. I'll come talk to you in a minute."

"I tried," Helen said to Saul. "I tried to make out like it was a kid thing, just youngsters fooling around. Which is exactly what it was. But I don't think that man was ever young. My poor Elaine, what it must have been like to be married to him. And he's furious you didn't say anything to him while you were both in the shop."

"You think he might cause a scene at work?" Saul asked. "In front of the workers? In front of the customers?"

"No," Helen said. "If there are any scenes, he'll save them for me." Helen got out of the car, looked at her husband. "And he doesn't scare me."

She walked over to where Rebecca was waiting and hugged her. "The first thing your father said when the car pulled up was, 'Where's my pretty girl who sent me candy?' I told him what happened. He's your father and he has a right to know. He's angry, but I think it'll be okay."

Rebecca nodded. She was remembering the weekends during which Helen had mandated Harvey spend time alone with his children. Her aunt had no idea what "okay" meant when it involved time with her father.

Marvin was pulling Rebecca's arm, trying to get her to move. Rebecca pushed him away. "Papa said immediately," Marvin said loudly. "You have to come. Come into the house. Right now."

"He's right. Go inside now," Helen said. "Try to be extra good for a while. Phone or come over if you need me."

It was a hot day and Rebecca was wearing shorts and a sleeveless shirt tied under her bust so her midriff was bare. Helen untied Rebecca's shirt and ran her hands over the wrinkles. Then she reached into a large straw bag, pulled out one of her beach cover-ups and put it on Rebecca. The shirt reached Rebecca's knees.

"You keep this," she said. "It's a good color for you."

"Don't worry," Rebecca said, staring straight ahead. "I'll be okay. He's been mad before. I can handle it. Thanks for the vacation. Sorry I messed things up."

She turned to her cousin who was standing beside the car.

"So long, Sarri," Rebecca said. "Too bad about the necklace. Okay, Marvin, let's go in."

Harvey called the shop the next morning and said he was taking a few days off to help the children settle in. Morris and Saul were relieved, they'd been afraid of his making a scene in front of customers.

Helen went to Rebecca's house the day after they all got back, the day after that and the following day. She didn't stay long.

The first time she went, Harvey ignored her knock. Helen waited a few minutes then rang the bell. There was no answer so she rang it again. And again. Eventually Harvey opened the door. "You didn't hear the bell, Harvey?" Helen said. "Maybe you should see the doctor. I just wanted to see how everyone was getting along. We packed in a hurry, something might have gotten misplaced."

The next day she brought a jar of lotion and asked if Marvin's sunburn was bothering him. A day later she asked if Rebecca had found the sandal that went missing their first week at the beach.

"Everything is fine. The children are fine," said Harvey each time. "They're in their rooms. Studying. Getting ready for school."

"I'm sure they could use a short break. I won't stay long." Helen pushed her way into the house and quickly walked up the stairs. She knocked on Marvin's door, went in and spoke to him, then knocked on Rebecca's door and spoke to her. Neither child was eager to speak to her.

"Harvey doesn't like my being there but he's not man enough to stop me," she told Rachel after each visit. "The kids are quiet, say they're okay. They seem nervous about talking to me, and I don't push. I just don't want them to feel deserted."

Sarah called Rebecca a few hours after they all got back to ask what had happened with her father, but Harvey picked up the phone and said she was busy unpacking and couldn't talk. Sarah went over there a few days later when she knew he was back at work, but Rebecca just shrugged and said it was no big deal. "You should go play with kids your own age," she said. "I don't have time to hang out with babies anymore."

The following week, while Harvey was at work, all of the Rosen women and children went to Macy's. The Jewish holidays were coming up and traditionally everyone got new outfits to wear in the temple.

Helen took Rebecca and Sarah to the girl's department; Rachel took Marvin and her sons two floors below to the boy's department. The women compared notes that evening. No one had seen any bruises. No one had received any pertinent information.

If something upsetting was going on in that house the children didn't want to talk about it. There was nothing the aunts could do but wait, keep their eyes open and hope for the best.

9.

A MIDNIGHT VISIT

Elaine had been gone for almost two years when Helen's doorbell rang in the middle of the night. She looked through her bedroom window, saw Harvey on her front porch and buttoned a floor-length gingham housecoat over her nightgown.

"My daughter has run off," Harvey said before Helen had fully opened the front door. He didn't sound surprised. He didn't sound upset. He seemed planted on the doorstep.

"What's going on?" asked Saul. He'd gotten to the door a few steps behind Helen.

"Go back to sleep," said Helen. "I can take care of this."

Saul looked at his wife, then he looked at Harvey. Harvey didn't meet his eyes. Saul went back to his bedroom. "Call if you need me," he said to Helen.

"Let me check on Sarah and make sure the bell didn't wake her then we'll talk." Helen took Harvey's jacket and told him to sit in the dinette, which shared a wall with her daughter's room.

Sarah had awakened as soon as the bell rang and was lying very still in her bed, her eyes closed, evenly breathing in and out as she always did when she listened to her parents sit in the dinette at night discussing "grown-up matters."

Helen smoothed a strand of hair that had fallen onto Sarah's forehead. "My good girl, my very good girl," she whispered. This one sleeps like a rock, she said to herself as she closed Sarah's door and returned to Harvey.

"Tell me what happened," she said to Harvey. "What do you mean Rebecca's run off? And where's Marvin?"

"He's sound asleep," said Harvey. "He'll be alright."

Helen shook her head but didn't say anything about Marvin being left alone. She spoke calmly, as if there was nothing unusual about Harvey coming by at an hour when all normal people were asleep.

Harvey started talking as soon as he sat down. "We were watching TV and around 10 pm Rebecca got up and politely explained she was going to study in her room before going to bed. She said goodnight and leaned over and gave me a kiss," he said. "A sweet peck on the cheek," Harvey pointed to his face. "Right here. The way a dutiful daughter should. But I'm not a fool. As soon I heard her door close I moved to the sofa where I could see the front door: the only way out of the house."

A little before midnight, Harvey explained, he went upstairs and quietly turned the knob on Rebecca's door. There was no lock; he had forbidden that long ago. Enough light streamed in from the hallway for him to see that the room was empty.

"She must have slipped out when I went to the kitchen to get a snack," Harvey said. "Imagine her crouching at the head of the stairs for over an hour, like an animal waiting to pounce."

Helen didn't reply. She went into the kitchen, took tea bags down from the shelf and poured water into the bright silver kettle.

Harvey closed his eyes. He could still see Rebecca's empty room. It was all so horribly vivid. He took a deep breath. His nose still contained the room's odor, *goyische* perfume, a strong chemical smell that would not be attractive to a pious girl. The room reeked of filial disobedience. He had seen the unmade bed where dirty underwear was tossed, and he was unable to suppress the thought that his daughter had the body of a whore. Still a young girl in years but already she filled cups larger than her mother's.

Harvey had stared at the luridly colored garments. Her mother wouldn't have chosen such items, not such colors, not so much lace, not so little coverage, he thought. Elaine wouldn't have allowed her daughter to bring them into the house.

There was a smiling photo of Elaine next to Rebecca's bed and Harvey had looked into his dear wife's face. Such a good wife, my Elaine, he thought. She was obedient, virtuous. Maybe a little too close to her family and their ways, but that couldn't be helped.

So why did she die? Why did she die, despite all my prayers? Harvey thought about all he had done. He had even written to Israel to receive a special blessing from one of the highest rabbis. How could Elaine die and leave him with children to raise in this country, a country with no respect for values?

Harvey turned and watched Helen make tea. Helen, my sophisticated sister-in-law, she probably bought those things for my Rebecca or gave her money to shop for herself, he thought. Helen, the one who demanded I hire housekeepers to cook and clean instead of expecting an older daughter to behave dutifully. Who asked her to mix in?

He watched Helen fumble for the teacups, still half asleep. He didn't offer to help, just sat still and looked at her. "What a *klutz*," he said softly.

"Did you say something, Harvey?" asked Helen. "The kettle is rattling. Speak up."

"Nothing," said Harvey. "I'm just mumbling. I've become a mumbling old man who still misses his wife and doesn't know what to do without her."

Helen didn't need to hear Harvey's words. She knew what Harvey thought about her, about the other members of the Rosen family. She remembered one Rosh Hashanah when she'd lingered in front of the *shul* to talk to neighbors. Harvey and his religious friends were nearby but, as usual, Helen wasn't worth his notice.

"Did you see my sister-in-law Rachel's hat?" Harvey asked his friends. "Did you ever see anything so silly? And my other sister-in-law, Helen, the American one who thinks she's so smart but can't read a word of Hebrew. She might as well hold the *mazur* upside down, it would mean as much to her. But she was smart enough to marry into the Rosen family. She grew up in a family that suffered during the Depression in this country and jumped at the chance to become part of a rich clan, a family of crooks, merchants, traders. People who make money, not righteousness."

Helen had overheard every word, knew the men Harvey was talking to. Her husband, Saul, called them *shnorers,* people who didn't pay their fair share. They always gave the lowest donations to the *shul.* You have a lot of nerve criticizing me, Helen had thought. You schemed your way into the Rosen family and you don't appreciate them or anything they've given you.

When Helen first met Saul, she had struggled with the idea of dating an uneducated immigrant with a heavy accent, but he was obviously smitten with her. Saul frequently showed up with flowers and made a point of speaking respectfully to her parents. Of course, it didn't hurt that, in the middle of the depression, Saul was financially well-off, a partner in a growing family business. He was devoted to his family and could be expected to be a devoted husband to her. As she learned the history of the Rosens, Helen became proud to be part of this group that accepted her so warmly.

Soon that pride turned to love.

In the 1930s, many of the Jewish people who had fled small villages in Poland settled close to each other, near Crotona Park in the Bronx. Few adapted to this new country as easily as the Rosens, who quickly established a prosperous business while Harvey had struggled to make a living. He was too proud to become a menial worker in a shop and didn't have the money or initiative to start his own business.

He lacked the credentials to be a rabbi in an established synagogue and the patience to teach young children in yeshivas, so the religious community had little in the way of material opportunities to offer him. But he was educated, good-looking and well spoken. Soon neighbors were mentioning Elaine to him, who was already in her 30s: the spinster Rosen girl.

In this country, no one remembered he'd been one of the chief readers in their village synagogue, the most learned among the young men. The Rosens? They had been unlearned boys who skipped school and got in trouble. In Europe, the Rosens would have been grateful if Harvey even spoke to them, much less thought about marrying into their family.

But they had all been forced to leave that village in Poland, where piety meant something, and come to America, where only money mattered. Now, instead of seeking the light that shines on those who study the Torah, Harvey spent his energy working for the Rosens, doing money-grubbing business that was dirty, like Rebecca's room, like Rebecca's clothing... like Rebecca.

The tea kettle whistled, and Helen turned off the flame. "Here, this will calm you," she said to Harvey. "You can't let yourself get sick over this. Remember your responsibilities."

Harvey's spoon clinked against the china sugar bowl. He put a lot of sugar in his tea, like all the men in the family did. Sometimes the older people asked for small cubes of sugar, which they held between their teeth as they sipped the tea. Usually, Helen warned people that too much sugar was bad for them, but now she didn't say anything.

Harvey told Helen what had been happening at his house during the past year, how Rebecca had started running around, staying out late and sometimes not coming in until the sun was ready to rise.

"I try to discipline her, but it doesn't do any good," said Harvey.

Helen flinched at the mention of "discipline." She disciplined her child by banning TV for a few days or assigning extra household chores. Coming from Harvey the word had a different, more ominous sound.

"I turned to the Holy books to see what advice they offered on how to treat such a girl," Harvey said. "But even the words of God and all of the holy scholars provided no assistance. I felt abandoned. For a while I ignored the whole situation. I went to bed hoping it would all be better in the morning. I didn't care what time she got in; I didn't ask. The next day she just took a shower, put on her clothes and went to school as if nothing had happened. But things got worse. What can I do? What does the Lord expect me to do? I've prayed for her, I've punished her until my arm aches, yelled until my throat is sore. What else does the good Lord expect me to do?"

Not for the first time, Helen wondered if it had been wrong to tell Harvey what had happened in Atlantic City. Maybe she should have at least tried to keep it a secret. Maybe then Rebecca would have trusted her and come to her instead of running around.

"You could have swallowed your pride and turned to the

family," Helen said. "We would have helped. I had no idea Rebecca was in such a bad way.

"Lately, whenever I've seen her, she didn't seem happy, but I thought it was merely teenage moodiness. She didn't say a thing about what was going on. I wish she had talked to me. A girl who gets into Bronx Science, one of only a few girls who were admitted last year, who would have expected this from a girl who's so smart?"

"Not so smart that she avoids the police." Harvey told Helen about the times in recent months that the police had brought Rebecca home after they found her wandering the streets of City Island. Each time he had humbled himself by thanking the large policemen for bringing his daughter home safely.

When the police left, Harvey took Rebecca inside, away from the prying eyes of neighbors, and slapped his daughter's face as hard as he could, the face that was covered with makeup, yelled at her and resisted the urge to pull out the dirty hair Rebecca had dyed a brassy yellow color. She ran to her room, was quiet and respectful for a few days and then went off again.

"And Marvin?" asked Helen.

"Undoubtedly he heard what was going on, but he always stayed in his room, never said anything. I didn't know what to say to him, so I said nothing.

"Last week when the police brought Rebecca home a fat, sloppy policeman, an uneducated man who spit when he spoke, actually took me aside and started lecturing me about how to be a father. It took all of my self-control to stand there quietly and let him talk to me that way. This policeman said Rebecca was a chronic runaway. That the next time they found her wandering the streets they wouldn't bring her home, they'd take her to a special jail for teenagers. 'The court will control your daughter if you can't.' That's what he said to me, to me, to her father, an educated man. That's what I had to listen to.

"He gave me his card with the phone number of the police station, 'in case there's any more trouble' he said. I wanted to spit on it, to throw the card on the ground, but I held on to it. I knew this wasn't the end of my troubles."

Harvey handed the card to Helen and stared at his open palms as if waiting for a vision to appear. But his hands were empty.

"I'm at the end of my strength. I can't do this anymore. I can't believe my own child, my own blood, would act this way," he said. "When the phone started ringing in the middle of the night tonight, I knew who it was, and I couldn't bear to talk to the police again. I just sat in the living room without moving. I counted seven rings before the phone went quiet."

Harvey believed it was the Rosen blood that caused Rebecca to act the way she did. That was why he'd come to Helen's house at that hour. He couldn't stand the idea of the Rosens sleeping peacefully while he was being bedeviled.

Helen didn't want to look at Harvey anymore. She walked back into the kitchen as if she wanted to refill her cup. She started to say something, but her voice and hands were shaking. Her teacup fell into the sink and broke.

"What happened?" asked Harvey. "What did you do?"

"I'm just being clumsy," said Helen. "Nothing to worry about. It's only a cup." She picked up the shards of china from the sink, careful not to cut her hand. She stood quietly, running cold water over her wrists. Then she patted her hair and straightened her shoulders. She returned to the dinette, walking with determination. She wasn't carrying any more tea, didn't offer Harvey any cake.

"Go home and take care of your son," she said. "Marvin is a little boy; he shouldn't wake up in an empty house."

She looked at the card with the police insignia. "I'll call the authorities and figure out what's going on, make sure our Rebecca is okay. We need to understand the situation better, then we'll decide what to do next."

Harvey stood, mumbled goodbye, and the front door closed behind him.

Sarah sat up and opened her eyes in her dark bedroom, trying to understand what she had just heard. Rebecca had been arrested. Rebecca had been running around. How exciting!

Sarah tried to imagine herself doing something like that, walking down the streets in City Island at night, boys eyeing her, calling out to her. She visualized the City Island streets and was stumped as to why Rebecca had chosen that as the place to have her adventures.

The whole family frequently visited this tiny strip of land jutting into the Long Island Sound, tethered to the Bronx by a narrow bridge. In the early morning, boats took people from the island piers to fish for flounder, bass and bluefish, or just drink beer with their friends in the fresh sea air.

In the evening, seafood restaurants were crowded. City Island was where the Rosens freely ordered shrimp and lobster, non-kosher foods forbidden in their own kitchens. It was also where greasy fish and chips places blasted loud music and sold beer and cigarettes to underage teenagers. Couples strolled up and down the single main street late at night or disappeared into dark alleys that led to deserted boatyards.

Sarah decided that if she was going to run away, she'd go someplace classier, more exciting. She'd go into Manhattan, maybe head for Greenwich Village find a boy with long hair who wrote poetry and played the guitar. She'd wear a black leotard and smoke cigarettes while he serenaded her. Maybe she'd hitchhike all the way across the country. By the time she got to San Francisco she'd have long hair and a bust; she'd be sexier than Rebecca and people would want her to join their band and become famous.

Sarah sat up straight in her bed. I'm not as brave as Rebecca, she admitted to herself. I'd be scared to walk midnight streets alone.

Sarah wondered what her family would do now. She knew her mother wouldn't sleep for the rest of the night. I have to behave, Sarah thought. Let Rebecca have the adventures. For now. Mom doesn't need more aggravation, can't afford to break any more teacups.

Early the next morning, Helen called her sister-in-law and told her about the midnight visit. "Oh my God," said Rachel. "What kind of man listens to a phone ring in the middle of the night, knowing his child could be in danger, and doesn't answer?"

"I know. I agree," said Helen. "I was afraid to say anything, afraid to say the wrong thing. It's important he feels comfortable turning to me, so I can stay involved, whatever happens."

"You did the right thing," Rachel said. "But I don't know how you had such self-control. I'd have told the man he's a monster."

"Of course he is. I spent the whole night trying to figure out how this could happen. Eventually I realized that, why, doesn't matter anymore. Coming here and not having any more to do with the police was probably the smartest thing Harvey could have done. This situation has gone on too long. He's made a mess. If he kept trying to cope he'd only make everything worse.

"As soon as that terrible excuse for a parent closed my door I called the police. They told me Rebecca was at the station and wasn't hurt, but she had to stay there overnight. Maybe she can come home today. I have to call back after 8 and speak to the person in charge. I'll call you as soon as I know anything."

Helen hung up, walked into the kitchen, took out the step ladder and reached behind the top kitchen cabinet where she'd hidden a box of chocolate fudge cookies. She finished six cookies, resealed the box and watched the clock tick, waiting till it was time to call the police. She finished the rest of the cookies after she made the call.

While Rebecca remained in custody, Helen was constantly on the phone during the following week. She discovered that late night excursions to City Island weren't the only reason the officials had intervened in Rebecca's life. There were also reports of her being drunk, shoplifting, damaging property and truancy. All minor offenses, but they added up.

A few times, Helen got dressed in her dark blue wool suit and was gone for the whole day. Sarah asked why her mother was so dressed up, and Helen said there were things to take care of for Rebecca. She had to go to court, to see a social worker. Sarah didn't ask what went on in court or what a social worker was.

One day Helen got a call early in the morning, quickly threw on her going-downtown clothes and rushed out the door.

Sarah walked into her parents' room and saw that the bed wasn't made. Her mother, who frequently said she didn't know how anyone could get a good night's sleep if they got into an unmade bed, had left the pillows and blankets in a tangle. Sarah quietly made the bed.

Helen came home late, too tired to speak, and went right to sleep. Sarah didn't think she had noticed that the bed had been made for her.

Grandmother Leah, Helen's mother, took over Helen's household chores. One evening, she put a big bowl of stew in front of

Saul and Sarah. "Okay," she said, "everyone dig in."

Sarah leaned over the bowl, inhaled and made a face. "We had this yesterday and I didn't like it then," she said. "Now it smells funny in addition to looking weird. I'm not eating it." She pushed her chair away from the table.

Leah looked at Saul. "She's becoming a spoiled brat just like Rebecca," she said.

"We do not say anything against Elaine's child in this house," Saul told her sternly. Leah looked away. "And you," he said to Sarah, "you know you're supposed to always be respectful to your grandmother."

Sarah knew he didn't like the stew any more than she did and wasn't surprised when he suddenly pushed his chair away from the table, put on his coat, and left the house. A few minutes later he was back with a pizza.

Leah shook her head but didn't say anything. She'd never criticize her son-in-law.

"You have to remember that in the long run the only people you can count on are your family," Saul told Sarah as they pulled long cheese strings from their mouths while Grandmother Leah ate her stew. "A cousin, a grandmother, any relative. Even if they do something you don't like, they're your blood."

"What about friends?" Sarah asked. "My friends are important to me."

"Friends are good," her dad said, tearing off a second slice. "In Poland I had lots of friends, even friends who weren't Jews. They were fun, and we had good times together. But as the War got closer the friends got further away and one day they were gone. Maybe they had no choice, maybe that was the only way they could keep their own families safe.

Blood doesn't disappear.

You can have fights with relatives. Some people don't speak to relatives for years, but, in our family, we don't turn our backs on each other.

You remember Uncle Bernie?"

Sarah nodded. She knew he liked to tell this story.

Uncle Bernie wasn't really an uncle; he was some sort of distant cousin. He had lived near her father's village in Poland. When he tried to escape the Nazis, the routes to the US were closed, but he was able to get to South America. After the war, Bernie contacted the Rosens from Mexico to say he wasn't happy and wanted to join them in the States.

U.S. Immigration was flooded with applications, but, as Saul explained, family was family and where there was a will, the Rosens often found a way. Someone located an American-born woman who needed money, and they paid her to travel to Mexico and marry Bernie. Some more cash wound up in the pockets of government officials. Within two years, Bernie was happily divorced, living nearby and working in the family shop.

Unfortunately, the Rosens soon realized that having Bernie in the next village, or in Mexico City, was one thing; having him live a few blocks away was another. There were fights about family matters, his friends, his activities and then, one day, Uncle Bernie revealed that he was a communist.

"Bernie didn't like Poland, he didn't like Mexico, and now he didn't like America," Saul explained. "He wanted to organize the workers. Not just any workers, our workers. Somehow, he forgot that because we had figured out how to run a profitable business we were able to buy him his new life in America where he was free to become a communist.

"I was ready to wash my hands of the whole thing. Let him go to Russia, I said. But my mother wouldn't let me walk away. Even a distant cousin was family, she said, especially after the war when so many relatives were gone."

Someone found an apartment for Bernie near Allerton Avenue, part of the Bronx that was a hotbed of communist sympathizers. Bernie soon had a new job and new friends among people who shared his philosophies. He married and had a few red-diaper babies. The Rosens rarely saw him or his family.

Eventually the revelations about Stalin's activities in the Gulag and the repercussions of the McCarthy Commission dampened the spirits of the Allerton Avenue communists. Uncle Bernie stopped talking about politics and ceased to be such an embarrassment to the Rosens. Sometimes he and his family were invited to the very largest family celebrations. But he was always seated at a table near the band.

"Bernie is family. A lunatic, but family," Saul explained. "While he waits for the revolution, we know he's safe. We did the right thing."

Sarah's dad turned to her. "Now, just because we're family doesn't mean that it's okay for you to steal all of the pepperoni," he said. "I've got my eye on you."

The next week, Helen didn't spend so much time on the phone. She'd hired a lawyer, a friend of a neighbor, highly recommended. Now she was busy reading documents, long sheets of paper with closely printed words. She kept a dictionary close-by and looked up words as she read.

Sometimes she called and asked to have something explained, but she didn't like doing that. And the person on the other end of the call wasn't always polite.

A week later Saul drove Helen and Sarah to the Bronx House of Detention for Girls, and they wound up in an empty classroom waiting for Rebecca.

10.

SENT AWAY

After fifteen minutes in the silent classroom, Helen started squirming in her chair, staring at the maps posted on the side walls as if trying to figure out where she was, where in her world this place could be located. Sarah stared out the window at the dismal playground. She had her back to the door when Rebecca appeared.

"Oh no," she heard her mother gasp. "My beautiful child, what happened to you? Who did this?"

Rebecca ignored her aunt. "Hey, Sarri," she called. Sarah turned around and Rebecca struck a model's pose, one hand behind her head, the other at her hip. "How do you like me as a redhead?"

Rebecca's shoulder-length hair had been unevenly chopped off and she had spiky bangs. The color wasn't like any redhead Sarah had ever seen. It was the rusty color of water that comes from the faucet when the pipes are corroded.

Before Sarah could reply, Helen was out of her chair and had her arms around Rebecca. "It's only hair," she said. "It'll grow back. The color can be fixed. Are you hurt anywhere else? You can tell me."

"Aunt Helen, relax," said Rebecca. She didn't move from the embrace. Helen finally let go and pulled out a chair. "Come, let's sit down," she said. "We need to talk." Rebecca took a chair beside

Helen and patted her aunt's hand. Sarah usually tried to be as close as possible to Rebecca, but her cousin looked a little scary, so she sat next to her mother.

"First of all, there's no reason for you to be so upset," Rebecca said. "No one has hurt me. It's boring here, but no one has done anything bad to me. I decided I needed a change and did this myself. One of the girls had some hair dye, and she traded it to me for cigarettes. The only scissors I could get were the kind with rounded edges that little children use, so it was hard to cut my hair properly."

Sarah waited for her mother to lecture Rebecca about the dangers of smoking, but Helen let it pass. "You're still a pretty girl," she said. "That'll always be true."

They made small talk for a few minutes, and then Helen leaned over and looked into Rebecca's eyes. "Ever since your father came to me in the middle of night and told me that you'd been running away, and that the police were involved, I've been wracking my brain trying to figure out how all this happened, what to do about it."

Rebecca turned away. "He doesn't care," she said. "I've told everyone I don't want to see him. I'm glad you came without him. If he were here I'd leave."

Helen nodded. "I've been running all around, talking to court officers, social workers, lawyers, anyone I could think of who might help."

"The social worker wasn't bad," said Rebecca. "I didn't think much of the rest of them."

"You know I only want the best for you," Helen said. "Everyone seems to think that that Hillsdale place would be the best."

Sarah didn't know what place they were talking about. She didn't ask.

"I don't care," said Rebecca, turning away from Helen and staring out the window. "That place, any place, no place would be worse than living with my father," she said.

"There'll be people there who can help you, that's what they said." Helen spoke in a gentle voice. "I promised your mother I'd take care of you. I don't know what else to do. Now that the police are involved it's out of our hands. Anyway, we couldn't go on like this, with you constantly running away, missing school. It was only a matter of time till you got hurt, badly hurt."

Helen's hands were trembling. Sarah put her hand on one of her mother's.

"I'll visit as often as possible," Helen said. "This place isn't so far away. In the Catskills, near the hotels. Sarah will come too. And Marvin, I'll bring him. I'm sure there'll be a phone, we'll call each other. We'll write. You'll let me know if you need anything and I'll send it. You're still part of a family that loves you. Don't forget that."

"I know," said Rebecca. "I know." They all hugged. Rebecca started to leave. Helen reached out and stopped her.

"Before you go, please do me one favor. I need you to answer a question. Tell me how this happened. What went wrong? I know when your mother died you were full of grief. Could we have helped you better? I know your father didn't respond properly, but why didn't you say anything? Why all the running around with boys? A smart girl like you, what did you think was going to happen? Please, explain it to me."

"I don't know," said Rebecca. "At first it was fun. There were all those guys who liked me, thought I was pretty, cared for me. It was exciting. And then all of a sudden it wasn't as much fun. I don't know. I honestly don't know."

A stout woman in a uniform opened the door. "Time to go,"

she said. Rebecca hugged her aunt and her cousin and walked out of the classroom.

Sarah spotted their car as soon as they left the detention center. Saul was parked exactly where they'd left him. The shabby old man was still sleeping on the street.

Helen told Saul about the visit and started to cry.

Saul took out a box of tissues that were in the glove compartment and handed them to his wife. "There was nothing else to do," he said. "We had no choice."

Sarah sat quietly in the back seat, not saying anything while her mother cried softly all the way home.

• • •

Years later, when Sarah tried to put all of the pieces together, she kept concluding that it shouldn't have happened like this. Not this quickly. Not to someone like Rebecca. Not according to all the movies and the newspapers and the TV shows.

Everyone knew that kids who got sent to reform schools come from slums; they grew up surrounded by addicts and drunks, neglected and uneducated. But Rebecca grew up in a nice house with a sandbox and swing set in the back yard. She had a caring middle-class family. She went to a school for the gifted.

Everyone knew that kids in reform schools had juvenile crime records, belonged to gangs, used drugs. But Rebecca merely stayed out late. Chronic runaway, they called her. Okay, some shoplifting, a little underage drinking, but was that so wrong? Didn't the police have better things to do? Even the City Island police? Wasn't there any real crime in that place?

But when her makeup wore off and she was tired, when you looked beyond the mature figure, Rebecca did look much too young to be out alone at 3 or 4 a.m. Maybe the police were trying to help. And their help generated an official record.

If only.

If only they'd hired a lawyer who specialized in this type of case instead of someone who was a friend of a friend, competent in real estate or business matters but unfamiliar with the juvenile court.

If only there were more experts involved, like private therapists who specialized in adolescent behavior, provided therapy for the whole family and treated Rebecca while she lived at home.

If only Rebecca had seen such people would the family have avoided all of this? Would Rebecca have become the nice Jewish girl everyone wanted her to be?

Well, remember, grandma wasn't a trolley and she wasn't a grandpa. And the Rosens weren't the type of family who went to doctors who treated people for mental problems, crazy people. Harvey wouldn't have gone to such a person even if there was one available.

They relied on American-born Helen who was so proud of her high school diploma. But Helen wasn't equipped to argue with court officials, with people who sat behind large desks in towering Manhattan office buildings and said the Rosens couldn't handle this situation by themselves, who said a girl like Rebecca needed a more supportive environment. Helen didn't know how, or if, she should argue with administrators who had college and graduate school diplomas on their walls.

What choice did they have?

• • •

A few days after her visit to the detention center, Helen gathered the younger members of the family together in Rachel's house and explained that Rebecca was going to go to a special school and would be gone for a while.

"No one is ever to use the word reform school," she said sternly. "If you hear that from anyone in the neighborhood or in school or anyplace else, you immediately correct them. Rebecca is in a boarding school. A fancy place. Like where the rich *goyim* send their children."

"When will she be back?" asked Marvin.

"As soon as possible," said Helen. "We don't know for sure."

No one else had any questions. They'd all overheard the grown-ups talking about this; they weren't surprised. Sarah stayed behind while all the cousins quickly left the room. She helped straighten the room. She wanted to hear if her mother had anything else that she'd say to her sister-in-law.

"So, what are we going to tell the old lady?" Rachel immediately said. "And when?"

"Soon. We can't delay," said Helen. "Rebecca's her favorite, she probably already misses seeing her around."

As if she were listening at the door, *Bubbe* Golda walked in. "I heard the children were here and by coincidence I made a fresh batch of candy just this morning." She looked around. "Did I miss everyone? Here Sarah, have some sweetness."

Sarah bent over, kissed *Bubbe*'s wrinkled cheek and took a piece of the candy. She was a full head taller than the old woman.

Bubbe settled herself in the middle of a large, plastic-covered yellow velvet couch. She looked from Helen to Rachel and back again, staring at each of them with her deep blue eyes.

"So," she said. "What's happening?"

"We were just going to talk to you," said Rachel. "There have been some problems with Rebecca."

"You think I don't know about that?" said Golda. "I live next door. My bedroom faces the street. Old ladies don't sleep well. You think I don't know my Rebecca has been having problems? You think I don't see her leave the house after dark and not come home until dawn? That I don't know the police have been here?"

"Why didn't you say anything?" asked Helen. "I only recently found out."

"I thought you knew everything," said *Bubbe.*

"I spoke to Harvey. He said he was taking care of it and I shouldn't worry. Of course I knew better than to believe him, so I spoke to Rebecca. She said everything was okay. My Rebecca was always a good girl, a little high-strung, but a good girl."

Bubbe offered some rock candy to Helen and Rachel. They shook their heads. The old lady shrugged, took a piece for herself and sucked it while she waited for her daughters-in-law to explain what was happening.

"The law is involved now, the courts, social workers, all kinds of people," said Rachel. "We've been talking to them. They think that the best thing for Rebecca is to go to a special school. For a little while. There'll be people there to help her."

"They're taking away my Rebecca?" *Bubbe* looked at Rachel and then Helen. "You're letting this happen?" Her small hands formed fists and she banged the marble coffee table, making a crystal ashtray jump. *Bubbe* started to breathe in long, loud gasps.

Rachel hurried into the kitchen, filled a glass with water and rushed back to the living room.

"This is a nice place. They'll take good care of her," Helen said. "We'll be able to visit.

"Now that the police are involved there's nothing else we can do."

"Nothing we can do," said *Bubbe* ignoring the water. "Nothing we can do. That's what they said about Shoshanna, and about Rifka. When they were sent away and there was nothing anyone could do."

Everyone knew the story. Shoshanna had been *Bubbe*'s oldest child, Saul and Morris' big sister for whom Sarah was named. When it looked like there would be war, one by one the Rosen boys and their mother started to leave Poland. But Shoshanna was already married and had a child, Rifka, for whom Rebecca was named. Shoshanna's husband had a successful business he didn't want to leave. He didn't believe Hitler would reach Poland. He and Shoshanna and Rifka died in a concentration camp.

Rachel and Helen put their arms around *Bubbe*. Sarah sat in front of her grandmother, on the coffee table, and held her tiny hands, no longer in fists. *Bubbe* shook them off and stood up.

"I have to go. It's time to start making supper," she said.

Everyone knew she wanted a drink of whiskey.

"This won't be for very long," said Helen. "Rebecca will be home again soon. We'll arrange to have her call you on the telephone so you'll know she's okay."

Bubbe stumbled toward the door. She seemed to have gotten even shorter since learning about Rebecca. She was muttering to herself.

"Little Rifka was such a sturdy child. The last time I saw her she was beginning to crawl. I wonder if she lived long enough to learn to walk."

11.

THAT PLACE

Helen called the Hillsdale Treatment Center for Girls to find out what her niece should bring. She listened carefully, made some notes, hung up and shook her head. "This can't be right," she said to Sarah. "They think a teenage girl barely needs anything. I'll just double the list and add a few special things."

Throughout the week, piles of clothing for Rebecca accumulated in Helen's bedroom. The day before Rebecca was to be released from the detention center, "going off to boarding school," as Helen (and only Helen) said, she washed and ironed everything she'd taken from Rebecca's room and unwrapped the new purchases. She carefully packed everything, rolling t-shirts and slacks so they wouldn't get wrinkled, stuffing the toes of expensive sneakers with underwear to save space.

Helen got up early the next morning to add last minute items like family photos with glass frames and clothes likely to wrinkle no matter how carefully they were packed. She wrapped a sweater around the box filled with *Bubbe* Golda's rock candy, which the old lady had brought over the night before.

"Rebecca will need some sweetness in her new place," Golda said, holding out her package. Then she turned and shuffled down the street. Helen stood on the stoop until Golda was out of sight, wondering how her mother-in-law had found out about the move, not surprised that she knew.

Sarah watched the suitcase fill up, tactfully not mentioning that she was sure Rebecca would hate many of Helen's purchases, like the gingham ruffled shirt and matching pedal pushers with over-sized pockets. Aunt Rachel came by with a makeup kit crammed with expensive cosmetics. Helen tucked five $20 bills into one of the zipper compartments under a tube of toothpaste and a bottle of expensive shampoo. Twenty $10 bills went into a box of fancy stationary along with a flowery message urging Rebecca to write often.

Finally, there was nothing left to pack. Sarah sat on the suit-case, and Saul snapped the locks. Then he drove to the detention center, where it was tagged and left with a guard. There wasn't any-thing else to do.

Rebecca was told she'd leave the detention center for her new residence at 7 a.m. She was ready on time, but there was no one to pick her up. And people say I'm irresponsible, she thought as she paced the hallway.

At about 7:30 she asked one of the guards about the delay. "It'll be here when it gets here," he grumbled. "You in a hurry to leave us?"

Rebecca didn't answer. She went over to the front door where three other girls were standing, presumably waiting for the same transport. Rebecca wanted to ask if they had any idea what was going on, but the girls were chatting animatedly in Spanish. She didn't understand what they were saying and didn't want to interrupt.

So much for the guidance counselor's advice that learning Latin would make it easier to know all other foreign languages, thought Rebecca. I'll bet they're not discussing Virgil. And if I demonstrated how well I can conjugate Latin 101 verbs I doubt they'd reward me with a cigarette, which I could really use right now.

Two of the girls held stuffed duffel bags, and the third had her possessions in a black trash bag. Rebecca carried a colorful tote bag with the things she had used while at the center. The large, expensive leather suitcase left by her uncle was at her feet. Rebecca hadn't bothered inspecting it's contents when the guard handed it to her this morning.

At around 8:15 a.m. a matron walked out of the office, announced it was time to leave and led the girls outside. Rebecca had expected some sort of armored car where they'd be locked into their seats. But the vehicle waiting just beyond the gate was a bright yellow school bus. The driver got out, grabbed everyone's bags and tossed them onto a steel rack inside. Then he called the names on his clipboard and each girl climbed aboard.

Rebecca paused at the top of the steps and looked down the narrow aisle. The bus was half-full. No one looked friendly, no one said anything. She slid across an empty, scuffed, two-seat bench behind the driver and settled herself next to the window.

When the last girl got on, someone in the back called out, "Carrie, hey Carrie. How you been?" The girl waved, smiled, called out some names and started down the aisle.

"Keep it quiet back there," said the driver. He shut the door and drove off. The bus made one more stop in the city, and six girls got on; no one sat next to Rebecca. Then they headed upstate.

About three hours later, the bus pulled off the thruway, drove through a small, drab town and stopped in front of a large, industrial-looking building surrounded by a sturdy fence topped with barbed wire.

Rebecca stared through the bus window thinking this building looked worse than the detention center, that spending a long time there would be awful. The driver started calling out names, and Rebecca listened carefully, relieved that she didn't hear her name. The girls who'd been called walked down the aisle and got off the bus. One of them was from the detention center Rebecca had just left, the girl with the trash bag. Rebecca thought about saying goodbye, good luck, something like that. But the girl walked past without a glance, so Rebecca didn't say anything.

An hour later the bus pulled off the thruway again. This time it drove through narrow country roads before it stopped. The driver called four names; one of them was Rebecca. The sun was in her eyes as she stumbled down the bus's stairs and she pulled a pair of large dark glasses out of her tote bag. The driver said hello to a stocky, middle-aged woman in a shapeless grey dress who was waiting by the bus door and handed her some papers.

"How've you been?" said the woman in a deep, husky voice. "You're late. Any trouble with this batch?"

"Nothing I couldn't handle. Just hit some traffic," said the driver. He tossed their bags out of the bus and drove off.

The woman looked at her clipboard. The girls looked at each other. They looked around. They were in a rural, campus-like setting. The bus had deposited them on a circular drive with three large brick buildings in a row. Gravel paths spoked off the circle and led to a series of two and three-story buildings, each painted a different color. There were grassy fields as far as they could see.

"Wow, we're really in the sticks," said one girl nervously. Another nodded.

When the girls stopped fidgeting the woman spoke up. "Hello, I'm the head matron. Welcome to Hillsdale. This is a treatment center, not a jail, but it is a secure facility. That means you have to obey the rules. While you're with us you'll receive counseling, attend school and perform assigned jobs. We're going to do everything we can to make this a positive experience for you. This is a special place for girls who need help dealing with their problems. If you cooperate, you will greatly benefit from your time here."

"I could really benefit by leaving," whispered one of the girls. "I wonder what kinda jobs they're gonna have us doin.'"

"Just be glad the driver didn't call your name at the last stop," said the other girl. "I've heard about that place. Definitely bad news."

The matron ignored the chatter and turned to the next paper on her clipboard. She told each girl where she'd be living and how to get there. "Now, go to your cottages. Your house mother and roommate are waiting to meet you and help you get settled. In an hour come back here and go to that large building behind you." All of the girls turned their heads. "That's the school building, and you'll be given placement exams. Then it'll be time for dinner. The cafeteria is right next to the school building."

The other girls picked up their bags and started off. Rebecca didn't move. She kept looking around, trying to wrap her mind around what was going on. She thought she could make out a fence in the distance, but it might have just been a line of darker-colored trees. She wanted to ask where the guards were but figured that was a dumb question. If there was hidden surveillance of course no one would admit it.

"Are you waiting for a bellhop, dear?" said the matron. The other girls laughed.

"Sorry, guess I'm a little dazed."

"Well, Rebecca is it?" said the matron. "It's time to pull yourself together and get on your way." She kept staring until Rebecca lifted the suitcase and started walking.

The suitcase was heavy. Very heavy. She walked down the road for a few minutes. It was a warm afternoon, she started to sweat, took some tissues out of her tote bag and wiped her face. She picked up the suitcase again, carried it for a few more minutes and then put it down. She looked around. The other girls from the bus were ahead of her.

Rebecca knew her Aunt Helen would have put some money in her bag. She wondered if there was a maintenance man or gardener who would be willing to help her if she tipped enough. But the only people around were other teenage girls who didn't look friendly. She picked the bag up again. Then she put it down, changed hands and kept walking.

When she got to her cottage, Rebecca saw that the house-mother had been standing by the door watching her come down the road, not making any effort to help with Rebecca's suitcase. She was a tall, thin woman and she nodded to Rebecca when she'd crossed the doorway. "Your room is on the third floor," she said in a lilting Caribbean accent. "Sorry, no elevator." Rebecca thumped the suitcase up the stairs.

The room was at the end of the hall. Rebecca knocked twice and, at the same time, turned the knob. The door was unlocked. She shoved her suitcase into the room with her foot and it fell over with a loud thud.

A thin girl with caramel colored skin and long black hair was lying on the bed near the window. There were a bunch of stuffed animals next to her pillow and two fuzzy pink slippers peeking from under her bed.

"Hi, I'm Rebecca."

"I'm Maria."

It was a pleasant room, large enough to accommodate two twin beds with pale green sheets and beige blankets that matched the window curtains. There was a wide dresser, two desks with a big, empty trash basket in between and a closet with sliding doors.

Maria looked at Rebecca's suitcase. "The three drawers on the left side of the dresser are yours, and there's a bunch of empty hangers in the closet."

The girls looked at each other for a minute.

"Guess I should start unpacking," said Rebecca. She put her suitcase on the bed and it sprang open as soon as she touched it.

"My God, look at all this stuff," she said as she scooped up a batch of clothes and dumped them next to her suitcase. Store tags flapped from many items. "My Aunt Helen packed for me, and Aunt Helen is often out of control. I don't recognize half of this stuff. She must have bought out every store in the Bronx."

"Are you from the Bronx? So am I. Near Crotona Park." Maria paused for a minute. "Well, that's where we used to live. My mom and her boyfriend recently moved to 174th Street under the El. So I guess I live there now."

"Oh, I know that area, my dad's business is nearby. I live in the North Bronx. No mom, just a hateful father and lots of nosey relatives." Rebecca haphazardly dropped clothes into bureau drawers and then stopped and held up one of the new outfits.

"Will you look at this?"

She was holding a ruffled, pale pink blouse and pedal pushers with matching ruffles down the outside seams. "Aunt Helen obviously thinks I've been sent to clown college." She dropped the outfit into the trash can and pulled out a tee-shirt with a large sequined rose in the center. "This goes too."

Rebecca unpacked some knitted vests. "And this, and this too." The can was filling up.

When Rebecca discovered the money, she turned her back to Maria and slipped the cash under a pile of t-shirts she'd already put in the drawer

Soon Rebecca uncovered the box filled with *Bubbe*'s candy and smiled. "Here, would you like some?" She walked over to Maria who was still lying on her bed, transfixed by Rebecca's unpacking. "It's rock candy. My grandmother makes it. She says it adds sweetness to your life. She'd want me to tell you to watch out for the string, that it might get wrapped around your insides."

Maria smiled and took a piece. "My grandma used to make candies with chili pepper. We gave them to our friends and laughed if they couldn't handle the spicy taste."

The suitcase wasn't totally unpacked when the housemother knocked on the door and said it was time for Rebecca's placement tests. She said goodbye to Maria and left her belongings scattered around the room.

Rebecca grabbed a test from the stack piled at the door and sat down in the back of the room. She recognized the girls who had been on the bus with her that morning, but there were several others. A bunch of buses must have arrived today, she thought.

Rebecca quickly finished the test and looked around the room. A few girls were just staring into the air; most had their heads down. She realized that there were only a few white girls in the large room. In Rebecca's elementary school there had been a handful of Black and Hispanic kids in each class, at Bronx Science there might have been one or two non-white students in the whole school. Well, those Science kids were pretty boring, she thought. This will be different. The proctor told Rebecca to keep her eyes on her own paper.

In less than an hour, Rebecca raised her hand and said she was finished. "Sure you don't want to try to answer a few more questions? There's plenty of time left," said the proctor.

"Nope, all done."

"Okay, just go back to your cottage until dinner time.

Rebecca decided to explore instead. She was walking around the central area when she saw a girl wearing the same gingham pedal pushers Helen had packed for her. Damn, someone actually bought those, Rebecca thought. She studied the girl. With a plain black shirt, the pants didn't look half bad. Maybe she should reconsider. Then Rebecca saw a tag hanging from the slacks, a tag from a store near her house. She cut in front of the girl.

"Excuse me, I was wondering where you got those pants. Do you shop at Ronnie Lees?" Rebecca pulled the tag off the back of the pants and held it up.

The girl stopped walking and looked Rebecca up and down. "Never hearda that store," she said. "I got this particular outfit in a local place. The red cottage. Some princess just moved in and didn't want it. Left it for the peasants."

"My name is Rebecca, and yes, I just got here. But I didn't intend to throw that out, just haven't gotten around to putting everything away yet."

"Just storing some clothes in the trash bin, huh?"

"Look, I'd appreciate it if you'd take those slacks off and return them as soon as possible. And if you took anything else bring that back too."

"I'm Alice, glad to meet ya, your highness. But no, I don't really feel like returning these pants. I've kinda gotten used to them." She pushed Rebecca aside and started walking away.

Rebecca moved in front of Alice. "I'm sorry, but it's not really your choice. I'm not familiar with all the rules here, but I'm pretty sure you're not allowed to steal stuff from my room."

"You calling me a thief, your majesty? I saw you struggle with that suitcase, guess you're used to being taken care of. Sorry to tell you, but your servants rebelled. You're on your own here. Better move out of my way if you know what's good for you."

Alice was slightly taller than Rebecca, thicker, sturdier. But being at a physical disadvantage wasn't why Rebecca felt like she was going to cry, why she was trying to keep from shaking. Rebecca had seen her share of teen gang movies and prison sagas. She'd read trashy novels. If I give in now I'm doomed, she thought. Everyone will pick on me. She didn't move. Just stood in front of the girl, staring, every muscle clenched.

"What's the matter? Low on energy? Maybe you need something to eat." Alice reached into the pants' pocket and pulled out *Bubbe* Golda's rock candy.

Rebecca was confused. She was hot. She was tired. She was anxious. And then suddenly all she was, was mad. "You lousy bitch," she yelled as she raised her hand and slapped Alice across the face as hard as she could. "My *Bubbe* made that for me!"

Alice stumbled backwards, more surprised than hurt and smiled. "What's a bubby?" she asked as she grabbed Rebecca with one hand and raked her long nails down Rebecca's neck with the other. Rebecca got hold of that arm and twisted it, twisted as if she could tear it off. Both of them fell to the ground. Alice knew how to deliver a punch, and Rebecca screamed and pulled her hair. They rolled around for a few minutes.

Two large men in uniforms pulled the girls to their feet. "Okay, cut it out," one of them said. When the girls were both standing, he took out a notebook. "Alice, you know better. You're getting 20 demerits." He turned to Rebecca. "And you, whoever you are, I guess you're new, so you're only getting 10 demerits. But just in case there's any confusion in your mind, let me tell you Rule One around here. No fighting. At all. Ever. Now I know Alice is in the red cottage, room 32," he said. "How about you?"

Rebecca looked at the other girl. "I'm in the red cottage too. Room 34."

The guard grinned. "Well, I guess you're both going to have to learn to be neighborly."

The two girls started walking back toward their cottage, Rebecca rubbing her neck where Alice had scratched her, Alice rubbing her arm where Rebecca had twisted it. They were both covered with dirt. No one said anything for a few minutes.

"Damn, I broke two nails," said Alice.

"I've got a pretty complete manicure kit in my bag, I can fix that for you," said Rebecca. "Unless you also took the case with all my cosmetics. Do you check out all the new girls?"

"No, most people here don't have much. But when Maria told me about her new roommate who arrived with a ton of clothes and then threw most of them away, well, I thought I'd take a look."

Alice started to brush the dirt off her slacks. She looked at Rebecca who was trying to shake gravel out of her now tangled hair. She knew exactly where Rebecca would have black and blue marks tomorrow. It was clear this girl didn't know how to fight, but she had landed a few good hits. "Listen, if you really want these pants, I guess you can have them back, but I think a seam ripped when we were on the ground."

Rebecca looked at Alice. "No, keep them. They look better on you then they would on me," said Rebecca. "I'll bet my aunts put a sewing kit in my suitcase, we can probably fix the seam."

Alice laughed. "These aunts of yours, they scout leaders or something? Want you to always be prepared?"

"They had no idea what I was getting into, just sent everything they could think of."

They walked quietly for a few minutes.

"What does 10 demerits mean?"

"Not much. The more demerits you have the more the house-mother can mess with your life. But the woman in charge of the red cottage is pretty cool. She'll just assign extra chores or take away TV time. Not really a big deal. They censor our TV anyway, no porn or super violent stuff. Like we'd see anything we don't already know. If the demerits really mount up, she might take away trips into town for a movie or something like that.

"The closest town is really a dump, but it's someplace to go. Sometimes local guys sneak onto the grounds. They think girls from this place are really hot, and they're willing to spend their money to get you booze or drugs or presents. Let me know if you want to get fixed up."

"I'm not interested in putting out for some hillbillies," said Rebecca. "But thanks for the offer."

"Oh, yeah, I forgot. You're loaded."

Rebecca stopped walking and looked directly at Alice. "Look, don't let the stuffed suitcase mislead you. I have a couple of rela-tives who try to look out for me. They're the only reason I'm even half sane. Okay, I'm not poor, I've got some things going for me. But I don't have a mom and my dad is a real bastard. If it were up to him, I'd be in a real jail wearing stripes and getting served gruel and water, not some half-assed Sunnybrook Farm for delinquents. Or maybe he'd just throw me out on the street."

"Relax," said Alice. "Welcome to Hillsdale. As bad as your old man is, somebody here has one that's worse. Plus an uncle, or a neighbor, or a teacher that's been up to some kind of funny business with them since they were kids. So I landed a couple of punches today and you'll be a little black and blue for a while, bet you don't have no other marks on you. When you're in the shower room, take a look at the scars on the other girls."

"I don't want to get into a contest over who had it worse. I just want to be left alone and not have my stuff stolen."

"Look, I'll do you a favor. Seems your kingdom is on shaky grounds, so I'll return your cash. Well, most of it. Already spent one of the twenties on cigarettes and snacks. Consider it the cost of education. You can spend those bills in town when they take us on outings or deposit them in the canteen so you can buy stuff you need when your suitcase runs out."

"The envelope with the money was in my bureau drawer," said Rebecca. "Did you go through everything?"

Alice smiled. "I was curious about what you were keeping, what was worthy of a princess."

12.

THE VISIT

It took almost two months before Rebecca was allowed to see her family.

"They want her to get adjusted to the place before she deals with visitors," Helen told Rachel. "I had to bite my tongue to keep from asking how a visit from her aunt who practically raised her could be a disturbance, but, you know me, I don't like to make a fuss."

Instead, Helen called Rebecca's counselor, a young man who insisted everyone call him Bill, at least once a week and pumped him for information. He was always polite, rarely informative.

"This Bill must be quite a guy," Saul confided in Morris one day at work. "If she was one of our customers and constantly called to hint she knew my business better than I did I'd have stopped taking her calls a long time ago."

Helen and Sarah wrote regularly. "We want Rebecca to remember we love her," said Helen. "And the school should be reminded that Rebecca comes from a family that's concerned about her."

Rebecca didn't write back often.

"She's busy making friends, getting used to her new classes," Helen said to anyone who asked for news. Sarah suspected Rebecca's mail was censored, and she was being careful.

At the start of Rebecca's stay, Helen sent her niece weekly care packages. She filled wax-paper lined boxes with homemade cookies and cakes, along with *Bubbe's* rock candy and new clothes. Sarah encouraged her mom. Helen's baked goods were envied throughout the family, and Sarah thought they might come in handy to bribe guards or appease gang members. Eventually Bill asked Helen to stop, explaining it was unfair for Rebecca to have a supply of sweets that weren't available to the other girls.

"They're afraid you'll bake a file into the middle of a *babka* and she'll use it to break out," Saul joked. Helen frowned and turned away.

She decided to compromise by sending fewer, but larger, packages, occasionally including more substantial food, like a brisket or roast chicken. She sent Bill a note letting him know that she always reminded Rebecca to share the food with her friends.

"Okay," said Bill. "You win. I know better than to try to get a Jewish mother to stop sending food."

Finally, Helen got permission for a family visit. Rebecca asked that Marvin be included; she also said that if Harvey came, she'd lock herself in her room and refuse to see anyone. Harvey said Marvin was too busy to go, and Helen decided not to argue. No one knew what to expect.

Helen, Saul and Sarah started off early. They took the thruway upstate a few hours until they spotted a small sign that told them to turn left for the Hillsdale Treatment Center.

"Why didn't they just say The Hillsdale School?" said Helen. No one replied.

Sarah stared fixedly out the window, eager for her first glance of a reform school. She saw a fence, just a steel mesh fence like people had in their backyards, no barbed wire. At the gatehouse a bored looking man pressed a button that lifted a flimsy barricade when Saul explained who they were visiting. On the other side of the gate, she saw a very green lawn, a few buildings in the distance. And a bunch of ducks.

A reform school, Sarah thought, should not have ducks. Anyone could have told you that. Anyone could have told you that a reform school had bars and thick walls and guards in stiff grey uniforms who carried electrified clubs.

Rebecca's reform school seemed to have none of these things. But it did have ducks. Fat honking creatures that waddled out of a pond onto a bright green lawn and left a trail of duck shit on the cobbled paths.

"*Katchkas!*" Saul called out. "Look, Sarah, look at them all." She remembered a Yiddish children's story about a pair of ducks that wandered into a butcher's shop. The tale doesn't end well for the ducks.

They located the main building where Rebecca was waiting. As soon as she spotted their car she ran over, barely waiting for Saul to stop before she opened the door and put her arms around Helen.

"You've gotten so skinny," Helen cried. "I should have brought more food." Everyone laughed and hugged, and Rebecca took them on a tour.

As far as Sarah was concerned the whole place was a disappointment. It had cottages, not cells. It had house mothers in polyester housedresses, not guards. Rebecca had a roommate who was a small, quiet Puerto Rican girl, barely bigger than Sarah, who had expected Rebecca's roommate to be a tattooed giant with missing teeth and a hidden shank carved out of her toothbrush.

Helen took one look at the campus and handed Sarah a package of tissues so she could wipe her shoes. "Be careful where you step. Watch out for the duck droppings."

Sarah had Rebecca's most recent letter tucked in her pocket. It was more exciting than anything Rebecca had previously written. Sarah had read it over and over. Especially the ending.

Clearly trying to escape the prying eyes of censoring guards, Rebecca had written the last few words phonetically in Yiddish. They both assumed that no guard would be able to read the message because, well, Jewish boys just don't become prison guards.

"*Krig mir gelt,*" she wrote. Bring me money.

Rebecca knew it was easy for Sarah to get money. Pocketbooks were open in her family. Wallets were left on Formica counters. "Sarah, get $20 dollars from my bag for the boy at the front door," Helen would call. She wouldn't notice if her daughter took a few extra bills.

As soon as the girls were alone, Rebecca asked, "Did you get the money?" Helen and Saul were behind them, walking slowly, pointing out attractive features of the school to each other.

Sarah clutched the wad of bills squashed into the bottom of her pocket. She remembered the trouble she'd gotten into keeping secrets for Rebecca in Atlantic City. But she also remembered the thrill of being part of her world. Without Rebecca, Sarah would have been just an ordinary junior high kid. Now, having a cousin in reform school made her special. She didn't want to let Rebecca down again. She gave her the money, $40.

"Is this all?"

"You didn't say how much you needed. Are you in trouble? What's going on? Can I help you bust out?" Sarah desperately wished she was old enough to drive a getaway car.

"Nah, it's not so bad here," Rebecca said. "There's an endless amount of bullshit, but no more than at my father's house. Play your cards right you don't get any real punishment. Just some demerits which means stuff like extra chores or no TV.

"Some of the people are okay. My counselor's pretty good. And he's good looking, which makes it easier to spend time with him. Maybe he can help me sort things out, deal with all the crap in the world.

"Meanwhile, the damn duck shit ruined the expensive shoes," Rebecca said. "Someone must have thought the ducks make the place look less like a prison. They weren't thinking about the duck shit.

"Now I need to get another pair of shoes, ones with better soles, but still stylish. I figure they'll cost more than the few dollars I have left from the money your mom stashed in my suitcase. I have to wait until they decide to take us into town, and they keep track of how much we withdraw from our accounts. I guess they're afraid we'll buy drugs. Anyway, thanks for this cash. I'll manage."

Rebecca slowed down to talk to Helen and Saul. Sarah knew that, before they left, her parents would push some money into Rebecca's hand. She wasn't worried about Rebecca going barefoot.

They took the tour, they met the people, they fed the ducks some stale bread provided by the helpful house mother. They hugged Rebecca and got back in the car to drive back to the city.

Saul glanced into the rearview mirror, at the lawns and the cottages and the ducks. "It looks like a picture from a children's book," he said. Helen was quietly crying. Sarah quietly stared out the window.

Let everyone pretend this was a place in a story book. Sarah knew better. Despite the cottages, despite the pond, despite the friendly housemother and despite the god-dammed quack, quack, here and a quack, quack, there, this wasn't ol' Mc Donald's farm.

Her cousin was buying shoes with stolen money, her family

needed permission from strangers to see her and their whole family was changed.

Rebecca was in jail.

Everything was all full of shit.

13.

WHILE SHE WAS AWAY

The aunts dropped in at Harvey's house regularly to oversee the housekeeper. If they were dissatisfied, they replaced her. The switch was barely noticed. Harvey and Marvin weren't very demanding.

The housekeeper made Marvin breakfast and packed a lunch for him to take to school. Harvey ate breakfast and lunch at a diner. The housekeeper left dinner, which they reheated. Frequently Marvin ate with Aunt Rachel and her boys and Harvey ate at home by himself, reading a book, oblivious to the food.

Everyone told Harvey how lucky he was to have his sisters-in-law and the rest of the devoted family. Everyone knew a man without a wife couldn't manage children and a house by himself. They should only know, Harvey thought. All of this help isn't always free, and it isn't always helpful. But he said he was grateful.

When they were alone together Harvey and Marvin were cordial, but they had trouble thinking of things to say to each other. Marvin answered Harvey's questions about school, said he was doing fine. Sometimes he needed a permission slip signed or money for books or a special excursion. He explained these activities with as little detail as possible.

Marvin wrote to Rebecca several times a week, mailing the

letters on his way to school. He told her there weren't many stars in the Bronx sky, so he no longer talked to their mother in the sky. He asked about the skies where Rebecca was. He asked about her new school. "Bet you're still the smartest kid in your class," he said. Sometimes he sent drawings he'd made when he was supposed to be studying. He always closed with the words, "miss you, love you."

Rebecca didn't write back often. She knew their papa would make Marvin show him the letters she sent so she was careful not to say anything personal. "Take care of yourself," she said at the end of each letter.

Sometimes Marvin asked Harvey about his day. His papa always said everything was fine. Marvin didn't know enough about Harvey's work to ask anything else, and Harvey was reluctant to provide details.

The family thought Marvin was doing well. He was a first baseman on his little league team and a top hitter, popular with classmates and spent a lot of time at the homes of other boys. Occasionally friends visited him, and, if he was home, Harvey greeted them, told them they were free to help themselves to snacks and then he retired to his study. He didn't know what to say to these boys. When there were no other children around, Marvin stayed busy with his large collection of baseball cards and comic books which seemed to require extensive curating.

Harvey attended a few little league games but was uncomfortable there. The games were played in the late afternoon, and Harvey worried about missing work. The ballfield was noisy and dusty, full of children and parents he didn't know yelling things he couldn't follow.

The bleacher seats were hard and there was little shade. Harvey got headaches from being in the sun. He was going bald, afraid to get his scalp sunburned, afraid of winding up with greasy-looking hair if he smeared lotion on the top of his head. He felt wearing a regular businessman's hat was inappropriate but didn't think he looked good in the baseball caps he saw on other men.

Marvin was just as uncomfortable with his father's presence. His dad didn't know how to cheer, how to yell at the umpire or how to take a group of kids out for pizza and ice cream when the game was over.

Eventually Marvin told his papa it really wasn't important for him to attend the games. "I'll let you know if we make the finals," Marvin assured him. "That'll be a game you should come to."

Apparently, the team never made the finals. Marvin didn't report on his team's progress. Harvey didn't ask.

While Harvey's absence at little league games was fine with Marvin, it was an issue to Rachel. Having three boys on three different little league teams meant Rachel knew a lot about baseball, including the fact that it was important for a boy to have someone cheer for him, or console him, after each game. When one of her sons did something special the whole family sang "Take Me Out to the Ballgame" before dinner and there was a special dessert.

When a few weeks went by without any of the boys performing any dessert-worthy feats, Kenny complained to his brother, making sure his mother overheard, that it was too bad they couldn't celebrate their cousin's accomplishments. "I heard he hit a triple that brought in two runs today," he said. "His team is now a sure thing to get to at least the semi-finals."

Rachel got the hint. "How would you all feel if once in a while I went to one of Marvin's games instead of yours?" she asked her sons at dinner that night. "And when he does something special, we can have him celebrate with us."

The boys grinned. Marvin was one of the stars of his team,

the Ben's Hardware Bombers. "That's a terrific idea. With him in our family league we'll be having hot fudge sundaes every night," said Kenny, imagining unlimited chocolate sauce dripping off his spoon.

Harvey was glad to miss Marvin's ball games, but he never missed a meeting with the public-school teacher. And he was even less comfortable at those meetings than when he'd been in the little league bleachers.

Life would have been a lot easier for Harvey if Marvin had been the smart one and Rebecca the average student. As far as Harvey was concerned, Rebecca's As had been a waste. Who cared about a girl's grades? She only needed to be smart enough to run a household. He had looked forward to raising a son who inherited his brilliance, a young man who would make Harvey feel his genius hadn't been wasted. He had dreamed of a son who would one day be a leader in American society. Even a son who was rebellious like Rebecca would have pleased Harvey; he imagined a son who'd question values and engage in intellectual arguments with him, maybe citing Talmudic arguments to back up his beliefs.

Rebecca's teachers had complained about her behavior but always gave her straight As. Marvin's teachers said, "He's a lovely boy, attentive, polite, he tries hard. Just a pleasure to have in the class." They gave him Cs.

Harvey suggested extra homework for Marvin, but the teachers shook their heads. "One of these days something will spark his interest," they said. "Why put pressure on him now?"

Harvey sat through these meetings quietly, nodding, trying to show respect for the teachers while thinking, these people have no idea what they're talking about. They should know how we studied in Europe. A little pressure would do the boy some good.

14.

AMIGAS

Rebecca had been at the school for a few months and was getting used to it.

She and Alice had patched things up after the fight on her first day, and Rebecca really liked hanging out with the street-smart, witty girl who was always ready for a new adventure.

And Rebecca was especially fond of her roommate, a quiet Puerto Rican girl with a soft, melodic voice. Maria parted her thick brown hair in the middle, and it hung straight down the sides of her face like velvet drapes. Rebecca thought that, in repose, her roommate looked like one of the Spanish Madonnas art teachers at Bronx Science had projected onto the screens they set up in front of blackboards.

Today there was a strong wind and, as the two girls walked to class, Maria's hair streamed behind her, revealing the jagged pink scar that followed her hairline from slightly above her eyebrow to the bottom of her ear. Rebecca had seen the scar before it was visible when Maria brushed her hair, when she tossed in her sleep and muttered in Spanish, or when she was upset and ran her fingers through her hair. She'd never had the nerve to ask Maria about it. In the strong sunlight, the scar looked darker, and Rebecca couldn't help noticing it.

"See something interesting?" Maria said in a harsh voice. She pulled two rubber bands from her pocket and gathered her hair in front of her ears into two ponytails that hid the sides of her face.

"I'm sorry," stammered Rebecca, taken aback by the nasty tone from her usually gentle roommate. "I didn't mean to stare."

"Yeah, well, it's no big deal."

They walked quietly for a few minutes.

Rebecca took a deep breath, spoke softly without looking at Maria. "Were you in an accident?"

"Yeah, an accident. It was quite an accident that the knife only caught the edge of my face, it was supposed to totally slice me up."

"Oh my God. Who did it? When? Did the police catch him? Put him in prison?"

Maria stopped walking and looked at Rebecca. "Sometimes I forget you come from a different planet. It was just a guy my mom was involved with. Not her current boyfriend. This one was a drunk, he liked to look at me. My mom told him not to, but he didn't listen. One day, when I was about twelve, I was playing with my mom's makeup when she was out. I saw him in the mirror, staring at me. I said I'd tell my mom, she'd kick him out. He'd wind up living on the street like the dog he was."

Maria stood still, glanced away but continued talking.

"He got mad, said he was going to do something so looking at myself wouldn't be so much fun. It was my fault. I was stupid to goad him. I should have remembered we were alone, that he was probably drunk, that he carried a knife."

Maria looked directly at Rebecca. "I'm lucky I got away. It could have been a lot worse. I ran down the street to my *abuela*, screaming and bleeding. She took me to the hospital. They did a pretty good job stitching me up. Sometimes the people in the ER aren't that good and leave worse scars."

"Didn't the doctors call the police?"

Maria shook her head. "We told the medics I'd fallen and there was glass on the sidewalk. We left while they were messing around with paperwork. My *abuela* didn't speak English very well but she understood how things worked and had given them a phony address when we arrived because we couldn't pay the bill. She called my mom and said she'd kill the guy herself if my mom didn't get rid of him. I lived with *abuela* for a while. Eventually mom and the guy broke up, and I moved back in with her.

"*Abuela* only had one room and a small kitchen, but I knew I could go back to her if things didn't work out." Maria shrugged. "But she died soon after I left her place. That's when I started stealing, in case I needed money to move away from my mom. That's how I wound up here."

Rebecca didn't know what to say. She stepped towards Maria, wanting stroke her face, but the other girl moved back. "It's not such a big deal," Maria said. "You should know that by now."

There were a lot of scars at the school, self-inflicted and otherwise. Some girls quietly exchanged make-up tips to cover disfigured body parts, others dressed to show off marks they regarded as badges of honor. Counselors talked about damages that couldn't be seen.

Rebecca remembered the times she'd suspected her father of hurting Marvin. But he'd always denied it. Anyway, this stuff Maria had gone through was different. Wasn't it? Of course her father had slapped her. Slapped her hard. A bunch of times. But a knife? No one in her community carried a knife. No one ever hurt a girl. Really hurt her. Did they? She'd never heard of it. But of course she'd never heard of anyone sending their daughter away to a place like this.

The girls reached the school building, impulsively hugged and hurried off to their classes.

15.

WORSHIP

Marvin's performance at Hebrew School was even worse than his performance in regular school, and even more upsetting to Harvey.

Like all the Rosens, Harvey and his family were members of a nearby temple, which Harvey thought of as "American *shul*" which meant not up to his standards. Nevertheless, Marvin went to Hebrew school there with his cousins.

Marvin dreaded the times when Harvey asked to see his Hebrew lessons. He knew his father was ashamed of him. Marvin's written work was barely legible, and he stumbled when he tried to read the Hebrew text. Clearly whatever Marvin had learned when he was trying to earn money for the magic kit hadn't stayed with him. Harvey shook his head and told Marvin to try harder. Harvey couldn't understand why Marvin didn't do better. After a few years it dawned on Harvey that maybe Marvin's poor performance wasn't all his son's fault.

The teachers in the synagogue's Hebrew school were young American men from religious families: some were studying to become Rabbis, some just needed to earn extra money. There were no grades in Hebrew school, no report cards; students progressed from one level to the next until they became thirteen and were Bar Mitzvahed. There was a very sparsely attended post-Bar Mitzvah class.

"They don't know what they're doing," Harvey told Morris. "We're sending our sons to a school with incompetent teachers. How can boys excel in a place that doesn't care about providing a proper education for Jewish youth?

"We should look for a yeshiva for them, a place where they'll get the right kind of education--an English education and a Hebrew education provided by knowledgeable teachers. A place with high standards, where they'll be surrounded by students from families who expect their sons to meet the highest levels."

Harvey imagined himself leading the parents' group at such a school, having Marvin be proud that he had one of the most accomplished fathers.

Morris shook his head and looked at Harvey as if he were crazy. "They'll get Bar Mitzvahed," he said. "What more do you want?"

• • •

The *shul* the Rosens attended was originally an Orthodox synagogue, a one-story brick building a few blocks from their homes, where men prayed on the main floor of the sanctuary, and women prayed in a small balcony above. There was a cement Jewish star on the outside wall and an embossed sign that identified the place.

By the late '50s, the Jewish population of the area had changed. Younger, more modern Jewish people moved in, people who had made enough money to leave the tenements and buy private homes with gardens in the North Bronx. They wanted a synagogue that followed the Conservative style of Judaism, where women sat next to men and more English was heard during services.

These people raised funds and attached a larger, more impressive structure to the old sanctuary. Conservative services were held in the new building, and Orthodox services were held in the old building. The old *shul* was primarily for elderly people who clung to the old ways and for younger people who wanted to save money. Seats in the old *shul* cost about a third of the price of seats in the new *shul*. Children from both *shuls* attended Hebrew school together in the refurbished classrooms attached to the newer building.

The addition was taller than the original structure so that the new sanctuary could have a soaring ceiling. There was a big bronze candelabra on the outside wall. Inside, the place was comfortable, heated and air conditioned, and had polished hardwood floors and cushioned walnut benches with bronze tags to show which families had paid to reserve certain seats for themselves. Elaborate floor-to-ceiling-stained glass windows displayed the names of deceased family members whose relatives had donated money.

During the high holidays, the Rosens of course, prayed in the newer sanctuary. As a member of the family, Harvey purchased a seat next to them. But sometimes Harvey arrived early and spent a few minutes standing alone in the old *shul*. He would become immersed in the patina of piety that he felt was missing in the new *shul*. He looked at the faded, worn carpets and saw the footprints of men who had been his mentors when he was a boy in Poland, men who, every Friday night and Saturday morning, walked down the aisles to chant prayers that echoed in their hearts and minds. He saw his father and his grandfather among those men. From the time he was a young boy, demonstrating exceptional fluency in Hebrew, he had walked down that aisle, and sat among the older men.

Harvey looked at the worn steps that led to the *bima,* the dais where the Rabbi stood. At his own Bar Mitzvah, Harvey had been proficient enough to lead the entire service, not just the portion usually chanted by the Bar Mitzvah boy. Harvey had used the same long pointer that the rabbi used when he read from the sacred scrolls. Other boys pointed with their fingers.

At the end of the service the rabbi embraced Harvey. "You did good, Heshy," he told the newest member of the congregation. "You've earned your own place on the *bima*."

Harvey looked at the pile of old prayer books printed only in Hebrew, books with broken spines, yellowed pages and crumbling corners, and saw old men clutching them, swaying back and forth, carefully reciting the same prayers year after year after year. Harvey now stood up straight when he prayed. People in the new *shul* would snicker if he swayed and slowly beat his chest in the Orthodox fashion.

Harvey gazed up at the balcony in this Bronx *shul* and thought of the pious women of his town. He remembered sneaking glances into the balcony where those women had sat, wondering if he was looking at his future bride. More than once he had overheard his proud mother say it was too bad their rabbi didn't have a daughter because she was looking for a special girl, a worthy girl, for her son. She wanted to be sure there would be grandsons who would follow in the family's tradition of producing exceptional men.

Harvey remembered how proud his parents had been at the party in his home that followed his Bar Mitzvah, how everyone had congratulated his parents for having such a boy. Harvey had never doubted that one day he, too, would be congratulated for the achievements of his own child.

Of course, this had been before the War. Before the destruction of his village. Before the concentration camps that destroyed its people. Before the war that killed his parents and his family and his religious career.

"Happy New Year to you, Harvey," said an old man, confused because Harvey was standing in the aisle, not moving. "Are you looking for something?"

Startled out of his reverie, Harvey shook his head. "I just wanted to say hello to someone," he said, stepping aside. "I'll greet him later. Looks like services are starting. Happy New Year to you."

Harvey scurried out of the old *shul* and into the new *shul*. He sat down on the bench where his name was engraved on a brass plate above his seat, next to the window with the name of his departed wife. He noticed Marvin sitting on the end of the bench, laughing with his cousins. Unless Marvin was seated next to him, he wouldn't stay in *shul* very long, but Harvey didn't feel like making a fuss. He nodded resignedly when Marvin slipped out half an hour later. His son wouldn't go far; he'd be in front of the synagogue clowning with classmates.

Sitting amidst his in-laws, Harvey watched the women spend as much time looking at their neighbors' wardrobe as at their prayer books, and the men holding whispered business conversations in between prayers. Harvey thought about Rebecca's absence. He wondered if there'd be a service in that place where she lived now. Even if there were, Harvey knew she wouldn't go. He said a prayer for her, reminding God to watch out for his daughter.

• • •

A few weeks later, midway through dinner, Harvey stopped eating and looked at Marvin. "I got a call from the director of the Hebrew school today," he said.

Marvin put his fork down. His father was trying to sound casual, always a bad sign.

"I was told that soon you'll be starting private lessons to prepare for your Bar Mitzvah." The director had also told Harvey the cost of these private lessons, more than the usual fee. The teachers thought Marvin might need something the director called, "intensive preparation."

"I know you'd rather be playing baseball or having fun with

your friends than going to these lessons," Harvey said slowly, trying to sound casual. "If you'd like, I could prepare you for your Bar Mitzvah. We could figure out a schedule convenient for both of us."

Marvin looked up at Harvey. "No," he said. "That's not a good idea. I'll stay in my Hebrew school. I'll study harder."

"Don't you remember how much fun we had learning Hebrew together?" Harvey said softly. "The problem with the magic game was unfortunate, but this time there won't be any misunderstanding about why we're studying."

"No!" said Marvin. "No! No! No! No! No! No! And No!" Each word was spoken louder than the one before. By the end Marvin was screaming.

Harvey stared at Marvin, his "good child." The obedient one, the one who didn't cause trouble.

"Calm down," he said. "Let's talk about this like sensible people."

"If you make me do that again, I'm going to run away!" yelled Marvin. "Like Rebecca!"

"You're talking like a fool. Behave."

"I won't! I don't care if you call the police. I don't care if you send me away. I don't care!" Before Harvey could say another word, Marvin bolted out the door.

Harvey watched through the window as his son ran to Rachel's house. At least this child doesn't go very far away, he thought. In a few minutes the phone rang. Harvey didn't ask who was calling. "I know, Rachel," he said into the phone as soon as he picked it up. "I know. I'll be right over."

Harvey braced himself for another visit to another interfering sister-in-law, another woman who would make him tea and tell him how to raise his own child. Another woman who thought she had the right to meddle in his life because her husband knew how to make money. God bless America.

Harvey saw no reason to rush out the door. He knew where his son was, knew what he was doing, knew he was safe. Harvey finished his meal, changed his shirt, looked in the mirror and smiled as he combed his thinning hair. He was proud of the way he looked. The stumpy Rosen men always looked sloppy, always seemed to need a shave, their wrinkled shirts stretched over their pot bellies. Harvey was tall and thin, neat and clean.

He told himself that this time, he wouldn't give in easily. Marvin was his son, and he'd make sure Rachel and the whole Rosen clan remembered that.

He wasn't going to lose Marvin like he had lost Rebecca.

Almost half an hour after Rachel called, Harvey rang her bell. He was surprised when Morris let him in. The two men shook hands and exchanged greetings as if they hadn't seen each other just a few hours before in the shop.

"Is everything okay?" said Harvey. "Where's Rachel?"

"Rachel is upstairs with the boys," said Morris. "Our boys and also yours. I guess there's a problem. Don't worry, she'll get things under control."

"I'm sorry if my son is keeping Rachel from attending to her husband," Harvey said. "She must be pleased you've come home early."

"That was my plan," said Morris. "Every night, when I come home at 7:30 or 8 o'clock or even later, my children ask me why I can't get home earlier, like their Uncle Harvey. They tell me they see Uncle Harvey coming home in time for dinner with his son. This sounds funny to me because I know their uncle's son frequently eats in my house while I'm out working."

It didn't occur to either man that, as a single parent, Harvey was entitled to special consideration, that he should rightly be spending more time with his child. They believed a man's primary obligation was to care for his business.

"So, tonight I thought I'd come home early, have a nice quiet evening with my family. Instead, I walk in and there's your Marvin sobbing, my Rachel comforting him, my boys yelling their opinions and no supper for me on the table."

"I'm sorry if Marvin disturbed you," Harvey said. "I didn't know he was in the way. I'll tell him not to spend so much time here in the future."

"Don't be silly. I never said we minded seeing Marvin. Rachel has to feed three boys, what's one more? It's good the cousins are close. Family should be that way. Blood should always be able to count on blood.

"Sit down now, tell me, how did things go with that guy on Jerome Avenue? You weren't too busy to see him today? He's moving in this week, and we'll start collecting at the end of the month, right?"

Harvey shrugged. "There's a problem with the permits. Until the inspector gives his okay there's no way the store can open."

"And I told you to take care of the inspector," said Morris. "A few dollars and the violations will disappear. We can make repairs later. Maybe. If they're really needed. Sometimes inspectors say there are violations just so they can make a few extra dollars from businessmen in a rush. You should know that by now."

"And you should know by now that I don't like breaking the law," said Harvey. "We'll make enough money from this customer when the building is safe."

Morris shook his head. "Okay Harvey," he said. "I'll grease the inspectors for you, your hands will stay clean. Like always. And

I'm sure that as soon as the deal is settled your conscience won't give you any problem about taking your share. A commission, you should keep in mind, higher than any other salesman in the shop even though you make fewer sales."

"And each of those sales I do make increases the value of the business you and your brother Saul, my brothers-in-law, own," said Harvey. "After all these years, I'm still a salesman when everyone knows that when I married Elaine you promised I'd become a partner."

"No one ever said anything about partner. We promised our mother, and our beloved sister, to take care of you," said Morris. "We promised Elaine and her children would have everything they needed. We are keeping our word. If you were a better businessman, maybe you'd be a partner by now, but you act like you're doing us a favor by showing up for work."

The two men glared at each other.

"In respect for Elaine's memory, not another word," said Morris finally. "It's not good to argue about business at home. Business problems are for the business place."

They sat in silence. Morris went over to the refrigerator and took out an apple. He reached into the silverware drawer and pulled out a small knife. He sat down across from Harvey and carefully peeled the apple, skillfully manipulating the sharp blade so the skin came off in one continuous swirl, which he dropped on the table. He cut off small chunks, popped them into his mouth and chewed carefully. He didn't offer any to Harvey.

"I heard Marvin's upset about Hebrew school," said Morris. "Those boys don't know how good they've got it. Here our boys get gold stars for good lessons. Nobody got gold stars in our school. But we did get hit if we didn't do things right. Then the teacher would tell our father, who whacked us again."

"You're not embarrassed to recall those times?" Harvey asked.

Morris shrugged, looking amused. "We had some fun. I remember one of my teachers, Reb Haskowitz, a skinny man who thought he knew everything, an expert on every subject. He had thick curly hair and a narrow little beard like a nanny goat. Whenever we saw him Saul and I would start to bleat. He'd wave his cane, and we'd run away.

"Once, we pushed a goat into his classroom while he was teaching and locked the door from the outside. The poor animal was so scared it ran in circles and shit all over the floor. Of course, we were discovered. The farmer who owned the goat saw us take it and ran to our father, who told the rabbi as soon as he heard what had happened. We had to scrub every inch of that classroom, and then our father made sure we couldn't sit down for a week." Morris was laughing so hard tears were running down his cheeks. "But it was worth it."

"I remember Reb Haskowitz," said Harvey. "He was a very wise man. A true sage. I always thought I was so lucky to have the privilege to study with such a man. I can't imagine why anyone would ridicule him."

Neither man said anything else. At the sound of Rachel coming down the stairs they both turned towards her.

"So, you finally came over, Harvey," said Rachel speaking slowly, quietly. "I was wondering what took you so long. I suppose you were finishing your dinner. I've been too busy to give my own husband dinner."

She took the apple peel and the core off the table where Morris had left them and dropped them into the garbage. "Marvin said he'd run out in the middle of his meal. I tried to give him something to eat, but he wasn't hungry. I'll try again later. I fed my boys quickly so they could all go upstairs and calm Marvin down."

She started to get Morris' dinner ready. She didn't offer Harvey anything.

Rachel turned around with a heavy pot in her shaking hand. "What were you thinking, telling him you were going to take him out of Hebrew school and give him lessons yourself?" she said. "All the boys go to Hebrew school together. His friends are there. Don't you remember how it ended the last time you tried to teach him? Why bring all of that up again? Marvin was hysterical when he came here. It wasn't easy to quiet him."

Rachel turned away and slammed the pot on the stove.

"You don't know what you're talking about." Harvey spoke to her back. "Marvin getting so upset that time had nothing to do with my teaching him Hebrew. He was upset because he knew his mother was dying and he couldn't cure Elaine with his magic."

Rachel sniffed loudly as if there was a bad smell in the room.

"Until now I've tolerated that Hebrew school because your family and everyone in the neighborhood thought that was how a Hebrew education should be provided to our children. But I've always had my doubts, felt it wasn't serious about the study of Hebrew. I didn't want to make a fuss. I thought, Rachel is a mother, a loving aunt, she knows what's best for my boy. Now I realize that was a big mistake. I'm more learned than anyone in that place. All those people know is how to ask for money. Those incompetent people wouldn't have been permitted to step foot in my yeshiva, a place of holiness, not business. That's what my yeshiva was like."

"Your yeshiva? Your yeshiva? That's where you want to send your son? You've forgotten that your yeshiva is a pile of ashes today. Marvin doesn't live in a Polish *shtetl,* he lives in the Bronx, in America."

Rachel pulled back her shoulders, stood tall and stared into Harvey's eyes.

"Marvin should go to the Hebrew school his friends go to and have the kind of Bar Mitzvah instruction his friends have. At our *shul* they'll prepare him for the ceremony. They know how to do this. Lots of boys in that school aren't scholars, but they get by. And, if it comes to it, Marvin won't be the first boy who's stood on the *bima*, faced the congregation and stumbled a few times as he chanted the Torah. Such a fine, well-behaved, good-looking boy. We'll all be proud of Marvin whatever happens. And you should be too. You want to be his teacher? Try instead to be his father."

"To tell you the truth," Morris added. "At his Bar Mitzvah our Kenny had to have part of his prayers written out in English. But who knew? Who cared?"

Morris shrugged, picked up the plastic bottle on the table and poured a thick stream of dressing over the salad Rachel had just placed in front of him. "That was the year his little league team won the city-wide trophy," said Morris. "He had other things on his mind. He didn't want to go to Hebrew school at all. I almost had to take off my belt a few times. But in the end, he went, he had his Bar Mitzvah and it all turned out fine."

Harvey noticed a small glob of pink salad dressing on Morris' shirt. He quietly watched it sink into the material.

"And for after the ceremony in the temple, I'll help you arrange an affair you can be proud of," said Rachel.

"And that's where you collect," said Morris. "Bar Mitzvah gifts add up. The bonds, you have to keep for your son. But the checks, you can put them into your own account. Rachel will make sure the right people are on your guest list. All our suppliers should be invited; they know what to do to keep our business. Trust me, you'll be happy."

"You won't have to worry about a thing," said Rachel. She put a plate of cookies in front of Harvey. "After three Bar Mitzvahs

I know how to get a good hall, a good band, arrange a smorgasbord. Maybe we can get the artist who does sculptures of the Bar Mitzvah boy, in chopped liver or in ice. Definitely a full roast beef meal with all the trimmings. Everyone will dance: the hora, the bunny hop, some rock n roll for the youngsters and some show tunes for the old folks. A traditional Bar Mitzvah."

Harvey pushed away the cookies.

"You dare to talk to me about tradition!" he said. "Chopped liver sculptures! The bunny hop! That's your idea of tradition? Do either of you understand what a Bar Mitzvah is? It's a holy occasion. A boy comes of age, takes his place in a congregation, becomes a man in the eyes of the Lord. You've never heard of that?

"Presents to a Bar Mitzvah boy should be things like an engraved prayer book, an embroidered prayer shawl, other things with religious significance. Not checks from people who mean nothing to him. This isn't a business transaction. You think the whole ceremony is just a prelude to a fancy party where everyone can eat too much and dance in their fancy clothes. You dress up the Bar Mitzvah boy in a shiny tuxedo, red, yellow, aqua satin, as if he were a tiny clown instead of a young man at a sacred ceremony."

Morris looked at his empty salad plate and shook his head. This nonsense about Bar Mitzvahs was taking too long. He wanted the rest of his dinner.

"I remember the Bar Mitzvahs you had for your sons," Harvey said. "I remember that at the end of that feast for gluttons they announced a special event. The lights went off, loud Russian music blared and spotlights shone on a line of high stepping men dressed like someone's idea of a Russian Cossack, bright red silk coats with gold sashes, gleaming knee-high black patent leather boots and tall fur hats. Each of them was carrying a flaming sword as they ran around the room. Was this meant as a bizarre commemoration of the times Cossacks burned down our ancestors' villages, I wondered? But no. According to the enthusiastic voice yelling loud enough to be heard over the blaring music, this was the special, famous, renowned offering of Parkway Gardens Catering Flaming Cherries Jubilee a la Russe."

Harvey paused for breath. "That's your idea of tradition, Rachel? Morris?" he said. "A bunch of Cossack peacocks with flaming cherries and brandy on swords like shish-ke-bobs to crown our desserts," he said. "That's the way you remember the atrocities done to our grandparents?"

Morris started to laugh. Not an everyday laugh, but a deep, breath-catching belly laugh. He clutched his stomach and looked at Harvey. "Hey, I hope you remember they put the cherries over fake ice cream, ice cream made without milk since the whole affair was kosher? You have to give us credit for following that tradition." He started to laugh again. Harvey scowled.

"Harvey, my friend," Morris added. "I was angry at you before, but I have to thank you now. I haven't had such a good laugh since the days when we saw Milton Berle and Buddy Hackett at Grossingers in the Catskills."

Harvey stared and then marched toward the stairs. "I'm going to get my son," he said. "I can handle his Bar Mitzvah myself. I don't need your help. And I can raise my son by myself. Please, don't help me anymore."

"Wait." Rachel stopped laughing and put her hand on Harvey's arm. "Let's talk some more. You don't want the cherries jubilee, we won't have it. No one meant to be offensive. And Marvin's such a nice-looking boy, he'll be a dreamboat in a regular suit."

Morris didn't want to talk to Harvey anymore. He saw enough of this man at work. But one look at Rachel and he knew the chicken waiting in the stove would have to stay there. No way his

Rachel was going to give up her relationship with Marvin. No way anyone in the family would ever allow Elaine's son to have a shoddy Bar Mitzvah. Rachel could reheat the chicken once this matter was settled. It wouldn't be the first time Morris would be served a dried-out dinner because he was delayed with business matters.

"Harvey," he said calmly, "don't get excited. Sit down like a *mensch*. Do you want anything?" Harvey shook his head. He was still scowling, but he sat down.

"Look, everyone wants the best for Marvin, for your son, for our nephew, for Elaine's memory," said Morris. "We all agree on that."

Morris and Harvey stared at each other. Rachel kept her position by the stove. "Now, let's talk money," Morris said.

"I should have known that sooner or later the Rosens would reduce a religious rite to a financial transaction," said Harvey.

"Just state your position, there's no reason for insults," said Morris slowly.

Harvey nodded. He would retain his dignity. "First of all, there's no reason to waste my money on Bar Mitzvah lessons from incompetent teachers and a gross display at some hall," Harvey said. "I can teach my son at home and have a tasteful reception in the *shul* after the ceremony. That's the way it should be done."

"That plan is off the table. Saul and I won't hear the end of it from our wives if Marvin doesn't have a proper affair, and you know that Marvin won't want you to instruct him. Let the teachers do their job."

"That's easy for you to say, Mr. Bigshot. It's easy to ignore expenses when you're a partner in a business with underpaid salesmen making money for you."

"If you're thinking we'll offer you a partnership, forget it. Saul and I will listen to our wives *kvetching* and moaning about this affair until we both go deaf before we destroy our business. But about your commission, about the cost of this whole thing, maybe there's room to negotiate. What did you have in mind?"

Harvey was taken aback that Morris was ready to negotiate specifics, but he tried not to let his surprise show, not to seem ill equipped to take advantage of a financial opportunity. "Well, something substantial, of course. Let me think," Harvey said.

"Okay, while you exercise your big brain I'll call Saul. This is now a business matter. He should be part of the decision."

Morris went into the next room and picked up the phone. "Saul," Harvey heard him say. "You'll never guess what's going on at my house tonight."

Rachel walked over and closed the door. Even so, Harvey could hear murmurs and, once in a while, laughter. Finally, Morris reappeared.

"Okay," said Morris. "Here's the deal. Take it or leave it. Saul and I will pay the Hebrew School for Marvin's lessons. Maybe we can write it off as a contribution to the *shul* we'll ask the accountant. Anyway, no more talk about your teaching him. Next, Rachel will help you plan the affair and make sure it's a proper party." Morris looked at his wife. "You'll try not to go crazy with the costs. And remember. No matter what else, Cherries Jubilee are off the menu." He turned back to Harvey. "And since we don't want you going around crying about your poverty, we'll increase your commission by one percent, and Saul and I will each give Marvin $1000 cash for his Bar Mitzvah present, which you can use to pay the bills."

"Make that a 5% raise in the commission," said Harvey. "And I want your Bar Mitzvah present money now, not at the party."

"The money you can have now, and the raise will be 1½ %.

"I won't settle for less than 3%. Agree and you've got a deal."

"Okay, we'll call it 2% and end this arguing."

Harvey and Morris shook hands. Morris suggested they have a drink, but Harvey was eager to leave.

"I'll just get my son and go home," said Harvey.

"It's late," said Rachel. "Why not let him sleep over? He has pajamas and a toothbrush here."

"I'm taking my son home. Now!" said Harvey.

From their doorway, Morris and Rachel watched Harvey and a sleepy Marvin walk down their front steps. "What a fool, what a *schlemiel*," murmured Morris. "Doesn't he know anything about how the world works? Of course Marvin has to have a proper Bar Mitzvah. We have to make sure of that. We can't violate our promise to our mother, or to Elaine's memory and, of course, we have to remember our position in the community. Everyone knows Harvey is part of our family, and he works with us. If it looks like he can't afford a proper Bar Mitzvah, people will think our firm is in trouble. Saul said to go as high as a 4 % bump in his earnings and a $2,000 cash present from each of us."

Morris turned off the outside light and looked at his wife. "Now Rachel," he said, "maybe you remember that I still haven't had any dinner? Stop standing here before I die of hunger."

The next day Harvey called the director of the Hebrew School to arrange for Marvin's special tutoring.

"While I have you on the phone, I want to tell you I've been thinking about the conversation we had last week," said Harvey. "About that woman you know. Maybe you're right, maybe it's time I looked for someone instead of relying on my sisters-in-law so much.

"You said her name was Batya? Tell me more."

16.

THE ROAD TO THE CHUPAH

When the phone rang that morning, it seemed to ring much more loudly than normal, a piercing, drop-whatever-you're-doing-and-get-this ring that meant Rachel had important news. Helen recognized that sound, ran across the house, grabbed the receiver and clutched it tightly to her ear.

"Harvey has a girlfriend!"

"What?" Helen asked. "What are you telling me?"

"The past few Saturdays he asked if Marvin could have supper with us and then spend the night," said Rachel. "And each week, shortly after Marvin gets here, I look out the window and see Harvey getting into his car. And he's all dressed up, preening like a peacock. And I realize that, every time, he is leaving right after sundown. So I add two and two and you know what I get?"

"He's seeing a woman! A religious woman," said Helen.

"Of course," answered Rachel. "How could this happen? If one of our friends wanted to set him up, they would have asked us first. Where did this woman come from?"

No one suggested that Saul or Morris ask Harvey who he was dating since, officially, no one knew he was dating. Anyway, this was clearly not a topic to be entrusted to a man. This was women's work.

For the next two weeks, both of their families ate precooked, reheated food as Helen and Rachel spent endless hours on the phone. Their husbands made lame jokes about buying stock in AT&T, but they knew better than to suggest their wives mind their own business. The welfare of Marvin and Rebecca, the two children they'd practically raised, was at stake. And, as they reminded their husbands, a new wife would undoubtedly affect Harvey's performance in the business.

Of course, not all Jews know each other. But if you narrow the group to, say, first generation Jewish immigrants who live in New York City, and you spend enough time and energy on the project, there's a good chance you can find connections forged during the struggle to overcome US immigration restrictions.

Helen and Rachel resurrected contacts with HIAS, the Hebrew Immigrant Aid Society, one of several groups that lobbied for changes in Jewish immigrant quotas immediately before, during and after WWII. These groups helped new arrivals deal with procedures at Ellis Island and provided housing, job, health and education services and set-up networks so refugees could contact family members who had previously arrived.

In immigrant groups, friends often started the tales of their early days in the United States with stories about such agencies. "When I was at the HIAS," they'd say, "I met Albert, who offered me a job; they found a doctor who cured me; I started learning English; my family was housed next-door to the man I wound up marrying."

Refugees formed social clubs and printed newsletters that were eagerly scanned for information about friends and relatives who hadn't been heard from since the war. With the slim hope that their sister or her child might have survived, the Rosens had registered with some of these groups. In the late '40s, they sometimes received calls from people who had gotten their names from one of these organizations. The callers said they knew about Rosen family members who had been left behind. Everyone would be hopeful for a while, but nothing ever came of these calls.

Yiddish language newspapers flourished after the War. Some included classified columns listing people looking for mates. Helen and Rachel collected these papers in case Harvey had placed an ad or they found an advertisement they thought might appeal to him.

They tried calling match makers, posing as single women looking for a husband with Harvey's characteristics. The agencies refused to give information over the phone, so Rachel got herself all dolled up and went to one of these places in person. "I found out that if I'm willing to pay the price I can bring home a prince," she told Helen. "But without cash up front, no set-up. I couldn't even peek at the book of eligibles to see if Harvey was there."

They decided Harvey was unlikely to pay the high fees charged by these services and looked closer to home. "He'd be looking for a middle-aged woman, someone who could keep house and care for his children," said Rachel. "One thing you have to say for Harvey, he's not a playboy."

"And of course, for the man who thinks he's a great Hebrew scholar, it would be an advantage if the woman was educated in addition to being religious," added Helen.

And where was the first place someone would look for a religious woman? Why, the *shul*, of course. They contacted synagogue members who prayed in the old sanctuary, concocting excuses to call people they barely knew and always ending with a thinly veiled request for social information. After a week of these calls, Rachel and Helen had several unwanted lunch invitations, committed to donate to charities they'd never heard of, collected a bunch of recipes (one of which turned out to be very tasty and became a standard in both households) and learned lots of only mildly interesting gossip. But they hadn't learned anything about Harvey's love life.

And then, one day, Rachel was entering the dentist's office when the Hebrew school director walked out. She barely knew him and was surprised when the man gave her a big hello and seemed determined to talk. "Hope you're here just for a check-up. I had a really painful session," he said. "Well, I won't keep you with the gory details. But I do have to say I'm glad things seem to be going well with Harvey and Batya."

Rachel was confused, fortunately the director kept talking. She learned that his father had been a rabbi in a small village in Romania and, when he arrived in this country, HIAS helped get him an apartment that was next door to a rabbi who had escaped with his daughter from a small village in Hungary. The two men became friends.

Eventually both rabbis found jobs and moved into their own homes. The director's father, a younger, better educated man, quickly learned to speak English and adopted American ways. He became the assistant rabbi in a prosperous Reform synagogue in Riverdale.

The other rabbi, older and extremely devout, felt he owed God eternal gratitude for allowing him to survive the War. He started his own strictly Orthodox congregation on the Lower East Side. But as the Jewish population prospered in New York City, many people moved away from that area. The synagogue struggled to pay its bills. In the last few years, it was composed primarily of elderly people.

About six months ago, the director's father heard that his old friend had died. "My father wanted to pay his respects to the daughter, a divorced woman who had been keeping house for her father. He asked me to come with him. As soon as I met the daughter, Batya, I thought of Harvey. I waited until the mourning period was over before saying anything to Harvey, and it took him a while to get around to calling her, but after a slow start this relationship seems to be warming up. Don't you think so?"

"I just stared at him, unable to say a word, like a real dummy," Rachel told Helen over the phone. "I wanted to ask a million questions, but I realized he thought that, as Harvey's sister-in-law and neighbor, I must know all about what's going on. I said we all wished the best for Harvey."

"So, okay, we've got a start," Helen said. "An Orthodox rabbi's daughter. And Hungarian. And divorced. Now we find out the rest."

Helen and Rachel scoured back issues of Yiddish newspapers and found the obituary of a Hungarian rabbi from the Lower East Side who had a daughter named Batya. Once they had a name, it wasn't hard to locate people who'd had contact with this family. They found friends of friends who still lived on the lower east side or had attended the Orthodox *shul*. Chassidic, Orthodox, Conservative or Reformed, Jewish women might differ about religious rites, but they found common ground in gossip.

Helen and Rachel learned that Batya was around their age and neither pretty nor homely enough for people to comment on her looks. The one thing mentioned by everyone was that she was bright. She was an only child; her mother died in Hungary when Batya was young, and her father apparently studied with her the way he would have with a son, so she had a much greater knowledge of Talmud and other sacred Jewish texts than the typical woman would have.

Soon after arriving in New York, Batya married another Hungarian refugee. Two years later Batya and her husband discovered she couldn't have children. A few months later she was divorced, keeping house for her father and attending classes at night.

After an extensive search, Batya found a way to piece together an educational program that satisfied most of her needs. The Jewish Theological Seminary offered a program for women who wanted to teach in a Yeshiva, the City Colleges had philosophy courses, libraries were open to all and featured bulletin boards that told of additional places to study and people, both men and women, who wanted to form study groups.

While she lived with her father, Batya organized functions for the Sisterhood, but many of the members considered her too bossy. Young women who needed advice about marriage and children and would ordinarily go to a *rebbitzen* didn't want to talk to a barren, divorced woman.

As her father's synagogue started to lose membership, there was little money to pay a salary adequate to support an elderly Rabbi and his daughter. Batya complained about having to economize while her father grew older and weaker, ignoring their financial situation while he devoted himself to his religious duties.

When the Rosen women hinted to their informants that Batya might be involved with someone who wasn't strictly Orthodox, someone who frequently followed Conservative doctrine, many weren't surprised.

By the time her father died, Batya had borrowed against the meager insurance policy the synagogue had provided for him, and there was very little money left in their savings. "She could have always taught in a girls Yeshiva. That would get her a living wage, but not a luxurious life," said a friend of a friend who was willing to talk to them. "But since she couldn't be a subsidized scholar, I don't think Batya would have minded being a more modern woman. I'd notice her glancing at American magazines like Vogue and Glamour in the public library. She had an eye for materialism. I never thought she was content being the righteous daughter of a sickly Orthodox rabbi."

Rachel and Helen tallied up all they had learned about Harvey's new girlfriend. She was smart enough to keep Harvey happy, experienced in running the type of kosher household he wanted and had no family obligations of her own. But she'd never dealt with children.

"If she wants to spend her time *davening* with Harvey and keeps him happy without interfering with his work or the children we raised, that wouldn't be so bad," said Rachel. "Of course it'll have to be made clear to her that she'll be expected to water down a lot of her Orthodoxy."

"And none of us are getting younger. If she's a gold digger, thinking she'll be entitled to a share of the Rosen money, which should go to Rebecca and Marvin, this Batya is going to be very disappointed," said Helen.

And what of the husband who left her? Was he likely to show up and become a distraction? Did he leave because of something about Batya that the Rosens should know? It took a while to track him down, but one morning Helen's phone made that special ring.

"I found him!" announced Rachel.

"Sylvia's friend Laura's cousin Miriam married a man from Hungary who lived next door to her family in HIAS housing. This man insists she go all the way to a special Hungarian deli, way out of her way, just to buy food like his mother used to make.

Rachel took a breath. "And, when she gets to the shop, which is always crowded, she reads a local Hungarian newspaper they have there. Imagine, she's even learned Hungarian for this man. Anyway, just last week she opened the paper and there he was!"

"Her husband went back to Hungary?" asked Helen.

"No," said Rachel. "Pay attention. Turn's out that Batya's ex-husband came from the same village in Hungary as this Miriam's husband. So I called her and she was very friendly, told me she has been reading about this man for years.

"Like Batya, he's considered a very bright man. In fact, he learned English so well he got a high paying job with an American insurance agency.

"After he dumped Batya this guy didn't want to stick around their community so he asked for a transfer. His bosses decided to see if he could develop a Jewish customer base in the Midwest. I'll bet he fell over when he found out he was going to Indiana."

"There are Jews there?"

"There are now. He found a Jewish girl, married her, and within five years he and this woman had two sets of twins. All boys. He's always sending family pictures to this newsletter. Just like a man. He has to make sure people know it wasn't his fault he didn't have any children with Batya. Anyway, we don't have to worry about him. He's got his hands full."

Helen and Rachel decided to retire their positions as private investigators. There was nothing to do now but wait and see.

Sarah wrote to Rebecca, "Your dad is dating someone. It sounds serious."

"I don't care what he does," Rebecca wrote back. "Any friend of his is my enemy."

17.

ONCE UPON A TIME

The girls were sitting in a tight circle in a wooded section of the reform school grounds, keeping an eye out for guards who might approach from any direction.

Rebecca inhaled the joint deeply. The contents hadn't been properly cleaned, and a seed flared and crackled as she drew the smoke into her lungs.

"So how come no one ever complains about Cinderella's father allowing his daughter to be abused by the evil stepmother?" She managed to get the whole sentence out without exhaling. Then she coughed, let out a puff of smoke and passed the joint to Maria.

"He died before the stepmom showed her true colors," said Maria. Then she exhaled a long stream of smoke and handed the stubby roach to Alice, who pinched it between long fingernails and took a drag.

Alice offered it back to Rebecca, but she shook her head. "I'll roll another one." Rebecca picked up a stick, dug a small hole, pushed the roach into the ground and buried it.

"Well, maybe Cinderella's father didn't know." Rebecca pulled an envelope out of the pocket of her tight jeans and got out the fixings. "But there's no doubt Hansel and Gretel's dad was around and a willing accompanist when their stepmom decided to leave the kids in the woods."

"You're really spoiled," said Alice, taking the new joint and smiling. "In my neighborhood we would have gotten a few more hits out of that last one. But I have to admire your skill, you really know how to roll 'em nice and tight, Princess."

Rebecca didn't smile back. "I told you not to call me Princess."

Alice shrugged. "Just looking at your smooth blonde hair and thinking you should let it grow. In case you ever get locked in a tower, prince charming can climb your golden tresses and rescue you."

"Sounds painful," Rebecca said. "I'll keep my hair short and get away on my own. Goldilocks managed to eat the porridge, grab a nap and still escape the bears."

Alice giggled and threw back her head; the tightly woven braids that striped her skull in a zig-zag pattern didn't move. The week before, Rebecca had stared, fascinated, as another girl spent an entire afternoon creating this hairdo for Alice.

"What's the matter?" Alice had taunted Rebecca when she realized she was being watched. "You didn't know some people don't have good hair?"

Rebecca shrugged. "Your hair is okay. Some of the girls in my neighborhood with really curly hair used to talk about going to beauty parlors in Harlem to get straightening treatments."

Alice laughed. "Yeah, I've seen white girls come to our area to get their hair done. They never came alone, always looked nervous, afraid to walk on our streets. They don't get the best service and get charged double the usual rate."

Alice was wearing black, wide-legged slacks with bright yellow flowers embroidered up the seams, one of the items taken from the suitcase Helen had packed for Rebecca. Matching buttercup charms jingled from the bracelet around Alice's wrist as she passed the joint.

"I wish I could tell my aunt how clever my friends are at finding ways to accessorize the clothes she bought," said Rebecca.

"Be sure to tell her I only steal the best," said Alice. "I made sure the charms were 24 karats before I slipped them into my bra. Fortunately, the shop owner was freaking out because a group of non-white delinquents just walked into his store while the counselor was having a cigarette break outside."

The girls had signed out of their cottage and told their housemother they were going to take a walk and do homework outside. They'd kept their word. Rebecca had done Maria's algebra and edited Alice's history essay while Maria did both of their Spanish assignments and Alice stood watch.

"I can't get over what lousy teachers they have here," Rebecca commented. "This stuff isn't as hard as your teacher makes it look," she said to Maria. "I can show you a trick for this type of equation that'll let you ace the next exam."

"Gracias," said Maria. "And we can speak Spanish while we discuss how dumb this math class is. No one ever teaches that the people from different Spanish speaking countries pronounce words differently. I can show you how to fit in if you travel."

"And if you had anyone for English except that old witch, Mrs. Hardwick, this would get an A- paper, or at least B+," Rebecca told Alice. "Your ideas are really interesting, it's only the spelling and punctuation that needs work. She always takes off way too much on your papers. Even with my help you probably won't get more than a B- on this. She really has it in for you."

"Maybe I should have gone to Bronx Science," smirked Alice. "Gotten the benefits of a superior education. Like you." Alice shook her head. "Oh wait. Turns out even Science girls can wind up in the red cottage. It's a lot easier to have you write my papers."

No one said anything for a few minutes. The girls stared at the trees, watching the leaves rustle. Maria stretched her legs, gracefully pointing her toes in her well-worn sneakers.

"In the Disney version of Snow White the queen is a stepmom and the father is dead, but in the original version she was a vain mother who was jealous of her own good-looking daughter," said Maria. "My abuela used to read to me from an old copy of Grimm's Fairy Tales in Spanish. Those stories weren't sugar coated."

Rebecca looked at Maria and could easily imagine her as a little girl with large dark eyes, and long brown braids, curled up next to her grandmother for story time. She was shorter and thinner than Rebecca and Alice, with the delicate wrists and ankles of a child. But everyone at the school knew Maria could stand up for herself. She had an extensive collection of demerits accumulated at the expense of girls who'd tried to bully her.

"That can't be right," said Rebecca. "A mother wouldn't send the hunter after her own daughter."

"You never heard of a mom's boyfriend who developed a roving eye?" said Maria. "It's not always easy for older women to hold on to their men when their daughters get ripe."

"I guess you're right," mumbled Rebecca. She knew the authorities were looking for a foster home for Maria who was due to leave the school soon. Her mother had said there wasn't room for her daughter in the apartment she now shared with her new boyfriend.

Maria watched a fat caterpillar crawl up a thick blade of grass near her wrist, picked up a flat rock and swiftly squashed the bug into the ground. "That's one less butterfly to get caught in someone's net. Or maybe just a troublesome moth.

"Let's get back," she said. "It's almost dinnertime and I don't need any more demerits for being late."

The girls stood up, brushed themselves off and walked toward their cottage.

18.

RUN AWAY

Rebecca wasn't in her room the next morning. The housemother had seen her at bed check the night before. Maria said she'd slept soundly all night and had no idea what had happened to her roommate.

She didn't mention that a noise in the night had woken her up and she saw that Rebecca's bed was empty. That had happened before. Maria went back to sleep, sure that Rebecca would return in time for breakfast.

As per procedure, local police were contacted when the school's guards failed to find Rebecca within two hours. Harvey was informed and told to notify the school if Rebecca showed up.

"Again," muttered Harvey as he hung up the phone. "Again the police are calling me about my daughter." He thought about calling Helen but decided not to. She'd just make a fuss. If Rebecca was hiding at her aunt's house, it wouldn't be for long. Helen wouldn't have the nerve to disobey the police.

Harvey had an appointment with a customer but paused to ask God to help, to let this situation finally end, to give him some peace. He looked at the picture of Elaine he carried in his wallet. "Watch over our child," Harvey said, grabbed his car keys and went off.

The town police found Rebecca asleep in the Greyhound Bus terminal early the next morning, called the school and brought her back to Hillsdale. She was dirty and disheveled but unhurt. The school's night watchman, alerted to the situation, signed for Rebecca. Like an unwanted package marked, return to sender, she thought.

She was told to wait in the empty administration building hallway next to a silent guard. She wanted to say there was no reason to keep the guard there, that she wasn't going anywhere. But she kept quiet. When the school day started she was taken to the director's office.

"We'd expected a girl raised with the advantages you had to behave better," said the director, who was sitting behind a meticulously arranged desk, flipping pages in Rebecca's folder. "I hope you realize this is a very serious matter."

He didn't ask her to sit, so she stood in front of him, counting the hairs carefully combed over his skull. There was a plain white mug full of BIC pens on his desk. Each pen had a pointy blue plastic cap pointing upwards.

The man informed Rebecca that for the next two weeks she would spend all her free time cleaning toilets and halls and washing dishes. She was banned from the canteen and all school entertainments.

Rebecca nodded. "You mean there's no dungeon? No torture rack in a moldy cellar? At the very least I expected a few days of bread and water."

He grabbed one of the pens, dug the pointy cap into his ear, twisted it, then returned the pen to the mug. "Just keep shooting off your smart mouth and you'll be a lot worse off. Pull something like this again and you'll get transferred someplace much less pleasant."

Disgusting pig, thought Rebecca, but she didn't say anything, just nodded and kept her eyes down until the man waved his hand, dismissing her.

Rebecca returned to her room, and Maria and Alice hugged her.

"Have fun?"

"Not really," said Rebecca.

"Want to talk?"

"Maybe later," she said. "I need some sleep now."

"We're here when you're ready."

"I know. Thanks."

She saw her counselor, Bill, a few hours later. As usual, the door to his office was open. Rebecca stared at him for a minute. He was in his late 30s, good looking, with thick curly dark blonde hair. He needed a shave. Maybe he spent the night with his girlfriend, Rebecca thought, and had to rush to get here on time.

Bill's desk was a mess. He had just received a thick pile of papers which included instructions to meet with town officials and try to pacify them. A local merchant had reported that one of their girls had tried to steal from him. This wasn't the first time something like this had happened. The town wanted the school to pay for extra police protection.

Bill noticed Rebecca standing by the door and waved her in. "Good to see you here," he said, emphasizing the word, 'here,' and smiling slightly. Rebecca noticed there was a gap between his two front teeth, and he had a slight overbite. His parents couldn't afford braces, she thought.

"So, sitting in the Greyhound terminal by yourself, that's pretty exciting," Bill said as soon as she was seated. "According to the police you didn't have a bus ticket, weren't with a guy, weren't high and weren't drunk."

"Nope, just fucked up."

"Want to tell me about it?"

"Not much to tell."

"Okay. Want to just stare at each other for an hour? See who blinks first?"

Rebecca raised one eyebrow.

"That's a good trick," said Bill. "Want to see me wiggle my ears?"

Rebecca rolled her eyes. "What do you want to know?"

"How about starting with how you got to town. Your house-mother is sure you didn't use the front door, and I'm pretty sure you didn't fly out the window like Super girl."

Rebecca smiled. "Not Super girl. Maybe Spider girl. It wasn't my first midnight climb on that wall, but I don't usually go down, I climb up. The pipe outside my window is attached with bolts thick enough to get a toe hold. I've spent quite a few nights on the roof. I like to watch the stars. There are lots of them here, a lot more than in the Bronx."

"You know that in addition to being against the rules you could get seriously hurt making believe you're some sort of insect who can scamper up concrete walls."

"Yeah, yeah, yeah. I know."

"But I understand the appeal of star gazing. I remember lying in the field at night when I was a kid, wondering about the world, watching for shooting stars."

"So you're a country boy? I wondered why someone as smart as you didn't go crazy in this hick town."

Bill didn't react to the remark and Rebecca walked over to the window. "I'd really love a cigarette."

"Can't allow that. But I've got something a lot better."

Bill opened his desk drawer, pulled out a mound of napkins

and unwrapped a thick slice of cake. "This arrived for you yesterday. We confiscate packages sent to students who go AWOL. This was a big hit in the staff lounge. I was lucky to get a piece."

"It's called a babka," said Rebecca, pulling the pastry apart and handing half to Bill. "Aunt Helen's specialty." Rebecca took a large bite and smiled. "It tastes like her kitchen."

"Mrs. Hardwick was really crazy about it. Bet she'd love the recipe. Might be willing to trade a few extra points on the next exam for it."

"That witch?" Rebecca wiped some sugary flakes off her sleeve. "She almost flunked Alice for no reason. I can ace her course on my own. Let her buy cake from the supermarket."

They were both quiet for a minute, eating the babka. "So, I know your father's family went through the Holocaust, that he's religious. How about you? Were you on the roof talking to God?"

"I'm not sure about God myself," Rebecca said. "That's my father's department. He has a pretty tight relationship with the Almighty, but I think he'd say that even God can make mistakes."

"What kind of mistakes?"

Rebecca finished her cake, wadded her napkin into a ball and tossed it at the wastepaper basket. She missed and left the napkin lying on the floor.

"Of course there's the big question as to why the chosen people were led into concentration camps. But, closer to home, my dear father thinks if someone in our house had to die it shouldn't have been my mother. It should have been me."

"Why do you say that?"

"My mom wasn't as religious as he is, but she always respected his beliefs. She made sure her family treated him properly. She was a good wife. I was never a good daughter. Never showed him the proper respect. Well, now he's getting a new wife, a religious one, the type of wife he thinks he deserved to have in the beginning."

"How do you feel about his marrying again?"

"You mean, do I think I'm Cinderella? Afraid of an evil stepmother? I'm not. I'm not afraid of anyone, especially some old religious fanatic. My cousin Sarah told me this new wife can't have children. Too bad. No chance he'll get a new daughter."

Rebecca walked across the room, picked up her ball of napkins and held them. "He's not the only one who thinks God can make a mistake. I remember my mom's funeral. I remember sitting there watching him cry and carry on and pray louder than anyone else. I remember thinking we all would have been better off if he was the one who had died and we were consoling my mom."

Rebecca slammed the napkins into the basket, went back to her chair, sat down heavily and crossed her legs.

"When I called to let him know that you'd been found, that you were okay, he sounded really relieved. Said he'd been praying for you."

"That's the kind of thing fathers have to say, isn't it? Did you expect him to say he was disappointed I hadn't been eaten by wolves?"

"You think he felt that way?"

"I never said the man was a monster."

"Glad to hear you say that."

Bill looked at his watch. "Okay, enough stalling for today. Why don't you tell me why you decided to go to town?"

"No special reason. Something woke me up around daybreak, maybe a bird. I was afraid it would fly into our room. Maria likes to sleep with the window open. I looked out and everything seemed so calm and peaceful that I decided to take a walk. I started exploring the grounds, found a break in the fence. It didn't take long to get to the main road and hitch a ride into town."

Rebecca stopped talking and looked at Bill.

"Don't worry, you're not revealing a secret passage. We found the hole and fixed the fence. For now."

Rebecca nodded. "I walked around and explored the town for a while. Not much to explore. That is one really small town. One really boring small town. I found a fancy shopping area, well, fancy for this area. There was a soft, fuzzy sweater in a shop window. It was a pale, burnt orange shade, cashmere. I knew it would look great on Maria."

"Not on you?"

"I've got plenty of clothes. Maria could've used this. I don't think she has many cashmere sweaters.

"The name on the window was the Chick Shoppe," she said, spelling out the words. "I'm not kidding. Can you imagine the dumb jerk who came up with that name? I'll bet he thought he was really clever. There was an overhead bell that jingled when I went through the front door and a tall man behind the cash register wearing bib overalls. Real folksy.

"The shopkeeper didn't look up when I walked in. I browsed through the racks, picked up several items including the sweater in the window and went into the fitting room, glad to see there were individual booths, not just one big dressing room. I closed the door firmly and pulled on the sweater. It fit really tight across my chest. Perfect for Maria. I put my own stuff on over the sweater and walked out of the dressing room."

"Done much shoplifting before?" asked Bill. "Sounds like you knew what you were doing."

"I picked up a few things in the days when I wanted to attract boys in City Island. But you can tell Clyde not to dump Bonnie.

I'm not really made for the outlaw life. Soon as I got near the front door the owner called out, 'Hey you! You with the sweater! Where do you think you're going?'

"I'll bet there were two-way mirrors in the dressingroom and that pervert was getting off watching girls change. He grabbed my arm, twisted it behind my back. 'You kids think you can get away with everything don't you? Well I'm sick of it. I'm calling the police right now.'

"I immediately started to cry. I'm pretty good at turning on the waterworks when I want to, but these tears didn't do any good. The guy just twisted my arm harder and pulled me into a small office behind the cash register."

Rebecca remembered the moldy smelling office. It was cramped and dirty. There were cardboard cartons stacked along the walls, a cardboard coffee cup with some decomposing cigarettes inside rested precariously on one box.

"He picked up a baseball bat that was leaning against the wall and poked me in the chest. I backed up against the wall. He asked if I'd ever had a broken rib. 'Not too serious, but it can really hurt,' he said. Then he said it might be a better idea to break my legs so I couldn't run around causing trouble for everyone. By then I was crying for real."

Rebecca walked over to Bill's desk, grabbed a handful of tissues and roughly wiped her face. "Could have used these at that horrible shop," she said. "My nose always runs when I cry." She remembered feeling like she was going to throw up. Rebecca took a deep breath. She was not going to vomit in front of Bill. She blew her nose.

"Take your time," said Bill.

"He told me to take off my own stuff so he could see what I was hiding. I got undressed, I told him I was really sorry, said my father was a drunk who would beat me if I got arrested. I offered to pay for the sweater, even took money out of my wallet and put it on the desk. But he wasn't listening."

When she'd revealed the stolen sweater, the owner told her, "just keep going." Rebecca pulled the tight sweater over her head so she was left standing in her bra. The shop owner looked at Rebecca's bra, then he looked at the money she'd left on the counter.

"He twisted his ugly face into a nasty smile and said, 'Well, you've got a pretty full wallet. And that bra of yours is pretty full too. Any chance you're hiding something in there?' Then the bastard grabbed my breast and squeezed. It really hurt.That's happened to me before, but it's still frightening. I was very scared. I offered him more money, but he didn't seem interested."

Rebecca was quiet for a minute. She remembered the shopkeeper's hand kneading her breast. He'd pinched her nipple, and she gasped, which made him smile and grab the other breast.

Bill waited for her to continue, moving the box of tissues towards Rebecca. "Then what happened?" he said softly, hoping she knew he was on her side.

Rebecca wondered if he would hug her. She paused for a minute, decided that probably wasn't allowed in a place like this. She looked at the tissues. Thanks, but I'm okay. The story gets better.

"All of a sudden the silly bell over the front door started to ring, and we both jumped. I heard a woman call, 'Jim? Jim where are you? I need to get a present for one of my kids.'"

"That prick manager turned to me and said, 'Damn it! Get the fuck out of here.'

"I grabbed my stuff, left his sweater and the money and ran out as fast as I could. I think I knocked over the customer as I charged through the front door. He wound up getting double the price of that damned sweater, and he could still sell it to someone else."

Bill's face relaxed. He wasn't going to have to listen to a rape story. He'd heard such stories before; he was trained to deal with them, but it was never easy.

"The shopkeeper didn't buy your story about a drunken father waiting at home," he said. "He figured out you came from this school and filed a complaint."

"I kept running till I was out of breath," Rebecca said. "I noticed there was a movie theater at the end of the block. Guess what it was playing? *Nazi Zombies from Hell.* Doesn't that sound perfect for a nice Jewish girl?"

Bill smiled. This was good, he thought. The tension was broken.

She didn't tell him there weren't many people in the chilly theater, that for two hours she sat in the dark, screaming as loud as she could, pulling her hair, digging her nails into her arm. She was hoarse by the time the film ended, empty, drained.

• • •

A few days later, Rebecca was sitting on the freshly mopped bathroom floor, right next to the three urinals she'd just scrubbed until they were bright and shiny. She had two more to clean this afternoon, but she was sure she'd finish in time for her appointment with Bill whose office was just down the hall.

She'd never been in a men's bathroom before, never seen a urinal up close. At first it'd felt creepy to go in, but soon it was just another room with lots of porcelain to clean. It had just occurred to Rebecca that Bill must regularly use one of the urinals she'd been scrubbing this week. Did he have a favorite? She was sure he hadn't made the mess in the one at the head of the row. Pee stains all over the floor. Really gross. That was probably done by that fat jerk who'd assigned her this job as part of her detention.

She decided to take a cigarette break. One of the few perks of cleaning bathrooms was the "Wet Floor, Do Not Enter" sign she could post in the doorway to make sure she wasn't disturbed. Alone time was rare in this place.

Rebecca needed to get her story straight. When she'd told Bill what happened when she ran away, she'd only told the first part of the story. Now she had to decide whether to tell him more. And, if so, how much.

After her last session with Bill, she'd felt better. Maybe just leave it there. No need to let him know there was more to the story. But maybe telling the whole story was the right thing, maybe it would help. He did sincerely seem to want to help her.

When she'd told the first part of her story, she'd left behind a wad of snot filled tissues. The story didn't get any more attractive. But now that she was rested, she would be in control of the session. Before she went into his office, she'd have time to put on some make-up, run a comb through her hair and get her act together.

Rebecca lit a cigarette, blew some smoke rings and watched them rise. Should she tell Bill the rest of the story? If she did, what should she say? How would Bill react?

She crushed the cigarette on the rim of the unwashed urinal, dropped it into the hole at the bottom. She'd been meaning to try to pee standing up. She'd try that before she started to scrub. In case she missed.

Rebecca got to Bill's office on time and pushed open the door. "How're you doing?" she said, plopping down in the chair across from his desk.

"You seem in good spirits. I'm glad to see that."

"Nothing like a morning spent cleaning the admin building to make you eager to see the people you're slaving for."

Bill opened his desk drawer and held out a box of hard candies. "On behalf of the staff of the third floor, I thank you. Sorry, this is the best I can offer, didn't confiscate any homemade goodies this week."

Rebecca looked at the candy and shrugged. "Bet my grandmother's rock candy is better than this stuff. Next time she sends a package I'll bring you some." Rebecca put Bill's candy in her pocket.

"Hey," she said. "Want to hear another story?"

"Okay."

Bill had known that the shoplifting episode wasn't all that had happened to Rebecca when she ran away. He'd been planning to go over the events of that day in more detail. He was glad she'd volunteered to tell the rest of the story without prompting.

Rebecca studied her broken fingernails.

"So, stories. You want more stories. I got a million o' dem. How about starting with a standard? A girl walks into a bar. But she doesn't have a priest or a rabbi with her. And there's no talking horse. All she has is the memory of the asshole who almost raped her over a stupid sweater. Just an underage girl who's had a terrible day, who really needs a drink. A girl who's been in enough bars to know she won't have any trouble getting served in this place.

As soon as Rebecca approached him, the bartender looked at her figure, her dyed hair and asked, "What'll you have, honey?"

Just what she expected from a bartender who looked like he'd been built with the place, someone whose skin was as grey and pitted as the linoleum, whose sparse brown hair was the same faded color as the bar and probably hadn't been cleaned anymore recently.

She asked for a beer, refused his offer of a glass. She liked the image of a tough girl who thought glasses were unnecessary. Rebecca didn't really like beer, had never gotten used to the bitter taste, but she'd learned to swig it down. She remembered the sweet wine her uncles had allowed her to sip at holiday meals when she was little. But this was hardly the type of establishment where you inquired about the house red.

She wasn't sure how much money she had in her wallet; most of it had been left with that horrible store manager. Forget about him, Rebecca told herself. No need to worry. Rebecca rarely paid for her own drinks.

"You one of the girls from that school off Route 17?" asked the bartender.

Rebecca lowered her head, looked up at him through her eyelashes. "Are you looking for a schoolgirl?" she purred. "Is the mean teacher gonna spank me cause I forgot my homework?"

The bartender startled, then grinned and went to help someone else. Rebecca had spoken loudly and, as she intended, the group of guys sitting at a nearby table overheard her remark and laughed.

She glanced at them as she drank her beer. They weren't much, but probably the best she'd find in this town. "Got room at that table for one more?" she asked.

They called out a greeting. Someone pulled out a chair. Someone got her a drink. They introduced themselves. She didn't try to keep track of the names.

"I'm Becky," she said.

The guys asked where she was from, and Rebecca started telling a story about her brother, Sid Arthur, who had left their fabulously rich and famous family looking for the meaning of life. Now she was looking for him. "Anyone seen a chubby, bald guy trying to hitch?" she asked.

They hadn't, but promised to look out for him.

They kept trying to tell funnier and funnier stories. There was a lot of whispering among the guys at the table. They're trying to think up something to impress me, Rebecca thought. Good luck with that.

She laughed at everyone but laughed loudest when the guy sitting across from her told his stories. She smiled at all of them but gave her brightest smile to him. They all looked basically the same, but somehow he was a little more put together: his hair combed, his face shaved, his shirt most recently washed.

Without saying anything, the fellow she'd been focusing on got up from the table. Walked away. Uh oh, she thought. Did I lay it on too thick?

But of course she had played her cards just right. No dumb redneck could outsmart her, after all, she was a Bronx Science girl. Rebecca giggled at that thought and almost choked on her drink.

Of course the guy wasn't leaving, he was going to the juke box. He dropped in some change and came back to the table with his hand out. "How about a dance, princess?" he said.

Rebecca finished her drink sometime during the night she'd switched from beer to whiskey and got up. They kept dancing together, fast dances and slow dances. She'd grind against her partner, whirl away and then get pulled back. She got dizzy and started to stumble.

"How about taking a break?" he said. "My van is right outside."

Rebecca nodded and walked with him to the parking lot, his arm around her waist, holding her up. She didn't notice that behind her back he gave the rest of the gang a thumbs-up sign.

"He was a regular prince charming," she said. "His coach awaited me. Of course it turned out to be a dirty van. But, to be fair, the mattress inside was covered by a sheet that was pretty clean."

She took a deep breath. Paused. Took a candy out of her pocket, held it in her fist. Rebecca walked across the room and looked out the window.

"He started to undress me and then stopped. At first I didn't understand why the delay, but I followed his eyes. We were both staring at the bruises on my body."

Rebecca looked at Bill. "Why do they call them 'black and blue' marks? They're not just black or blue. The bruises on my arms were red and purple. The bastard in that crumby store had left his dirty fingerprints all over me. The marks on my body had turned dark green and brown and yellow. My breasts looked like they'd been smeared with a diaper full of baby shit."

The guy had just stared at Rebecca. She looked at herself and got dizzy. Then her stomach heaved, and she vomited. All over the place. On herself. On the formerly clean sheet.

The guy from the bar didn't say anything, just stared and handed Rebecca her shirt. "Looks like you've had enough," he said. "You should leave now before the rest of the guys come. They're waiting for their turns. Some of them won't mind that you're sick."

"Waiting for their turns! Their turns! That's what he said. Like I was a fuckin' ride in an amusement park, like the Atlantic City Ferris wheel and everyone had bought tickets," Rebecca yelled at Bill. "I thought I was so smart, that I could control a bunch of small town jerks, spot a guy who'd take care of me. For a few days anyway. What a joke! That bastard was probably the ringleader. Now he thinks he's some sort of saint because he felt so sorry for the poor bruised girl that he decided not to pass her around."

She turned away from Bill, lowered her head and spoke softly. "Or maybe he thought I was so ugly, so disfigured, he didn't want to bother with me."

Rebecca waited for Bill to come to her defense. She imagined Bill leaping over his desk, taking her in his arms and promising to protect her. They'd go back to town, beat that guy and his friends to a pulp and drive off to someplace exciting.

But Bill just looked at her. "Take a deep breath. And then listen to me," he said. "You're smart and attractive and have the potential to become a really terrific woman. We have some hard work to do, but we're going to do it.

"Lesson one. Running away is dumb and dangerous, so is shoplifting, drinking and picking up guys in places you shouldn't be in." Bill was staring directly at Rebecca. His voice was stern. "I really want to help you, but you have to cooperate."

Rebecca unwrapped the candy and chewed it, making sharp, cracking noises. She stared at Bill. He stared back.

"Okay, okay," she said. "I'll try."

"Glad to hear that."

"Just do me one favor," she said. "Seeing how this place is supposed to teach me how to get my shit together, could you drop a hint to the staff to stop behaving like animals? Those faculty bathrooms are really disgusting."

"I'll get the word out." Bill smiled and looked at his watch. "Now get back to work."

19.

NEGOTIATIONS

Two months after their first date, Harvey told the Rosens he was seeing a woman, an Orthodox woman, but flexible about her beliefs. In fact, she was considered very modern in her community.

"Mazel Tov," said the Rosens, wondering what it meant to be a flexible , modern Orthodox Jew.

Harvey said he wanted the Rosens to meet Batya, to see what a fine woman might soon be part of their family. He suggested they all have dinner together.

Actually, the dinner was Batya's idea. Helen and Rachel weren't the only ones who could do research. Batya had discovered what an important role Harvey's in-laws played in his life. She wanted to know if they'd be an obstacle on her path to the *chupah*.

Harvey's remarrying didn't surprise anyone. A nice-looking widower, from a good family, with a healthy financial situation, it was surprising he had stayed single for so long. People had tried to fix him up with suitable widows since the official mourning period ended. The problem was, she had to be suitable for Harvey, and for the rest of the Rosens.

Harvey wanted a religious woman, one who valued his scholarly mind. Helen and Rachel wanted a woman who would easily fit into their extended family.

An Orthodox woman, even one who was "flexible," whatever that meant, didn't sound appropriate. She couldn't eat where they ate, she wouldn't dress like they dressed. And who could guess what ideas a woman who'd never had children would have about caring for children, caring for the children that Helen and Rachel had been taking care of all these years. Morris and Saul just wanted someone who wouldn't cause trouble in the family, who would let Harvey get on with his work.

They needed to personally check out this interloper. Right away. They owed it to Elaine. They arranged to meet for dinner at a kosher restaurant. Not just any kosher restaurant, as Harvey reminded them, but a *glatt* kosher restaurant, one that was super kosher so Batya would be comfortable.

An appropriate restaurant was found. Helen and Rachel made beauty parlor appointments and warned their stylists that they needed hairdos that would withstand the predicted rainstorm. The stylists used extra strong spray, promising that their creations would stand up to a tornado.

Batya had no coiffeur concerns. When her divorce was granted, she had briefly stopped wearing her *sheitel,* the wig all Orthodox women put on when they marry. Batya believed that this action would signal to the outside world that she was open to moving to a less strict community. But she had little contact with such people. As the years went by and no worthy outsider appeared to ask for her hand, Batya realized that, in her community, a middle-aged woman without a *sheitel* looked like a spinster, someone who'd never married because she was somehow defective. She went back to covering her head with a stylish wig.

Batya hadn't decided if she would continue wearing a wig once she married Harvey; she'd see how things went. But she was sure of one thing. Batya had always been proud of her thin, shapely legs, and marrying someone who wasn't Orthodox would finally give her a chance to show them off. She'd shortened her dress a little, from mid-calf to just below her knees, not enough to scandalize the neighbors, but, she hoped, enough to stop her future in-laws from thinking of her as dowdy or unsophisticated. She'd gone to a midtown shop and blown her budget to purchase open-toed shoes with high heels. She loved taking them out of the box and looking at herself in the mirror, practicing walking across the room. But they weren't shoes to wear in a rainstorm. She found an old pair of her father's boots and a plastic bag to carry the shoes in.

The Rosens drove to the restaurant in one car. Helen and Rachel got out in front of the restaurant and stood under the canopy while the men drove off looking for a parking place. When Harvey and Batya drove by they saw the women waiting. Harvey asked if he should let Batya out, but she didn't want to be alone the first time she spoke to these women.

"I'll stay with you," Batya said. "We have an umbrella."

Harvey quickly found a parking spot and he and Batya started walking to the restaurant.

"She's a little pigeon," said Rachel as soon as she spotted them. "A smooth head, a plump round body and a big behind sticking out like tail."

"And all of it perched on long, skinny legs," said Helen.

The two women smiled, waved their hands and loudly called, "Hello, hello, here we are!"

Harvey and Batya stopped walking.

"Look," said Helen. "There's a big puddle in front of them. Maybe she's waiting for him to take off his jacket so she can walk across it. A regular Sir Galahad she thinks she's got."

Batya was taking tiny steps through the puddle so she didn't slip in her floppy boots when Morris and Saul came splashing up behind them.

"Hey Harvey, how you doing? What a night, huh?" said Morris as he slapped Harvey on the back. Surprised, Harvey stumbled. Batya lost her footing and would have wound up sitting in the puddle if Saul hadn't grabbed her. She sprang away, startled. A strange man was touching her.

Saul quickly put up his hands. "Don't be nervous, I'm your future brother-in-law," he said. "What a night to meet. Let's get to the restaurant right away."

Everyone introduced themselves, and they went inside. While the Rosen men got the table, Harvey asked the head waiter where he could wash his hands and the ladies hurried to the restroom. Helen and Rachel's hairdos had been blown askew, but they easily molded them back into shape. Batya's wig hadn't moved. She quickly replaced the boots with her new shoes and washed her hands.

When the women were ready to leave the bathroom Helen pulled Rachel back and they watched Batya wobble on her high heels. "A pigeon has better balance," she whispered.

As soon as everyone was seated, a waiter brought over a basket of the onion rolls for which the restaurant was famous. Saul leaned across the table, grabbed the largest one and took a big bite. At the same time, Harvey looked at Batya, smiled, pulled a yarmulke out of his pocket and stood up.

"For the past few weeks I've been washing my hands and then reciting a blessing before each meal. I remember all the Jewish families in our village doing this, sanctifying family meals. But in America many of us abandoned this practice," he said, looking at his in-laws. "Fortunately, I met Batya, who encouraged me to resume this custom. Everyone should remember to thank God for our food."

Helen narrowed her eyes and looked sharply at her husband, who was chewing as Harvey spoke. "It's a kosher restaurant, the food is already blessed," Saul whispered, but he put the half-eaten roll on his plate. When Harvey was finished, everyone quietly mumbled, "Amen," and Saul took another bite. Morris, who had noticed Helen and Saul's interchange, grabbed a roll for himself. "A man works hard all day he gets hungry," he said to Helen.

Before anyone else could speak, the waiter came over and distributed menus. "On a night like this everyone should start with some hot soup," he said. "I recommend the vegetable soup, which will keep you nice and healthy, or the matzo ball, which is always light and fluffy like your *Bubbe* used to make."

"I'll start with a salad," said Batya.

"That won't warm you up," said the waiter.

Batya stared at him. "I'd like the salad. And not too much dressing."

The waiter shrugged. "Okay lady, you're the boss. I won't be the one suffering when you get a cold."

The Rosens laughed. Batya looked at Harvey. Harvey looked at the waiter.

"I'll thank you not to insult this lady," he said. "You should apologize."

"Who's insulting?" said the waiter. "I haven't got time to be a diplomat. You're not my only table. What do the rest of you want?"

"I'll have the vegetable soup," said Morris. "Because not even a fancy restaurant chef could make matzo balls as good as my wife."

"I'm not going to argue with you," said the waiter. He took everyone's order and left.

"What Morris said about Rachel's matzo balls are true, they're the best," Helen told Batya. "But don't bother asking for her recipe.

She's keeping it a secret. Won't even tell family members."

Everyone smiled at Rachel. "Oh, it's not such a big deal," she said.

"It must be nice to have time to concentrate on cooking. I understand it's very creative," said Batya. "I've always been busy helping my father, he should rest in peace, run the *shul* and working on my studies."

"If you want to talk about books, just ask Helen. She has a diploma from an American high school," said Saul. "No one reads more than my wife. As soon as she walks into a drugstore, a supermarket, any place with a book rack, that's the first place she goes. We've got the Readers Digest Condensed Book series from the past five years in our living room, right next to the complete World Book Encyclopedia. And she never leaves the house without a paperback in her purse."

"I've seen those books with the flashy covers. I'll bet it's fun to read stuff like that, to just turn off your mind and relax. I've never had the time," said Batya. "I take college courses at night. With the Lord's guidance, right now I'm studying the ancient Greeks, reading Plato and Socrates."

"I've never read those books," said Helen quietly. She reached for a roll and looked around. "That waiter is certainly taking his time. Next time he passes, someone grab him and tell him to hurry-up. And ask for more bread."

By the time the entrees arrived, Saul and Morris were busy discussing business. Sometimes they asked Harvey a question, but he was clearly not interested, just kept smiling at Batya. Saul poked Morris. "He looks like a schoolboy with his first sweetheart," he whispered, and they laughed quietly.

The women ignored the men, talked to each other about their lives. Batya was very interested. She kept asking for more details, peppering her remarks with Yiddish phrases. As if we didn't know she was Jewish, thought Rachel.

How big were the houses which the Lord had granted them? How about Harvey's house? What was the furniture like? Did they have maids? Their own cars? Did they take vacations? Where? How often?

Finally, Batya turned away to respond to Harvey's question and let him know she wasn't happy with the fish she'd ordered. Helen whispered to Rachel, "Too bad we forgot to bring our tax returns for her. Next time we get together remember to invite the accountant."

Over dessert the discussion turned to the children, and Batya remained attentive while she listened to the trials and tribulations of motherhood. "Of course, all of these problems are offset by the joy we receive from our children," said Helen. "It must be so hard to be childless."

Batya took a long drink of tea. "Yes, it's true I haven't been as blessed as both of you. I am eager to get to know Harvey's children. But he's so shy about them." Batya looked at Harvey. "I guess he doesn't want to boast. Harvey's such a modest man."

"Helen and I have practically raised those children since their dear mother, may she rest in peace, passed away," said Rachel. "I'm sure we can make up for Harvey's shyness about them."

When she heard that all Harvey had said about Marvin was that his teachers were fond of him, Rachel launched into a long speech about what a lovely child he was, so smart, so polite, and a star athlete. Everyone loved him.

"And what about Rebecca?" asked Batya. "I understand she doesn't live at home. What is that all about?"

The waiter had removed the breadbasket when he brought dessert. When he heard Batya's question, Harvey jammed a heaping forkful of apple strudel into his mouth and chewed vigorously.

"She's a prize," said Helen. "A straight A student who made Bronx Science. Also a beauty. Because of her many gifts, Rebecca didn't always find it easy to fit in. Everyone thought it was best if she went to a special boarding school. Just for a little while. We all miss her terribly."

Harvey put down his fork. "Well, I'm certainly glad we were all able to get together," he said. "But it's getting late. I think it's time to head for home."

Saul called for the waiter, who was suddenly attentive, and got the check. "I'll take care of it," he said to Morris, opening a gaping wallet and pulling out a pile of cash. No one expected Harvey to pay.

Batya retrieved her boots from under her chair and put them on. She said goodbye to everyone, hugging Rachel and Helen, smiling at Saul and Morris. It was still raining when they got outside and hurried to their cars.

"Well, looks like we've got a new member coming into the family," said Morris as soon as everyone was settled in the car.

"Unless she breaks her neck trying to walk in those ridiculous shoes," said Helen.

"Don't underestimate her," said Saul. "That Batya's a tough cookie. She hasn't had it easy. You're not the only ones who can ask questions. I've been talking to Harvey when we're in the shop alone and found out a few things. She's a smart girl born into a society that doesn't always value smartness in girls. Her mother dies when she's young, she comes of age as the Nazis take over her country and flees Europe with just the clothes on her back and a helpless father. When she gets here she manages to quickly grab a husband, but he dumps her and she winds up living in poverty with a rabbi who probably thought whatever the Lord provides is enough. But a woman like this, she thinks the Lord could have done better."

Saul stared through the windshield, steering the big car through the heavy rain, trying to ignore the glare of oncoming headlights.

"She's no spring chicken, no beauty," he said. "Harvey is probably her last chance. She'll give him all the religious stuff he wants, that's her ace in the hole.

"Harvey could have found someone long ago, but he would have had to make a choice. He could marry a woman who was the kind of Jew we are, somewhat religious, but not too much, one who wouldn't understand all of his scholarly stuff. Or he could have gotten matched-up with a truly Orthodox woman who wouldn't have accepted the way he lives, the way he has to live if he's going to make enough money so he and his children can live the way they're used to living. This one is special Orthodox, but flexible." Saul shook his head, "what a phrase. Wonder where Harvey heard that.

"The two of them can moan together about how America robbed them of their faith. She'll sacrifice her religious principles for him. But there'll be a cost. She's not a push-over. I don't think Harvey knows what he's getting into."

Morris interrupted the conversation, remembering an appointment he had the next day that he had to discuss with Saul. The subject of Batya was dropped until they got home.

"Tell me everything," Sarah said as soon as her folks walked into the house. She was eager to write to Rebecca and give her all the dirt. Sarah thought of herself as the family's Walter Winchell.

"Later. First, I have to take off my girdle and call your Aunt Rachel," said Helen. "We still have things to discuss."

Annoyed, Sarah turned to her father. "What did you think?

What happened? What did mom and Aunt Rachel say? How did they act?"

Saul shook his head again. "I'm not sure they understand the full situation. Your American-born mother, your aunt whose family came over well before the War started, they think they know what it was like in Europe because they heard stories. They think, just because they drop off old clothes there, they know what it was like to desperately need places like HIAS so you don't starve in the cold.

"A woman like Batya knows things they don't. I just hope they'll be careful. This isn't a competition for president of the Sisterhood. If they can't figure out a way to get along it'll be bad for the family. And that'll be bad for our business."

That night, Sarah wrote a long letter to Rebecca, telling her all she'd learned about Batya.

A week later, Rebecca wrote back. "I don't care what my father does."

20.

THE HOLIDAYS

The first Rosh Hashanah that Harvey and Batya were together she arranged to stay at the home of a friend of a friend who lived near the Rosens so she wouldn't have to ride in a car on the High Holidays and could attend services at Harvey's synagogue. This would be the first time Batya would pray someplace where men and women sat together.

She arrived with her own prayer book. An heirloom she'd inherited from her father, Batya explained as she unzipped the dark blue velvet pouch with a large Jewish star embroidered in the center in thick gold thread.

Batya read Hebrew fluently, much more skillfully than anyone in the Rosen family. When the congregation read aloud, she whipped through the prayers with perfect pronunciation. No one complimented her.

Helen just skimmed the English translation on the facing page. Her mind wandered during services. She whispered to her neighbors, looked at her watch, planned meals and didn't try to keep pace with the congregation.

Quickly realizing the situation, Batya decided she would be "helpful" and frequently reached over to turn the pages in Helen's prayer book. Helen just nodded.

Batya was wearing a dark blue suit, a boxy jacket with large gold buttons, not very flattering for someone who was small and busty. It had an A-line skirt, mid-calf length, and she wore thick, seamed nylons and pointy-toed blue leather pumps with high gold heels.

When the congregation had to remain standing during a long Torah passage, Helen whispered, "if your feet hurt you can slip off your shoes, no one will notice."

Batya nodded and kept her shoes on.

Midway through the service, Rachel leaned over and loudly whispered to Batya, "Have you seen our beautiful stained-glass windows? The one on your right is dedicated to our beloved Elaine. Harvey made sure it was installed next to our seats."

"Very decorative," said Batya. She stared at Rachel. Women's hats were a big thing in *shul*, and that year no one's hat was more elaborate than Rachel's, a bright blue concoction of beads and feathers and netting.

"I always wondered what a Ziegfeld girl looked like," Batya whispered to Harvey.

Like many houses of worship, this synagogue relied on member donations to meet expenses. And the leadership knew that the best way to maximize donations was peer pressure. Since Rosh Hashanah was one of the few times that the entire congregation came together, it was the prime fund-raising opportunity.

Conservative Jews don't write on High Holidays, at least not while they're inside the *shul*, so a card with each member's name was placed on their seats before services began. Around the edge of the card were tabs with numbers printed on them, $50, $75, several tabs with $100, and a few with $500. To donate, all you had to do was bend the appropriate tabs.

During the afternoon break, the cards were collected and

reviewed by the membership president and then read aloud. In front of everyone. If the president was satisfied with the donation, he might just read out the donor's name.

"Joseph Berger, thank you, Joe.

"Robert Rosenblatt, thanks, Bob."

But soon he got to a card that made him pause. He stared at it and shook his head.

"Morty Gottlieb, this says $200, but that's what you gave last year. I know you just had your first grandchild. For the new baby, let's say I raise this to $250. Okay?"

There were a few more thank-yous, and then the president paused again.

"Sam Blum, only $300? I can see the next card says that Milton Shapiro is giving $400. You guys are in the same line of work, aren't you? Do you want the competition to show you up? Tell you what. I'll raise each of these cards to $500 and you guys can start the New Year on an equal footing. Okay?"

Surrounded by their friends and family, no one ever said no. A few days later the bills went out. On Rosh Hashanah the Lord records your fate—and the bookkeeper records your contribution.

Usually Harvey got away with a quick, "thank you," and the membership president saved his jibes for Saul and Morris, who always indicated less than they wanted to contribute. They enjoyed the game, admired how the president always knew how far he could push each member. "What a *goniff*, a real finagler," Saul would say to Morris. "We should hire him to work for us."

This year, things were a little different. Briefed by the Hebrew school director, the president saw an opportunity to make some extra money.

"Harvey," he said. "You must have made a mistake. You only turned down the tab for $100. But I see there's a lovely young lady sitting next to you. And a little bird told me we may be seeing more of her in the future. You don't want this charming woman to think she's joining a *shul* that isn't financially secure, do you? Remember last year when there was a heat wave, and the AC didn't work properly? Wouldn't you be embarrassed if something like that happened in front of your lovely guest?"

He turned to the next two cards. "And Morris and Saul Rosen, it looks like you were as distracted as your brother-in-law. I'm not even going to tell the congregation which tabs you turned down this year.

"I'll tell you what, guys," he said. "To show this lady that she's sitting with a family she can be proud of I'm going to turn down $500 on each of these cards. Okay?"

Saul and Morris started to laugh. They shook their fists at the president but then nodded in agreement. Harvey sat up straight and gave a thin-lipped smile.

Batya looked at Harvey and then at the laughing Rosen family. She was quiet for a minute, and then she started to laugh too. "Well, that's certainly something I've never seen before," she said. "My father always worked so hard to raise money for the temple's necessities. While he had a superior knowledge of Torah, it looks like he could have learned something from the Conservatives."

After services they all walked back together. Batya wanted to use the bathroom, so everyone went into the house with her, eager to see Batya's first reaction to Harvey's home.

Batya came out of the bathroom, turned towards the living room and pronounced it charming. "But I always imagined people with money wouldn't have to keep their furniture covered," she said, fingering the plastic slip covers on the couch and armchairs.

"It keeps them clean," said Rachel. "No one has so much money they can afford an unsanitary household." In Rachel's house, as in Helen's, and most of the homes in the neighborhood, all the living room furniture was covered in clear, heavy plastic.

"And are these antiques?" Batya asked. "They're lovely." She was looking at the tall ceramic lamps with Asian dragon designs standing on either side of the couch. She ran her fingers through the long gold fringes on the lampshades.

"Not antiques," said Rachel. "Just tasteful."

Batya glanced briefly at the ornately framed paintings, an old man painted on velvet, a vase of flowers that matched the color of the couch.

"And your study?" she said to Harvey. "Surely a scholar like you has a study in a house this size."

Harvey showed her to the study, everyone followed. Batya looked at the collection of Hebrew books, pulled out a few volumes by renowned Talmudic scholars and flipped through the pages. She praised Harvey's taste. "These are certainly well worn," she said with a smile. "Just like the editions in my house."

"I try to study regularly," said Harvey. "With my job it's not always easy to find time, but I make it a priority." He smiled back at Batya.

"Could I have a glass of water?" Batya asked. She spotted the kitchen and walked in without waiting for a reply. Although there were water glasses on a shelf above the sink, Batya opened all the cabinets and scanned the contents. "Only one set of dishes," she murmured. She picked up a plate, turned it over to see the brand name and quickly replaced it. She spotted the good dishes, turned over a soup bowl and smiled. "Wedgewood," she said. "How lovely."

"Do you need a Baccarat goblet for your water?" asked Helen. "Sorry that's not available. But there's crystal behind you." Batya laughed, drank her water from a plain glass and went outside.

As everyone waved goodbye, Helen turned to Rachel. "Too bad it was unseemly for her to visit Harvey's bedroom. She could have checked the thread count of the linens and measured the thickness of the towels."

21.

THE COURTSHIP

A few weeks later, Batya told Harvey she wanted to spend some time with Marvin without the rest of the family around and the three of them wound up having lunch together at a kosher delicatessen. As soon as they sat down Batya handed Marvin a carefully wrapped present. He tore off the paper and grinned widely when he spotted the new first baseman's mitt.

"This is perfect," he said. "How did you know which position I play?"

"Oh," said Batya. "When I saw you in *shul* you just looked like a first baseman."

Harvey looked at them blankly. One baseball glove was different from another? Who knew?

He had mentioned to Batya that Marvin played in a neighborhood little league, and she located the organization and got a list of the players and their positions. A quick scan of a few books and Batya knew enough about baseball to make conversation with Marvin. He was so busy with the new glove that he barely noticed when she pulled a yarmulke out of her purse, put it on him and Harvey said a quick blessing before they ate. And he was delighted she didn't criticize him when he spilled his soda, just told the waiter to bring another. At the end of the meal, Batya suggested she and

Harvey attend Marvin's next baseball game.

"It's not a comfortable place," said Harvey.

"It's outdoors, with hard benches, no shade and lots of noise," Marvin said, quoting his father.

"Don't be foolish," said Batya. "We're not so old we need to be protected from the outdoors. Marvin, don't worry, we'll be there."

At the next game, Harvey and Batya showed up on time, waved to Marvin while he was warming up, and quickly found seats. Batya wore a simple cotton dress, neither longer nor shorter than the other women. She'd brought along seat cushions so Harvey would be comfortable.

At the beginning of the second inning, Batya heard the girl sitting next to her loudly crunching. She looked at the bag the girl was emptying and saw that it read, "pork rinds." Batya poked Harvey and tilted her head toward her neighbor. They found other seats.

Batya had no qualms about cheering loudly for Marvin's team and quickly learned the lingo. Harvey was too reserved to participate in the cheers, but he looked at her with admiration. He was wearing the yarmulke he now carried in his pocket all the time, it did an excellent job of protecting his bald spot from the sun.

Marvin's team won the game by a score of 12 to 10 and, along with all the other parents, Batya and Harvey ran over and hugged him. Batya politely turned down invitations to join the rest of the team and their parents in a celebration. She had the address of a nearby kosher pizza restaurant for the three of them.

"That was so exciting," she said as soon as they were seated. "I can't wait to see more. When's the next game?"

"We're in the quarter finals now," said Marvin. "It's this Saturday."

Batya looked at Harvey. "There are little leagues that don't have games on Saturday, you know," she said. "How did he choose this group?"

"This is where Rachel's boys play," said Harvey.

Batya looked at Marvin. "I'm sorry, but I won't be able to come. You understand, don't you?"

"Yeah, I know you're religious," he said. "It's okay. We probably won't win anyway. I'll let you know how the game goes."

Batya nodded. "I want to hear all about it. Everything. Maybe next season you can find a league that doesn't play on Saturday, and I can go to all your games."

Marvin stared at her. "I want to be in the same league as my cousins."

Harvey looked from Batya to Marvin and back again. "Well," he said. "That's a long way away. Now, what type of pizza should we order?"

• • •

Two weeks later Saul came home from work early.

"What a nice surprise," said Helen. "What happened?"

Saul looked at his daughter. "Sarah, why don't you make your mother some tea? And see if there are any cookies."

Sarah didn't move.

"Who died?" asked Helen.

"No one died," Saul said. "And no one was in a car accident. The business didn't fail. The earth didn't quake. No fire, no floods, the stars will come out tonight and the sun will rise tomorrow."

"So why are you home early and why do I need tea and cookies?"

"Harvey came in today and told us he's going to marry Batya."

"So? Everyone's known that for weeks."

"He wants to sell the house and live someplace else when he's married."

"And you said?"

"Just let me get settled," he said and walked down the hall into the bedroom.

Saul took his wallet and keys out of his pants pockets along with the things he'd collected that day loose change, candy wrappers, paper clips, two business cards, a crooked nail and a thumbtack. A small statue of a pseudo-Greek nymph wearing a diaper and holding up a clamshell stood on his dresser. He added the contents of his pockets to the detritus that almost filled the clamshell. The statue was artificially antiqued with dabs of brownish-gold paint that would rub off if the cleaning lady scrubbed too hard, which she had done a few times before Helen told her to stop using Ajax on the artwork.

"Morris and I spent all day yesterday trying to change his mind," he said.

"You knew about this yesterday?"

"I didn't want to make a fuss for no reason. We thought we had him convinced. He wanted to talk it over with Batya. But today, well," Saul shrugged. He opened one of the dresser drawers and stared at his socks. Each pair was neatly rolled into a ball. His underwear was folded and stacked next to the socks.

"Do we have any seltzer?" asked Saul. "I feel like having a glass of seltzer."

"And you thought you'd find it in the drawer with your socks and underwear?"

Saul walked back into the living room. Helen and Sarah followed.

"Batya has a point, you know," he said. "When Rebecca comes home it might be best for her to start over in a neighborhood where people don't know her. And in a new school Marvin might do better. Maybe new teachers wouldn't accept mediocre work because they think that's the best he can do."

"And, of course, a woman who's never had children knows what's best for children." Helen spoke slowly. "Especially for these children, children Rachel and I have been taking care of since they were babies. Batya knows the best thing for them is to be taken away from a home filled with memories of their dear, departed mother and live with someone they don't know, following Orthodox Jewish practices they don't understand."

The phone started to ring. "That'll be Rachel. Morris will have spoken to her by now," Saul said as Helen went to answer the phone.

Saul walked into the living room and sat on the couch. He picked up the newspaper, flipped to the sports section, put it down again.

About 15 minutes passed before Helen came back. "Okay, Rachel agrees with me. This is not good. This is not going to happen. We won't allow it."

"You know, it is his house," Saul said. "And they wouldn't be too far away. Harvey still works for us and has to be able to get to the shop. Maybe just a few miles away."

"Just far enough so Rachel and I won't be able to mix in," said Helen.

"Maybe Batya won't turn out to be so terrible," said Saul. "And the children aren't going to die if they have to eat kosher food and observe the Sabbath."

"You really think Rachel and I are just a couple of crazy Jewish mothers?" said Helen. "Have you forgotten why you and Morris are paying for Marvin's Hebrew lessons? That not so long ago Marvin ran into Rachel's arms crying hysterically because his father wanted to teach him Hebrew at home? You think he'll run a few miles the next time he wants to feel safe? That we want our Marvin far away from us with a father who left his little boy covered in bruises because he turned to a magic set instead of joining Harvey in praying for Elaine's recovery?

"And my Rebecca?" said Helen, her voice rising. "You think when she comes home from that place her biggest adjustment will be learning the blessing so she and Batya can light candles together? You think the biggest problem she'll cause is mixing up the meat dishes with the dairy? A girl with Rebecca's intelligence, with her fire, Harvey couldn't handle her before, you think with what she's been through in that place, he'll be able to handle her now? That Batya will be any help?"

Saul started to say something. Helen put up her hand.

"No. No more getting slapped around for my Rebecca. Last time I didn't know what was going on. Now I'm smarter. I'm going to be watching, staying nearby to put a stop to anything like that. And before you start, I don't want to hear a word about how it was in Europe. I don't want to hear about your father punishing his children. I don't care if your father's father, and his father, and every father in your village and all over Poland and all over Europe and maybe all over America thought you should use a strap to show you cared for your children.

"Today is today, not years ago. We're here, not someplace else. And these children are Rebecca and Marvin, and God knows that I know they're not perfect. I'm not a fool. I know Harvey is their father and a father has rights. Maybe he is trying to start a good home for them. That's what I pray for. I know that living with two happily married people in a nice stable home, even an Orthodox home, would be the best thing that could happen to them. Rachel knows she's not Marvin's mother, I know I'm not Rebecca's mother. I know everyone has problems. We just want to be close by to make sure the problems don't get out of hand."

It took a moment for Saul to reply. "So you and Rachel have figured out how you can stop Harvey from selling a house he owns and moving away with his own children and the woman he's going to marry?"

"Yes, I think we have," said Helen. "Be quiet and listen. This solution is right up your alley. It's money."

"What do you mean?" he said.

"It takes money to sell a house, it takes money to buy a new house, and money to keep a new wife happy. And we know Harvey is too busy with the holy books to worry about money, which is why he's never had any and wouldn't know how to manage it if he did. But you and Morris, whom Harvey fervently believes are money-loving heathens, you two know how to manipulate money and the people who deal with money."

Saul listened to Helen speak. He raised his eyebrows, he nodded his head. Then he got up, put his arms on her shoulders and kissed her lips. He turned to his daughter. "You've got a smart mother. Don't ever forget that."

The next week Saul had a word with the manager of the local bank, and Harvey discovered he'd have trouble getting a mortgage. Morris had a word with the local realtor, and Harvey learned that the cost of buying homes near their area was going up while the amount sellers were receiving for homes in the area was going down.

• • •

Helen and Rachel decided the final push was up to them. They asked Batya to join them for lunch at a nearby kosher Chinese restaurant to celebrate her engagement.

Batya was already seated when Helen and Rachel arrived, and it took them a minute to locate her. Batya looked just like every other woman in this Orthodox restaurant, neat brown wig, calf length grey skirt and long-sleeved dark blue blouse buttoned all the way up.

Helen was wearing a green pastel polyester pants suit, and Rachel had on her baby-blue knee-length dress with a rose-print jacket. Two heretics among the faithful. Bewigged heads turned as they walked over to Batya.

As soon as they were all seated and had ordered vegetarian chow mein and kosher beef with broccoli, Rachel gave Batya a big smile. "The whole family is so happy about this joyous occasion. You and Harvey make a terrific couple."

Batya smiled. "I'm really looking forward to being part of such a nice family. I can't wait to invite you to our new home."

"Have you told Marvin you're thinking about moving?" asked Rachel. "I'm sure he'll be excited, although he'll miss being near his cousins. They're like brothers, you know. But you shouldn't worry about having no experience raising children. Marvin's always been a very easy kid. Of course, he'll be a teenager soon, and who knows what'll happen then."

Rachel reached for the bowl of crispy noodles on the table and dunked a few into the duck sauce, which, she had to admit, tasted just like the duck sauce in real Chinese restaurants, even if it was made from kosher ducks.

She leaned over the table. "I remember when my Kenny reached puberty. Hormones, you know? What a commotion." Rachel rolled her eyes. "Harvey always sent Marvin to my house when there was any trouble, not that there were many problems. And you can call me for advice any time." Rachel patted Batya's hand. "Any time, day or night."

"And that goes for me too," said Helen. She took Batya's other hand. "Rebecca's always been a handful. But two years in that special school, I'm sure she'll come home a perfect lady. And before you know it, you'll be busy getting ready to send her to college. She's so smart, I'm sure she'll qualify for a scholarship, certainly for low-interest student loans."

Batya freed her hands and picked up her fork. There were no chop sticks in this Chinese restaurant.

"Loans, scholarships," said Batya. "Do partners in the Rosen Corporation really think about such things? With all that the Lord has already provided for them?"

Rachel and Helen exchanged glances. "Harvey didn't tell her," Rachel sighed. "Did you know she didn't know?"

"Not me," said Helen. "Otherwise I never would have opened my mouth."

"Well," said Rachel, "I guess the cat is out of the bag, and, one woman to another, I think she really should understand the situation."

Batya shifted her position in the chair and stared at the women across from her. "The situation?" Her eyebrows pressed together, her forehead was wrinkled.

"You see, Morris and Saul are partners. Harvey just works for them," said Helen. "I'm sure Harvey is one of the top salesmen. With his personality, so charismatic, how could he be anything else? But he works on commission. Our husbands always made sure Elaine had everything she needed, that she lived as well as we did, and if that meant pitching in a little extra for the children's expenses, picking up the bill for some of Elaine's needs, that was okay. They would do anything for their sister, for dear Elaine, may she rest in peace."

"Our husbands have promised their mother they'll always make sure Elaine's children are well cared for, and with Morris and Saul it's always, 'whatever Mama wants, Mama gets,'" said Rachel.

"Family is very important to them. And, of course, it is to us, too."

Batya pulled a tissue from her purse, covered her face to hide her surprise and pretended to sneeze. She wouldn't give these two *yentas* the satisfaction of seeing she had no idea Harvey wasn't a partner, and that she was upset by the news.

"Gesundheit," said Rachel. "Have some more tea. It's important you take care of yourself. You don't want anything to get in the way of the wedding."

No one heard from the happy couple for a few days. Then Saul came home with a big bouquet of flowers for Helen. "To celebrate your victory," he said. "Harvey was asking about contractors today. He and Batya are staying put, but she's getting a top-grade new kitchen, kosher enough for the biggest rabbi in Israel."

"And the cost of the renovation?" asked Helen.

"Taken care of," said Saul. "Harvey was surprised to find out how popular he was. The electrician, the plumber, the carpenter, everyone was willing to do the job at cost. As a wedding present, they told him."

Helen smiled. "Admit it," she said to Saul. "You didn't think Rachel and I would be able to change Batya's mind about moving, did you?"

"I had my doubts. But I also knew Batya wasn't going to sabotage such a good arrangement because she didn't get everything she wanted. That's not the way a good negotiator works," Saul said. "Wait 'til you see the plans for the fancy kitchen Harvey promised her. It's going to cost us a fortune to reimburse everyone whose arm Morris and I twisted to get this deal done."

"It's money well spent," said Helen. "And probably nothing compared to how much Batya will make Harvey pay for deceiving her.

22.

YAHRTZITE

Rebecca hung up the phone and closed the notebook she'd been clumsily writing in while balancing the receiver between her neck and shoulder. The housemother put a check next to her name on the list taped to the wall and Rebecca quickly moved aside so the next girl could make a call.

Maria and Alice were waiting across the room. "How's *Bubbe* doing?" asked Alice. The girls had picked up the habit of referring to Rebecca's grandmother as *Bubbe*, and Maria's grandmother as Abuela. Alice rarely spoke about her family, had no special names for relatives.

"How did you know who I was speaking to?" asked Rebecca.

"Elementary, my dear Watson. You were talking louder than usual, like someone conversing with an old person who might be a little deaf. And you were talking in a language no one else understands, so you didn't care if you were overheard."

Rebecca smiled. "No shit, Sherlock. You paid attention to my book recommendation, huh?"

Maria looked puzzled.

"Sherlock Holmes, the famous detective," said Alice. "Watson was his slightly dimwitted assistant." She nodded towards Rebecca who stuck out her tongue. "I'd finished all the paper-back detective stories in our library and Rebecca kept telling me not to be afraid of the hard stuff, the hard-covered stuff. I cracked a binding, as intellectuals say, and found out she was right."

The girls found a place to sit in the rec room. They were all wearing jeans, t-shirts and dirty sneakers. Rebecca and Alice looked like sexy young women out to attract neighborhood guys. Their pants were tight, and their V-necked shirts revealed the tops of young breasts. Large brass hoop earrings jutted from Alice's thick hair. Rebecca wore a pearl drop on a gold chain that sparkled and invited eyes to follow as it skimmed her cleavage. Maria looked like a kid ready to go out and play. Her jeans were baggy, her crew-neck shirt was loose and, Rebecca knew, underneath the shirt was a pewter cross dangling from a long, silver chain.

"So how is *Bubbe* doing?" Alice asked again, once they were settled. "I saw you carefully writing something down while you were on the phone. She give you the combination to her safe? The location of the family jewels? Did she relocate her stash so your dad's new bride wouldn't find it?"

"Safe? Family jewels? Her stash? I doubt my *Bubbe* has ever had more than a dollar or two in her pocket since she arrived in this country. My aunt gives her that money so she can pay the kid across the street who sneaks pizza to her, so the other old people don't know she eats non-kosher foods."

"Aren't all Jews rich?" asked Alice with a smile.

Rebecca rolled her eyes. "Oh come on, you're really going to start that stuff. Again? Remember, we settled it all? Jews are conniving merchants and slumlords, all blacks are crooks and most are junkies and Puerto Ricans are lazy slobs who only want to lie in the sun and eat cuchifritoes. And I still don't know what that is."

"And I still don't see any reason to tell you. You Jews know enough already." Maria giggled and turned to Alice. "With all their money you'd think they'd be able to find someone to teach them to dance."

"Look, if it's not in the blood, it can't be taught," sighed Alice. "Like how to produce star athletes on a ghetto diet."

Rebecca joined in as the three girls laughed, wondering what her friends were really thinking while they kidded around this way. No one in her neighborhood had looked like Maria or Alice, and there was always gossip about houses shown to non-white potential buyers, how last-minute arrangements always guaranteed those deals didn't go through.

The women who cleaned Rebecca's house and nearby houses all looked like they could be the mothers or grandmothers of most of the girls in this school. These women who, their employers boasted, just had a knack for ironing, were inherently limber and didn't mind getting on their knees to scrub floors no matter how old they were. Rebecca wondered if her friends would have cared that her neighbors spoke fondly of their "girls," saved used clothing for them and were proud to allow them to take home leftover food.

"I'm not up for another debate about who was worse, slave owners, Nazis, or imperialists," Rebecca said. "I thought we'd decided there have always been a lot of cruel, ignorant dopes in the world. Just look at this crowd."

They glanced around. Some tables were full of girls talking animatedly in Spanish, at one they spoke Italian, there were tables for white girls and tables where girls with a variety of dark skin colors laughed and chatted together. There were few tables at which girls of different races or cultures sat together.

"No doubt about it," said Maria. "We're the brightest, most tolerant people in this place."

Alice tried to grab Rebecca's book. "I'm still curious about what *Bubbe* had to say that deserves to be written down."

"You can look, but it's not going to mean anything to you." Rebecca opened the notebook to the page in which she'd been writing and slid it to Alice, who stared at the page and shook her head.

"So now you and Bubs have a secret code?" she said.

"It's *Bubbe* or grandma. Show some respect," Rebecca said. She took back her notebook. "This is a phonetic transcription of Hebrew."

"Didn't mean to disrespect the lady," said Alice. "And you can stop showing off your Bronx Science vocabulary."

"Sorry," said Rebecca. "I'm a little shook up about our conversation. *Bubbe* told me it was my mom's Yahrzeit. That means it's time to say the prayer that marks the anniversary of the death of someone close to you. I'd lost track of the date, but of course *Bubbe* hadn't. She wanted to talk about her daughter, I guess because my dad is getting married, replacing her. I wasn't ready to start talking about my mother, to hear what she was like as a child, as a new mother.

"*Bubbe* and I speak to each other in Yiddish, but prayers are said in Hebrew. Both languages use the same characters, like this." Rebecca wrote a few squiggles from right to left. "I don't really know how to write in either language. I just wrote the sounds in English letters."

"Jews have two languages?" Alice smiled at Rebecca. "No wonder you talk so much."

"We have a lot to say." Rebecca smiled back.

"So, do you want to mark the anniversary of your mom's death or ignore it? By yourself, or should we join you?" asked Maria. "What would happen at home?"

"It's really simple, few people make a fuss. You just light a candle, quietly say the short prayer and let the candle burn all night.

You use those glasses they sell at supermarkets, the glasses with Hebrew labels. They have just enough wax to last a whole night."

Alice and Maria looked at each other. Rebecca understood. "Well, those glasses that are sold at all supermarkets in areas where Jews live," she said.

"Of course my father, being my father, makes a fuss about everything. When he lights the candle, everyone has to stand around and listen to him wail the prayer, weep and carry on about how God has been so hard on him. I wonder what he'll do once the new wife moves in."

"Never mind him," said Maria. "What do you want to do?"

"I wouldn't mind going through the ritual. *Bubbe* would be happy, and if, by any chance, there is a heaven, if my mom is watching me, I'd like her to know I miss her. However, just saying a prayer doesn't feel like enough, and the housemother would have a fit if she found a candle burning in my room."

"People light candles in the chapel," Maria said softly.

The Hillsdale Non-Denominational Inter-Faith Chapel was in the administration building, one steep flight of stairs above Staff Conference Room A. The space used to be called Staff Conference Room B, but five years ago the director realized there was really no need for two staff conference rooms, and the room which housed the chapel was near the kitchen and would make a perfect faculty dining room.

Every Sunday a rotating crew of neophyte clergymen from surrounding towns delivered sermons judged suitable for teenage girls from all faiths but of dubious morality. Maria tried to show up when she knew a Catholic priest would be there to administer the sacraments and hear confession. Alice went occasionally; she didn't prefer any particular type of spiritual leader, just sometimes felt it was time to pray. Rebecca had never been there.

"Do you think *Bubbe* would mind if your mom's candle was in a plain glass? If it was next to a Catholic candle?" asked Maria. "Sometimes the service is delivered by a Rabbi, are there any Jewish holidays coming up?"

"No Jewish holidays on the horizon as far as I know," said Rebecca. "*Bubbe* will be so glad to hear I listened to her. I think she'd be thankful if I did it at a Hari Krishna service."

"No need to shave your head," said Maria. "But we'll all have to be up and dressed before 8 a.m."

"*Oy* vey," said Alice and they all giggled.

By 7:45 a.m. the next Sunday the three girls were ready. Rebecca had a pale blue silk scarf tied around her neck. A black lace square that could be pinned onto her hair was tucked in Maria's pocket. Alice had simple pearl studs in her ears. Everyone's outfit was neat and clean and fit properly.

The housemother studied them as they came downstairs. "You must have been involved in something really sinful to get your entire crew up and dressed at this hour. I hope you get properly forgiven and blessed."

When the girls got to the doorway, Rebecca paused and glanced around. The chapel looked exactly like what it was, a spare meeting room decorated to look like something more important. Heavy gold colored cotton curtains covered the back wall. Three religious photos hung from the folds, a large cross in the middle, a Jewish star on one side and a Muslim crescent and star on the other. At the front of the room stood a table covered with a cloth that almost matched the curtain. There were metal folding chairs on both sides of the central aisle. The girls signed in and sat in the last row.

Maria pointed to the left wall where candles were spread out on a table lower than the one in front of the room, covered with a yellow cloth. There were two iron trays on the table and five two-inch tall glasses on each tray, each glass nestled in a scalloped, iron candleholder. A large box of wooden kitchen matches rested between the trays.

"Those candles won't last all night," whispered Rebecca.

"That's the best we can do," said Maria. "I'm sure your mom will understand."

When there were about a dozen girls in the room, a clean-cut young man came in, walked to the front and stood behind the table. He introduced himself, unzipped the leather portfolio he was carrying, took out some large index cards and spread them in front of himself.

"Protestant," whispered Maria. "The service won't be long."

"White Protestant," whispered Alice. "It'll be boring."

Ten minutes into the service Rebecca gave up counting how many times the good reverend used the words "respect" and "reform." She wondered if there was a manual for clergy-in-training called *The Little Golden Book of Sermons for Naughty Girls*.

Rebecca leaned over to Alice. "How long do you have to listen to this stuff before you're guaranteed to get into Heaven?"

"If you stay awake for the whole thing it makes up for having sex with your best friend's boyfriend," said Alice.

"SHHHH!" said Maria.

When the service was finally over, they waited while several other girls lit candles and then went over to the table. A few wooden matches were lying in an ashtray, and the area smelled of sulfur. Rebecca took the scarf off her neck and draped it over her head. Maria bobby pinned the lace square to her hair.

Maria knelt, crossed herself, then stood up, struck a match, lit a candle and spoke softly.

"*Lord Jesus, look kindly on my work and the work of my friends today. Help us in our difficulties and decisions. May this candle be a light for you to enlighten us. May it be a fire for you to burn out of me all pride, selfishness and impurity.*"

She crossed herself again and stepped back.

Alice bowed her head, lit a candle, stared into the flame and whispered something no one could hear.

Rebecca pulled out the paper on which she'd written *Bubbe's* dictation and read the Hebrew words, noting that her mother's name had been included:

"*Neir Adonai nishmat Adam. Yehi Raton milfanecha, Adonai eloheinu veilohei avoteinu, shetchei nishmat* Elaine *tzerurah betzeror hachayim, im nishmot Abraham, Yitzchak ve 'Ya'akov, Sarah, Rivkah, Rachel, VeLeah. Tehi Menutchatah kavod, Selah.*"

She stumbled only once, put the paper back in her pocket and lit the candle.

When all the flames were burning steadily, they took off their head coverings and left the chapel. The sun was shining as the three girls quietly walked to the dining room for breakfast.

23.

THE BEST MAN

Rachel looked through her kitchen window and watched the boys rolling around her backyard. Eventually they untangled themselves and started shooting hoops into the basket above the garage, and she was able to distinguish the players—two of her sons, Marvin and a few preteen neighborhood boys.

They were clearly involved in a heated conversation, but the window was closed, and Rachel couldn't hear what was being said. Probably complaining about the ball, she thought. Her boys wanted a better basketball, said they were too old for the toy they were using, which was softer and smaller than a regulation basketball. She and Morris planned to get a professional size ball for Kenny for his birthday next month. He'd share it with the others. Until then, they could just manage with this ball.

Actually, Rachel's sons were negotiating the cost of renting a collection of girlie magazines from the boy who lived across the street. "We'll do it while Marvin is staying over so he can see them and chip in," Kenny said.

"My dad's getting married," Marvin explained to the other boys. "Afterwards he and the woman he's marrying are going away for a few days, and I'm staying here."

"Honeymoon trip, huh?" said the boy who owned the

magazines. He bounced the ball a few times, took careful aim but missed the ring. "You know what that means." He grinned and jabbed his index finger through a circle made with the fingers on the other hand.

Marvin waited until it was his turn, looked at the boy who'd made the sex comment and threw the ball as hard as he could. It was a perfect shot. The ball connected with the bridge of the boy's nose, which started to bleed profusely. The injured boy fell down, his brother jumped on Marvin and Marvin's cousins ran to his defense. Soon all of the boys were rolling in the dirt again.

Rachel rushed out, made sure no one was badly hurt and sent the neighbor's kids home. "What were you doing?" she said angrily. She looked at Marvin. "Since when are you such a hoodlum?"

"No big deal," said Kenny, putting his arm on Marvin's shoulder. "Just goofing around."

Marvin nodded. "Yeah, still good friends."

Rachel brought them into her house to get cleaned up. "Marvin, put on a pair of Bobby's pants," she called. "Yours are torn. I'll fix them before you go home."

When the boys came downstairs, Rachel noticed that her son's pants were too short for Marvin. "You're really shooting up," she said. "You're going to be tall like your father." Marvin glanced at his feet as if amazed that two long protuberances had suddenly sprung from his body.

"I guess," he said and shrugged.

Rachel looked at him carefully. "When was the last time you wore your good suit?"

Marvin shrugged again. "Dunno."

Rachel shook her head. "How did Helen and I overlook this? You need a new suit for your father's wedding."

"My old suit is okay."

Rachel ignored him. "I'm driving you to the shopping center next Saturday, right after lunch. We'll buy something sharp."

Rachel spotted the salesman she wanted as soon as they got off the escalator. He was a plump, balding man with a tape measure around his neck. He looked like someone who would recognize that she'd only settle for top quality merchandise.

"I need a suit for this young man for a very special occasion," she said ignoring the nearby woman who was trying to get the salesman's attention. "Stand up straight Marvin, let the man get a look at you."

"Well, that shouldn't be hard," said the salesman, smiling. He recognized a good commission when he saw one. "Such a nice-looking boy, everything will look good on him. What did you have in mind? Navy? Charcoal? Pin Stripe? Double breasted? Single breasted? We have everything. You'll also want a shirt, plain or white on white? And of course a tie. Does he need dress socks? You're in luck, there's a special sale on everything today."

"Plain white shirt," said Rachel. "And make sure the shirt has buttons. Boys lose cuff links. Let's try a variety of jacket styles and colors and see how they look on him."

"Absolutely right," said the salesman. He turned to Marvin. "What about you, young fellow? Any preferences?"

Marvin looked up, surprised he was being addressed. "Yeah, no cuff links," he said.

The salesman had Marvin try several jackets to determine his size. Rachel picked her favorites. "Now let's see the whole look," said the salesman. Rachel started to follow them to the dressing room. Marvin stopped walking. He looked at Rachel. "I'll try the pants now," he said. "I'll show you when they're on."

Rachel understood. "As if I didn't change his diapers not too long ago," she said to the salesman. "Okay, go. Don't take too long or I'll come get you."

The first suit Marvin tried on was perfect. So was the second. "This youngster makes all of our merchandise look good," said the salesman. "He's a great model."

"If he only knew how to use a comb," Rachel said. She stepped closer and pushed Marvin's hair off his forehead with her hand. He had Elaine's fine, pale brown hair that always fell into his eyes. "Your mother would be so proud of what a handsome young man you've become." Marvin turned away, but Rachel could see in the mirror that he was smiling.

They eventually decided on a navy blue, pin-striped suit and a blue and crimson striped tie. "This looks so good with your eyes," she said. "You're the only grandchild who inherited Golda's deep blue eyes."

"Yeah," said Marvin. "*Bubbe* says we have blueberry eyes."

"And now," Rachel said, turning to the salesman. "I'm going to stand over the fitter. And you're going to make sure this suit is altered perfectly. I don't want to have to come back for adjustments. But if everything's not just right you can count on my coming back, and I won't be in a good mood."

Marvin tried not to fidget while the fitter worked. When the sleeves were being pinned, he glanced at the price tag on the cuff. "Aunt Rachel, isn't this kind of expensive? Are you sure it'll be okay with my father?"

"Don't worry. This is quality merchandise, worth the price. I know how to judge such things. Anyway, there's no reason it should bother your father. A perfectly dressed best man will be part of my gift to him."

As they pulled out of the crowded parking lot, Rachel turned to her nephew. "So, are you looking forward to the wedding? Nervous about making a speech? Don't worry, I'll help you write it, and there won't be much of a crowd. Mostly family."

Marvin turned away, spoke in a soft voice. "Do you think my mother was a good wife to my father? Did they love each other?"

Rachel kept her eyes on the road. She was trying to enter the stream of traffic on the street that led from the parking lot to the thruway. "What brought that up?"

"One of Batya's friends came by last week when she was inspecting the construction in the kitchen. I heard Batya tell her that now everything would be strictly kosher. 'Not like with that other one. Imagine a wife who couldn't be bothered keeping a proper Jewish household,' she said. Well, just more proof that she didn't really care about Harvey, didn't understand what was important to him. No one will ever accuse me of not doing everything to keep my husband happy. We're going to have a blessed home.'"

"I'd just come home from practice. Batya didn't know I was there, didn't know I could hear her."

Rachel didn't reply right away. She was seething. *That woman needs to learn that children are always around when you don't need them to be, and they hear all the things you don't want them to hear.*

The driver behind Rachel was annoyed that it was taking her so long to get on to the road and blew his horn. "Be quiet, you *momser,*" said Rachel. "You're not going anyplace so important that I should risk getting into an accident for you."

Marvin smiled. "Almost all the curse words I know are Yiddish."

"It's a bad habit. I'm not proud that I spoke that way."

"I remember hearing Mama and Papa yelling sometimes.

Sometimes they cursed in Yiddish. Not sure what they were yelling about."

Rachel took her eyes off the road, glanced at her nephew. She didn't know anything about arguments between Elaine and Harvey.

"Everyone fights once in a while," she said. "It doesn't mean anything. I've heard you fighting with your cousins, and I know you care for them. The other day I saw you throw a basketball at another boy, and then you told me you're still friends."

Rachel didn't say anything for a few minutes; she kept her eyes on the road, concentrating on merging onto the highway while she thought about Elaine and Harvey.

Elaine was almost 30 when her family settled in America, she knew people called her 'the spinster Rosen girl.' She knew she was plain, that Harvey had approached her only because her family had money. She knew her brothers didn't really like him, they had accepted him and taken him into the business because the family thought he might be Elaine's last chance.

Elaine believed that if she didn't marry Harvey, she would become the maiden aunt who lived with one of her brothers, resented by her sisters-in-law. Better she should marry Harvey and have her own household.

Unexpectedly, Elaine grew fond of her husband. She enjoyed his scholarly mind and the respect he showed her even though they disagreed about many things. She liked to listen to him explain the holy books, and he liked having an attentive audience. By the end of their first year of marriage Elaine began to blossom. She joined her sisters-in-law at the beauty parlor, found clothes that flattered her and learned to put on make-up.

When she was safely cruising the highway Rachel turned back

to Marvin. "Did you ever see your mother's ruby earrings?" she asked. "They look like red flowers."

"Yeah, I know which ones you mean. Sometimes, when no one else was around, mama would ask me to get them. They're in her top dresser drawer. She'd look at them for a few minutes, smile and read a paper inside the box. Then I'd put them away."

Rachel nodded. She was glad Marvin knew that the earrings were important to Elaine. She wondered how he'd react to the rest of the story.

"And did you ever hear anything about your mother being pregnant with another baby?" she said. "Before Rebecca was born."

Marvin turned from the window and stared at his aunt. "My folks had another kid? I have an older brother? Or sister? Where are they?"

Rachel met Marvin's eyes. "No, no, nothing like that," she said firmly. "There's only you and Rebecca. No one else. The two of you were all your mama and papa ever wanted, and they loved you both very much. However, life is complicated."

Rachel explained that soon after she was married Elaine became pregnant. She was thrilled. So was Harvey. Together they made elaborate plans for the baby. "But then, in her third month, your mama lost the baby. Such things happen, they're no one's fault," said Rachel slowly. "The doctor said she could have other children, but your mama was very upset. Do you know what depressed means?"

"Yeah, it's when you're very sad."

"That's right. She was sad and unhappy. She was tired a lot and not interested in going out and doing things."

Rachel vividly remembered that time. When Elaine wasn't sleeping she was crying or just sitting in the living room, staring straight ahead. She stopped taking care of herself, her skin became dry, her hair was frizzy and she neglected the house.

"Seeing your mama so unhappy made your papa unhappy," Rachel said, looking at Marvin. "Then one day he came home with a small turquoise jewelry box tied with a white ribbon."

Inside the box Elaine found the earrings, two small roses cut from rubies, nestled in white silk. Rachel remembered Elaine as she showed the earrings to the rest of the family how she beamed as she showed them the slip of paper also inside the box.

Written in Harvey's careful script were the words:
A Wife of Virtue and Noble Character,
Who Can Find her?
For Her Worth Is Far Above Rubies

"Your father told your mother that when he saw those earrings he thought of that proverb and realized he was the lucky man who had found such a precious woman. Your mother looked at the earrings, read the prayer and smiled for the first time in a long time."

Elaine had once confided in Rachel that when the Rosens criticized Harvey because he wasn't a good businessman, or made fun of his religious ways, she always remembered her earrings and reminded herself of the benefits of having a husband who knew the Bible.

"Within a year she was pregnant again, Rebecca was born without complications, and then, a few years later you came along, a wonderful baby boy. In those years your mama was always smiling. And whenever she entertained or went someplace special, she always wore her sparkling earrings.

Rachel watched a large grin sweep over Marvin's face. "Yeah," he said. "Mama had a great smile."

Rachel wanted to stop the car, brush his hair out of his eyes and give Marvin a large hug and kiss. But she didn't want to embarrass him and just kept driving.

They were both quiet for a little while. Then Marvin started to talk about the reorganization of the little league.

Rachel dropped Marvin at his house and watched him go inside with the packages. She went into her house and startled her children by giving each one a big hug.

"Did something happen?" asked Kenny as he squirmed away.

"I just wanted you to know I love each of you," said Rachel. "And I'm glad you didn't destroy the house while you were here alone." The boys looked at her for a moment and then returned to their game.

Rachel went upstairs, closed her bedroom door so she wouldn't be overheard, called Helen and told her about the conversation with Marvin.

"Whenever I saw those earrings I'd think, whoever would have guessed Harvey could be such a romantic?" said Helen. "And I'd wonder, what ever happened to the man who bought such a present, who wrote such a note."

"Who knows what really goes on between couples?" Rachel replied. "Most of what Marvin remembers about his mother is tied up with her sickness. He deserves memories of happily married parents, to be able to think about loving gestures from his father."

"You did a wise thing today," said Helen.

That evening, Harvey called Rachel. "I want to talk about the clothes you bought for Marvin."

"No need to thank me. You know I'm always glad to help. Marvin's going to be the best-looking young man at that wedding, and that's coming from the mother of other young men who'll be at the celebration."

"Yes, I'm sure he'll look good, but that's not why I'm calling. I saw the price tags on the items he brought home and know there are more clothes in the shop being altered, probably at an extra charge. I wondered if it was necessary to spend so much. Can some of these things be returned? Maybe they didn't start the alterations yet and you can cancel the whole order.

"It'll only be a small gathering, no need to make such a fuss. Couldn't you find someone to make a few adjustments on the clothes he has? Or borrow a suit from another boy?"

Rachel couldn't believe what she was hearing. She'd expected praise, gratitude, appreciation. "He's your only son, Harvey, the only one you'll ever have. And you're very lucky to have such a fine boy. You should be counting your blessings, not price tags."

"The purpose of the marriage ceremony is to sanctify a union, not display yourself and your children like prize animals," said Harvey. "Thank God I'm marrying a woman who respects holiness, doesn't waste her time worrying about nonsense."

Rachel took a deep breath and spoke very slowly and carefully. "The order cannot be cancelled. Marvin's suit will be ready next week. I'll drop it off along with the final bill, and you will pay me back. Every penny. You hear me, Harvey? The matter is closed. No more discussion. Every penny. You owe me."

24.

HERE COMES THE BRIDE

It was a small wedding, held at the Orthodox *shul* where Batya's father had once presided. The Rosens were all there, fidgeting throughout the ceremony, which was conducted almost exclusively in Hebrew.

Men sat in one area, women in another. Everyone dressed conservatively. Helen and Rachel wore calf-length, long-sleeved dresses and hats that covered their hair. The men wore *taliths,* dark suits and yarmulkes. They gave the newlyweds large checks.

Although children from a first marriage don't always attend their religious parents' remarriage, Helen and Rachel had insisted that Marvin be there and he looked terrific in his new suit.

After the ceremony there was a small reception in the *shul's* conference room, lots of cakes and wine, people sang traditional songs when Harvey and Batya walked in, men and women mingled together and made toasts but there was no dancing.

Rebecca wasn't there.

She had written to Harvey and Batya, sent her congratulations and, with her aunt's help, an ornate bowl that matched her mother's good china. She had told Helen she wasn't ready to face the event. "I'll get there, but I'm taking baby steps."

Bubbe Golda didn't attend either. She had no interest in watching Elaine's husband marry another woman.

Golda had become frailer in the past year and rarely left her apartment. However, she insisted on meeting Batya before she married into the family. No one remembered telling *Bubbe* that Harvey was getting married. No one was surprised she knew.

Batya and Harvey had arranged to meet Golda at her apartment a few weeks before the wedding. One of Batya's friends, a Jew from Poland like the Rosens, gave her a recipe for pastry popular in their region, and Batya spent the previous day making *kolaczki*, fried bowtie cookies filled with jam. She baked three batches before she finally made one she declared perfect. Batya packed the offering in a slightly dented baking pan to make sure there was no confusion about it being homemade.

As Harvey and Batya approached Golda's apartment, they were surprised to see her sitting outside on her bench. "It was such a nice day. I thought we should all get some air," said the old lady.

"What a wonderful idea," said Batya, although it was a little cool for her taste. She would have worn a heavy sweater if she'd known they were meeting outside. Golda looked perfectly comfortable in a wool kerchief, flannel housecoat, thick socks and worn leather slippers.

Harvey made the introductions, and Batya gave the cookies to Golda, who immediately opened the container. "How nice of you," she said. "I can't wait to try one. Harvey, go get some plates and napkins. Maybe a little schnapps, too. Batya and I will stay here and get acquainted."

"You want me to get those things now?" said Harvey. "From your apartment?"

"The ones in your house are much nicer. Get those."

Harvey glanced at Batya. She shrugged. The request was

peculiar, but she wasn't going to start her relationship with the old lady by contradicting her.

"I'll be right back," said Harvey.

As soon as Harvey left, Golda plunged her hand into the container and fingered through the assortment. "You didn't make any prune ones? Don't worry, I like cherry almost as much."

Golda popped the whole cookie into her mouth and chewed vigorously. "Please have one. They're very good even if you did forget to sprinkle on powdered sugar. Here, try this one, it looks tasty." Golda pushed her finger into a bright green cookie and some of the lime jelly squirted out.

Batya picked up the cookie and nibbled it, getting crumbs on her suede skirt. She took a deep breath. "I want you to know how happy I am to be joining your family. I've heard so many wonderful things about your dear Elaine, may she rest in peace. I know it'll be hard to fill her shoes. But I'm going to try as hard as I can."

Golda looked at Batya's feet. "Elaine's feet were smaller than yours. If you try to squeeze into her shoes, you'll get blisters."

Batya glanced at her feet. She moved her legs under the bench.

"I hear you're divorced. Well, those things happen," said Golda. "And you've never had children?"

"No, I wasn't blessed that way. But I've always loved children. I'm very excited to be a mother to Marvin and Rebecca. Maybe not exactly a mother, but close. I hope the Lord answers all of our prayers and things go well."

Golda bit into another cookie. Some of the apricot jelly remained on her lips and she slowly licked it off.

"Oh look, there's Harvey," said Batya.

The women watched him come down the front stoop of his house next door carrying a shopping bag.

"He's still a good-looking man. Quite a catch," said Golda.

"Although not much of a provider, not like my boys."

Batya quietly reached into the tin for another cookie.

Golda patted her shoulder. "Don't worry, just take good care of my grandchildren and I'll make sure my boys do right by you. From Marvin you won't have much trouble; he needs attention and affection, give him that and you'll be okay. My Rebecca will be a little more difficult. You'll have to try harder. But she's worth it."

"I promise I'll do the very best I can," said Batya as Harvey approached. Clinking sounds came from his bag. "I brought dessert dishes, napkins, some wine and wine glasses," said Harvey. "Now we can have a fancy picnic right here on the bench."

"That was very kind," said Golda. "But I've decided it's a little chilly to sit here any longer. And it's almost time for my dinner. I'll take the wine and drink a toast to you while I'm eating."

Harvey and Batya stared as Golda got up, reached into Harvey's bag, pulled out the bottle of wine and put it under her arm. She held the cookie tin in the other hand. Then she nodded and smiled at them. "I'm sorry I'm not strong enough to attend your wedding. I wish you both lots of luck."

Golda turned to Batya. "Remember, a little extra sweetness always helps," she said. "I'll send you some of my rock candy next time I make it."

Then she shuffled back to her apartment.

25.

HAPPY BIRTHDAY

Rebecca turned 17 a few months after her father's wedding, and Saul, Helen, Marvin and Sarah came to the school to celebrate her birthday. Rebecca hadn't accrued many demerits recently, so she was allowed off school grounds for the occasion.

Marvin arrived at his aunt's house anxious to get moving. "Let's get going," he kept saying, trying to hurry everyone into the car. "Rebecca's waiting for us. I haven't seen her in a long time."

"In a few minutes," said Helen. "We're all eager to see her."

Helen was putting Rebecca's birthday presents in their car's trunk. She'd bought her niece a tape deck and Sarah had bought tapes, spending a lot of time trying to figure out what type of music Rebecca might want. She selected *Jailhouse Rock,* by Elvis Presley and *Folsom Prison Blues* by Johnny Cash.

"Let me teach you something," Saul said to Marvin. "Trying to hurry a woman just slows them down. Don't worry, I'll hit the gas as soon as we get on the road."

Finally they took off and Marvin squirmed in his seat all the way there, groaning loudly when they had to slow down because of construction. When they reached the school he was the first one out of the car, hugged Rebecca who'd come outside to meet them and then stood shyly next to her, unable to think of anything to say.

They drove directly to the restaurant where Marvin insisted Rebecca open his present first. It was a beautiful blue cashmere sweater. Rebecca hugged her brother and kissed his cheek while he grinned.

Helen picked up the sweater and examined it carefully. "Thick cashmere from Bloomingdale's," she whispered to Saul. "Costs a pretty penny."

"What a beautiful color," Rebecca said to Marvin.

"Yeah, Batya brought home three blue sweaters, and I had to tell her which one matched your eyes," Marvin said. "I chipped in, wrapped the box and got the card."

"You actually know what color eyes I have?" said Rebecca. "You're usually in such a daze I'm surprised the sweater isn't polka dot."

"Your eyes are easy to remember," Marvin said. "I'm glad Batya wasn't trying to match your hair. I never know what color that's going to be."

Rebecca playfully punched Marvin, and he softly hit her back. They grinned at each other.

Helen turned to Marvin. "You did a good job helping Batya pick out that lovely sweater," she said. "It's nice you're getting along so well at home."

"Yeah, things are okay. Most of the time," said Marvin.

Sarah had started talking to Rebecca, and Marvin was trying to hold a conversation with his aunt while he emptied the salt shaker into Rebecca's glass, a common prank when they were little. But Rebecca quickly put her hand over the glass. "Just try it," she whispered. "You'll wind up with a saltwater shampoo."

Marvin shrugged, put down the saltshaker and turned back to Helen. "But you should have heard my dad yell when he saw the price of those sweaters."

"He's mad Batya buys a nice gift for his daughter?" asked Saul.

"I don't think he would have minded one sweater," said Marvin. "But he said he knew that when she took the other two back to the store she'd use the refund to get something for herself. Batya said next time he could do his own shopping. That's when I closed my door, so I couldn't hear anything else."

"Smart boy," said Saul. "Don't get involved."

Marvin got busy studying the menu.

"If you want a cheeseburger, no one will tell Batya or Papa," said Rebecca. "In fact, since it's my birthday I say we all have cheeseburgers. Maybe even bacon cheeseburgers."

"Sounds good," Sarah said.

"We'll have that too, right Saul?" said Helen. "But for me just a regular burger. No bacon. And no French fries. I'm watching my figure."

Sarah sighed. She knew her mom would steal fries from her plate.

When the food arrived, Helen leaned over to her niece. "You know, Rebecca when you come home, you'll be expected to keep kosher."

"I can handle that, it's not such a big deal," Rebecca said. "I don't really care what I eat. I've been working hard with Bill. I'm stronger now, smarter. Staying away from cheeseburgers isn't a big deal. I hope Papa and this Batya are happy together. Really. I'm glad my father has someone. He really took it hard when my mom died. I'm going to invite them to visit soon."

"I'm glad to hear that," said Helen, patting her niece's hand. "Very glad. Every day I pray that this school is the right place for you."

Rebecca leaned over and kissed Helen on the cheek. "Stop

worrying. You'll get wrinkles. Then what good will all the dieting do?"

"Rebecca is right. No more serious talk, this is a party," said Saul. He took a big bite of his burger and got ketchup on his shirt. Helen dipped her napkin into the water glass and wiped off her husband.

Then it was time for dessert. "I'll have the Tropical Fruit Bonanza," Helen said. That was a banana split and two scoops of strawberry ice cream, covered with pineapple and cherry syrup and shredded coconut. "No whipped cream or nuts," she told the waiter.

Sarah rolled my eyes. "That's on your new diet?" she asked.

Helen shrugged. "Fruit is healthy. Fiber is important."

Helen reached across the table and took hold of Marvin's hand. "And I'm glad it's not too hard for you to follow Batya's rules."

"Everything is fine," he said, pulling away his hand. "In the beginning, I got the silverware all mixed up. The meat and the dairy plates are different colors, but all the silverware has similar patterns. Now I've learned the difference. I know what I'm doing."

He turned to Rebecca. "You should see the size of our kitchen. There are meat and milk regular dishes, each has its own silverware. Then there are the fancy dishes and silverware for Shabbos dinner. Now she's talking about getting special dishes for Passover. At first Papa brought home dishes that he got at discount. Batya didn't like those plates. She wanted to go shopping with her friends for dishes. She got so mad she threw one of the dishes on the floor. It didn't break. That got her even madder. She yelled that only cheap plates don't shatter.

"When they get mad, Batya and Papa stop speaking English. He yells in Yiddish. She yells in a combination of Yiddish and

Hebrew. She talks really fast, really loud. When that happens, I go to my room."

Marvin looked down at the table and started playing with his ice cream. "Anyway," he said. "A few days later all the dishes Papa brought home were gone and eventually new ones were delivered. And they have special shelves where they belong. Everyone is calm now."

Rebecca stopped eating. She stared at Marvin. "Is Papa building cabinets for the dishes? Is he working in the basement?" She remembered past conversations about Harvey's woodworking. Remembered catching glimpses of bruises on Marvin. "Does he make you go downstairs? Make you help?"

Marvin stopped swirling his ice cream.

"No, no, everything's fine. Really. No problem. Plenty of shelves in the new kitchen. I can keep track of where everything belongs. Really, everything's okay." Marvin made more swirls in his ice cream. "But I miss you," he said softly.

Just then a group of waiters came over carrying a cake with flickering candles and sang "Happy Birthday" to Rebecca. Several people in the restaurant joined in. Rebecca smiled, closed her eyes and blew out the candles.

Sarah wanted to ask what Rebecca had wished for, but that wasn't allowed.

When they got back to the school, Helen told Saul to take Marvin for a walk while she and Sarah went to Rebecca's room.

As soon as Marvin was out of sight, Helen turned to Rebecca. "What did you mean about the woodshop?" she asked. "Does something happen downstairs that shouldn't happen?"

Harvey's house had a large basement, an unfinished room with cement walls divided by a sliding plastic partition. The smaller section of the room smelled like laundry soap and dampness from the washer and dryer along one wall. The larger section had metal shelves where Harvey neatly stacked his tools. It smelled of freshly cut wood.

When Elaine was alive, sometimes Marvin or Rebecca would help their mother carry laundry downstairs. If they wandered over to where Harvey's woodshop was set up, their mother would scold them, pointing out the many sharp, dangerous things there. The children stared at the saws and nails and long, skinny pieces of wood that made a whistling sound if you snapped them like a whip.

Helen remembered Rachel telling her about some scratches she'd seen on Marvin's arms. "He said he'd been trying to build something for science class with his father's tools and he messed up, broke something. He told me Harvey got mad at him for touching the tools. Really mad. I'm not sure what it was all about. Marvin wouldn't say anything else. He seemed sorry he'd said anything and left my house before he'd finished playing monopoly with my boys. And he was winning."

Helen didn't remember hearing anything else about the wood shop. Shortly after the incident Rachel had described, Elaine had taken a turn for the worst, and there was no time to think about Harvey's carpentry.

Rebecca didn't reply to Helen's question, so she asked it again, more forcefully. "Rebecca, I need to know. Is there something going on in that basement? Something that shouldn't be happening?"

"Maybe," Rebecca answered after a while. "I don't know. Marvin's too big to pick up and shake these days. Papa makes threats. There's lots of stuff down there, all types of boards, some have nails in them. I can't be sure."

"Sure of what?" Helen asked.

"You know Marvin, he's so athletic. He gets bruises. A couple of times I suspected my dad caused them. That was when I was running around almost every night. I had plenty of my own issues to fight with my father about. Marvin swore nothing was wrong. Maybe he did get hit with a baseball or get tackled too hard. I don't know what really happened. The older Marvin gets, the quieter he gets. He's very private. He's not like me, he'll never act out."

Helen ran her hands through her hair. "Aunt Rachel and I, you know we made sure your father and Batya didn't move away when they got married because we wanted to be able to keep an eye on Marvin and you. But now you're both too big for us to watch over all the time. Obviously getting bigger didn't mean you'd gotten smarter, not smart enough to let us know when something was wrong in that house. How come no one ever said anything about what was going on in that basement? What may still be going on there?"

"Look, I'm not sure," said Rebecca. "Maybe nothing is going on. Maybe my dad and Batya just yell at him when he mixes up the milk and meat silverware. Sounds like Marvin has learned to stay out of the way when plates are flying."

Helen was still upset when they got downstairs. Marvin and Saul were standing in front of Rebecca's dorm, cleaning their shoes. "You have to use one of your good handkerchiefs for that?" she said. "You still don't know enough to carry tissues when you walk around here? Now there's going to be duck shit mixed in with my laundry."

Saul didn't answer. He took the dirty handkerchief and threw it into the garbage can.

Everyone hugged goodbye and got into the car. Marvin kept looking out the back window until the school was no longer visible. "Doesn't Rebecca look terrific?" he said. "No one has a sister as smart and good looking as mine. I wish she was home again."

That night, as they were getting ready for bed, Helen asked Saul if he knew anything about Harvey's woodworking.

"I've never seen it, but I'll bet he's got quite a set up in his basement," Saul said. "He's always taking wood from our shop, I think sometimes he's also helped himself to some of the power tools. I was going to say something, but it's not worth fighting about.

"A few weeks ago Tony, the carpenter, was out sick. I told Harvey I bet he could do a better job than Tony, given all of his experience, and I'd send him over to the job, but I was afraid of getting into trouble with the union.

"Harvey didn't smile. The man has no sense of humor."

Helen nodded. "I don't think what's going on in that place is funny at all."

26.

BATYA'S FRIENDS

Sitting beside him in the car, on their way to a party of her old friends, Batya looked at Harvey as he concentrated on the traffic. He was a good-looking man, everyone said so. Much better looking than that good-for-nothing who'd left her with her impoverished father so he could live in the middle of nowhere and have a liter with some fertile dummy. As soon as she'd met Harvey, Batya knew this was a man she could marry. She was ready to start a new life, and if that life involved a man who was Conservative but would respect her Orthodox orientation, so be it. Let him drive his big car on Saturday for business if that business provided the comfortable lifestyle she was going to enjoy.

Batya had delayed introducing Harvey to her friends until after they were married. She had been worried something would happen at the last minute and the wedding would be cancelled. Almost no one who would be at this party had been at their ceremony.

She believed many of the women in her community had pitied her for not having a husband, and, at the same time, were jealous. Few of the women were as educated as she, few shared her desire to acquire knowledge. They certainly weren't happy when she made friends with husbands who attended classes with her. These women often tried to fix her up, always with a poor, starving scholar, someone who would expect her to pinch pennies in order to support his studies.

"Thanks, but no thanks," Batya said. She had had enough of that when she kept house for her father.

Since her wedding she'd been calling a few friends to tell them about her fabulous new life. They had spread the word. And tonight, everyone would see with their own eyes how well she was doing. Tonight, she would tell these women who still lived on the run down Lower East Side streets about her new home and introduce them to her husband, a good-looking man, who drove a fancy car, wore expensive clothes and was as much of a scholar as any of their husbands.

Batya was glad she'd bought her Harvey a new, expensive shirt that fit him so well. Since she became Harvey's wife, she'd begun shopping in high class stores. She'd kept her eyes open, watched what was purchased by people who were comfortable in these stores and learned that the most expensive merchandise was often the simplest. And tonight, Harvey looked like a prosperous husband should look.

She hoped she looked as good. It had been hard to decide what to wear. Something elegant to proclaim her new economic status. But nothing that looked like she was trying to show off. Something a little daring to show that she had become a modern woman, but not so daring that anyone thought she'd lost her faith.

She settled on a tan calf-length skirt, long enough to be appropriate for an Orthodox woman. But it would be a rare Orthodox woman who had a skirt made of ultra-suede and would pair it with high heeled boots that clung to her trim legs. Batya also wore a dark green cashmere sweater. She'd got it when she returned the two sweaters Marvin had rejected for Rebecca's birthday.

Batya's sweater would have looked better with some pearls or a gold chain. Batya had inherited a thick golden rope from her mother but had been forced to sell it a few years earlier to cover a rent check. There was a beautiful strand of pearls in Elaine's jewelry box, but Harvey didn't look happy when he saw Batya going through Elaine's things. She wanted him to be in a good mood for this party, so she didn't wear the pearls.

That Elaine had certainly had some nice things, Batya thought. She couldn't understand why Harvey wouldn't want her to wear the jewelry. It was just lying there. Gathering dust. Better it should get some use. Batya assumed Harvey would get her some nice jewelry for her birthday next month; she was dropping hints. She'd been upset when Helen and Rachel revealed Harvey didn't have nearly as much money as she'd thought he had, but if Harvey had been able to be so generous with his first wife there was no reason for him to get stingy with his second.

"Look," Harvey said as they drove to the party. "There's where my friend Morty used to live, his mother's sister was right next door. And Orchard Street is right over there. Morris and Saul and I used to take our wives and children down here on a Sunday every fall so they could get bargains on new winter coats. Then we'd all go out to eat at one of the kosher restaurants on Delancey Street. Those were first class places. We should come here to eat sometime, maybe with some of your friends."

Harvey had wondered why Batya didn't introduce him to her scholarly friends before. Why hadn't they been at his wedding? Of course, they had gotten married very soon after they met, not much time to meet each other's friends. At their age who needed a long courtship? But still. He was a scholar, too. She knew that. He was looking forward to an evening with men who talked about the world of ideas.

They parked the car and walked past a row of tenements to Batya's friends' apartment in a decaying building.

"It still smells of *Yiddishkeit* around here. Like it did when I first arrived in this country and lived nearby," said Harvey happily. "The joyful smell of happy Jewish families celebrating that they're alive and carrying on Jewish traditions."

"Well, some of them are still here, still Jewish, glad they're alive," said Batya, stopping in front of an old building. "But a lot of the people you're imagining have moved away, enjoying their Jewish lives in New Jersey, Westchester, the Bronx and Long Island like you and your in-laws." She pressed a bell, and they went inside.

Batya immediately started up the stairs, but Harvey hesitated, stopped and took a deep breath. Instead of the familiar odor of pickles and garlic, fatty meat and smoked fish he was expecting, Harvey smelled sharp peppers, sausage and spiced rice, and heard Spanish music playing through a doorway. He silently followed Batya up a steep, uncarpeted staircase. Many of the hall lights were out, the plaster peeling.

After three flights, Batya paused, patted her hair and straightened her skirt. Harvey caught his breath, reached into his pocket, pulled out a yarmulke and placed it on his head. Batya smiled. "I don't wear it all the time, but since we've been together, I always have it with me," said Harvey. Batya put her arm into his, and they strode through the door.

The room was jammed. There were people talking in English, Hebrew and Yiddish. A couple in the corner were having an animated conversation in Hungarian. There were clean-shaven men and men with unkempt beards and long *payes*. There was some sort of music playing, maybe a folk song; Harvey couldn't tell. He heard a baby crying.

Someone spotted them and called out, "the newlyweds have arrived. I'd say, 'carry them around the room on chairs' but in this crowd we'd never manage. Let's just have a song and a toast."

Someone put a glass of whiskey in Harvey's hand, glasses all over the room were filled, and everyone yelled, "*L'Chaim*" and began humming Yiddish melodies.

Batya started introducing Harvey. The men shook his hand and clapped him on the back. The women smiled at Harvey, hugged Batya and said they'd missed her. Batya went to get a plate of food for Harvey and wound up in the center of a circle of women all talking at once. Everyone had heard something about Batya's new life and wanted to know more.

"Looks like you got yourself some catch. No wonder you kept him to yourself."

"So, tell us. How's married life? It certainly agrees with you."

"Why did you stop going to school? Are you coming back?"

"What's your new house like? Are you really surrounded by your in-laws?"

"You're staying in the same house he lived in with his first wife? Whose idea was that?"

Batya laughed and smiled at her friends. She apologized for not being in touch, told them she and Harvey had been getting to know each other, and before she knew it, she'd been planning the wedding. It was a small wedding. But a lovely, joyous occasion. She'd send pictures.

"How are you adjusting to life among people who aren't religious?" asked her friend Chana, raising her voice so she was heard above the rest of the group. Not all of her friends were strictly Orthodox, but Chana was. Before she'd met Harvey, Batya and Chana had felt superior to the women in their group who didn't follow the religious rules.

"It's not as hard as I had thought," said Batya. "I overlook some things, like the fact that he drives on Saturday. That's necessary for his business. But when he walks through the door he wants a real Jewish home, and that's what we have.

"I don't want to criticize the dead, but his first wife, that Elaine, she failed him. I've seen pictures of her, certainly nothing to look at, and not much of a homemaker. When I went into that kitchen and saw only one set of dishes, saw the whole family, the rest of the Rosens, walking in and out of the house with uncovered heads, all I could think was, what kind of home did this woman make for such a learned man? As soon as he popped the question, I knew what I had to do. I ripped out the whole kitchen, bought new appliances, new dishes, everything the best. No arguments from my Harvey. He appreciates what I provide. And no one walks into our house bareheaded. They show respect or they stay outside. On a marble shelf in the entryway, the yarmulkes are stacked like soup bowls, available to everyone."

"The house isn't the only thing you've spruced up," said Chana. "Is that a new wig? And that's a new skirt and new shoes?"

Batya ran her hand over her outfit, smoothing imaginary wrinkles. "It's important for me to look fashionable for a man in Harvey's position. But the wig is one of my old ones, just remodeled." Batya smiled. "Yes, just like the house."

Batya glanced around and made sure that all the women surrounding her were wearing wigs. Some of the women, even in this neighborhood, didn't cover their hair.

"Let me tell you," Batya added, "non-observant women don't know how jealous they should be of the Orthodox. Not only do you feel better about yourself when you obey the rules of the Torah and dress modestly, but you look better. I was surprised to see that, in between trips to the beauty parlor, my new sisters-in-law are frequently a mess. I don't know how they have the nerve to walk in the street. On weekends they may have fancy blonde curls, but during the week they look like they stuck their fingers in an electric socket. They spend their money to have hair teased like a beach ball and every day it deflates a little more so that by the end of the week you want to offer a bicycle pump. And frequently you can see the line of grey creeping up from hairlines, like a ring around a bathtub no one's bothered to wash. It's no wonder their men work so hard. Who wants to come home to that?"

"And you like being surrounded by all of them?"

"We thought about moving but decided to stay in Harvey's old house because he didn't want to disrupt his son's education by making him change schools," Batya explained. "He's such a good father, he and Marvin are so close. That boy could be a scholar like his father, but he needs a woman's encouragement. I don't know why those Rosen women never bothered to help with the children. Marvin was running around on Shabbos playing ball, watching TV, and no one cared. It broke his father's heart. I found him a new little league with observant boys for next season. He's thrilled I'm going to be able to attend his games."

Batya laughed. "I haven't admitted to Marvin that before I met him, I'd never seen a ballgame. I've been studying the sport so when the season starts I won't be an embarrassment."

"Speaking of education," Chana said. "We miss you in women's study groups. You were one of the stars."

"I miss my studies," said Batya. "But I'm busy with my new life. I'm not sure what my studies will be now. Night school is out of the question; I need to be there when Harvey gets home. After all, I'm a wife now. Maybe we'll study together, maybe I'll take classes during the day. At least I no longer have to worry about how to pay tuition. I'll have to see. I've never been a mother before. I don't want to neglect the children."

"What about the daughter?" someone asked. "My sister-in-law's niece went to Science High School. I hear they threw her out, that she's a troublemaker."

"I guess everyone knows about her," sighed Batya. "A motherless girl whose aunts turned their back on her. Sent her away, away from her loving father. I'm going to visit her soon, let her know that there's a good home waiting for her. I'm certainly going to try my best for her. Harvey knows that, and he's grateful."

Across the room, Harvey was wandering around, smiling at strangers who were smiling at him. The party was mainly in the living room of a shabby two-bedroom apartment. In this room were several over-stuffed chairs, a sagging couch with a brightly colored slipcover and a large desk with a packed bookcase above it. The desk was covered by a plastic tablecloth where bowls of chopped liver, herring salad and gefilte fish were placed next to raw vegetables and crackers. A variety of cakes and cookies, whiskey, wine and sodas were on a bridge table.

The walls were beige and hadn't been painted in a while. The scuffed wood floor was covered by a few imitation oriental rugs. Harvey peeked into the other rooms where people were sitting on beds, leaning against dressers while they talked. Everyone was animated, enthusiastic. In the larger bedroom, there were child-size bunk beds and children's toys stacked against the wall. Two twin beds and a huge wardrobe took up most of the smaller bedroom.

Someone slapped Harvey on the back, wished him *mazel tov* and put a plate of food in one of his hands. A few minutes later there was another glass of whiskey in the other. He had no idea how to manipulate the food. There was no place to sit, no place to put the plates. Harvey didn't care; he was having a wonderful time listening to the conversations around him. He heard someone mention Spinoza, Maimonides and other sages.

"Every day I read in the papers about another Vietnam protest. There's always so much violence, and my son is right in the middle of it. You think the hippies will find a ben Zakkai, someone to keep the idea of living in peace alive before they're jailed or drafted or the police bash their heads in?" one man was saying to another.

Harvey allowed himself to be pushed aside before he could hear the other man's answer. He would have liked to hear more of this conversation, but worried that if he stood too close the men would ask his opinion. Harvey knew ben Zakkai had been a famous pacifist around the time that Jerusalem fell to Rome, but he didn't remember the rabbi's writings.

How amazing to be in a room with people who make such connections, thought Harvey. This is where I belong.

Someone else was complaining about a complicated change in the tax code. "Unless I can find a CPA who's descended from Rabbi Akiba, I'm going to keep getting violations," the man said as he spread chopped liver onto a cracker.

That, Harvey understood. Akiba had organized and systematized biblical text so it could be more easily understood. He should tell Morris and Saul to hire Akiba the next time they complained about city regulations, he thought, smiling. Harvey shook his head. No, that wouldn't amuse them. They wouldn't know what he was talking about.

Batya found Harvey in the middle of the room, both arms full. She got him a chair and cleared off a space at a small table where he could put his food. With Batya standing next to him, even more people started coming up to Harvey and introducing themselves. They seemed to know all about him, or all about someone they thought was him.

"Did you arrive in a limousine?"

"I also lost my wife to a terrible disease when my children were small. Today I work in that hospital as a volunteer. It helps. Now that you've found a new wife, maybe you should remember the old one with a contribution to our hospital."

"Do you have any tips about the stock market?"

Harvey looked at Batya, confused. "These people think I'm a Rothschild," he said. "What's going on?"

"They're just being foolish," she said. "Ignore them. Here comes someone I know you'll want to talk to."

Harvey noticed a heavy-set man determinedly making his way across the room. The man had thinning, grey hair and heavy eyebrows, so thick that long black hairs curled up toward his wrinkled forehead. He was wearing a faded cardigan in a mustard color that made him look sallow.

Batya smiled broadly. All of a sudden, Harvey knew who it was, put down his food, got up and stepped in front of Batya so he could hug this man.

"So, Heshy recognizes his old friend Zvi from Przemyslany," the man said, tightly embracing Harvey and then stepping back so they could look at each other. "It's been a long time my friend, a long time since we were the brightest young men in our province, a time when instead of hugging we fought each other to be known as the cleverest student in Galicia and beyond."

Harvey had tears in his eyes. "Of course I remember," he said and turned to Batya. "We were Yeshiva *buchers,* the best students in our respective schools, each vying to outdo the other, to make a name for ourselves in front of the top rabbis."

She smiled and nodded. "I've heard the story," Batya said.

"Who could have predicted that two young men like us would one day be old men embracing in a faraway country?" said Zvi. "That we would be known, not as Hershel and Zvi, religious leaders, but as Harvey and Zach, one a successful entrepreneur and principal of the prosperous Rosen Corporation and the other a member of the largest hardware store on the Lower East Side."

"Don't be so modest, Zach," said Batya. "You know you're not just a hardware store employee. Soon you'll have your degree and maybe will be able to get a job teaching at a university. Then you'll be able to finish your research, make a name for yourself as one of the leading Jewish scholars of the New Testament."

"A Jew studying the New Testament?" said Harvey. "That's a real thing?"

Zach laughed. "You've fallen behind, my old friend. Do you think Jews can only study the same things we studied in Europe? This is America. Times have changed. So have we. Do you think I ever imagined I'd be studying next to a female in a college level course on ethics and religion? If a woman ever tried to enroll in our old yeshiva it would be a scandal, everyone would think she was crazy. But that's how I met your lovely new wife. We sat next to each other the very first year I started to take night classes at City University. Let me tell you, I was relieved that if I was going to study next to a female, at least it was a religious woman. It wasn't long before I realized that this particular female was my equal when it came to learning."

Batya gave a small smile, trying to look modest.

"Since we lived in the same neighborhood, Batya and I got into the habit of taking the subway home together after class," he said. "One day she confided she'd met a man she was interested in and I soon realized she was talking about my old friend from Poland. Funny how it turns out. One day I'm studying with you, the next, I'm studying with your future wife."

Harvey turned to Batya. "How come you never told me you knew an old friend of mine?"

"I wanted it to be a surprise," she said.

Harvey looked at Batya, confused.

"Oh, there's Temima," she said suddenly, looking into the crowd. "I haven't had a chance to say hello to her. You two talk over old times, I'll be back soon."

"There aren't many serious female scholars; they have to support each other," said Zach, noticing Harvey's expression. "Although there are more every day."

"You should have been at our wedding," Harvey said. "If I'd known you were here, I would have made sure of that. I didn't even know you were in New York."

"That's okay," Zach said. "I understood it was a small gathering. If you invite one friend, you have to invite them all. To tell you the truth, my wife isn't as learned as Batya, and the two of them aren't very friendly. And anyway, I'm a pretty big group with my wife and my three children, and most people feel they also have to include my sister and her children when they invite me, since we're all so close."

"It's good you have your sister with you," said Harvey. "I lost all of my family in the War. All I have now are in-laws. And, of course, my children. And now there's Batya. So, tell me everything. Where do you live?"

Zach laughed again. "You're in my living room," he said. "I'm your host. And my sister is across the hall. My children are staying with her tonight. And that's my wife over there," he pointed to a very thin woman in a slightly faded flower-print dress that was too big. "She's the one refilling the bowls that are already full," said Zach. "We'll all be eating nothing but this stuff for the next week, but she wanted to be sure she had enough."

Harvey laughed. "Yes, my late wife, Elaine, she should rest in peace, was like that too, and her sisters-in-law are the same.

Batya and I haven't had a chance to entertain yet. We're redoing the kitchen, but as soon as the construction is finished, you'll be invited over. I'm sure Batya will overfill your plates."

"I don't know about her cooking, but that woman certainly has a top-quality brain. I thought she might become one of the first female Orthodox Jewish theologians," Zvi began to laugh. "Think how that would outrage all of the learned men in this community. Not an ordained rabbi of course, only the Reformed have female rabbis, but a torah scholar. Today there are women teaching religious topics in secular schools just like they had in the Middle Ages, like Deborah or one of Rashi's daughters."

"Something else I've never heard of," said Harvey. "You have to give me the name of a prominent woman writer in that area so I can buy a book for Batya. I've been trying to figure out what to get her for her birthday. That would be perfect."

Batya returned with a few other people who wanted to be introduced to Harvey. Zach stood nearby, explaining that he and Harvey had been close friends in Europe.

"You should join our study group," he said to Harvey. "A few of us get together every week or so and have friendly debates. We could use some new blood."

"Watch out for this guy," laughed one of the men, pointing at Zach. "He's a trickster. He'll maneuver you into the old Hillel versus Shammai argument. We all know Hillel's ideas prevailed, but Zvi keeps coming up with new theories."

"Don't worry, Heshy here, I mean Harvey, knows all my tricks," said Zach. "I wouldn't put it past him to come up with some point of view we haven't considered. What do you say, Harvey? We'll have fun. Like the old days."

Harvey looked at the men standing around him, men who had found a way in this new world to continue the studies they'd started in the old world. It had been a long time since he was surrounded by such men. Could he match their knowledge?

Maybe once. Not anymore.

"It sounds like a good time," said Harvey. "But it's a long ride to the Lower East Side from the Bronx, and this is my busy time at work. I don't know if I'd have the energy right now. Why don't I call you when things slow down?"

One of the men, a paunchy redhead whose faded shirt barely closed over his stomach, shook his head. "Yes, it's not easy to get from your big house to our tenements. We all know this. We've seen many people move away. Don't worry, we'll manage to keep our group together ourselves."

Harvey realized they were offended and thought he believed he was too good for them. He sighed and said nothing. It was better they should think he was a snob than to let them know he was concerned about keeping up with them, afraid they'd see he had wasted his education.

"You forget, Harvey doesn't need a bunch of old men like us to study with," said Zach, turning to Batya. "He's got a wife who knows as much as any of us. Maybe more."

"Yes, I know I've got a prize here," said Harvey with a smile. "Both a wife and a scholar. Who could ask for more?"

Batya put up her hands, smiled and backed away. "Too much flattery," she said. "I'm overwhelmed." She turned to face Zach. Thank you, she mouthed silently.

Batya asked where the bathroom was and walked across the room. It was occupied, so Batya stood there and watched Harvey as he listened to the conversations going on around the room, surprised that he didn't engage the other men.

At first she thought he was being polite, not wanting to intrude, holding back to avoid looking like he was showing off.

Then she saw Harvey repeatedly scratch behind his ear, a gesture he used when trying to recall something he thought he should know. Batya had learned that gesture when she and Harvey first started discussing theological concepts together. As she watched him turn from one group to another, Batya realized Harvey was trying to hide his inability to match wits with the other men.

Batya remembered the long train rides home from school when she and Zach had gotten to know each other, their mutual delight in intellectual sparring. Batya knew Zach's wife suspected there might be more than academics between them. She had wanted to let the woman know that as much as she admired Zach's mind she was turned off by his looks, and, equally important, by his poverty.

When she told Zach about her suitor, Batya was delighted to learn he and Harvey had been intellectual peers in Europe. It never occurred to Batya that Harvey might no longer be the Heshy who could easily match wits with Zvi, just as she hadn't doubted Harvey's wealth and business position until that luncheon with Rachel and Helen.

Well, she had always been good at making the best of things. She was now a wife, not a woman who had been tossed away. She had fancy clothes and a private house, big enough to impress her friends. And she had a good-looking man who respected her for her superior intellect. At least three nights a week Harvey and Batya would select a section of the holy books and discuss it in the study, in their newly renovated study, in their new leather chairs, munching on the cookies and cake Batya bought without regard for the expense. Not bad for someone who had been a starving rabbi's daughter not so long ago.

The bathroom door opened, and Batya almost bumped into Zach's wife. The women smiled, and each told the other how well she looked. Batya was surprised this woman looked so old and tired; she knew they were about the same age. Batya praised the party, and the other woman said it was nothing, that she'd been glad to do it.

When Batya re-crossed the room, back to her good-looking husband and the men surrounding him, she noticed that none of them was as well-groomed as Harvey and she knew that none would ever drive a car as expensive as the one in which she and Harvey had arrived.

The crowd began to thin out, and Batya told Harvey to find their coats. Zach took Harvey to a closet in the larger bedroom.

"Before you go, I have something I want to ask you," said Zach. Harvey looked confused. For a man who had been boldly proclaiming his opinions all night long, Zach was now mumbling, and Harvey had to step closer to hear him.

"I was wondering if, maybe, you might need an additional source for hardware," Zach said. He was facing the interior of the closet, not looking at Harvey as he spoke. "The store where I work has top quality merchandise. I would speak to the boss and make sure you got only the best. And at a good price."

Harvey sighed. "I'm not really involved in that part of the business," he said. "My brother-in-law handles the purchasing. I'll ask him about the situation with hardware. If we can do some business, I'll let you know."

Harvey took the coats and quickly walked back to Batya.

It took a while for them to say goodbye to everyone. Finally, they made it down the three flights of stairs. Neither of them said anything as Harvey maneuvered the big car through the streets and onto the highway.

"Well, that was some evening," said Harvey.

Batya nodded. "Yes, I'll be glad to get back to our own house," she said. "I'm tired."

They rode in silence for a while.

"So, Zvi came to this country and decided to continue his studies," said Harvey. "I envy his discipline and commitment. You really think he's going to become a professor one day?"

"No," said Batya. "I was just being kind. Earlier, you mentioned how, right after the war, these streets were crammed with Jews. What do you think happened to them? People got settled, worked for others until they started their own businesses, like the Rosens. Many enrolled in night school. Most realized that in the United States they should study something practical, become CPAs or learn about business and work for big companies like the insurance firm that hired my good-for-nothing ex-husband. Orthodox Jews became Conservative Jews, then they became Reformed. Eventually they moved to better neighborhoods.

"But not the people you saw upstairs. Regardless of where they were, they wanted to study religion and philosophy, not secular subjects. They're like my father, may he rest in peace; nothing was ever as important as religion. No other studies could provide so much satisfaction. That's why they're still here.

"Maybe Zach will eventually get his advanced degree, that wife of his seems willing to sacrifice for his continuing studies. Just like in Europe. But by then he'll be an old man who never had time to do proper research and publish articles in the right journals. Philosophy departments in this country aren't looking for people like that. If he's lucky, he'll teach a course or two in a second-rate school every few terms. On that he can't support a wife, three children and help out his sister."

"Of course some of the Orthodox have money, they've figured out how to work with *goyim* and maintain their faith, they acquire political influence as well as money, but not your friend Zvi. His head is only for school things. He isn't leaving that hardware store anytime soon."

Batya slipped off the high heeled boots and rubbed her feet.

"At the end of the party, when we got our coats, Zvi tried to have a conversation with me, businessman to businessman," said Harvey. "It didn't go well. He wants to do business with the Rosens. I said I couldn't help him. He was disappointed."

"His wife probably told him to ask you," she said. "You were right to refuse him. It wouldn't take him long to figure out your status with the Rosens, that they looked down on you. And he wouldn't be shy about spreading that information. He would want to demonstrate that maintaining the lord's commandments was more important than seeking mateiral success, that ultimately it brought longer lasting rewards and satisfaction. "

Harvey turned to his wife. "That I'm not a partner, that I have less money than you thought, it bothers you, Batya?"

"It is what it is," she said and slipped her feet back into her fancy boots.

Batya turned the radio on and spoke very softly, her voice almost drowned out by the music. She didn't know if Harvey heard her. Harvey didn't know if she had intended him to hear or was just muttering to herself. He didn't say anything.

"The Rosens are right," she said. "You're not much of a businessman. If you were going to sell your soul, you should have negotiated a better price, at least gotten a full partnership for it."

27.

SHOWTIME

A week after Zvi's party Batya called some of her old friends and arranged to meet them at the end of the following month. A few days later, just as she'd planned, Batya cancelled the get-together.

"I'm so busy these days I can't keep track of my schedule," she told the women. "I totally forgot I'm expected at the theater party my new *shul* is having that night. No, not a Yiddish show, I go to Broadway now. The top donors to the Bonds for Israel Drive got tickets to *The Sound of Music.* Yes, it's strange that a synagogue goes to a play about Catholics. Harvey said someone's brother-in-law's cousin had a connection, so they got a good deal on the tickets. That's his world, always wheeling and dealing. Given his position in the community, of course Harvey and I have to attend. I'm so disappointed, but we'll get together another time. I'll call as soon as my calendar clears."

Harvey's contribution to the bond drive had been considerably less generous than those received from Saul and Morris, but the three checks were recorded as a joint family donation so Harvey and Batya were among the invitees to the theater party.

Eager to make friends in her new temple, especially among the well-to-do members, Batya suggested to Harvey that they arrange to go out with some other people before the show. "I'd like to know who, in addition to the Rosens, is praying beside me," she said.

Harvey hesitated. "I don't think most of those people would be interested in eating at a strictly kosher restaurant," he said, expecting her to get annoyed. Instead, Batya laughed. "So, now I live in a world where members of my *shul* raise money for the holy land by eating *traife* and seeing a show about nuns." She shrugged. "Let them go with God. We'll eat a proper dinner at home and see everyone at the theater."

This was Batya's first Broadway show. She was determined not to let anything spoil the experience. She spent the week before the curtain went up deciding what to wear, where to sit, how to act.

Batya checked the seating chart and decided that, of the seats allocated to their family, the one on the aisle would give her the best view. She and Harvey arrived as soon as the theater doors opened and grabbed the seats Batya wanted. While he held their places, Batya did a full inspection, went to the balcony to see what people in the cheaper seats would see, tapped the walls and discovered that what looked like carved woodwork was just painted plaster.

She noted how the smell of the place changed as it grew crowded, as diverse perfumes and body odors were added. She was looking for her own signature perfume, a phrase she'd learned from fashion magazines, and often stood near the perfume counter in fancy department stores noting which scent was purchased by women whose appearance she admired.

When the Rosens arrived Harvey and Batya didn't offer to move down the row. They stood up and smiled as the family squeezed past.

As soon as they were seated, Rachel leaned over to Helen. "You saw?"

"Of course I saw."

Seated between them, Saul looked from his wife to his sister-in-law. "What did you see?"

"You didn't see Batya? Open your eyes. She's wearing the earrings Elaine cherished."

Saul craned his neck. Batya had turned around, talking to the woman behind her. He couldn't see her earrings. No matter. "You're right," he said. "How terrible."

Suddenly, the orchestra started playing. The lights dimmed, and the thick gold curtain kept rising until it disappeared. Batya took a deep breath. Show time!

Helen kept glancing down their row, watching Batya watch the show, noting that she was captivated, humming with the music and swaying with the dancers. She was laughing. She was crying. No one in the theater could be enjoying this show more than Batya, thought Helen. What was going on? It was good. But so good?

For Batya, this wasn't just a show. Seated amid her embattled, recently acquired family, Batya was watching the life she thought she would have, a life in which a woman of faith leaves her pious community for a rich, good-looking man and his adoring children. She vanquishes the wealthy, socialite countess whom others in his class preferred for him. Soon she's married, living in a castle, loved and admired by everyone, secular and religious. Then the music swelled, the curtain came down and everyone applauded. No one more enthusiastically than Batya.

Batya was ready to discuss the show and provide personal insight into what it was like in Europe when the Nazis came to power, but suddenly her hands were grabbed by Helen and Rachel, who practically lifted her out of her seat.

"Quick, quick," they said. "You have to rush to the Ladies Room, or you won't be finished before the next act. There's always a long line." Batya didn't resist; she didn't want to violate theater-going protocol.

Neither Helen nor Rachel wanted Batya's opinion of the play. "You look so nice tonight," said Rachel as soon as they got on line. "Those earrings are so pretty."

"Yes, thank you," said Batya with a knowing nod. "Harvey gave them to me. I know they used to belong to Elaine, but I'm not superstitious. Look how well they match my new dress." Batya twirled so they could admire her long-sleeved, shirtwaist dress. Helen and Rachel were in pastel, polyester pants suits.

Batya started to hum one of the show tunes. The woman in front of her smiled. "Aren't the songs wonderful," she said. Soon they were trying to recall lyrics.

"I can't just stand here and be polite," Helen whispered to Rachel. "Keep her away from the seats as long as possible."

Helen turned to Batya. "I've changed my mind," she said. "I'll wait 'til the show's over." She hurried back inside the theater.

• • •

Earlier that evening Harvey had walked into their bedroom as Batya was getting dressed. "How do I look?" she said, admiring herself in the full mirror on the closet door.

Harvey started to say she looked very nice, but his attention was grabbed by something sparkling in Batya's hand. He couldn't look at her dress. All he could do was watch Batya thrust the stem of one of Elaine's ruby earrings through her own earlobe.

Harvey took a deep breath. "You look lovely," he said. "But maybe you should wear different earrings."

"What do you mean? These are perfect with my dress." Batya turned away from the mirror and faced Harvey as she pushed the other earring in place.

Harvey understood the significance of those earrings, how much they'd meant to his late wife, how impressed the Rosen family was when he presented them to Elaine and how upset Helen and Rachel would be when they saw them on Batya.

Batya had discovered the box and the note with the Biblical quotation shortly after her birthday, after Harvey had given her a book which she already owned, not the jewelry she wanted. So, thought Batya, Elaine gets gems and poetry and I get dusty tomes. Batya immediately bought herself an expensive cranberry silk dress to match the earrings.

If Harvey had revealed the whole story right away, told Batya about Elaine's miscarriage, her fear that she couldn't have children, her depression, would Batya have sympathized and taken off the earrings? Would that have eliminated part of the friction between her and the Rosens? Or would she have seethed at the unfairness of Elaine receiving jewels for the possibility that she was infertile, the condition that had wrecked Batya's own life?

Who knows? Anyway it never occurred to Harvey to tell Batya the story.

Instead, he said, "those earrings were very special to Elaine," trying to sound casual. "People who knew her might be surprised to see them on you."

Batya narrowed her eyes. "People? You mean Helen and Rachel? Because I'm not as special as your precious Elaine, not a woman of virtue who deserves such jewels?"

Batya adjusted her wig so the earrings were more visible.

"Don't be silly. You and Elaine are each special in your own ways."

Harvey was trying to sound reasonable. Batya ignored him. She slipped on her high heeled shoes and checked her make-up.

"Now let's go," she said. "I don't want to be late."

He had lost many arguments to Batya; Harvey knew it was

futile to say anything more and meekly followed her out the door.

• • •

The intermission lights were still on inside the theater when Helen sat down in the seat Batya had vacated. She didn't waste time on pleasantries. "How could you give Elaine's ruby earrings to that woman?" she said in a harsh voice, not caring if she was overheard.

"Don't start with me, Helen. I tried. There was nothing I could do. For her birthday I got Batya an antique leather-bound book by a prominent Jewish woman scholar from the Middle Ages. Let me tell you, it wasn't cheap. I thought she'd be thrilled. But she wasn't happy. Tonight she insisted she wanted to wear those earrings. I don't want to fight with her anymore. I need peace."

Helen looked at Harvey. He looked tired and grey, his skin, his hair, his affect, all grey. She shook her head and moved down the row just as Rachel and Batya hurried back and reclaimed their seats.

Suddenly the lights went out, the curtain rose, a cymbal clanged and the Nazis came to power.

The Baron and his new bride were threatened but held to their principles. By the end of the play they'd escaped. Batya nodded and smiled. With a song in their hearts and two virtuous parents, she was sure the family was off to fame and fortune and a wonderful life in America. She was one of the first to stand and applaud and kept clapping through numerous curtain calls. She laughed happily when someone let out a loud whistle.

Helen barely glanced at Batya as she pushed past her and hurried to the bathroom. When she returned the theater was almost empty and the lobby was crowded with people from their synagogue discussing the show.

"You know, the real family didn't have it so good in America," someone said. "They were a so-so singing group. They ran a hotel in the mountains. Not the Catskills. Some other mountains."

"Well, how many people did have it as good in America as they did in Europe before the war?" said Harvey. "In order to survive we made sacrifices."

Morris shook his head and turned to Saul. "He spends a night listening to great music and he's still singing the same old song. Let's get going. The parking garages are going to be crowded."

Morris wound up walking with someone from their temple who wanted the Rosens to get him a discount on building material.

Saul walked next to Harvey. "I got a call from that Bill at Rebecca's school," said Harvey. "He thinks it's time Batya and I came to visit."

Both men were accustomed to speaking loudly to each other in the shop in order to be heard over the noise of power tools and arguing customers. Traffic noises didn't hamper their conversation.

"Are you going? It's not a bad drive," said Saul. "It's a nice-looking place. Wear sturdy shoes; they like to take you for walks, show off the grounds, talk about the joys of country life. Watch out for animal shit."

"Of course I'm going. I'm glad to go. I miss my daughter. And Batya is anxious to meet Rebecca. But that counselor, that Bill, he annoys me. He suggested we all meet with him. He wants to have a group session, a discussion of what led to Rebecca being there, what the future will be like. What do you think of something like that?"

"I like Bill. Seems eager to help. But we never had special meetings with him."

"Well, I don't like it. The past is the past. You can't change it. And no one can predict the future. You do your best and hope the Lord sees fit to make things right. If this Bill wants to talk to Rebecca about what happened years ago, I can't stop him. That's his job. But there's no reason for anyone else to be involved. I pray for this whole business to be over, for my Rebecca to come home. Then we can be a happy family, Rebecca, Marvin, Batya and me. We'll be fine without outsiders who think they can help."

Helen and Rachel were walking behind the men. Rachel looked at Helen. "You heard?"

"I heard," said Helen. "I'll call Bill tomorrow, make sure he knows what he's letting himself in for."

Saul was right, the garages were crowded. The woman who'd been walking with Batya promised to call her and followed her husband to the garage across the street where he'd parked. Batya stood by herself in the garage where Harvey and the Rosens had parked, smiling contentedly while her husband paid the parking fee.

Helen arrived a few minutes later and stared at Batya. Elaine's earrings twinkled under the garage's fluorescent lights, which were making an annoying buzzing sound and giving Helen a headache. Suddenly she realized the noise wasn't coming from the lights. Batya was singing.

Under other circumstances Batya might have become a great rabbi. But in even the most liberal synagogue she would never be a cantor. Batya knew the meaning of complicated Talmudic passages, she knew the works of medieval scribes, but she didn't know she was tone deaf.

Climb Every Mountain is a daunting song for even accomplished performers. It's frequently sung by someone with operatic training. When Batya reached the phrase, *"for as long as you live,"* Helen heard a chicken getting its head cut off.

Saul watched his wife clench her fists and approach Batya just as she sang, "*ford every stream.*" He took a $10 bill and his garage ticket from his pocket and found an attendant. "My wife isn't feeling well," he said. "My car should be the next." The attendant looked at the money and nodded.

Saul took Helen's hand and quickly pulled her toward the entrance just as their car came down the ramp. The attendant opened the heavy Oldsmobile door for Helen, waited until she got in and closed it with a thud.

"You enjoyed the show?" asked Saul as they made their way through the traffic.

"Pretty good."

"You heard Harvey's going to see Rebecca?"

"I heard."

"Looks like Batya is making friends with some of the women in the congregation."

"They'll figure out what she's like. Or maybe not. Some of them aren't so smart."

"You want to hear some music? I could put on the radio."

"I've had enough music. Let's listen to the news."

Saul was yawning by the time they got home, his wife was wide awake. He offered to keep Helen company if she wanted a cup of tea before bed. "Since when do I need a babysitter?" she said. "I'm fine and you've got work early tomorrow morning. There are a few things I have to take care of. Go to bed, I'll be up soon."

Helen found the frozen chocolate babka hidden in the freezer under a brisket she planned to make next week. With a sturdy, serrated knife she sawed the cake in half, put one piece in the oven and the other back in the freezer. Then, she found the new murder mystery she'd bought that morning, attracted by the cover photo of blood dripping from the decapitated head of a bald woman. By the time she reached the second chapter, the cake was defrosted enough to eat.

Helen finished all of the babka and half of the book before going to bed.

28.

HOMECOMING

"So, the big visit with your dad and his new wife is tomorrow. How do you feel about that?" asked Bill.

"Haven't we talked about this enough? You really want to go over it again?" Rebecca stretched and looked up at the ceiling. "It'll be tense. I'll behave. No weapons, not even a small switchblade. Although I can't speak for her, maybe she'll have a dagger tucked into her wig. Wonder if when she uses one of her knives on me, will it still be kosher?"

Bill frowned.

"Okay, no jokes. I'm nervous, but I think it'll be okay. What can they do to me if it doesn't work out? Send me to reform school?"

The visit went better than expected. Rebecca and Marvin hugged tightly, Harvey and Rebecca sort of patted each other and Batya and Rebecca shook hands. Everyone was nervous. Everyone was stiff. Batya and Rebecca kept sneaking looks at each other. Rebecca's friends kept walking by to get a glimpse of this family unit so they could discuss it later that night. Batya was smaller than Rebecca had expected; Rebecca looked younger than Batya had anticipated. Everyone behaved. Everyone was relieved when the visit was over.

Harvey started visiting Hillsdale with Batya and Marvin twice a month. It never became an enjoyable get-together but eventually a satisfactory routine was established. Batya brought Tupperware containers filled with homemade kosher food, which Harvey blessed before they ate at a picnic table as far from school buildings as possible. They talked about impersonal things: Marvin's sports, Batya's redecorating, neighborhood gossip, TV shows.

Bill kept repeating his request for a meeting, and Harvey kept turning him down. Finally, Harvey asked Bill to join them for lunch. He brought an extra yarmulke, and Bill put it on without discussion. Although they stayed away from personal matters, Bill was glad of an opportunity to observe how the family interacted. When he tried to bring up anything personal, his question was deflected. "How did you feel about that?" he'd say. "Like anyone would feel," was the answer. The invitation wasn't repeated.

Bill and Rebecca regularly dissected the family visits and thought they'd gone as smoothly as possible for four nervous people with too much of a past and no common idea of what the future could be like. But they were clearly decent people.

• • •

Almost two years after Rebecca's arrival, Bill met with Hillsdale's administration committee and they decided she was ready to leave. Rebecca would return home two weeks before Labor Day when she'd start her senior year at Christopher Columbus, the local high school. Returning to Bronx Science High School was judged too stressful even if the school had been willing to readmit her.

Rebecca's family arrived early. Harvey had gotten the car cleaned inside and out, mats, hubcaps, even the inside of the trunk. The whole car had the sweet, piney smell that said you'd paid an extra fee for the golden nugget cleaning package.

"She's having her final interview with Bill," the house mother said when they pulled up. "You can just walk around for a while."

Batya glared at the ducks strutting down the path. "We'll just sit in the car," she said.

Finally, Marvin spotted Rebecca and Bill heading towards them. "We're over here," he yelled, ran over and hugged Rebecca.

Batya and Harvey got out of the car. Bill shook hands with Harvey, nodded to Batya.

"Marvin, go upstairs and help your sister with her bags," Harvey said. "We'll wait here."

Bill turned to Batya and Harvey. "You've got some nice kids there," he said. "Hope everything goes well."

"We expect it to," said Batya. "Now that Rebecca is back with her own family."

Rebecca's room in the red cottage was empty when they got there. The girls had thrown a goodbye party for her the night before. Alice had cried and hugged her tightly. Maria had recently left the school to live with a foster family.

Marvin picked up the large suitcase, the one Helen had packed for Rebecca when she was first sent there. "I'm glad you're coming home," he said.

"Me too. Let's get going before they change their minds."

The bags were put into the spotless trunk. Bill gave Rebecca a final hug, which Batya thought lasted too long. "I think you'll like the guy in the city I recommended," Bill told Rebecca. "And you know you can call me anytime."

Then Bill stepped back. Rebecca and Marvin sat in the back, Harvey and Batya in front. Harvey blew the horn to scatter the ducks, and they took off.

"Rebecca, Bill said something to you, something about some-one else to talk to," Harvey said as soon as they were out of sight of the school. "Aren't you finished with all that stuff?"

"Just a referral," said Rebecca. "If I need it."

"All of this talking, it's about our family? You tell him what goes on in our house?" said Harvey.

"Don't worry, it's confidential," said Rebecca."

Harvey decided to drop the subject of Rebecca's therapy. Hopefully that kind of stuff would all stay in the past. "Helen expects you for breakfast tomorrow morning," he told Rebecca.

"You mean, I shouldn't expect to see her marching down the street, leading a brass band, when we arrive?" she said. "Did you break both of her legs?"

No one laughed. Rebecca shrugged.

"I thought for the first night it would be best to just have a nice, quiet meal with your own family," said Batya.

"Batya prepared a terrific dinner," said Harvey. "Roast beef, vegetables, all kinds of things. She even baked her own bread. Marvin and I eat like kings these days, don't we?"

"Yeah," said Marvin. "Great food."

"But now meals should get even better," said Batya. "Now there'll be two caring women in the kitchen. Don't worry. It's not hard to keep a kosher kitchen. I'll teach you. With just a little effort you can be kosher and a gourmet."

Rebecca laughed. "No one in this family was ever a gourmet."

She watched as Marvin picked at his fingernails, his new habit.

No one had anything more to say for a while.

"Did everyone forget there's a baseball game going on right now?" said Batya. She turned around to Rebecca. "Marvin has taught me all about baseball. Now I'm a Yankee fan just like he is. I'm going to go to all his games this season and cheer for his new team."

"I'm in a different little league now," said Marvin. "This one doesn't play on Shabbos." He glanced at his hands. The thumb and index finger nails were cracked.

Batya turned on the radio. The announcer's voice filled the car until they got home. The Yankees lost.

Bubbe Golda had shuffled out to her bench shortly after she woke up. She knew this was the day Rebecca was coming home and didn't want to miss her arrival. When the clouds covered the sun and it began to look like rain, Morris tried to convince her to go inside, promising he would get her as soon as Rebecca came, but the old lady shooed him away.

"My granddaughter, my Rifka, is coming back to me today," *Bubbe* said. "After all this time you think a few raindrops will stop me from welcoming her?"

Morris didn't correct his mother. Let her confuse the grandchild lost in the war with the grandchild coming home from reform school, no reason to make a fuss. He and Rachel kept glancing through their window, prepared to come out with an umbrella and sit with Golda if necessary. But the clouds soon disappeared.

Finally Harvey's car pulled into his driveway. Golda bolted from her bench, moving faster than anyone would ever have thought she could. Rebecca jumped out of the car and ran to her.

"You're here, you're here, you're here," said Golda. She reached up to Rebecca, a full head taller than she was, and stroked her granddaughter's hair. "You're here. You're here," she repeated. "And healthy, and beautiful and alive."

"I'm so glad to see you," said Rebecca. She hugged the frail old woman so tightly she became afraid she'd hurt her. They each took a step back, stared at each other, tears in their blue eyes, then hugged again.

Harvey and Batya walked over. "Isn't it wonderful," said Harvey. "Rebecca's back. Everything is fine now."

"Please, come inside. We'll have some tea and relax," said Batya.

"No, I'm alright. I needed to see for myself, to make sure she was okay," Golda said. She turned to her granddaughter. "You'll come visit me when you're rested. We'll talk then."

Golda started walking slowly back to her apartment then turned and watched Marvin carry Rebecca's luggage into the house. She looked straight up into the bright sunshine and said, "Thank you for bringing her back. Now, take good care of her."

As soon as they walked into their house Batya told Rebecca, "I'll get dinner on the table while you get settled. Marvin will help you.

"Meanwhile, you relax," she said to Harvey. "It was a long drive."

Rebecca quickly went upstairs and stared into her old bedroom. It was immaculate. It was sterile. The beige walls had been freshly washed. The single bed was made with a tight, fitted, white sheet. There were no pictures on the walls. The hardwood floor had been waxed until it shone. Her radio and record player were missing.

Rebecca sat on the bed and started to laugh. "I have to hand it to our papa," she said to Marvin. "Reform school wasn't enough. Now my beloved father has me living in a convent. And he managed to find a convent with an Orthodox Jew for the mother superior."

Rebecca opened her suitcases and revealed a multi-colored cornucopia: sweatshirts, sneakers, books, underwear, tops and bottoms and see-through plastic cases with flowered designs that held

262

cosmetics in squiggly, uncapped tubes and oddly shaped bottles. It all poured into the room. There was a carefully wrapped framed photo of her mother that Rebecca put on the nightstand.

She grabbed a long-sleeved flannel shirt, sniffed the armpits and put it on. "Okay, I'm ready. Nice sturdy bra and no bare arms for this girl," said Rebecca. "I'll put everything away later. Let's go downstairs. I can't wait to see what the rest of this place looks like."

Neither Rebecca nor Marvin noticed Batya, who was standing behind the open door of the linen closet at the end of the hall, supposedly getting more towels. When Rebecca left her room Batya went over, opened the door, stared at the mess she'd made in the formerly immaculate area and shook her head.

Over dinner, Rebecca assured Batya the meal was delicious, praised the kitchen renovation and paid attention as she was told where everything went so the kosher rites were observed. She volunteered to do the dishes, but Batya wouldn't hear of that on Rebecca's first night home.

When everything was cleared away, Marvin went to his room while Rebecca watched the news on the living room TV with Batya and her father. An hour later she said she was tired, kissed both of them on the cheek as she'd become accustomed to doing after their visits to school and went upstairs.

Rebecca wasn't sleepy. She walked down the hall and stopped in front of Marvin's closed door. "Hey, you up?" she called.

"Sure, come on in."

Marvin was lying on the floor with his baseball cards spread around him. He started to explain his system for classifying players, but Rebecca cut him off. "So, any gossip about the last two years you want to share?" she said. "Any booby traps to warn me about?"

'Well, there's all of the Jewish stuff. It'll be a new ball game now that you're here."

"Speaking of ball games, what's the story behind your changing teams? You really prefer playing with religious kids?"

"They're alright. Some of them aren't bad players. I'm still one of the best on the team. It keeps Batya happy. She's really enthusiastic, when she starts yelling it's like there's a whole cheering section on my side. She's even gotten papa to come a few times."

"Well, now you've got another fan. I'll come to the next game."

"That'll be great."

Marvin began putting his baseball cards in piles, stretching rubber bands around each pile. When he finished, he looked at Rebecca. "Hey, do you know the story about mama's earrings? The red ones shaped like flowers?"

Rebecca knew the story but let him tell it. She wanted to know the version of their family history he'd been fed. Aunt Rachel had done a decent job with that story she thought when he finished. She was happy Marvin believed Papa cared about Mama and he hadn't learned that their parents' betrothal was more of a financial arrangement than a love match.

"From now on, anything you want to know, just ask me," said Rebecca. "I know where a lot of bodies are buried. *Bubbe* likes telling me family stories no one else tells. And I can ask Sarah, she's always spying on people."

Rebecca hugged her little brother and went back to her room. She pushed her things from the bed onto the floor and got under the covers. The house was very quiet, quieter than she was used to. It took a while for her to fall asleep.

• • •

The next morning Rebecca carefully made her bed and politely said good morning to Batya and Marvin. Harvey had already left for work. Then she headed around the corner to Helen's house.

She was halfway up the stairs when the door flew open, and Helen ran out yelling greetings. Rebecca started to laugh. Her squat little aunt looked ready to start jumping up and down. Rebecca felt like doing the same, but they were on the steep front steps and Rebecca worried they would tumble into the street.

"Hey Sarri, how're you doing?" she greeted her cousin as she walked into the house. "I made it. Thanks for sending me a pickaxe and shovel so I could dig my way out."

"No problem," Sarah said. "Don't forget you promised to show me how to make a shiv out of a toothbrush."

Helen gave both of them a dirty look. Complying with Harvey and Batya's request, she had waited a full day before she greeted Rebecca. She didn't want to waste time listening to nonsense.

"Sit down, sit down," she told Rebecca. "We have so much to talk about. I thought you could use a *nosh* so I got some bagels and appetizing."

Rebecca looked at all the food spread before her and grinned. "This is fantastic. All I've had for two years were frozen, packaged bagels from the supermarket."

Helen and Sarah chanted, "*Oy, oy, oy.*"

The Rosens had strict beliefs about bagels. Mass marketed, mass produced products, frozen or packaged or stored in a grocer's display case until they achieved the consistency of a brick, were often deceptively labeled as bagels. That was a *goyische* trick.

Likewise, a cinnamon-raisin bagel was a fraud. Maybe it was a scone. Maybe it was soda bread. Somewhere buried in a book of *goyische* fables there were probably tales of blueberry, cherry, or chocolate chip bagels plucked from a stack displayed on the horn of a unicorn.

True bagels, however, come from a bagel store, like the one Helen had gone to that morning while the rest of the family was asleep. The inside of the bagel was chewy, the outside crisp. Crusts were coated with salt, onion, garlic, poppy or sesame seed. Some bagels had all of these ingredients. Some had none. No other type of bagel was authentic.

When Rebecca had selected her perfect bagel, it was time for her to select the *shmear*, cream cheese, plain, scallion or vegetable, was available.

"Now, have some appetizing," Helen said, using the word, "appetizing" in the Bronx way, as a noun and not an adjective, the generic term for the cured fish that was piled on top of the *shmear*. The appetizing stores patronized by the Rosens sold slabs of belly lox or nova (which was less salty than regular lox) and sturgeon, whitefish, carp and sable. There were also platters of herring and of cheese.

Helen had bought an adequate amount of everything, enough for twice the number of people who would be eating plus some extra for Rebecca to take home in case she got hungry later. In the kitchen, the coffee percolator was perking, and freshly baked babka and rugelach were waiting to be served.

Rebecca looked at all of the food. She looked at her aunt.

"I love you too," she said and dug in.

29.

THE END OF AN ERA

Rebecca began making weekly visits to *Bubbe* Golda. She didn't stay long, just enough time to reassure her grandmother that she was still there, still well.

Sometimes *Bubbe* told her a funny story about how Elaine and her brothers and sister got into mischief when they were children in Poland, sometimes they sang Yiddish songs, and sometimes *Bubbe* told dirty jokes and Rebecca promised not to tell anyone that Golda knew such stories. While they talked, Golda stroked Rebecca's hand, and they drank tea and ate the cake Rachel bought when she did her mother-in-law's shopping.

Each time she visited, Golda told Rebecca, "If you ever have serious trouble with Batya or with your father you tell me. Tell me right away. No more hiding things. Remember, Harvey works for my sons. They listen to me, and they can make him behave. But if the problems aren't serious, you work them out yourself, no need for us to talk about them."

"You're a smart woman, *Bubbe*," Rebecca said.

About six months after Rebecca returned, Rachel went to Golda's door to deliver her groceries. She entered the unlocked house and called out. There was no response. Rachel went into the bedroom and found Golda in bed, small and shrunken, barely making a lump under the blankets.

Rachel called her name and shook her. There was no response. Rachel held a mirror to the old woman's face; Golda was no longer breathing. Her faded nightgown had ridden up to her waist and Rachel pulled it down before she called the doctor. Next, she called Helen, who called Saul and Morris at the shop. They all arrived quickly.

A heart attack, the doctor said. "She went quickly, quietly, painlessly, in her sleep."

Golda hadn't liked doctors and rarely went to one. Whenever her children convinced her to get a check-up, the doctor invariably said there were a variety of things wrong with her heart, her blood pressure and other things. They told her to change her diet and stop drinking whiskey. She'd nod, smile and ignore him. She was 91 when she died and had outlived most of the doctors.

At the funeral home, almost everyone mentioned that Golda had waited for Rebecca's return before she died. Now she was at peace. There was nothing more to say.

Saul and Morris chanted some prayers in Hebrew. Neither of them wanted to make a speech. They had been good sons who loved their mother and cared for her. Everyone knew that.

The Rabbi noted that the death of each Holocaust survivor is more than a loss to one person's family, it is a loss to the collective memory of the Jewish people. It means that there are fewer actual witnesses to that tragedy, fewer people with numbers on their arms, fewer people who can give those events personal meaning to the next generation.

Golda's grandchildren walked together to the lectern. They'd chosen Rebecca to read a poem she thought their *Bubbe* would like. Rebecca was crying, and mascaraed tears ran down her cheek.

As she left the podium, Harvey whispered to her to wash her face. She ignored him.

There was a brief ceremony at the cemetery and then everyone went to Rachel's house for the *shiva*.

No one tried to stop underage grandchildren from drinking. One cousin commandeered a bottle, and they all sat on the back porch toasting *Bubbe*'s passing, mourning the loss of the endless supply of rock candy.

"Here's to sweetness," they said as glasses clinked. "To enjoying the good stuff."

The youngsters all woke up with terrible headaches the next day. *Bubbe* would have enjoyed a good laugh at their expense.

30.

OIL AND WATER

Everyone in the Rosen family had talked about how bright Rebecca was. Batya was used to being considered the smartest in any group. She told friends she was looking forward to some intellectual companionship.

Soon after Rebecca arrived, Batya told her that sometimes, after dinner, she and Harvey chose a section of scripture and spent the evening discussing its implications. She didn't say that she had been disappointed to realize that Harvey wasn't her intellectual equal. "I know you have no background in this kind of thing, but you might find it interesting. I could find some good English translations for you."

Batya envisioned finding a few other bright young girls and leading the type of study group that had been forbidden to females in Europe, about becoming a feminist icon in American-Jewish studies.

But Rebecca wasn't interested. "Sounds interesting, but I'd better concentrate on my own schoolwork for now. Maybe when I'm more settled."

A few months later, Batya saw an ad for a performance of *The Merchant of Venice* at a small theater downtown. A play about Jews, she thought. Perfect place for her and Rebecca to have an intellectual experience together. "Let's get tickets," she said.

"That sounds great," said Rebecca. "I read it in honors English when I was at Science. Are you very interested in Shakespeare?"

Batya had seen this play performed in the Yiddish Theater; she regarded it as an example of the age-old persecution and slander of Jews by gentiles. She told Rebecca it was important to remember that anti-Semitism has been around for a long time, prevalent among all classes and all over the world. Even a world-famous figure like Shakespeare hated Jews and tried to spread the idea that Judaism was evil.

Rebecca shook her head and began to explain the play in the context of Elizabethan times.

Batya remembered it was time to start dinner.

The next day Rebecca came home with a copy of Cliff Notes for the play. "I thought you might read this before we go. Lots of kids at school used them, said they were really helpful."

Batya recognized the bright yellow and black striped booklet. "When I was taking courses at college I saw students with such things, students who were too lazy or too stupid to read the original text. I speak four languages; I've analyzed works that would cause your eyes to cross. Who do you think you are, giving something like this to someone like me?" She tossed the booklet into the trash.

They never went to the play.

Batya gave up her idea of having an acolyte.

Batya and Harvey had discussed how much spending money Rebecca should receive when she came home. They thought they'd come up with a figure that would cover necessities, but not enough to allow her to get into trouble. Batya assumed she could control Rebecca by threatening to withhold her allowance. But Rebecca had never relied on her papa's generosity.

Within a month of starting at her new school, Rebecca had established a flourishing tutoring business. Her good-girl-gone-bad reputation made her a celebrity. Hanging out with Rebecca appealed to classmates who would have balked at spending time with some nerd tutor. Many parents knew Rebecca's family and were ready to overlook her background and employ a girl who was polite, dependable and had a history of getting top grades, despite personal problems. She promised parents that, in addition to teaching kids to solve quadratic equations, she'd tell them the dire consequences of defying your parents. She earned hefty fees

I guess I shouldn't be surprised Batya thought, she is a Rosen. She's certainly got a head for business.

Batya had discovered that many of the things she'd assumed Harvey owned, like his car and insurance policies, were actually owned by the Rosen business. If something happened to Harvey—after all he was no spring chicken—much of what she had thought of as her inheritance would go to the Rosens' company. There were trusts for his children, the Rosens' lawyers had made sure of that. But what about Batya? Who was looking out for her? She began accumulating her own money. This family had so much, they wouldn't miss a little.

When she had lived with her father, they didn't have much money, but what there was, was Batya's to use as she saw fit. Being married to Harvey meant she had to account for everything she bought. She was constantly negotiating for more money to spend on the house while figuring out how to use some of that money for herself.

"What happened to the picture of my mother in the silver frame by my bed?" Rebecca asked Batya one day.

"It's right where it's always been. Unless you've moved it. Or buried it under the junk that should be put away."

"The photo's there, but it's in a cheap steel frame, not the antique silver frame *Bubbe* gave me."

"Are you sure? Your *Bubbe* wasn't very worldly. Who knows what the frame was made of?"

"She knew more than people thought she knew. One of the few things she could say in English was 'good stuff, make sure I get the good stuff.' She wouldn't have given me a cheap frame for my mother's photo. *Bubbe* always said she wanted me to have the most life could offer because the child I'm named after, her first grandchild, had so little."

"It must have been nice to have a grandmother who was so generous."

Rebecca didn't mention the incident again. However, a few days later, when Batya opened the kitchen cabinet, she saw that the meat and milk dishes were mixed up. One dish could have been a mistake, but this was done very neatly, very deliberately, one meat saucer on top of a milk saucer on top of a meat saucer.

About a week later, Rebecca was in the living room which Batya was refurnishing, piece by piece, as she accumulated the necessary funds. Rebecca was sitting on the plush burgundy chair she'd pulled next to a stiff couch, across from the TV. On her other side was the ugliest lamp in the world.

Rebecca was sprawled with her legs resting on one of the chair's wide arms while she read a book and watched TV. She pushed her hair behind her ears. She had dyed it auburn last week but wasn't happy with the results. She was thinking of cutting bangs. The telephone was on the table, right next to her, as was her half-eaten sandwich. Her dad and Batya refused to let her have a phone or

TV in her own room.

Rebecca heard the front door open. She listened for the sound of Batya limping, but there was nothing irregular about her step. Rebecca had made a small nick on Batya's shoe last week, but apparently the strap was still holding. Oh well, no rush, she thought.

She could sense Batya standing in the hallway staring at her, but didn't look up. "You know, sitting that way can loosen the arm of the chair," Batya said.

"Good thing I have a father who's such a good carpenter and will be able to fix it." Rebecca didn't lift her eyes from the book.

"If you're going to eat in here, and you know you shouldn't, you could at least put a plate under your food so the crumbs don't attract ants."

"Don't worry. It's a tuna sandwich on fresh, squishy white bread that doesn't make crumbs. Strictly kosher. It won't attract any heathen bugs. And I have a napkin under it. See?" Rebecca picked up the sandwich with one hand and the paper napkin with the other hand. The book fell off her lap. She put the sandwich back on the table, picked up the book, folded down the corner of the page she was up to and closed it.

Batya sighed. "You want me to tell you again that books are precious? That they should be treated with care? If that book is giving you pleasure you should return the favor, treat it kindly. Maybe someday I'll want to read it, or your father or your brother. You should make sure it will be in good shape for someone else." She made the noise she made when she was annoyed, a cross between a sigh of sadness and a snort of contempt. "I don't know why I bother. You have no respect for knowledge."

Rebecca did a perfect imitation of Batya's sound. "You wouldn't like this book. It's modern American literature. Nothing about Jews."

"Well, if you're finished reading, you can help me put these things away so I can start dinner. I've got two heavy shopping bags and my purse broke."

Rebecca left her sandwich on the table and carried one of the shopping bags into the kitchen. She smiled as she saw Batya quickly scan the cabinets to make sure the meat and milk dishes were properly arranged.

For a while, they silently put away the groceries. Then Batya looked at her pocketbook. The strap had torn and the shine on the decorative clasp was peeling. "I don't know why this happened," said Batya. "This was an expensive bag. A Gucci handbag. I found a place that gave me a good deal but still it cost me a lot."

Rebecca picked up the purse, dumped out the contents—a wallet, a small notebook in which Batya wrote in Hebrew, Harvey's expensive fountain pen, keys and make-up—and looked inside.

"It's a fake," Rebecca said. "A knock-off. The label is counterfeit, the stitches on the leather aren't even and the lining is a synthetic fabric."

Batya took the bag, stared at it carefully, inside and out.

Rebecca was right.

Rebecca smiled. "My friend Alice in reform school taught me how to spot counterfeit merchandise. She would sneak into town and check out the local shops for stuff she could trade for drugs and cash. It was important that she get quality merchandise—her dealer knew the difference.

They didn't spend much time on academics at that school, but there was a very diverse curriculum. I got quite an education."

Batya rubbed her eyes, smudging her mascara onto her cheeks. She felt old. She wanted to lay down in her nice, clean, freshly made bed with the new, thick linen next to the fresh-smelling closet where all her new clothes hung neatly. But she couldn't just walk away from Rebecca.

Batya had spent that day traipsing from one store to the next, all of the shops near her current home that carried the type of the strictly kosher food she required. The stores had been crowded, and her shopping bags were heavy. The fancy purse she'd bought with money from the silver picture frame she'd sold to the second-hand shop was heavy. When the strap broke, she'd had to carry it awkwardly under her arm. And her shoes didn't seem to fit properly anymore.

Batya wanted to smack the smug look off Rebecca's young face. But she knew if she hit Rebecca her sisters-in-law would find out. They seemed to know everything. Damn the whole family, always prying, always making trouble. As if she hadn't had enough trouble in her life.

"Poor little American girl," Batya said. "You think you've had such a hard life, don't you? Your mother died, you got sent away to a fancy school. Too bad for you. I'm so sorry. Hand me some tissues. I think I'm going to cry.

"You think you're the only one who saw a beloved relative die? But when my mother died, when my friends' mothers died, they weren't in clean beds surrounded by people prepared to provide the very best. They were in hovels. And the people around them secretly counted the dear departed's last breaths, knowing that when they passed there'd be more food for the rest."

Rebecca was no longer smiling, but she didn't feel sorry for Batya.

"You ran away?" said Batya. "I know what that's like. You think I didn't run? But I ran for my life, not because my daddy didn't understand me. You think the Nazis sent young girls to fancy schools that cared for them? They sent people to places where there was nothing but pain and misery. Real pain, not the pain of spoiled teenagers who think no one understands them."

Rebecca stood up. She picked up Batya's purse and threw it against the kitchen wall so hard the china cabinet shook. They heard glass clinking but didn't check to see if anything was broken.

"No!" Rebecca yelled. "No! No! No! I can't hear another Holocaust story. I won't listen to you hold me responsible for the Nazis. I'm sorry for the camps and the torture and the starvation. I'm sorry that my father had to give up his life as a scholar. And I know your family had to endure terrors much worse than my family did. I grew up hearing those stories. What makes you think I don't curse the Nazis as much as you do? But that doesn't give you the right to take my family's things, my room, my house, my life."

"So many, many things," said Batya. "It must be very difficult to keep track of all that you have."

"Do I have to have numbers on my arm before you can leave me alone?" yelled Rebecca. She grabbed her father's fountain pen, pulled off the cap and put the point against her inner arm where she had seen tattoos on concentration camp survivors.

Batya stared at Rebecca, her eyes wide. "Stop," she said sharply. And then louder, "Nazi! You Nazi! Stop!"

Rebecca pushed the pen point into her arm and felt it break the skin. She saw a drop of blood mix with the ink. She pushed the pen down harder. The hand holding the pen started to shake. It shook so violently she dropped the pen. Rebecca grabbed her own shaking hand with her other arm and ran out of the house.

Batya sat at the kitchen table, unable to move.

Rebecca ran towards the City Island bus stop, to her old haunts. But it was still early; no one would be at the places where she used to go. She headed to the park, and, still running, tripped over a tree root and wound up sitting in the dirt.

Rebecca picked up a handful of grass and threw it as far as she could. It didn't go far, but the motion felt good, so she did it again. And again. Soon her hands were filthy, her carefully manicured nails chipped and broken. Rebecca examined her arms. There was a tiny black dot in the spot where she had stabbed herself with the pen. She rubbed the spot, put some spit on her finger and rubbed it again; the dot remained.

She didn't realize it then, but she had accidentally tattooed herself. A tiny, easy-to-overlook tattoo. But still a permanent reminder of that day.

Rebecca sat in the park for about half an hour. She thought about calling that guy Bill had recommended for more counselling. But she knew her father wouldn't pay for it.

She threw a stone at a passing squirrel, missed it and watched the squirrel run away. She missed talking to Bill. But not enough to let them send her back to that place. That's what Batya would demand, especially if she went to City Island and got picked up again.

Rebecca stood up, realized she was hungry. She'd only had half a sandwich for lunch. She started to laugh. Where had she always been told to go if she needed anything, especially if she was hungry? Why, to her Aunt Helen, of course.

Rebecca arrived at her aunt's house looking dirty and disheveled. "Oh my God," said Helen. "What happened? Have you been mugged? Should I call a doctor? Call the police?"

Rebecca started to laugh. "I was wondering if you'd ask if I was hungry before you asked what had happened to me."

Helen looked at Rebecca, wet her finger, rubbed away some of the dirt, saw that she was okay and began to laugh. "I would have made something for you to eat in the ambulance. Now, go wash up and then tell me what's going on."

Rebecca went to the bathroom to wash, and Helen found Sarah and pulled her aside. "What's been going on in that house? What do you know?" she whispered.

"I know Rebecca and Batya keep fighting, but I didn't think either of them was ready to throw punches."

Rebecca came into the dinette and smiled when she saw a hefty corned beef sandwich waiting for her. As she ate, she recounted the scene with Batya and the knock-off designer purse.

"The woman is crazy," said Helen. "Imagine getting so mad because you pointed out she couldn't recognize quality merchandise and you could."

Then Rebecca got to the part of the story where they were screaming about the Nazis.

"No. Rebecca, my beloved child, no," said Helen. "You know better than to imitate those monsters. Never mind Batya, you know about what happened to your own family. You got mad and broke some dishes, I'm not going to criticize. But what you're saying. How did you even think of such a thing?"

"I don't know. I really don't know what happened to me, why I said what I said, did what I did."

Rebecca started to cry. She held out her arm, there was one small dot just above her wrist; otherwise her arm was clear. No one said anything about the dot. They didn't yet know it was permanent. Helen handed her a tissue, patted Rebecca on the back and walked into the kitchen. Sarah and Rebecca listened to the water run without saying anything. When Helen decided she'd had time to calm down a little, she brought Rebecca a glass of water to drink until the tears stopped.

"All the time I spent talking to *Bubbe* Golda, hearing her describe the horrors she went through in Europe. I know who

Sarah is named after, who I'm named after, I know about all the dreams my father left behind. I don't know what happened to me. I was ready to take a knife to Batya, to smash in her face in that fancy kosher kitchen, but I ran out of there before I did anything. I thought about running away, but I knew they'd catch me. I don't want to be sent away again."

"Well, thank God you're grown up enough to sensibly think some things through before you act," said Helen. "Listen, in June you'll graduate from high school. That's the time to think about going out on your own. For now, let's figure out a way to keep Batya quiet, something we can do before Harvey comes home and hears Batya's version of what happened. I don't like to think how your father would react to that."

Batya had straightened the kitchen and was preparing dinner. She'd gotten rid of the fake pocketbook. She wished she could clean up the mess with Rebecca as easily. Clearly something had to be done about that girl, but not right now.

Batya was afraid Rebecca would tell Harvey about the picture frame. She should have known Rebecca would notice the replacement. Harvey didn't seem to care that she switched lamps or chairs, but a frame that held the photo of his precious Elaine, that would bother him.

That's when Rebecca walked into Batya's kitchen and held out an expensively wrapped small box. She was following the script worked out with Sarah and Helen.

"What's this?" said Batya.

"It's a peace offering. I'm sorry about the argument, especially for bringing up all that stuff about the Nazis."

Batya didn't say anything. She unwrapped the package and saw a wallet with a designer's logo on the leather.

"This one's authentic. I made sure," said Rebecca. "You know, it matches that handbag of my mother's on the very top shelf of the hall closet. You could use this wallet with that purse. It would look very smart."

When Elaine died, her sisters-in-law went through her clothes to see what should be given to charity, what should be thrown out or given to someone else. Helen remembered finding the expensive bag that Elaine purchased just before she got sick. Someone would like this she thought. Helen put the bag someplace safe and then forgot about it. Rebecca and Batya's fight about the leather purse reminded her.

Batya looked at the gift carefully. It was easy to see the wallet was of superior quality to the handbag she'd bought. Batya was intrigued at the idea of an expensive bag hidden in a closet. What else was secreted in this house? What else did Rebecca know about?

Batya took a deep breath. "I guess we both got overexcited," she said. "Anything connected to the Holocaust is a very emotional subject for me. I forget you were raised so differently. I can't expect you to understand."

Rebecca nodded, trying to look repentant.

"I know we both care for your father and your brother and want to live together in peace," said Batya. "Let's not talk about it anymore. Come, it's almost dinner time. Why don't you help me get ready?"

"Sure, something smells really good."

"It's Hungarian goulash," said Batya. "A little different from the way your aunts cook. If you like it, I could show you how to make it."

"That would be great," Rebecca replied.

At dinner, Harvey was pleased to see Batya and Rebecca finally getting along. "It's so good to come home from a hard day at work to such a loving family," he said as he took a second helping of the goulash that he knew would give him heartburn.

During the months that followed, Batya and Rebecca tried to get along. Rebecca admitted she liked Batya's Hungarian cooking and learned to follow a few of her recipes. Batya admired the pop art posters that lined Rebecca's room and borrowed a book on modern art from the library so she could say something knowledgeable about them.

Rebecca saved her tutoring fees and bought a new silver frame for her mother's photo.

Batya saw the frame, didn't say anything about it.

31.

BLAME THE BLONDE CHIPPIE

For many years, Abraham and Estelle Lapidus sat four rows behind the Rosens in the synagogue. The families didn't know each other very well, but the Lapiduses seemed to be nice people. They lived in a pleasant looking house, bought Israeli bonds and gave reasonable donations to the *shul*. They greeted each other warmly if their paths crossed.

When Estelle was involved in a fatal auto accident, the Rosens sent a donation to the appropriate charity and visited the Lapidus house during the *shiva* period, bringing a large fruit and cheese platter.

Two years after that sad event, Helen glanced behind her during the Rosh Hashanah services and noticed Abe. He looked great. He'd lost his paunch, his thinning hair was obviously styled by a professional, and he had a healthy tan.

Shirley Rappaport, who was always up to date on *shul* gossip, sat in front of the Rosens. Helen tapped her on the shoulder. "Have you seen Abe Lapidus?" she said. "Being a widower certainly agrees with him."

Shirley twisted around. "You don't know?" she said. "He's got a girlfriend. They just got back from a week in Boca."

"I didn't hear a thing," said Rachel who was sitting next to

Helen. "We've been busy lately." She nodded toward Batya, who was at the end of the row, her head buried in her prayer book.

"I've heard," said Shirley. "Well, Abe certainly didn't befriend a rabbi's daughter. I hear in the *schmatta* business there are naked models running around the factory all the time. One of them didn't run very fast. Frieda from the Sisterhood Hospitality Committee got a glimpse of the happy couple getting into a cab last week. There was Abe holding open the door while his companion stuck out her *tush* and actually wiggled it in his face as she got in."

"*Oy*, that little bald-headed *pisher*," said Rachel. "So, as soon as she's gone, he figures out a way to make himself feel like a big man."

The women tried not to laugh too loudly and disturb the services. "You're sure it was Abe?" said Helen.

"These are Frieda's exact words," said Shirley. "Abe Lapidus, upstanding member of the community, former vice president of the Pelham Parkway Synagogue, is running around with a blonde chippie."

• • •

The Rosen clan came out in force for Rebecca's high school graduation, and cheered loudly when her name was called.

After the ceremony, families lingered to pose for pictures with cap and gown-clad offspring and share news.

"My son is going to CCNY," one father said.

"My daughter to Hunter," someone's mother replied.

"The twins are both going to NYU," added a beaming *Bubbe*.

"We made Columbia," said a mother in a huge, flowered hat. "We're Ivy Leaguers."

And Rebecca? Rebecca, who always got straight A's. Where was she going? To a rundown apartment and a minimum wage job.

Rebecca had answered a classified ad and found an aspiring

actress who worked as a waitress and leased a fourth-floor walk-up in Manhattan. Her current roommate was leaving at the end of the summer, and Rebecca could move in after Labor Day.

With few secretarial skills and a confusing high school transcript, Rebecca couldn't get hired in a fancy office. She found a job at a small finance company that made high interest loans to people who didn't qualify for bank loans.

Saul approved. It sounded like a place where Rebecca could learn about finance, how to make money and how to avoid scams. "Never forget, rich or poor it's good to have money," he said.

Rebecca agreed. "I want to be around people who know about money. I want to be able to take care of myself," she said.

"A place for a Rosen," said Harvey shaking his head. But he didn't try to stop Rebecca from taking the job. Batya was delighted but tried not to show how happy she was at the thought of Rebecca going anywhere. Anywhere out of her home.

Helen didn't like it. None of it. "A girl like Rebecca should be living at home with her family and going to a good college, not spending her time with who knows who, doing who knows what," she said to anyone within hearing distance.

Rebecca told her to stop the rant. "When did I ever do what everyone else did?" she said. "You know that if I stay in that house too long it'll be a disaster. Either Batya will kill me, or I'll kill her. There's been enough bloodshed." She pointed to the spot where she'd pressed the pen into her arm. It looked like a freckle or a wart; Rebecca thought of it as a badge of honor.

"Just give me a little while to get settled. By next year I'll be in night school, showing up everyone else's child. Don't worry, you'll have a chance to *kvell* about me yet."

Helen decided they should celebrate the graduation with a

family dinner in a big, fancy Manhattan restaurant. Things had seemed fairly amicable between Batya and Rebecca recently, both were looking forward to Rebecca leaving home.

Batya said she was willing to go to a non-kosher restaurant because, "I know that's what all of you prefer and this is a special day for you. The family should enjoy it however they want. You know I don't like to make a fuss."

Batya had just purchased her first pair of dressy slacks and thought this would be a great time to show them off since no one who had known her before her marriage would be in such a place.

"We'll go to a seafood restaurant, that'll be easiest for her. But that means no shellfish for the rest of us," said Helen. "Let's not pull apart lobsters while she sits there making disapproving faces. We'll meet her halfway."

So, there they all were, a typical family celebrating a graduation at Catch O' The Sea. Everyone was behaving well. They'd all ordered salads and fish that was kosher: salmon, filet of sole, and halibut.

Batya smiled a lot. She told the waiter to give Harvey extra vegetables instead of French fries. "I want you to stay healthy," she said, patting his hand. "We have a long, happy life together ahead of us."

Harvey nodded but didn't look happy.

Morris ordered a bottle of wine and, when everyone's glass was full, stood to make a toast, "To the first of our children to graduate from an American high school," he said and, turning to Rebecca, "Your mama in heaven is *kvelling.*" He looked at the rest of the children. "Remember, I expect to celebrate lots more of these *simchas.*"

Suddenly, Rachel grabbed Helen's arm and put her hand over her mouth. "Don't look now, but Abe Lapidus just came through the door," she said in a voice everyone could hear. "With the blonde chippie!"

In unison, all the Rosen heads spun around.

"This is a family restaurant," Helen said. "The man has no shame."

Rebecca started to laugh. Unlike her aunt, she didn't cover her mouth, a mouth which, thanks to Morris, was full of wine. It sprayed all over Batya who was seated next to her.

"*Oy vey!*" cried Batya, furious about the purple splotches seeping into her new outfit. She grabbed a passing waiter. "Quick!" she yelled at him. "I need club soda before it stains!"

Saul and Morris noticed the commotion and looked up. "Hey, there's Abe Lapidus," said Morris. "And look who he's with."

"Hey, Lapidus, how's it going?" said Saul in a voice that carried across the place.

The expression on Abe's face made it clear he wished he had walked into any other restaurant, anywhere else in the world. He nodded at their table and smiled, desperately looking for someone to seat him, but the head waiter was escorting another party.

Saul waved his hand. "Come say hello. We're having a celebration."

Batya was furiously plunging her napkin into the glass of club soda and dabbing at her new slacks. She hissed at Rebecca, "Look what you've done."

No one cared about Batya's stained clothes. All eyes were on Abe Lapidus' companion. The chippie was standing directly beneath a chandelier, and the light shone on her, from the top of her towering, platinum, French twist hairdo, down to the rhinestone buckles on her red satin spiked heel shoes. She was wearing a silky turquoise jumpsuit with a wide gold zipper that strained to hold the outfit together. A jeweled chain circled her neck and disappeared into her ample cleavage. From her arm dangled a beaded purse shaped like a French poodle.

Resignedly, Abe slowly approached their table. "What's the occasion?" he said.

"You know my niece, Rebecca," said Saul. "She just graduated from high school."

"Well, congratulations young lady," said Abe, patting Rebecca on the back. "I remember when you were just a little girl running up and down the aisles in the synagogue."

He turned to Harvey and reached out his hand. "And congratulations to you, may you have lots more *naches* from your children." The chippie stood silently next to Abe.

Harvey stood and extended his hand. "I don't believe you've met my new wife," he said, nodding toward Batya. "Batya, say hello to Abe. He's a prominent member of our congregation."

"Oh yes," said Abe. "I heard about the joyous event. Well then, even more congratulations are in order."

"Thank you," said Batya. "I'd like to stand up and shake your hand, but I'm indisposed. I apologize for the way I look. And smell." She indicated her stained clothing.

"Oh, that's happened to me lots of times," said the chippie. "Sometimes a drink gets frisky. You have to go bottoms up before the liquor jumps out of the glass." She laughed, revealing large, irregular teeth, and bent over to hug Batya's shoulder with the hand holding the poodle purse.

Batya gave her a tight smile and a nod.

"What a cute bag," said Rebecca.

"Thanks, I just love it," said the chippie. "I was so excited when I woke up Christmas morning and found what Abie had hung on my tree."

All minds were whirring. Abe Lapidus celebrating Christmas!

Hanging presents from a tree!

"Guess what?" said the chippie. "If you pull its little jeweled tail it barks. Try it."

Rebecca reached up and tugged the tail. The purse emitted a loud "Woooof, woooof, woooof" which is apparently how a sequined dog barks if it has a French accent. As she pulled her hand away from the purse, Rebecca bumped into Batya's wineglass, which toppled over and spilled its contents into Batya's still damp lap, creating a larger, deeper purple blotch.

"Oops! Need some more club soda?" asked Rebecca sweetly.

"I think our table is ready," said Abe Lapidus. He grabbed his companion and pulled her away.

"Nice to meet all of you," called out the chippie.

Batya sat perfectly still, feeling the dark red wine seep into her lap, permanently staining her first pair of slacks, very wide-legged, expensive slacks she'd bought for her first trip to a fancy, non-kosher restaurant, a deviation from the Orthodox dress code that she'd justified to herself by noting that when she was still it looked like she wearing a skirt.

"They're the latest fashion," the saleslady had said. "They're a little pricey, but you'll know they're worth the money when you see every other woman in the place envy you."

For a moment Batya thought the stains might be God's retribution for her immodest outfit but immediately dismissed the idea. It was all Rebecca's fault. She turned to Harvey. "I hope you don't expect me to sit here reeking like a drunkard."

"It was an accident," said Harvey. "Don't get so upset. No one cares."

"I'm really sorry," said Rebecca as she took another drink of wine.

"Only someone with no respect for me could do such a thing to me, in public, in front of a synagogue official," Batya hissed loudly. She stood up and marched towards the door. Aware that all eyes were on her, Batya straightened her back, head high, determined to maintain her dignity, hoping the wide legged slacks wouldn't catch on her high heels and cause her to trip.

Harvey watched Batya walk away. She paused a few feet away from their table. He knew his wife was waiting for him to join her exit from the restaurant.

But it's a celebration, he thought. After all she's been through, my Rebecca got top grades this year. She's an American high school graduate, becoming an attractive grown woman, and every day the resemblance to her dear mother grew stronger.

Harvey leaned over to Rebecca. "I have to go. I'm sure you understand." He kissed Rebecca on the cheek. "I'm very proud of you. Your mother would be proud too. Enjoy yourself."

Everyone watched Harvey catch up to Batya, take her arm and leave the restaurant. Rebecca didn't move, didn't say a word. Then she heard her uncles whispering.

"With a *tuchis* like that she shouldn't wear such pants," said Saul.

"If she stumbles on those stilts her wig could fly into someone's soup," said Morris.

"And what if it's clam chowder?" laughed Saul. "The wig will become *traife*. Can you make hair kosher again? Quick, find a rabbi."

"Never mind a rabbi, find the waiter," said Morris. "See if we can still change our orders. Salmon I can get at home. When I go to a fancy restaurant like this, I want shellfish." He grabbed the arm of a passing waiter. "Get me a shrimp cocktail and a jumbo lobster tail with extra butter."

About half an hour later, as they all sat around the messy table, wearing lobster bibs, having a great time, Morris ordered a bottle of champagne. "I'm making another toast," he said, standing up. "This time, Rebecca, remember you're supposed to swallow your drink."

"Okay," she laughed. "I'll try."

"To family, and celebrations and good food," he said, holding up his glass. "And, for making it possible for us to enjoy this dinner in good company, to the blonde chippie!"

32.

EXILE

Almost an hour after they got home from the graduation celebration, Saul, Sarah and Helen heard their doorbell ring. It was late and their minds flashed to that time, years ago, when Harvey had appeared in their doorway in the middle of the night.

This time it was Rebecca, shaking and talking as soon as the door opened. "He did it again," she said. "He sent me away. My father doesn't want me in his house."

Helen put her arms around Rebecca and brought her inside. "Take it easy, my child," she said. "Come in. Sit down. Calm yourself."

Rebecca came inside, but she wasn't calm. Her hands were trembling. Helen put her own hands over Rebecca's until her fingers relaxed. "Take your time," said Helen. "There's no rush. Sarah, get a glass of water. We'll all just sit here quietly until you're ready to talk."

Rebecca quietly sipped the water, relaxed a little and closed her eyes, seeing the whole scene all over again.

She and Marvin had been laughing as they climbed the stoop to their house. "Shhh," said Rebecca. "If I'm lucky they've gone to bed, and I won't have to deal with the fiasco in the restaurant until morning. If I'm really lucky, Batya will have calmed down by then, compensated by dad's offer to have her buy a new, more expensive outfit."

As Rebecca reached for her keys, the door swung open. "Get in! Right away!" said Harvey. "Stop carrying on and disturbing the neighbors."

They walked into the house and saw Batya standing in the living room. Standing very still. Batya had taken off her makeup and stained clothing and was wearing a floor length dark purple robe. She wasn't wearing her wig. A cotton scarf was wrapped around her head covering her thin, grey-streaked hair.

She looks so old, thought Rebecca. She looks so crazy.

Batya was standing in the middle of a puddle of splintered, multi-colored glass. Elaine had collected glass figurines. Five miniature farm animals had stood on the mantel when everyone left for the graduation celebration. Now they were gone.

Rebecca and Marvin didn't ask what had happened. They knew Batya liked to throw things when she got angry.

Marvin looked at the floor. "I'll get a broom," he said.

"Just go to bed," Harvey said. "There are things to discuss that don't concern you."

He didn't move, just looked at Rebecca. When she nodded, he slowly started towards his bedroom.

"Now!" yelled Harvey, and Marvin tripped running up the stairs. Everyone was silent until they heard Marvin's door slam.

Then Batya looked at Harvey. "You tell her. Tell her right now!" she hissed.

"Look, I'm sorry I got some wine on your outfit. It was very pretty. I'll take it to the cleaners first thing tomorrow and pay to have the stain removed," Rebecca said.

"You'll pay? Just like your crooked uncles, you think you can buy your way out of everything," said Batya.

Rebecca's eyes opened wide. She'd never heard anyone say such things about the Rosens aloud. Harvey was startled too. How nice to finally have someone who's on my side, he thought.

Harvey turned towards Rebecca. "First of all, congratulations again on your graduation and your plans for the future." He was speaking softly, trying to sound calm. "Now, there's no reason to get excited but, since you're planning to move anyway, maybe you should arrange to go a little sooner. Maybe very soon. Things have gotten uncomfortable here; that would be for the best."

Batya stamped her foot, splintering one of the larger glass shards with her heavy leather slippers. "Things are uncomfortable? It's for the best?" she screamed. "Tell her the truth. Tell her that she's made life unbearable. Tell her she has to go! Has to go immediately! It's too bad her aunts will take her in. I wish she had to spend time on the streets where such a person belongs." She stared at Rebecca, her hands in fists. "You don't get to ruin my life, to rob me of my place. Get out of here before I throw you out. We never want to see you again."

Rebecca stared back, her eyes wide. Nothing like a reform school to teach you how to deal with crazies, she thought. Take one step towards me you horrible old witch, and I'll pick up that ugly lamp and smash it over your head.

Rebecca turned to her father and spoke softly, her muted voice startling after Batya's screeching. "We? She's speaking for you? She has the right to throw me out, like you threw me out once before? Out of her house? Her place?"

Rebecca was almost as tall as Harvey. She looked into his eyes. "Are you still my father, or do you belong to her too?"

"Of course you're still my daughter, and I'm still your papa who loves you." Harvey spoke slowly. "The last time you left, when you went to that place, I was heartbroken, but everyone said it was for the best. I was so glad when you came back; I thought we would all live happily together. Be a happy family. But it hasn't worked out. We're all unhappy. This is no way to live, not for any of us. You planned to move out soon. What harm is it for you to move a little sooner?"

He really can't see the harm, thought Rebecca. It's just a scheduling issue to him. She looked at her father and Batya standing together.

I don't want to be around such people anymore she thought, turned and walked out of her home before Batya could see her cry.

When Rebecca finished her story, Helen hugged her, and they rocked back and forth slowly.

The phone rang, startling everyone. Saul picked it up, listened for a few minutes and handed the receiver to Helen. "It's Rachel," he said. "Marvin is at their place. He walked out of his house in his pajamas without anyone noticing. He said there was too much noise for him to sleep. He's lying in the bed they keep ready for him pretending he's asleep."

Helen took the phone and filled Rachel in on what had happened.

"Oh my God," said Rachel. "And our husbands thought we were crazy when we insisted on staying close to those children. Where would Marvin have gone--alone, scared, in his pajamas--if I wasn't nearby. Let me know if I can help you. As for Marvin, he doesn't seem in any condition to talk. I'll kiss him goodnight and leave my bedroom door open. He knows that means he can come in and talk to me during the night. I'll speak to him tomorrow morning when he's had some rest and we know more."

Helen told Rebecca about Marvin. "He's such a good kid," said Rebecca. "And smarter than people give him credit for. I wonder how long it'll take before they notice he's missing."

She nibbled on a cookie Helen had given her.

"You did the right thing to come here," said Saul. "You know you're part of us."

"You look exhausted," Helen said. "Try to get some sleep. We can talk more tomorrow."

"The extra bed in my room is always ready for you," Sarah said. She wondered what it was like to be kicked out of your own house. She believed that no matter what she did, Helen and Saul would never act like this. The ties between Sarah and her parents were strong, sometimes stronger than she liked, but not tonight.

"Do you want to talk?" she whispered into the darkness when Rebecca was settled in her room. But Rebecca fell asleep immediately.

"Again that man turned his back on his own child," Helen said to Saul as she put away the plate of cookies she'd brought out. "What kind of person can do that? They think they're such good Jews, Harvey and Batya. But that's not the way our people behave. Even animals take care of their young."

"Such a fuss over such a stupid thing," said Saul. "Breaking up a family because a child knocks over a glass? I don't understand such things."

"All I can think about is going over there, picking up that lamp myself and swinging it at Batya," said Helen. "And I'd take a swing at Harvey, too."

Saul chuckled softly. "So now you're Mickey Mantle?" he said. "Come on slugger, time for bed. We'll talk more tomorrow."

The next morning, Batya rang Rachel's doorbell at about 6

a.m. "Is Marvin here?" she demanded, obviously distraught. She'd thrown a raincoat over her long nightgown, a faded kerchief tied around her head.

"You finally noticed he was missing?" said Rachel. "He's asleep, being watched over by people who love and care for him, like a child should be."

Batya didn't say a word, just ran upstairs. Rachel was right behind. Her children were still asleep, but Marvin was up, quietly getting dressed in clothes he kept at Rachel's house. Batya ran into the room.

"Don't ever do that again," she said, hugging Marvin. "I almost had a heart attack when I got up this morning and saw you were missing. I was ready to call the police. Quick, finish dressing, and let's go home."

The boys woke up. "What's going on?" they asked. "When did you get here, Marvin?"

Rachel put her arms out to Marvin. "You don't have to leave," she told him. "Come downstairs, have breakfast with the boys, with your family, we'll figure out what to do next."

"There's nothing to figure out," Batya said to Marvin. "Breakfast is waiting for you in your own house."

"Where's Rebecca?" asked Marvin.

"At Aunt Helen's house," said Rachel.

"She's okay?"

"Yes," said Rachel. "Do you want to go see her?"

"I'll go later," said Marvin.

He finished getting dressed and hugged Rachel. "Thanks for letting me stay. I'm okay. Honest."

Batya put her arm around Marvin's shoulder as they walked out the door but he pulled away.

Rebecca woke early and announced she had no intention of

apologizing to Harvey and Batya. No one disagreed.

After breakfast they started playing Monopoly, but halfway through the game everyone lost interest. They played blackjack for matchsticks; Helen wiped everyone out, and no one cared. Saul turned on a baseball game and turned it off in the middle of the third inning. Rebecca worked on a crossword puzzle, broke the point on her pencil and walked away. Sarah kept walking around the house to see what everyone was doing.

Saul was the first to crack. A little before noon he picked up the phone. "Harvey," he said. "In case you're curious, Elaine's daughter is here. We're taking good care of her. Like family should." Then he hung up. A few minutes later, Harvey and Marvin rang his bell.

Rebecca answered the door. Marvin stepped next to her. "You okay?" he asked.

Rebecca put her arm around his waist. "I'm fine. Don't worry." She turned to Harvey. "Anything changed?"

"I don't want you to be mad. I love you. I want the best for all of us."

"You still want Batya to stay? Want me to go?"

"But you want to leave, you've never been happy living at home."

"Let's take a walk, Marvin," Rebecca said. "Papa and I have nothing to say to each other."

Harvey watched his children walk away. Marvin was almost as tall as Rebecca. Soon he'd be as tall as his father, maybe taller.

"If you want to talk you can come inside," said Saul. Harvey went into the house. No one offered to take his jacket. No one offered him a chair. No one offered him anything to eat. Harvey put up his hands, his fingers spread wide. He had large hands. He could really hurt someone, Helen thought.

"Before you start yelling, hear me out," he said. "Remember,

Rebecca has been talking about moving for months now. Okay, maybe Batya overreacted last night, but even before that Rebecca and Batya haven't been happy living together."

"You choose that woman over your own flesh and blood?" said Saul. "How does that happen?

"I choose a chance for a life with happiness, with peace and contentment. Don't I deserve that?" Harvey faced Helen. "You think it didn't break my heart when Rebecca wound up at that place. But what choice did I have? Then I met Batya, I got married, I had a new life. A happy life. The kind of life I always wanted. A real Jewish home, with a woman who understands what that means and wants it too.

"Now I come home from work, from a job where I'm not respected." Harvey turned to Saul, who shrugged. "I walk through my door, and I inhale the blessedness in my house. My body relaxes. I know I'm where I belong."

"And the times you look like you've been whipped? When you're afraid to say anything about Elaine's earrings, about financial issues, those are part of the blessings?" Helen said.

Harvey put up his hands again. "Are there problems, you're asking? Of course. We're human," he said. "But overall Batya has given me a good life. And not just me. Marvin is happy too. Or, he was happy until Rebecca came home and he wound up living in a house where there's always fighting, where he feels disloyal to his sister when he remembers how good Batya has been to him."

Helen looked at Harvey. "These things you're saying, they're things Batya told you to say to prove you can stand up to the Rosens?"

"You're doubting I can think for myself," Harvey said. "You think you have the right to do that because of all the years you've mixed in between me and my daughter? I don't understand why

299

Rebecca is so mad at me when you were the one who arranged for her to go to that place."

"Mixing in? That's what you think I've been doing?" said Helen, her fists clenched. "You don't remember you couldn't even be bothered to pick up the phone and talk to the police when Rebecca was arrested. You kept it all a secret until the situation was so bad there was no way to help her but to get her away from you."

They glared at each other. Harvey gave in first. He slumped and turned away.

"You've had your say," said Helen. "Now it's time for you to leave. We'll talk to Rebecca and let you know what's decided."

Harvey opened the door. "When Marvin gets back send him home," he said. "To his own home. With his own family."

When the door closed, Saul looked at Helen. "You stayed calmer than I expected. So, what do you say?"

"I say that Batya is certainly an impressive woman. Not enough she's a Talmudic scholar, it turns out she's also a *moyle*. But maybe not such a good one, maybe a little too enthusiastic with the knife. If Harvey loses anymore of his manhood, he'll have to sit down when he pees."

• • •

Rebecca called her future roommate to see if she could move in earlier. They arranged for Rebecca to arrive the following week, sleep on the living room couch and pay half the rent they'd agreed upon until the other girl moved out.

Rachel waited until she saw Batya leave the house, then slid a note under the door to let her know that she and Helen would be there from noon to 3 p.m. the next day to get Rebecca's things. Batya should be absent.

In Rebecca's room, Helen kept thinking of the last time she went through this closet, this chest of drawers, the day she packed a suitcase for Rebecca to take to that school. She walked into the master bedroom and started opening drawers and closets, careful not to disturb anything. "I couldn't find a jewelry box," she told Rachel. "I wanted to get Elaine's things. I guess Batya hid them."

"Imagine that," said Rachel. "She doesn't trust us.

Rebecca left for her new job from Helen and Saul's house and returned there each night for a week. "Everyone is friendly," she said. "The other clerks told me that, if I go to the beach over the weekend and a client admires my tan, I should say I'd just gotten back from the Bahamas. 'Tell them it was the best vacation of your life. Then add that in just a few minutes you can get their loan refinanced so they could go there too.'" Getting a client to renew a loan earned an employee points that added up to bonuses.

Saul laughed. "Sounds like a place that knows how to make money," he said. "You can learn things from such people." Helen just frowned. Sarah asked if any cute guys were working there.

Marvin told his cousins that things were tense at home. Batya had told Harvey and Marvin not to have any contact with Rebecca. No visits, no letters, no phone calls, no discussion of her.

"Such a *shanda* that Elaine's child should wind up without any parents," sighed Helen.

"Well, Marvin and Rebecca know we'll always be there for them. I told Marvin to use my phone if he wanted to call Rebecca," said Rachel. "If Rebecca wants to call him, send something or come by and see him, my house is open."

On Saturday, Rebecca's belongings were loaded into Saul's car, and he drove the family to Rebecca's new walk-up apartment. Sarah looked around. So, this was what a first apartment looked like. The place hadn't been painted in a while, posters were thumb-tacked to the walls, rugs were faded, an armchair looked like it had been picked up from the street and the glassware and dishes didn't match. I'll do better, she thought; no one would be rushing her to move out.

Helen looked around carefully. It was old, but clean. It could be worse, she decided. The two girls who lived there introduced themselves politely.

Saul whispered to Sarah, "You hear the accents? *Very* American. *Shiksas*. Definitely not from New York."

Helen went into the kitchen and opened the nearly empty refrigerator. The freezer compartment contained only a bottle of vodka and some TV dinners. Helen filled it with things she'd bought earlier that week, neatly labeled packages of lamb chops, roasts, chicken and hamburger. Although the freezer badly needed to be defrosted, Helen managed to find room for the Tupperware containers of beef stew and noodle pudding she'd made yesterday. She filled the rest of the fridge with juice, milk, eggs, cold cuts and a brisket, cooked and ready to be served.

"Come back anytime," said the roommates.

Saul offered to take everyone out for dinner, but Rebecca said she was tired. "You'll feed us another time," she promised. Everyone hugged, and then, finally, walked down the stairs.

They managed to reach the car before Helen began to cry.

33.

DIPLOMACY

Within a month of her move, Saul told Helen that Harvey was asking about Rebecca. "He wants to know if we hear from her. What her apartment is like. Who she is living with."

Helen wrote down Rebecca's phone number. "I'm glad he still has some humanity in him," she said. "Give this to Harvey. When things get a little slow at work, you can say, 'Now would be a good time for you to call Rebecca.'"

"When things get a little slow at work it's time to call customers and try to find more business," Saul said, but he took the note.

Soon a channel of communication was established. Harvey and Rebecca called each other from work almost every other week. "Not bad," said Helen. "Not what Elaine would want; not what Rebecca deserves, but a normal relationship will have to wait a while."

Rebecca worked hard and soon landed a better job, one that offered more money, more opportunity and evening college tuition reimbursement. She relocated to New Jersey, where rents were cheaper, and found a nicer apartment. Helen showed up with a house-warming present that filled her new refrigerator.

But Rebecca's new job frowned on employees making personal

phone calls at work. Harvey and his daughter would have to speak to each other in the evenings.

"I need to call Morris and check something for tomorrow," Harvey said, making a call from his study when Batya was busy in the kitchen.

He rushed to pick up the phone if it rang at a time Rebecca was likely to call. "I think it's a customer with a complaint. I don't know how they get my home number. I'll take it in my study and get rid of him as soon as I can."

But Harvey had forgotten that the New Jersey area code was indicated on the phone bill, which Batya carefully checked each month. She had taken over all the household finances, telling Harvey it was her duty as a good wife to make sure they didn't get cheated.

She spotted the calls to New Jersey and became suspicious. She had been waiting for Harvey to revisit the question of contact with Rebecca. He had been too quiet for too long.

Batya called the number on the phone bill, and a strange voice answered.

"Is Rebecca there?"

"No, she's out. Want to leave a message?"

Batya hung up.

Batya was in the hallway, phone bill in hand, when Harvey came home. "You're making calls to her? To *her*? To that girl who practically spat in my face! Who said things to me I can't bear to repeat! That's how you spend your time?" Batya pushed the phone bill into Harvey's hand. There was a red circle around each call to New Jersey.

"She's my daughter," he said. "She's all alone. How can I turn my back on her?"

304

"Is that what your sisters-in-law tell you?" yelled Batya. "What their husbands say? Alone? That girl has more people looking out for her than anyone needs. Certainly more than I ever had. So this is the cause of all those calls about work you've started to get at home? I was feeling so sorry. 'My poor husband has to work night and day,' I thought. Now I find out what's really going on."

"Batya," said Harvey. "It's a call. Every week or so. To my only daughter, the child of my poor Elaine, may she rest in peace. What's so terrible?"

"It's a lie, a lie between a husband and a wife," she said. "You need me to explain why that's so terrible? You don't know how many times it says lying is forbidden in all the sacred writings you think you know so well. Did you lie like this to Elaine? The wife who wouldn't even bother to keep a decent kosher home for you like I do. What kind of man responds to righteousness with deceit?"

Harvey sighed. He knew he had made a mistake when he mentioned Elaine. But he was tired; he had had a hard day. He wanted a nice meal, some rest, maybe to read Torah with Batya and get his mind off the day's aggravation. He didn't want to fight.

Harvey apologized and promised he wouldn't have anything more to do with Rebecca. He asked Batya for forgiveness.

Graciously, she forgave him. This time.

Harvey tried to stick to his promise, but he missed talking to Rebecca. When they weren't fighting, he could see what a bright, funny daughter he had. He came up with a clever idea: he'd call her collect. There would be no charge on their phone bill. Batya would never know.

Harvey had forgotten there were no secrets in their family. Marvin had overheard the conversation between Batya and Harvey and called Rebecca from his aunt's house to let her know what was going on. Batya had ordered Harvey to cut off all contact with his wayward offspring. Again. And again, he had agreed.

When her phone rang and an operator asked if she would accept a collect call from Harvey, Rebecca didn't hesitate to reply. "Tell that no-good bastard his daughter thinks he's a fucking coward," she yelled and slammed down the receiver.

The next day Helen called Rebecca. She agreed with Rebecca's sentiment but was shocked by such language. Rebecca wasn't surprised Helen knew her exact words; the woman was psychic.

Actually, Harvey told Morris, who told Rachel, who told Helen. That's the way things work in a *shtetl*

Helen, of course, wasn't finished trying to reestablish contact between Rebecca and Harvey. She knew about feuds that lasted a lifetime, people who endured terminal separation from family members because of monetary disputes or unintended slights. "It's the principle of the thing," people declared and went to their deathbeds without acknowledging their flesh and blood.

Helen didn't have such principles. She believed in flexibility and compromise. In Helen Rosen's world, parents and children stayed in touch, with each other and, if possible, with the rest of the family. They might not like each other very much, they might not share beliefs, but they were never completely estranged. As Saul had told Sarah years before, "You don't turn your back on your own blood."

Helen bided her time. Tempers needed to cool down. And, sure enough, three weeks later Harvey rang her doorbell just before dinner. He had come directly from work so Batya wouldn't know of his visit. He didn't say hello, didn't ask how she was. He just bowed his head and said, "I miss my Rebecca. I need your help. Again."

Helen tried not to gloat. "Maybe it was Batya's experiences during the war, or her failed marriage, or maybe she's just a kind of person I don't know anything about, but whatever the reason she's the way she is, it's no excuse for you to forget who you are. You're a father. If you don't stand up for your own child, what good are you?"

Harvey stared at his shoes. Helen looked at him with contempt, wanting to throw him out of her house. If she hadn't promised Elaine, on her deathbed, that she would help; if he wasn't Rebecca's father; if he wasn't Marvin's father...but he was.

"Go home," she told Harvey. "Your strictly kosher dinner is waiting. You don't want your wife to be mad. I'll do what I can. But you should know I'm not getting involved to help you. I'm only doing this because I believe it will be bad for Rebecca to go through life with a living father with whom she has no contact. She's gone through enough."

Harvey didn't thank her. He didn't say anything. He turned and slowly walked home.

Helen phoned Batya the next day. "It's been so long since I've seen you," she said. "We should catch up. Would it be convenient for me to come over this afternoon?"

Batya said she was busy for the next few days but would be glad to see Helen next week.

"I'm going to eat some crow," Helen told Rachel. "Who knew it was kosher?"

Helen decided not to pretend she didn't know the whole story about the phone calls. Batya wouldn't believe that. As soon as she walked through the door, before Batya could say a word, Helen put her arms out and embraced Batya.

"You poor dear. What you've had to endure. These men, all of them, just terrible. A wife does everything for them, the least they could do is treat her with honesty. A woman like you, a woman everyone knows is so educated, so wise, how could Harvey think he could fool you?

"Of course I don't think cutting off contact between Harvey and Rebecca was the right thing to do, but ignoring a wife's feelings, that's equally wrong. You tell him not to make calls and he makes them anyway. Collect calls? What nonsense. The lack of respect for your intelligence is almost as bad as the lying."

Helen took a deep breath. She'd twice mentioned Batya's intelligence and her education. That should do it.

Batya smiled, a humble, but still victorious, smile.

"I know you and the rest of your family think Harvey married a religious fanatic with no sympathy for an unfortunate child. You should know that no one cares more about family than the Orthodox. Maybe my ways were uncomfortable for her, but I never meant to be unkind. And remember, I was adjusting to a new environment too. I'd expected challenges, but I didn't expect to be surrounded by people who had no respect for me or where I came from."

Helen started to say something, but Batya put up her hand.

"I didn't meet Rebecca until your family had sent her away. I expected her to be angry with all of you, but she turned her anger on me. I was the intruder. No matter how I tried, she always resented me. In order to survive, to have the family life I wanted, that Harvey and Marvin needed and deserved, she had to leave."

Helen tried to gauge Batya's sincerity but decided it didn't matter. "It must be hard to be such a sensitive person," she said.

The two women had coffee, ate danish and reached an accord. Batya would let Harvey make occasional telephone calls to Rebecca. Helen would spread the word about how magnanimous

Batya had been.

Batya claimed the moral high ground. Helen achieved her goal of enabling communication between Harvey and Rebecca.

The women kissed each other on the cheek as Batya closed the door to her house and Helen went home to call Harvey and tell him he could phone Rebecca.

It was said in the family that it was a pity Helen had never joined the diplomatic corps. Subjected to unlimited amounts of rhetoric, copious amounts of food, an intuitive spy network and an ability to inflict guilt derived directly from the pages of the Old Testament, Arabs and Israelis would have long ago thrown up their hands, thrown down their weapons and agreed to peace.

"Anything to get her to leave us alone," they would have muttered in various Semitic dialects. "Of course she acts from love. But even with love, enough already."

34.

THE NEXT GENERATION

Rachel's sons were all lackluster students. She suspected they'd do better if they paid more attention to their studies and less time to having fun. But when she tried to get them to buckle down, their father interceded. "They're only young once," said Morris. "Let them enjoy their youth." He reminded her that he'd never been a great student and hadn't done too badly for himself.

Both parents were proud of their American children: tall, good-looking boys, who played several sports, had lots of friends and were popular with the girls.

The war in Vietnam was on everyone's minds, and a student deferment was the best way to avoid the draft. Kenny was admitted to a small, non-competitive, business college a short subway commute from home. He studied management, helped school teams win championships, made lots of friends and kept busy making sure his parents didn't discover that he occasionally dated non-Jewish girls.

Kenny's college management courses were of little use when he worked at the Rosen Company during summer vacations. However, he liked the status of being the boss' son, the high salary and thought he'd enter the business when he graduated. Meanwhile, he was healthy and happy and safe. Rachel was satisfied.

Kenny and one of his brothers eventually took over the Rosen Company. They wound up making more money than their better educated cousins.

• • •

Sarah entered high school determined to become a different person. She had spent her early years in Rebecca's shadow; now it was time for her to shine. She declared herself a hippie: bought a few black turtleneck sweaters and some miniskirts, learned to smoke and wore white lipstick and heavy black eye make-up. She ignored her mother's threats not to let her out of the house if she didn't wash her face.

"So, is Sarah busy with dates?" inquired curious relatives. "Going to the movies every Saturday?"

Helen shook her head. "The movies Sarah wants to go to, what normal boy would take her?"

There were two date-movie theaters on the Bronx's Grand Concourse. The Paradise was large and ornate with faux Venetian balconies, a ceiling mural of a starry night and cushioned velveteen chairs that tipped back to facilitate necking. It showed all of the first run movies. Three blocks south was the Ascot, small and dirty with uncomfortable seats, and it charged more than the Paradise. The Ascot played the foreign movies shown at Manhattan art houses.

"Betsy Leibowitz tells me her nephew asked you to the movies and you said you'd only go to the Ascot," Helen said.

"Actually, I told him I wanted to catch a cinema in Greenwich Village and then get an espresso at the Fat Black Pussy Cat," Sarah said. "My second choice was the Ascot. Just to show I was flexible. I knew he wouldn't go."

"So only something by Antonionionio is good enough for my daughter. A black and white movie where no one speaks English, everyone is depressed and at least one person throws up before the film is over. Then you drink small cups of bitter coffee at a place with uncomfortable chairs. That's what you want?" Helen shook her head.

"No, I want to see Gidget Goes *Mishuganah*," Sarah said. "It takes place in Hawaii, the sun is always shining and a girl with a blonde ponytail gets so upset when she gets a pimple that she tries to throw herself into a volcano. Fortunately, her mom knows the best dermatologist on the island, and everyone lives happily ever after, dancing the hora while the volcano spews multi-colored lava."

Helen walked away.

Sarah's high school grades were good enough to get into City College. Her parents were thrilled. Sarah wasn't. She wanted to go to an out-of-town college. Helen and Saul said she could go to any college she wanted, as long as she lived at home. They weren't afraid of the tuition; they feared the exposure to the outside world, the gentile world where children lived with Cossacks, Nazis and who knew who else.

Years later, Sarah admitted to herself that she could have put up a stronger fight, maybe worn down her parents. She didn't like to admit she'd inherited her parents' fears of the outside world. It was easier to acknowledge defeat, attend CCNY and plan to get away when she graduated. Then she'd be ready to live an exciting, glamourous life, in a fabulous place far from the Bronx.

Marvin remained a good boy, progressing from junior high to high school without causing any trouble. Batya proudly told friends she couldn't understand why anyone had problems with adolescents. "I treat my Marvin with respect, and he treats me the same way. "Anyone with a little common sense can have a model teenager."

Of course, Batya never knew about Marvin's lunches with Rebecca.

Once every other month he'd skip school and head to their favorite diner in Manhattan. As soon as she saw him, Rebecca waved enthusiastically, and Marvin hoped people thought he had a date with the hot girl calling his name.

"Let me look at you," she'd say after the bear hug with which they greeted each other. "So that's what my natural color is," said Rebecca, ruffling Marvin's light brown hair. Her own hair was currently a pale auburn in a short pixie cut. "And your eyes are still a deeper blue than mine. Not fair."

"*Bubbe's* blueberry eyes," they said together and laughed.

Once they were seated and had ordered their traditional bacon cheeseburgers, brother and sister chatted non-stop, updating each other about their lives. Rebecca talked about her job, the guys she dated and the classes she was taking to get a college degree at night.

"Wow, you're really doing great," said Marvin. "Wish I could tell dad and Batya how successful you are."

"Not worth the trouble. I don't care what they think. Tell me how things are with you. What's happening in school?"

"Same old garbage. Nothing to talk about."

"How about your team? Anything happening there?"

Marvin's face lit up, and he described upcoming inter-school competitions. Rebecca asked a few questions, and within 10 minutes he'd covered three paper napkins with numbers, explaining box scores, batting averages and team odds.

"Wow, when did you become a math whizz?"

Marvin stopped writing and frowned. "Yeah, I'm a real whizz.

If things work out, I just might pass remedial algebra this term."

"I'm not kidding." Rebecca looked directly at Marvin, trying to make sure he knew she was very serious. "Manipulating numbers is what math is all about, any math. And that's what you're doing right here." She indicated the napkins he'd been scribbling on. "Remember, my allowance was always being docked, and I supported myself through high school as a math tutor. I'd be glad to give you a few pointers. I could call you at Aunt Rachel's house and go over your homework any time you want. Bet you'd catch on quick.

"Don't waste your time."

Marvin crumpled up the napkins and stuffed them into a soda glass. "School's just not my thing. Never has been. Everyone knows you're the one with the brains, I'm the dummy who can hit a ball. Let's talk about something else."

Rebecca wanted to protest, but Marvin looked close to tears. She didn't want to embarrass him so she let Marvin change the subject. He launched into a long story about their cousin Kenny's romantic escapades. Then he described Batya's continuing identification with *The Sound of Music,* how she walked around the house screeching show tunes.

Soon they were both laughing. Too soon it was time to leave.

Rebecca walked back to her office looking like someone who'd just stepped in dog shit. My dad and Batya are disgusting, she thought. The kid's convinced he's an idiot and they don't see it, or they just don't care enough to do anything about it. If I was around the house, I'd find a way to help him. I know I would. But there's nothing I can do from exile.

Marvin finished high school with a C+ average and received an award for athletic excellence. He had no idea what to do next.

With his grades, the free CUNY schools weren't an option. He could have gotten into a mediocre college like Kenny, but Harvey refused to waste money trying to educate someone not interested in learning.

Of course there would always be a spot in the Rosen business for Elaine's son, but no one was enthusiastic about that. "He's clumsy around tools and an even worse salesman than his father," Saul told Helen. And, of course, working for the Rosen Company wouldn't change his 1A draft status.

No one knew what to do with him. No one, that is, but the Selective Service.

Marvin had a low lottery number. Soon after his high school graduation he received a letter from his draft board telling him to show up for a pre-induction physical.

35.

MARVIN GOES TO WAR

The family tried to figure out some way to deal with Marvin's situation.

Rachel called Harvey and told him it was his fault. "It's because you're too cheap to send Marvin to a college like the one Kenny goes to," she said. Harvey hung up without saying a word.

Saul thought they should find a doctor who would say Marvin had a condition that made the star athlete ineligible for the army. He called dozens of people. No one knew such a doctor or would admit that they did.

Sarah thought Marvin should go to Canada. She reminded her family that going into exile to escape an unjust war was a Jewish tradition.

"If he goes to Canada, Marvin might never be able to come home again," Helen said. "Who does he know in Canada? What could he do there?"

"That sounds like the reason so many Jews stayed in Germany until it was too late," said Sarah.

Saul told her not to talk about things she didn't understand and walked away.

"If the border crossing isn't handled properly Marvin could

wind up in prison," said Rebecca. "Just because you attended a few rallies doesn't mean you know how such things work."

Sarah stopped talking about Canada.

"Not everyone who's drafted winds up in Vietnam," Marvin told his father. He sat in the living room staring at his notice, which had been folded and unfolded so many times it was ready to tear. "One of the guys in the class ahead of me in high school wound up in Germany. I heard he's having a great time."

"So we'll start praying you wind up in Germany," said Harvey. "Who would have expected such a thing?"

Marvin refused to allow anyone from the family to see him off when he reported for duty, afraid they'd cause a scene.

He wrote frequently from basic training in Virginia. He was living with boys who'd never seen a Jew; he'd never known anyone who didn't know any Jews. They were curious about each other and seemed to be getting along. Marvin was a welcome addition to base sports teams, and he didn't make a fuss about minor discomforts. The whole family wrote regularly, and Marvin shared the care packages they sent.

In a few months he was shipped to Vietnam.

He wrote once or twice. He missed everyone, it was hot and uncomfortable; he didn't say much more. Then the letters stopped. Family members called each other. Did you hear anything? Do you know anything? Is there anyone we can check with to make sure he's okay?

Finally a message arrived.

Marvin was coming home.

In a box covered with an American flag.

Harvey was at work when the news was delivered. Batya immediately called the shop, was told Harvey was out canvassing for customers and she said it was essential that someone find him and get Harvey to call home right away. It took an hour before he phoned her from a small bodega in the South Bronx.

When he realized what Batya was saying, Harvey dropped the phone, fell to his knees and started to weep. "No, God no," he yelled in Yiddish. "Why are you punishing me again?"

The Puerto Rican shop owner didn't understand what was happening. He tried to help Harvey to his feet but was pushed away. Harvey continued ranting. Some customers rushed over to help. Finally, Harvey stood up. Embarrassed by his behavior in front of strangers, he ran outside and drove home, where Batya was waiting with hugs and prayers.

Batya also called Helen and asked her to break the news to Rebecca. "You'll be better at comforting her," she said. "Harvey doesn't have the strength to speak to his daughter right now."

Helen didn't argue.

Before calling Rebecca, who was at work, Helen rushed over to Rachel's house. As she ran up Rachel's stoop, she met Batya coming down.

"I know how much Rachel loved Marvin. I felt I should tell her in person," Batya said slowly. She was pale and hunched over, a wad of tissues clasped in her hand. "I thought Rachel might join Harvey and me, we could pray together, maybe comfort each other. But that's not what she wants right now. You go to her."

Batya stepped aside so Helen could pass. "I'll call when the arrangements are made. Let me know if there's anything I can do to help Rachel."

Helen went through the unlocked front door and found Rachel in the living room. She had expected tears, but Rachel was sitting quietly, stonily. Helen tried to embrace her, but there was no response.

"Can I get you something?" asked Helen. "Something to drink? An aspirin?"

Rachel turned to Helen. "Did you see who just left? Did you see who thinks she was also a mother to Marvin so we should grieve together?"

"What a stupid woman," said Helen. "You were the one who was a mother to Marvin when Elaine died. The only one. Everyone knows that. You were the one he ran to when he needed something; love, attention, protection, affection, anything at all, you were always the one who provided it."

Helen decided Rachel needed some tea and was in the kitchen when she heard Morris open the door. She rushed back to the living room. He was just standing there watching Rachel stare straight ahead. Helen and Morris were waiting for her to break down, to tear her hair and sob. They didn't know what to do with this stone-faced woman.

"When they dig the hole for Marvin, they should make sure it's big enough so I can throw Harvey in. He should spend eternity alongside the son he never sufficiently valued," Rachel said. "Maybe it'll cost a few extra dollars to have such a large grave, but think of all the money Harvey saved by not sending his son to a college where he would be safe.

"When it comes my turn to throw earth on to the casket, I can use the shovel to hit Harvey hard enough to knock him out, then I'll roll him into the grave." Rachel spoke calmly, slowly, with no inflection. "Someone else can cover him. Or just let him rot there."

Morris sat down on one side of Rachel, Helen on the other. They each took one of her hands. No one said anything. The tea kettle began to whistle, and Helen ran into the kitchen, turned it off and went back to Rachel and Morris.

"Remember, when he was little, he was always drawing pictures?" Helen said quietly. "Elaine taped them to her wall. She wanted to be able to see them when she could no longer get out of bed."

"And such an athlete," said Morris. "Always the first one picked for any team."

"He was sorry to leave his friends when Batya forced him to change to a little league for religious children, but he never complained," said Rachel. "The team he left really missed him. Missed his friendship as well as his athletic skill. The year he left was the first time in ages that they didn't even make the quarterfinals."

"Always so kind," said Helen. "He never got into fights, never hurt anyone."

When Saul walked in, a few minutes later, Helen, Morris and Rachel were all in tears. "I didn't bother going to our house. I knew where you'd be," he said to Helen. "Have you spoken to Rebecca yet? Harvey said it was better if the news came from you. I thought, a father should call his own daughter with such news, but I didn't argue."

"I'll call tonight, when she's home, not surrounded by strangers at work," said Helen. "Then we'll drive over and get her. Rebecca shouldn't be alone with such news; she'll stay with us."

The phone rang. Morris went into the hall to pick it up and was back in a few minutes.

"That was Batya," he said. "They're sending Marvin home next week. The funeral will be two days later at Parkside, where we had the service for Elaine."

"We'll sit *shiva* here," said Rachel.

Everyone looked at her.

"*Shiva* will be at Harvey's house," said Morris.

"You can speak at the funeral," said Helen.

Rachel turned to Helen. "I'll think about whether I want to say anything there," she said. "I'm not as nice a person as you are. You might not like what I have to say. And I don't care if I never speak to Harvey or to Batya ever again. I'll mourn for my Marvin in my house where he was always comfortable, secure and knew he was loved."

Her voice was steady. It made everyone nervous.

"Well, there's time to decide," said Helen.

She turned to Saul. "It's time for us to get home. Sarah will be back from school soon. I need to tell her what happened."

"And we need to talk to our boys," said Morris. Everyone stood up and put their arms around each other. No one said anything.

As they walked down the steps, Saul looked toward Harvey and Batya's house. "Do you want to go there?" he asked Helen.

"I need to save my strength for Rebecca, for Sarah," said Helen. "Batya will be saying prayers with Harvey. They're good at that, they don't need me."

Helen didn't reach Rebecca until late that night; she'd been out with friends. When her aunt softly told her the news, Rebecca cried into the phone. Helen held the receiver until Rebecca's tears subsided. "I never said this aloud, but I didn't expect Marvin to make it home from the war," Rebecca said softly. "If there was ever anyone who wasn't cut out to be a soldier it was my good-natured little brother. I always wanted to teach him how to stand up for himself, but I didn't know how."

"Uncle Saul and I will come get you right away," Helen said. "You'll stay here as long as you like. This is no time to be alone."

Rebecca refused her aunt's offer, insisting she'd be better off in her own apartment spending the next few days by herself.

As soon as she heard her mother hang up, Sarah called Rebecca. The phone rang for almost ten minutes. Sarah held on, and eventually Rebecca answered. "I can't talk right now," she said and hung up.

Sarah waited an hour and called again. No one answered. And no one answered two hours later. At four a.m. the phone rang, and Sarah rushed to answer it before her mom got there.

"Tell your mother it's me, that I'm okay, just couldn't sleep, and she should go back to bed," said Rebecca.

"Rebecca sounds calm," Sarah said to her mother. "I'll tell her to call you in the morning." Helen went back to her room.

"Okay, it's just us," Sarah said.

"I'm okay, but I just got back from the hospital. I need you to lend me some money."

"The hospital! What happened? Are you hurt? Of course you can have the money. What's going on?"

"Don't get excited. I'm fine now. There's nothing like a two-hour wait in the emergency room to sober you up," Rebecca said.

After learning about Marvin, Rebecca had cried for a while and then headed to a nearby bar. She had a few drinks and saw a young guy in an army uniform who looked a little like Marvin and said he was leaving for Vietnam soon.

"I know you have to be pretty lame to fall for that line, but I was really drunk," Rebecca said. "I brought him to my place, we had a few more drinks, smoked a joint and, while we were getting undressed, I told him about Marvin. Suddenly I started shaking him, saying, 'Vietnam is too dangerous. You'll get hurt. You have to stay here. I'll hide you.'

"That sobered him up. Soldier-boy confessed that his parents had pulled strings, that he was a draft office clerk in New Jersey and likely to remain there. He was at the bar looking for action. I tried to throw my drink at him. He grabbed my arm and pushed me away. I lunged at him, the glass broke, and suddenly there was blood all over the place and I had a deep gash on my forearm."

Sarah heard Rebecca put down a glass, hoped she was drinking water, but didn't ask.

"He took me to the hospital in a cab and said he was really sorry about my brother before leaving me there. I wound up with four stitches and a bill for services not covered by my insurance. I gave them a check, but it's going to bounce. That's why I need the money."

Sarah heard Rebecca light a cigarette. "I think I'm going to have another scar. Same arm but more noticeable than the dot from my Nazi tattoo."

"Oh my God, Rebecca, how awful," Sarah said. "Are you sure you're okay? Don't think about the money, that's no problem. Look, my folks are upset that you're all alone, maybe they're right. Why not get in a cab and come here? Or I'll come to your place. I can leave right now, stay as long as necessary."

"No, I'm all talked out. Exhausted. I'll be asleep as soon as I hit the pillow. I'll go to work tomorrow; it'll be good to be around strangers, to talk about something else. I'll just tell my boss so I can take time off for the funeral."

"I was always jealous of you for having such a great little brother," said Sarah. "I know he really loved you."

Sarah heard Rebecca crying softly and hung on until the crying stopped. "Thanks for being there for me, Sarri. Thanks a lot."

Then they both hung up and went to bed.

At the funeral, Harvey described what a good son Marvin had been. "And now he is with his blessed mother in Paradise," Harvey said. He had told Batya it wouldn't be appropriate for her to speak at the service. She didn't agree but decided not to argue.

Rebecca told a funny story about Marvin playing lifeguard at Atlantic City and watching over the grandmothers in the ocean even though he couldn't yet swim. She wore a long-sleeved dress that covered her bandaged arm.

Rachel didn't go to the podium. At the cemetery, when the shovel was passed to her to help fill the grave, Helen and Saul and Morris glanced at each other nervously, but nothing unusual happened.

The rabbi announced that the family would be sitting *shiva* at 1155 Astor Avenue, Harvey and Batya's house and at 1159 Astor Avenue, Rachel and Morris' house. Most of the mourners had been informed of this plan beforehand. No one had ever heard of two *shivas*, but no one had been able to talk Rachel out of the idea.

"Anyone doesn't like it, doesn't have to come to me," Rachel said.

During the mourning week people would show up at one house, pay their respects, then walk down the steps, go to the other house, walk up the steps and pay their respects again. The Rabbi led prayers at Harvey's house at 11 a.m. and at Rachel and Morris' house at noon. Everyone was welcome to come to either session, or both.

Batya told the rabbi she thought this arrangement was ridiculous.

"It's certainly unusual," he said. "But no religious laws are being violated. At times like this, the best arrangement is what gives the most comfort to the mourners."

Batya turned away. What could you expect from a Conservative Rabbi?

The religious observance was stricter at Harvey's house. The food was better at Rachel's. At the end of the week both *shivas* were over. The men went back to work. The women went back to managing their households.

No one ever heard of another double *shiva*.

Rebecca had saved the drawings Marvin sent her while she was at Hillsdale. One showed a plump, curly haired woman who resembled Rachel jumping up and down, cheering at a kid's baseball game. There was a tall, blonde boy, obviously Marvin, with a big grin on his face as he caught a fly ball.

Rebecca had the drawing framed and sent it to her aunt. It arrived a week after the funeral and Rachel hung it on her bedroom wall.

36.

BATYA MAKES IT EASY

Almost four years after Marvin's funeral the Rosen family was back at the Park Side Funeral Home. This time Batya was the star of the event. A large, air-brushed photo of her was displayed in the entranceway. It included the dates of her birth and death, revealing she was 68, five years older than she'd told her Rosen relatives.

Batya always claimed she was a better wife to Harvey than Elaine had been, and she would have said that, in the end, she proved it. Elaine had suffered a long, painful illness, depleting the family's emotional, physical and financial resources. Batya had never been sick once during the years she was married to Harvey. "I don't like to make a fuss about myself," she would say if anyone commented on her excellent health.

And then, one minute she was demanding the *glatt* kosher butcher move aside so she could be sure she wasn't being charged for his thumb along with the rib steak, and a moment later she was lying on the sawdust-covered floor. Twenty-four hours later she was wearing a clean, white shroud and resting in a plain, pine box.

"Look at Rebecca," Helen said to Rachel as they waited for the service to start. "Doesn't she look lovely? An accomplished, professional woman in addition to being such a beauty

Rebecca hadn't planned to go to the funeral, but her father sounded so pitiful when he asked her to attend that she relented. "I don't want to sit on the front bench without anyone I care about beside me," said Harvey. She kept awkwardly patting her father's arm, and wishing she had a cigarette. Several times she turned around and nodded to her Rosen relatives.

The room was crowded. In addition to the Rosens, who, Harvey whispered to Rebecca, "were only here because it wouldn't look right if they didn't come," there were several business associates, neighbors and many of Batya's religious friends, who offered sympathy in Yiddish and Hebrew.

"Such a brilliant woman," said a man with a scraggly white beard.

"She willingly gave up her studies to create a good Jewish life for you and the children," said a woman with a long grey skirt and bright red wig.

"Yes, she brought us all closer to the word of God," said Harvey.

The group nodded.

Rebecca was wearing a simple, long-sleeved black dress. Her chin-length hair was chestnut brown, straight and pushed behind her ears where her mother's ruby earrings sparkled.

Sarah walked over to her as soon as the services ended, didn't bother offering condolences on Batya's death. "You finally got your mother's earrings, *Mazel Tov!*"

"I think your mom was at my dad's house going through the jewelry box as soon as Batya's body hit the floor," said Rebecca. "She grabbed anything that looked valuable but all I want is these earrings. I remember how beautiful my mom looked when she wore them."

The Rosens weren't going to the service in the cemetery. "I'm not sitting on the LIE for three hours for that woman," Helen declared. Maybe they'd go to Harvey's house in a day or two when it wasn't crowded and participate in the *shiva*. Helen hadn't decided yet.

Sarah kissed Rebecca as she got into the long black limousine with Harvey, and they made vague plans to get together. Rebecca would go to the cemetery and then back to her own apartment. Harvey knew she wouldn't participate in the *shiva* for Batya. That was too much to ask.

The Rosen family plot was in the B'nai Moses Cemetery, visible from the Exit 35 cloverleaf on the Long Island Expressway. Coincidentally, B'nai Moses had a section patronized by the Orthodox, which was where Batya's father was buried and where she was to be placed, in the designated spot right next to him.

No one had anticipated Batya's marriage when arrangements were made to bury her father, and his synagogue had purchased a double plot so their rabbi would be with his daughter. There wasn't room there for Harvey. When his time came, Harvey would be next to Elaine. In the Rosen plot. Next to his in-laws for eternity.

When Batya's burial was over, after Harvey put a shovelful of dirt on the casket, after he said goodbye to the people who'd come to the cemetery and told them he'd be at his house in a little while to start the *shiva* for Batya, he motioned to Rebecca to follow him. She understood.

When they reached the Rosen plot, Rebecca bent down and scooped up a handful of dirt, shaking it in her palm so the soil fell through her fingers and only the rocks remained in her hands. Jews are practical people, she thought. Stones last longer than flowers.

Harvey said a short prayer in Hebrew, and Rebecca bowed her head. He picked up two stones, placed one on Elaine's headstone and one on Marvin's. Rebecca put rocks on the headstones for her mother and her brother and *Bubbe* Golda. "Rebecca, you'll come live with me now?" asked Harvey as they walked back to his car. "I don't want to be by myself. There's plenty of room in the house. You can come and go as you please. I don't expect you to keep strictly kosher. We could get a cleaning girl to help you."

Rebecca stood still. "I'd rather live on the street," she said and quickly walked away.

It took Harvey a few minutes to catch up. "Why are you so angry with me? I tried to be a good father, to bring you up properly. We had problems, but I always wanted the best for you. I always loved you."

"I love you too, Papa. But I can't live in that house. There are no good memories for me there."

37.

A DUTIFUL DAUGHTER

Rebecca stuck to her decision not to live with Harvey, but she started to see him regularly. Her aunts understood. He was still her father. She was still his daughter.

Sarah found this blossoming of filial devotion ridiculous and didn't hesitate to say so. "You're putting us all to shame," she told Rebecca. "All the cousins are being told, 'Rebecca doesn't mind spending time with her elderly parent. Why don't you visit more often?' After all these years you've suddenly decided to change your image, become 'the good kid.'"

Rebecca laughed. "I only see him once a week. We meet for lunch at a kosher restaurant."

"With everything he put you through, being sent away, rejected in favor of Batya, why bother now?" said Sarah "Why not just tell him to go to hell?"

Rebecca didn't answer immediately. She needed a few minutes to think about her answer. The silence made Sarah uncomfortable.

"He's still my father," she said, finally. "I can't change what happened. I didn't have much time with my mother. I lost my brother. This is my last chance to have a father. I figured someone should make an effort, and I knew he wouldn't do it."

Being a good daughter wasn't the only way that her cousin's

behavior baffled Sarah. Rebecca had been the first in the family to charge into the world beyond the Bronx, but she hadn't gone far and now was afraid to stretch her boundaries. Rebecca was afraid to fly, didn't like boat trips that took her beyond sight of land and had no interest in ever living outside the New York area. She'd also become a hypochondriac, going from one doctor to another, never trusting anyone and always seeking another opinion.

"I have to be careful," Rebecca said when Sarah warned that all of this second guessing risked letting minor illnesses get worse. "My mother died young. There's no telling what type of genetic condition I've inherited."

Harvey was finally proud of his daughter. He rarely missed a chance to tell people he was going downtown to meet his Rebecca. He was 78, not driving anymore and hesitant to spend money on a cab, so he figured out how to take the subway. He got dressed up for these lunches, always wearing a freshly laundered shirt, suit and tie. Rebecca wondered who'd shown him how to use the washing machine and explained which clothes went to the cleaners. She didn't ask.

She had learned about the embarrassing encounters with Zvi, Batya's friend and Harvey's old nemesis, how Harvey hadn't rekindled the relationship because he'd been afraid he wouldn't be able to match Zvi in intellectual conversations. Rebecca dug out an old college philosophy text and reviewed a few of the basics, just enough to ask questions that allowed her papa to show off his knowledge.

"You have a fine mind, Rebecca," her father said. "You should read more about these matters. You'd enjoy it, I'm sure."

"I'm tempted to tell him I got honors on a college paper I wrote about Hillel," said Rebecca. "I would never have chosen that topic if not for him and Batya. I wanted to prove I could understand the stuff they thought only they knew. I wound up acing all my philosophy courses. Bet I could have wiped the floor with Batya's crew in an intellectual debate. Of course I never told them. It was enough that I knew it."

When the trips to Manhattan became too much for Harvey, Rebecca finally agreed to visit him at the house she hadn't entered since she'd been thrown out. She brought takeout from kosher restaurants, blintzes, roast chickens, *kugel,* delicacies from a "kosher style" deli. It wouldn't have been allowed through the door when Batya was alive, but Harvey didn't mind.

Sometimes, after dinner, her father fell asleep while talking to her, and Rebecca explored the house, looking at the changes Batya had made, lamps she'd moved, drapes she'd replaced, gold leaf mirrors she'd hung in the bathroom. "You can't believe the horrible taste that woman had. I've found the most peculiar things," she told Sarah, who started to laugh.

"I know what you're doing," she said. "You don't care about the décor; it wouldn't matter to you if there was a gold-plated bidet in the living room. You're looking for a *knipple.*" Rebecca hesitated and then joined Sarah's laughter.

Their grandmothers had told them about *knipple,* the secret stash of money that women hid from their husbands. You scrimped on groceries and told your husband prices had gone up, went through his pockets when he was asleep, or started a small business like baking or embroidering for neighbors and didn't reveal exactly how much you made. The money was stored someplace a husband would never look: an old cooking pot, the bottom of a woman's underwear drawer, behind a loose brick in the kitchen.

"Even the happiest couples have secrets," the *Bubbe*s said.

"Every woman should have some money that's just her own. Things happen. You never know."

Sarah and Rebecca called their grandmothers old-fashioned. They were modern girls who would have careers and earn their own money, not people who hid coins in an old purse. Many years later, when they were married, Rebecca and Sarah admitted to each other that they sometimes contemplated getting their own safe deposit boxes or collecting bearer bonds that wouldn't show up on joint tax returns.

When Rebecca prowled the house she found her parents' wedding photos, once displayed in ornate frames, now stuffed into manila envelopes. There were receipts for rugs and crystal that Batya had sold to secondhand shops.

But no *knipple*.

"I'm sure it's there, somewhere," Rebecca said. "This is Batya's revenge for all of the nasty things I said about her, all the times I used a meat utensil for a dairy dish or ruined her expensive shoes. If there's a heaven, she's up there laughing at me as I crawl through dusty spaces, brush away mouse droppings behind the washing machine and scrape my knuckles on loose tiles."

38.

THE HOSPICE (1978)

When she told her friends how Harvey's life ended, Rebecca usually claimed she got the call at 7 a.m. on a Sunday morning while she was dreaming about her father. She liked that explanation; it implied a psychic connection, a loving bond with her aging dad.

Of course, she didn't try that when she spoke to Sarah, whom she'd called immediately. "I was still half asleep and hungover when I picked up the phone and a soft-voiced woman told me my father had passed away and offered her sympathy. Before I could say anything, she told me to come get his stuff. They needed the room."

Sarah started to say the things you say to someone in that situation, but Rebecca cut her off. "Please, no Hallmark messages. Not from you. I know who my dad was. The last few years haven't wiped out everything that happened when I was young."

Rebecca got in the shower and was surprised to find herself sobbing as the hot water beat down on her. She made some strong coffee, called the funeral parlor and told them to get her father. She didn't want to see his dead body.

Sarah had offered to go to the hospice, but Rebecca said she'd go alone. "There'll just be some paperwork to do. He didn't have much with him. It won't take long to go through his things," she said. "But I'd appreciate it if you could call your folks, deal with their reactions. Tell them I've already notified the funeral parlor. Your mom can call the rest of the family. And tell her there won't be any *shiva*. I'm not sitting in that house for a week with nothing to do but relive bad memories. Anyone who wants to say anything to me can do it at the funeral."

"You know my mom will want you to come over," Sarah said. "Or they'll come to you."

"I can't," Rebecca said. "I can't listen to them try to make believe they thought my dad was a good man."

Harvey had had a long, lingering illness and, as he got weaker, Rebecca found aides to care for him in his house, using up Harvey's limited funds. She didn't care. She'd never counted on an inheritance. She wanted him to know she cared, wanted to believe he was grateful and, maybe, finally, that he loved her.

Eventually he was too sick to be cared for at home and she put his name on the waiting list for St Joseph's Hospice. Of course, a facility named after a Catholic saint was an odd place for a religious Jewish man to wind up but it was "highly recommended by top people" as relatives would say.

Rebecca wasn't surprised when she got the call about Harvey's death. Just two weeks before she had coordinated his move to a hospice and, of course, hospice meant the end was near. He was there to die. It meant it was time to choose a funeral home, find the cemetery deed and send your good black suit to the cleaners. She had even written a speech to deliver.

But still. Still, she'd somehow thought her papa would last just a little longer.

Watching the staff go about their business, Rebecca had

learned that running a hospice is an administrative nightmare. People check-in for an indefinite stay; sometimes they're there only a day or two, sometimes a month or more—if it's much longer they might be asked to leave and come back when their condition worsens. There's no way to know when there'll be a vacancy, but when there is, it's quickly filled. There's a long waiting list.

"We were lucky to get a room for my dad. People were dying to get in," Rebecca said to Sarah. "That's hospice humor."

When Rebecca had inspected the place, she was shown a bare room with a narrow bed over which hung a simple cross.

"This won't work," she told the administrator. "If my father is at all conscious and looks up and sees a cross above his head it'll kill him."

"Don't worry," said the guide. "We have plenty of Jewish clients. By the time your dad gets here the cross will be gone. We even have a rabbi on call who'll be glad to talk to your dad or to you and pray with you both."

"He can visit my father," she said. "I won't be needing a rabbi."

The hospice kept its word. When they brought Harvey to his room the cross was gone; there was just a nail protruding from the wall above the bed. Later in the day someone hung a picture of some wildflowers from the nail. They even put a *mezuzah* on the doorpost, attached with a strip of Velcro.

Rebecca had expected the inside of a hospice to look like a hospital, but it was more like an old, genteel hotel, the kind seen in movies about ancient English ladies who are always drinking tea. The nurses wore regular clothes, not uniforms. There were soft chairs for visitors in the rooms, and the walls were painted muted colors. The common room had lots of alcoves where relatives could gather and speak to each other to make the type of plans they were uncomfortable making at the bedside of someone still breathing.

Harvey remained lucid until the end, but he was asleep much of the time. Rebecca bought a heavy novel she had been meaning to get to and tried to read while he snored softly. But the book didn't hold her interest, and she stared at her father, his body outlined by the light blanket. He'd gotten thinner, but he was still tall.

I used to believe you were a giant, papa, Rebecca wanted to say. You were always looming above me. I don't remember your ever picking me up or squatting down like I saw other adults do when they spoke to children. I could never reach you. Why didn't you try to get to my level, try to understand me? Why did you let things get to the point where you felt you had to send me away? She'd never said these things aloud and wouldn't say them now. She got a glass of water and went back to her book.

When her father was awake, they talked about the past, the very distant past. Rebecca bought a small tape recorder and a few cassettes of Yiddish music. Harvey sang along with the recordings and talked about the days in Europe when he was a prized student, stories Rebecca had heard many times before.

Helen and Rachel visited a few times. Their husbands didn't come. "Too depressing," they said. "We saw enough of Harvey when he was well."

Her aunts brought cookies, "so people will have something to nibble while they're here." But no one else came. The cookies got stale, and Rebecca threw them away.

No one was there when Harvey died.

Rebecca put on jeans and a sweatshirt, went downstairs and gave the cab driver the address of St. Joseph's Hospice, named for Jesus' father, the saint in charge of peaceful deaths. Joseph held this position as he'd been allowed to die in the arms of Jesus and Mary and therefore had the happiest, most glorious death of any saint. She'd learned that from the plaque under the plaster statue in the lobby, presumably of St. Joseph. She'd spent a lot of time in that lobby, the only place in the building you were allowed to smoke.

The nurse on duty recognized Rebecca and said she was sorry about her father. "You just missed him," she said. "The men from the funeral parlor left with him about 15 minutes ago."

The light was on in her father's room. The bed had been stripped, the picture of the wildflowers was gone and a cross was once again hanging from the nail.

Rebecca was carrying a large black garbage bag and a canvas tote. Her father's pajamas, his glasses, his toilet articles, dentures and underwear went into the garbage bag. She took the Yiddish music out of the tape recorder, put the recorder in her tote bag and the music into the garbage bag.

There were a few books on her father's bedside table; he'd chosen them himself when he left his house for the last time. There was a Hebrew book with black leather binding and Hebrew letters embossed in gold on the cover. It looked old and beat-up. Rebecca wondered if it could be the book that Marvin had abused when he was little. Was that what her father wanted with him at the hospice? If so, what memories did it have for him?

She started to put the book into the garbage bag then remembered that someone was coming to appraise Harvey's books next week. Maybe this was part of a set. She put it in her tote bag.

One doesn't pack very much for a stay at a hospice, so it didn't take long to go through Harvey's possessions. Rebecca looked around and noticed that the mezuzah was still on the doorframe. She peeled it off slowly, the Velcro making tiny popping sounds. The back piece of Velcro stuck to the wall, and she left it alone.

Rebecca went to the nurse's station, dropped the black garbage bag in a large trash can and handed the mezuzah to the woman at the desk, who thanked her and repeated her condolences.

Rebecca passed her dad's room again as she left. Someone had closed the door and she quietly turned the knob. The curtains were drawn, the lights were off, the room was completely empty.

39.

WASPS WITHOUT SOCKS (1982)

"Guess what? Don't bother, you'll never guess. I'll tell you. I have a date with one of the WASPy guys at the bank. And not just any WASP, the WASPiest guy in the whole program. So WASPy he wears his tasseled loafers without socks. The whole day."

"*Mazel Tov.* I'm *kvelling* from you. Try to find out if his tribe is born with that ability or if they have the sweat glands removed from their feet at birth, a top-secret Protestant rite."

Rebecca giggled so hard she got the hiccups, and Sarah started laughing at her.

"And wait 'til you hear his name. It's so authentic. You know how so many of them have first names that are really last names? He's got one of those.

Next Saturday night—let's hear a drum roll, da da da dah—I'm breaking bread with Mr. Warfield Harrison Earl."

"Pretty classy. What do people call him?"

"Oh, you'll love this. Most people call him Skip. I asked about the name, and he said it was short for Skippy, which was his boarding school name. He has a boarding school name. Maybe he was on his school's crew, or his family has a boat."

"Maybe he really likes peanut butter."

The age gap between Sarah and Rebecca had disappeared. They phoned each other every week or two but rarely got together. They were busy with their very different lives, but both valued the ability to talk with someone who knew their backgrounds, knew their truths. It was like running into someone with whom you could speak your native language when you were living among foreigners.

After years of shabby apartments in neighborhoods her aunts disapproved of, working while going to school and covering her own expenses, Rebecca graduated from college with honors and landed a prestigious internship at a large commercial bank. She had a salary that allowed her to move to a tiny apartment in a good area.

I'm on the Upper East Side, a couple of blocks off Park Avenue, she would say to herself and smile. Rebecca got some new furniture and threw away pieces she had found on the street. Occasionally she bought clothes in places other than thrift shops.

If she got good ratings from her supervisors, (and Rebecca had no doubt she would impress these people) she'd be entitled to free tuition at an MBA program. She planned to go to Columbia, become an ivy leaguer, as her aunts would say.

"This is where the money is, where all the right people are, where I'm going to belong," Rebecca told Sarah. "Forget about the Jewish girl from the Bronx, the child of immigrants, the juvenile delinquent thrown out by her father. In a few years you won't be able to tell I wasn't born with a silver spoon in my mouth and a safety net under my feet."

"Careful you don't choke and trip," said Sarah.

Sarah had followed a different route. She graduated college

with a liberal arts degree and mediocre grades, too busy going to demonstrations to study. Her parents subsidized her rent in a nice apartment in a trendy area where original settlers were being forced out. Sarah told people she'd wrangled a deal and wasn't a gentrifier.

She worked for minimum wage at a non-profit foundation. Sarah was thinking of getting a degree in non-profit management so could one day be a senior position in an agency that provided housing or food or medical care for poor people. She thought about spending time abroad and helping improve conditions in third world countries.

Sarah dated guys who were finding themselves, guys who refused to sell out. She sometimes helped them out, gave them small amounts of money. "We're all in this together," she'd say, not revealing she had a substantial trust fund from the Rosen Corporation's earnings in the South Bronx.

"What are you going to wear?" asked Sarah. "Going someplace elegant?"

"No, he grew up in a Connecticut suburb and is trying to prove he's now a real New Yorker. 'I hate pretentious places, don't you?' he said, assumed I'd agree, and told me we'd go to, 'a place real people go, where there's a fat old mama in the back cooking her heart out.'

That means we'll be eating off Formica countertops not linen tablecloths. I'll have to dress upper-class casual, designer jeans, a pure linen work shirt and a hand-woven native poncho, stuff which costs double what my designer clothes go for at the thrift shop."

The following Saturday, Skip picked Rebecca up in his sports car. He was wearing pressed chinos, a pale blue J. Crew shirt and his customary footwear. His pale brown hair was carefully combed, a few wisps conspicuously astray for a casual look.

Rebecca stared at his forehead and wondered if Skippy was going bald.

"I found a Spanish restaurant in Spanish Harlem, so you know the food will be authentic," he said. "Hope there's a garage close to the restaurant. We don't want to walk around in that neighborhood or leave this car in the street."

Rebecca didn't mention that she'd once lived in the area.

The place was called, *Restaurante de ma Abuela*. "Abuela means grandma," Skip said. "I spent some time in Spain during my junior year, so I know the language and can translate if you need help with the menu. Bet the kitchen is full of mamacitas making authentic food, recipes handed down by their grandmas. No pretentious cuisine in this place."

"I know what abuela means."

Rebecca walked into the restaurant prepared for the smell of greasy tacos, the sight of scuffed linoleum and walls covered with posters of bullfights and flamenco dancers. Then she stopped. The place smelled good. Really good. And it looked good. Soft lighting flattered the customers, comfortable woven straw chairs cradled them and floral wall tiles echoed the table-top mosaics. Servers in crisp Caribbean colored uniforms showed them to a table, made recommendations, took their orders and politely and promptly brought the food. The really terrific food.

Whenever a waiter did anything, Skip would look into their eyes and say "gracias, muchas gracias." The first time he did this he turned to Rebecca and explained, "that means thank you. It's good to show immigrants you appreciate their efforts."

"You really got your money's worth during your time abroad," she said.

Halfway through the meal a waiter brought out a luscious looking item and explained that it was compliments of the manager. "She noticed you enjoying our food and wanted you to try the house specialty, cuchifritoes." He turned towards Rebecca as he finished dividing it between them. "She said to explain to you that the term can be used for any fried food but usually refers to fried pork. She had the cook make this special pork cuchifrito just for you."

"See, I told you these people appreciate it when you talk their language," said Skip.

"I guess you're right."

Rebecca looked around uncomfortably, didn't see anyone watching them, shrugged and dug into the dish. The manager was right; it was delicious.

They were almost finished with their café con leche when they heard two women speaking loudly in the kitchen in Spanish. "See, I told you there'd be authentic Mexicans at the stove. That's why the food was so good," said Skippy.

"They're not Mexican. They have Puerto Rican accents."

"How can you tell?"

"In school I learned the different ways words are pronounced by various Spanish speaking people. I also learned about Hispanic cultures. This was Puerto Rican food."

"Guess you went to a really good school. Where'd you go? Sounds tough."

"My father had strict intellectual standards. My school was like a jail."

Skip didn't notice that Rebecca hadn't named her school. He was staring at a woman with a scarf wrapped around her head who had just walked out of the kitchen, still speaking Spanish to someone inside.

"I'll bet that's the cook," he said, getting up. "I'm going to give her an extra tip. It's important to motivate these people. You can wait here."

Rebecca had her back to the kitchen door, she turned and watched Skip walk through the room calling, "Senora! Momentito!" The woman stood still, looked across the room to the table where Rebecca was sitting. She took off her scarf and ran her hand through her heavy hair, revealing a scar that stretched from her eyebrow to the top of her ear.

Rebecca was out of her chair so fast it almost tipped over. "Maria!" she called as she dashed through the restaurant and threw her arms around the now smiling woman standing with Skip. "Maria, it's Rebecca!"

Skip stared at the two women embracing. "How do you two know each other?"

Maria, in her turquoise restaurant uniform, looked at Rebecca and Skip in their high-class casual clothes. She didn't say anything. Rebecca looked at Maria, holding the $20 bill Skip had just given her. She looked at Skip in his sockless tasseled loafers. "We went to the same boarding school," she said quietly. "Maria tutored me in Spanish."

"That's right," said Maria. "And Rebecca helped me and another girl, Alice, in math."

Rebecca stepped back and stood beside Skip. "Are you in touch with Alice?"

"Oh my God. You don't know. Alice died last year. She was doing community work in Harlem and was shot by a gang member who thought she was someone else. There was an article in the paper. People said she'd really be missed, she'd accomplished a lot."

Rebecca reached out and grabbed Maria's hand. "Oh no. Alice was so amazing. It was always exciting to be around her. I used to think about her, about both of you. I always meant to contact you two. But things were really crazy when I first got home. Last few years I've been working and going to college. No time for anything, not even to read the papers."

"It was a small article, easy to miss," said Maria. She squeezed Rebecca's hand and quickly dropped it. "Alice and I went separate ways, but we stayed in touch. We talked about you but didn't try to call, figured you were busy with your family, with school, had a fancy career, a boyfriend. Look, if you ever want to get together, well, now you know how to reach me."

"Are you a cook here?" asked Skip.

"I own the place," said Maria.

She turned to Skip and nodded at the money in her hand. "I'll give this to the people in the kitchen. They'll appreciate it. Glad you liked the food. Come again." She went through the swinging doors back to the kitchen.

Skip and Rebecca walked slowly to the nearby garage. "Wow," he said. "Gee. What a coincidence. What a night. Who'd have imagined such a thing? In Spanish Harlem we discover a great place to eat, and you run into an old school chum. Too bad about that other girl, but this one seems to be doing well. My school had scholarship students too. It's always nice to see them succeeding."

He handed the parking ticket to the garage attendant. "Say, it's still early. Let's go downtown and have a drink. I didn't realize you were also a boarding school brat. We can rehash preppie days. I remember some wild mixers, had some characters at my school too."

"I don't think so. I'm really tired. Just take me home."

When they got to her place, Rebecca leaned across the seat and quickly kissed Skip before he could get out. "Adios Skippy," she said and ran into her building.

As soon as she got inside, Rebecca dropped all her clothes on the floor. She noticed that her linen shirt was wrinkled, shrugged and kicked it into a corner.

She rummaged through a collection of fancy nightgowns saved for special dates, until she found a faded blue flowered flannel bathrobe and wrapped it around herself. Her aunts had worn such things in the evenings when they'd taken off their girdles. Rebecca had smiled all the way home when she found it for $1 in a thrift shop.

She made a drink, turned on the TV, turned it off, flipped through her records and books, couldn't find anything interesting and just stared out the window. She realized she didn't know the exact date of Alice's death. That seemed important. She'd go to the library and check old newspapers.

Good old Maria, always dependable. She'd remembered the joke about cuchifritoes, let Rebecca catch a glimpse of her scar so she could be sure it was her old roommate, didn't initiate contact. And even after Rebecca ran over to her, Maria hadn't mentioned the name of their reform school.

Rebecca wondered why she'd lost control and ran across the restaurant to embrace Maria. Why did she risk having someone like Skip find out she wasn't a normal person with a normal background?

She finished her drink and made another.

The people Rebecca hung out with these days talked about their dates, their jobs, their plans for the future. They kept things light. Rebecca wasn't close to anyone, didn't want to be. Superficial was fine; she liked superficial.

Rebecca picked up the phone to call Sarah, listened to the tone and hung up without dialing. She could make a funny story about what a jerk Skippy had turned out to be. She and Sarah would have a good laugh about the old skipper sinking into the sea. But should she mention Maria? Sarah would want to know all about her former roommate, ask if Rebecca planned to see her. Rebecca didn't know what she would answer.

I'm glad I know where she is, thought Rebecca. I'm glad she's doing well. I'm really sorry about Alice, but there's nothing I could have done for her.

Starting another friendship with Maria, even as discreet as Maria had shown herself to be, carried the risk of other people finding out about her background. Rebecca didn't want Maria to think she was ashamed of her, but she wasn't ready for her years at reform school, for all that led up to those years and followed them, to be revealed.

Rebecca knew there was a good chance that eventually word would get out about her past. But not yet. She wasn't ready. For the time being, it was hard enough to just be a neophyte in the finance department, not to mention female, and without any family or old school connections. She didn't need more baggage.

Being a finance exec with a wild history, a colorful resume, wouldn't hurt if she was a hotshot success. But would she make it? Her family thought she was so smart, but they lived in another world. And smart didn't always mean successful. Her father was supposed to have been some sort of genius in the old country and look what happened to him

When I get a promotion, when my career is more secure. That shouldn't take too long. I'll call Maria then, thought Rebecca. Maybe I could help her finance a chain of restaurants. We can be poster girls for the school, "former delinquents make good." I'll be the first one on the Forbes 500 list to include the Bronx House of Juvenile Detention on my resume.

That would really show my dad.

Rebecca dialed Sarah's number. She wouldn't say anything about Maria, just tell a few jokes about Skip. Then she'd make plans to get together with her cousin later in the week. They should see each other more often.

They were two smart American girls with bright futures. Just what their families had hoped for when they fled Europe.

Every immigrant's dream. Maybe it would come true.

YIDDISH GLOSSARY

Bubbe—grandmother

Bucher—student

Chupah—canopy under which a couple stands during their wedding ceremony Glatt kosher—obeying all Orthodox dietary rules

Goniff—thief, swindler

Goyische—non-Jewish

Katchkas—ducks

Klutz—clumsy

Kvelling—very proud

Landsman—someone from your native town

L'chaim—to life (generally used as a toast)

Mazel Tov—good luck, congratulations

Mezuzah—piece of parchment with Torah verse hung on door frame in protective cylinder

Mishugana—crazy person

Momsa—bastard

Moyle—person who performs circumcisions

Nachis—good fortune

Oy—cry of exasperation

Oy Vey—very exasperated

Payes—sideburns

Pisher—peeing, (slang term for someone acting like a baby)

Putz—penis

Rebbetzin—rabbi's wife

Schmatta—rag (slang term for dress)

Shandra—shame

Shiva—mourning period

Shiksa—non-Jewish woman

Shnorers—people who take advantage of others

Simchas—happy occasions

Shul—synagogue

Sheitel—wig worn by Orthodox women after they're married

Talith—prayer shawl

Traife—not kosher

Tsaddik—wise man

Tuchis—buttocks

Yahrzeit—anniversary (on the Jewish calendar) of the death of a
    beloved person

Yarmulke—skullcap worn by men

Yenta—gossip

Yiddishkeit—Jewishness

*People in areas with large Jewish populations may be surprised to learn that anyone thought there was a need for this glossary. If you live in someplace like NYC you've been shlepping bundles and listening to frustrated people intone, *oy, oy, oy* your entire life regardless of your race, creed, color or religious affiliation.

But apparently out in the hinterlands there are some people who think that *yenta* is a Barbra Streisand movie and I didn't want them to be confused by my book. If I failed to translate a word that was unfamiliar, I'm sorry. As a native-New Yorker, I'm not always sure which words that I commonly use are English and which are Yiddish. Hope you enjoyed the book anyway.

ACKNOWLEDGMENTS

First of all there's Kaylie, my editor, teacher, guide, cheerleader and friend. This book wouldn't exist without Kaylie Jones. I met her in a Stony Brook classroom, followed her to Manhattan's upper east side, Florence, Provincetown and San Diego. Along the way I became a writer.

The joy of being a writer includes the privilege of interacting with the talented people you encounter along the way.

Special thanks to my other talented teachers and guides: Judy Mandel, Kaylie's cohort and the first person I bother with questions about the bizarre world of publishing; Christopher Castellani at Bread Loaf; Julie Maloney, director of Women Reading Aloud who provided a beautiful environment where I could generate new material and brush up on my SCUBA diving; Matt Klamm at the Southampton Writers Conference and Stephen Merrill Bloch from The Center for Fiction Writers.

I'm a big believer in writing seminars. If you're as lucky as I was, in addition to learning the meaning of buzz words like objective correlative, you leave these places with new friends, talented people who get you on a special level. Such people include Ruth Bonapace, Diedre Sinnott, Stacey Lender, Laurel Brett, Heather Bryant, Mary Horgan, Rachel Wong, Cheryl J. Fish, Lee Esterling Stewart, April Bogle, Martha Chang, Holly Tappen and Susan Piperato.

Of course, none of this would happen without the support of family and friends. There's no way to adequately thank the people who've spent years helping me celebrate my victories, commiserating over my failures and endlessly listening to my kvetching—Michelle Gage, Edith Novack and Sylvia Netzer.

Apprentice House Press of Loyola University, Baltimore, made this book a reality and I'm forever grateful to Kevin Atticks and his talented group, Sophia Strocko, Rylee Miler, and Molly Gerard.

And in tried-and-true tradition of saving the best for last, I want to acknowledge my amazing son, daughter-in-law and grandchildren who give my life meaning. Josh, Miranda, Thomas and Julia, I love you all.

ABOUT THE AUTHOR

Jean Ende is a native NYer who is trying to exorcise her background by writing fiction influenced by her Jewish family in the Bronx, NY.

A former reporter for daily newspapers in Westchester, NY and Jersey City, NJ, she was a press secretary in the NY City government and for several political candidates. When she left politics, Jean spent several years doing communications work for public service organizations which led to her decision to go over to the dark side. An English major with a degree from CCNY, Jean got an MBA from the Columbia University School of Business. She became a VP at a major commercial bank, wrote for business magazines and taught marketing in college management departments.

Jean has had two dozen short stories published in print and online magazines and anthologies in the US and England and her work has been recognized by major literary competitions. This is her first novel.

Jean and her dog now live in Brooklyn which is a foreign country to anyone from the Bronx.

Apprentice
House Press
Loyola University Maryland

Apprentice House is the country's only campus-based, student-staffed book publishing company. Directed by professors and industry professionals, it is a nonprofit activity of the Communication Department at Loyola University Maryland.

Using state-of-the-art technology and an experiential learning model of education, Apprentice House publishes books in untraditional ways. This dual responsibility as publishers and educators creates an unprecedented collaborative environment among faculty and students, while teaching tomorrow's editors, designers, and marketers.

Eclectic and provocative, Apprentice House titles intend to entertain as well as spark dialogue on a variety of topics. Financial contributions to sustain the press's work are welcomed. Contributions are tax deductible to the fullest extent allowed by the IRS.

To learn more about Apprentice House books or to obtain submission guidelines, please visit www.apprenticehouse.com.

Apprentice House Press
Communication Department
Loyola University Maryland
4501 N. Charles Street
Baltimore, MD 21210
Ph: 410-617-5265
info@apprenticehouse.com • www.apprenticehouse.com